The Dark Lords Stir

Evil Arising Cycle

Book 1

S. M. Doll

First Edition

PAGE PUBLISHING, INC.
Conneaut Lake, PA

First originally published by Page Publishing 2021

ISBN 978-1-6624-6370-9 (pbk)
ISBN 978-1-6624-7567-2 (hc)
ISBN 978-1-6624-6371-6 (digital)

Printed in the United States of America

To Alyssa, Carly, and Alisha, whose inspiration
and encouragement started me writing down the
many stories that circle through my mind.

I would like to say thank you to my wife, Lori, for always being
there and encouraging me to follow my dreams and imagination.

To my children who listened to my endless stories for
years no matter how many times I repeated them.

To the people who read my rough drafts and gave me
very helpful feedback: Juanita, Gary, Corky, Louise,
and anyone else who I dragged into the process.

And I want to give glory to the God of Light for
giving me life, a mind, and an imagination.

CHAPTER 1

Thwack!

Daniel's eyes flashed open at the sound. A crossbow bolt quivered inches from his head, the shaft buried two inches deep into the bed-post. He threw himself out of the bed and onto the floor. His mind raced, trying to remember where he was.

Swish! Thwack!

Another bolt struck the mattress he had just vacated. Shaking the sleep from his head, he remembered, *I am in Staymos!*

Swish! Thwack!

A third bolt flew through the window and embedded itself in the wood floor next to his foot. Daniel wondered, *How did they find me?*

The full moon's light gave the room an eerie glow. Daniel crawled on his belly across the dusty floor, grabbed his clothes and travel bag, and inched his way to the door. Getting up on one knee, he opened it with care, glancing down the hallway from side to side, looking for other attackers.

Satisfied that he was alone, he crawled into the hall just as another bolt slammed into the door behind him. Standing up in the hallway, he pulled on his leather pants and silk shirt and stuffed everything else into his travel bag. He pulled the gold-handled sword out of its scabbard as he made his way down the wooden steps on his bare feet.

The old steps squeaked underfoot, but he was confident that the snoring of the large toothless woman who occupied the room at the top of the stairs would drown out the noise. Reaching the landing at the bottom of the steps, Daniel opened the door just a crack.

He caught his breath as the pungent odor of ale and sweat rushed through the opening to meet him. He pushed the door open a little more and peered around the corner into the common room. There was no one to be seen. He pulled the door closed and took the time to pull on his boots, slip the chain mail shirt over his head, and strap the scabbard to his back.

He opened the door once again and took another quick look into the great room of the Three Apples Inn. No one was there. Wondering again, he thought, *Someone had to have betrayed me, someone I trusted. There is no way the prize-seekers could have find me this quickly.*

Slam!

The door from the kitchen slammed open. He immediately pulled back into the stairwell. After pausing for a moment, he reopened the door and stuck his head around the corner; he could see the innkeeper walking behind the counter.

With great skill acquired from years of practice, he bounded across the room to the counter, quick as a cat, albeit an exceptionally large cat.

"Aahh! You're ali—awake!" the innkeeper squealed as he stumbled back against the wall.

Daniel held his forefinger to his lips to quiet the innkeeper. He glanced around the room one more time and asked, "Charsel, are we alone?"

"Yes, yes, we're alone. You're up early, Daniel," Charsel stuttered, looking confused.

Daniel questioned Charsel, "Have you told anyone that I was here?"

"No, of course not, not a soul." Charsel looked down, averting his eyes from Daniel's.

"Someone just tried to kill me," Daniel stated.

Charsel looked at him quizzically. "There was someone upstairs in your room?"

"No," Daniel answered, then said, "They shot through the open window from the rooftop across the street."

Charsel glanced down behind the counter but then quickly looked back up. Looking toward the front door to the inn, he said, "There seems to be no place safe in this town anymore."

Daniel was unsure of what Charsel was implying, but feeling uneasy, he replied, "Certainly not here, anyway." Then testing Charsel, he said, "I'm leaving early this morning. I will settle up with you for the room later."

Charsel reluctantly replied, "Tha...tha...that's fine, very good, whatever you like."

Daniel paused and thought, *So it was Charsel who sold me out. He would never let me leave without paying. Now he wants to avoid being caught in the crossfire.*

Daniel turned and walked toward the door. As he reached for the door handle, he heard a scuffling sound from behind him. He quickly dropped down onto one knee, his fingers grasping the hilt of the throwing knife hidden in the lining of his boot. Spinning on his knee, he drew and threw the silver blade all in one motion.

The would-be assassin was standing, aiming his crossbow at Daniel as the knife plunged into his throat. The assassin spun around from the force of the blow. He reached up for the knife with his left hand, but he inadvertently pulled the trigger on the crossbow with his right. The bolt slammed into the belly of the innkeeper.

Daniel's long strides brought him back behind the counter, where he bent down to check on the assassin. The crossbowman was as good as dead, blood gushing from the hole in his jugular. He pulled the blade from the assassin's throat and wiped the blood off on the man's shirt. Picking up the crossbow, he turned it over. Sure enough, it was Ramaahian, and he thought, *They found me way too quickly this time.*

Looking up at Charsel, Daniel queried, "How many are there?"

The rotund innkeeper's chubby hands held his belly, with the crossbow bolt protruding from between them, blood oozing down his fingers. With his eyes, he pleaded to Daniel for help.

"How many?" Daniel demanded.

"I…I don't know," came the weak reply.

Daniel questioned again, "Are there more than this one?"

"I…I think so. Help me, please," the dying innkeeper begged.

He snarled at the innkeeper, "I will gladly give you the same help you were giving me."

Daniel stood up and stepped over the dead assassin and walked through the door into the kitchen. He heard the fat man's body fall to the floor.

The cook had been stirring a large vat of something with a big wooden spoon but was now staring in disbelief and horror at Daniel. Taking the large spoon from the cook's hand, he withdrew some of the broth and tasted it. Frowning at the cook, he said, "Needs more salt."

Daniel pulled his cloak out of his bag and put it on as he emerged from the rear door of the inn. He stopped and peered deeply into the shadows and checked the roofline for more attackers. He thought, *How many people know that I'm here? I thought when I left the Eastward, they would give up.* He continued to watch for several minutes. When no one appeared, he crossed the street and headed for the docks. Maybe he could find a ship leaving tonight, or at least early the next morning.

He had hoped to be able to stay in Staymos long enough to pick up a few jobs from some of the rich merchants who lived here. He had made a large sum of gold on his last job, but a little more could never hurt.

Moving from shadow to shadow, cautious not to be silhouetted by the moonlight, Daniel knew there had to be others waiting for him. Alert for movement in the shadows, he worked his way toward the bay.

Daniel had chosen the Barbarian Kingdom for a few reasons. Cult Island was as far from the Ramaahian Empire as one could get. He had worked for several local wealthy merchants when he and the old man had passed through the island nine years ago. But mostly, there were a lot of thieves and kidnappers whom the rich merchants would need protection from. But tonight's activities put an end to any thoughts of staying.

The wind was picking up, causing dark clouds filled with heavy rain to obscure the light from the moon. With the deepening darkness came a foreboding of more danger. As the rain began to fall, Daniel stepped into a darkened doorway.

Daniel ran over the events at the inn. *I think the dead assassin behind the counter was a flunky, a backup in case the lead assassin missed. I am quite sure the lead assassin is Count Valkar. Valkar is the best the Ramaahian Empire has. Boy, I must have really made them mad this time!*

In the last five years, there had been ten attempts on Daniel's life by prize-seekers. Four of those, five now, were by Ramaahian-hired assassins. One of those attempts, four years ago, had killed Nathan. But none of the previous prize-seekers were as good as Valkar.

Daniel regretted having to leave Staymos. In general, the people here were good folks, except the thieves and kidnappers. Most of the people made their living off the busy port, working for the shipping companies. They were dockworkers, shipwrights, or as teamsters hauling freight into the interior of the giant island. Many of the rest of them worked in the numerous shops and small industries that provided for the city's services.

Daniel pulled the hood of his cloak up over his head as the rain poured down in sheets. With the rainfall reducing visibility to a few yards, it was time to move. He stepped out into the street, looked around, and headed for the docks. He still moved from shadow to shadow, watching his back trail carefully.

The buildings he past were constructed out of wood and stone, and the roofs were covered with slate and built on a steep slope to allow the heavy winter snow to slide off easily.

Charsel's Three Apples Inn was on the edge of town opposite the bay. Daniel had to walk all the way across town by houses whose windows were dark, the occupants still asleep this early in the morning. The streets he passed over were rough cobblestone with slate gutters running down the middle. All the streets sloped toward the bay. As he got closer to the port, the houses gave way to commercial buildings.

The rain was a torrential downpour by now, making his job of stealing through the town without being seen much easier. He reached the docks and slowly made his way down the waterfront street, to the Body and Sole restaurant. It was a well-used, run-down inn that served fresh fish and not-so-fresh women in a variety of ways. It also was the most popular inn for ship captains and their crews. He hoped to find a captain who would let him purchase passage out of the port town tonight without being noticed.

The smell of fish and unwashed men gagged him when he stepped through the door. Even this early in the morning, the place was full of sailors. Ships came into Staymos at all hours of the day and night, and the two things sailors wanted most, after a couple pints of ale, were fresh food and women, not necessarily always in that order.

Daniel stopped to look around. If it were possible, it seemed darker inside the tavern than out. Shaking the water from his cloak, he surveyed the great room. It was not overly large, with space for about fifty people.

Daniel walked toward the bar, all the time taking notice of the other patrons. Two guys sitting at a table in the middle of the room were fighting over a bawdy soul dressed as a serving wench. She was a buxom woman with brown teeth, stringy brown hair, and scars on her face. She did not seem like much to fight over. Daniel smiled to himself and thought, *But I guess if you've been at sea for an exceptionally long time, anything would look good.*

Standing at the bar, he motioned for the bartender and said, "I would like a half pint of ale, and maybe some information."

The bartender snickered and gave him a gap-toothed grin. "Ale, I have plenty of. Information, on the other hand, will cost you."

Daniel asked, "Are you the owner?"

"Yeah, sure, I am," replied the bartender, "and if I were, don't you think I would have something better to do than stay up all night, waiting on these pigs and handing out information to useless vagabonds like you?"

Some of the men around the bar laughed as they gulped down their drinks. The bartender continued to wipe the mug in his hand, moving the grease and grime from one side to the other.

Daniel was not in the mood for jesting, but he ignored the bartender's sarcasm. He said, "I was under the impression that the owner would be able to help me."

The bartender drew a mug of ale from the keg behind him, then set it on the counter. He placed both hands palms down on the bar and leaned forward toward Daniel. He spoke coarsely, the smell of rotting teeth leaking from his mocking smirk. "The owner went home hours ago, probably to count his gold and to niggle with his young wife. So for a man such as you, talking to me would be like talking to him."

Daniel could not decide—should he knock the few remaining teeth out of this fool's head or continue to endure his taunts? He opted for the latter and pulled two silver coins out of his pouch and dropped one of them on the counter, then asked, "I'm looking for a ship that would be leaving tonight or first thing in the morning. Do you know of any?"

Daniel began dancing the other coin from finger to finger on his right hand. With his eyes locked on the dancing coin, the bartender placed his left hand over the coin on the counter, stuck his right hand out, palm up, and grinned. "I don't think I can help you. What with all the sailors we get in here, I have trouble remembering those kinds of things. But a little more incentive might jog my memory, if you know what I mean."

Daniel reached across the counter and grabbed the man by the throat with his left hand and lifted him off the ground. "Let me see if I can help." Tightening his grip, he asked again, "Are there any ships leaving port tonight?"

The man struggled wildly, feet flailing in the air. His face was turning blue as he pulled desperately with both hands on Daniel's wrist. Looking toward the far side of the room, he croaked out, "That table in the corner." Daniel turned his head to look. The table had four men sitting around it.

Daniel dropped the gasping man onto the floor and spun the coin in his right hand onto the counter. Picking up his mug of ale, he walked to the table in the corner.

The men were better dressed than the rest of the customers. They had full plates of food sitting on the table in front of them. The serving girls sitting with them were cleaner and healthier looking than the rest.

Daniel stopped at the end of the table and waited for one of the men to finish his story. The men boomed with laughter, and all the girls giggled and scrunched in closer to the men beside them. As far as Daniel could tell from what he had heard, the story did not seem all that funny. But he knew that most men like to think they are funny, and they especially like it when attractive women think so too. These women clearly understood this, and they probably also understood that their appreciation loosened the men's purse strings.

He interrupted their revelry. "Excuse me, I am looking for a captain who might be sailing east, maybe tonight or in the morning?"

The oldest one in the group, a big man with a long scar on his face, chortled, "You're out of luck, laddie. We all arrived late yesterday or early last night. There's a big storm blowing in. I doubt anybody will be leaving here for any eastern destination for three or four days."

The door of the inn opened, and Daniel's eyes darted toward it to see who was coming in. It was just an old fisherman. As he turned his head back to the table, he spotted a dark figure moving deeper into the shadows on the other side of the room, but he could not see a face. Looking back at the captains, he replied, "The destination is not that important."

The old captain smirked and asked, "Got some little lassie's angry husband after you?"

Everyone at the table laughed. Two of the girls bent over the table toward Daniel, one arm wrapped around the other's shoulder, the cut in their blouses sagging low. Rocking her shoulders back and forth, one of them cooed in a taunting, husky voice, "If you had come to Doreen and me in the first place, you wouldn't be worrying about no angry husband."

Again, everyone at the table laughed. The oldest one of the girls, who had long black hair, dark-brown eyes, and brightly painted red lips, surveyed Daniel like a tree cat getting ready to pounce. Licking her red lips, she smiled and cautioned the other girls by saying, "From the size of this one, girls, it might take two or three of us." Her mouth widened and her white teeth gleamed as she purred at Daniel. "What do you say, Blue Eyes? You want us to save you from that angry husband?"

Daniel knew they were just flirting, not making an offer. They would not trade their wealthy captains for him. Still, he flirted back and said, "I will have to pass. I don't have the time now, not even for ladies as pretty as you three."

The three of them giggled again and thrust out their bottom lips, pretending to pout.

Daniel surveyed the common room again, peering through the smoky gloom. He looked to the other side of the room, where he had seen the dark figure earlier, but he was gone. He thought, *Curse it! I should have paid more attention.*

The youngest of the captains interrupted Daniel's thoughts as he said, "Well, if you don't care where you are going, then you might be interested in Captain Short's brig. He's leaving at daybreak, but he's not going east. He's headed south."

Daniel replied, "Like I said, I'm not too picky about the destination."

The old captain spoke up again. "Still, you might not want to sail on the *Johansson's Pride*. She plies her trade with the Three Sisters and the Pact of Brothers."

With that, everyone at the table grew quiet and pulled back in on themselves, as if a cold draft had just blown through the room.

The young captain shuddered and said, "I believe he makes for Hog Snout Bay this trip."

Again, they all shivered.

Turning back to the table, Daniel gave them a puzzled look. "Where's Hog Snout Bay?"

The old captain whispered, "In the Lands of Chaos."

Chapter 2

Captain Jovan stood at attention as Colonel Campbell and his Majesty, Brother Samuel, talked to each other at the far end of the long room. He surveyed the room; it was easily five spans across and ten spans long. Moving his eyes from painting to painting and tapestry to tapestry, he noted that they all were filled with depictions of bloody battles fought sometime in the past. The pieces of furniture were covered with different kinds of animal skins.

He would have liked to sit down on one of them, having ridden hard for four days to get to this meeting, but when he arrived, they did not even wait for morning and called him directly to the palace while it was still extremely late.

The two men on the other end of the room looked like they were in disagreement over whatever they were talking about. If the situation did not make the captain so uncomfortable, being this close to two of the most powerful men in the kingdom, it might have been funny. Brother Samuel was the ruler of all the Pact of Brothers, the largest kingdom in the Westward, and Colonel Campbell was the commander of the Pact of Royal Lancers, the most elite cavalry division in the entire army. But by their physical looks, no one would think much of either of them.

Brother Samuel was a short compact man with a wiry build. His face looked calm on the surface, but the tension in his posture was obvious to Captain Jovan. The man was wound as tight as a saddle strap on a green broke colt. He wore a simple brown priest robe, designed to make him look humble, but it only accented the leanness of his build and the intensity of his demeanor.

Colonel Campbell stood a good two heads taller than Brother Samuel and was twice the small man's weight. Where the ruler's eyes were sharp and keen, the colonel's eyes were droopy and almost sad. His uniform was also a study in opposites of that of the monkish robes of the king. He wore the powder-blue coat and white pants of the Royal Lancers, but the gold braid on the shoulders, sleeves, button face, and leg piping was intricately designed and overly ornate. He wore a bright-red sash, from which his sword, encased in its gold scabbard, was suspended. In his position as commander of the Pact of Royal Lancers, he was entitled to wear the uniform of a commanding general, and of course, he did.

Jovan felt a little underdressed as he waited patiently in his simple and unadorned short captain's uniform. He really did not understand why he was here at all. He was supposed to have left with his patrol for the Lands of Chaos two days ago. His lancer patrol was to head north up the coast highway from Crome Castle, headquarters of the Royal Lancers, to relieve the patrol that was returning south from Devil's Pass. Instead, he had received orders a week ago to come to the capital city of St. Michaels to meet with Colonel Campbell about a change in his mission. Another patrol headed north in his place.

So here he was in full dress uniform, scared, uncomfortable, and unsure of himself, standing in the office of Brother Samuel. What could they possibly want him to do that they would not send for someone more senior and with more experience? As a young short captain with less than a year of combat experience, he did not feel qualified for a special detail. He had led only four patrols into the Ebony Forest during his time as a short captain, and he had never commanded more than a half score of lancers at any one time.

Jovan looked up from his thoughts and found Colonel Campbell staring at him, the colonel's booming voice calling him. "Captain Jovan, will you come join us, please?"

Marching smartly toward the pair of leaders, he responded, "Yes, sir."

Brother Samuel turned to him with a smile that held no humor. "Captain, how has your time been while on patrols in the Middle Kingdom?"

Jovan thought, *The Middle Kingdom! Why do this nation's leaders insist on using the archaic name for the Lands of Chaos? It certainly was not a kingdom, for it had no king, or laws, except for those that the lancer patrols brought with them.* Then he replied, "Your Majesty, I have been privileged to lead four patrols into the Ebony Forest. Each time we encountered small bands of the hadrac or orcs, my men showed themselves to be more than a match for them. We have been able to kill all we have found. Fortunately, to this point, we have had no casualties."

"That is most impressive, Captain." The colonel's voice boomed again as his eyes looked right through Jovan. "So you feel confident about your men and your ability to lead them?"

"Sir, I have great confidence in my men. They are well trained and very eager to fulfill any order they receive from His Majesty, and I am prepared to lead them," Jovan boasted, only lying a little bit. The truth was that none of the men understood why they were being sent into the Lands of Chaos to fight the hadrac and orcs. The people who lived in the Ebony Forest and the Midland Plains seemed to be, at best, outcast from civilized nations or, at worst, liars, thieves, and murderers. He himself knew that they patrolled the coast highway to keep the road open for commerce and trade with the Three Sisters. The patrols on the old Queen's Highway made no sense to him. The people of L'ke L'fe did not want anything to do with the Pact of Brothers or their Royal Lancers.

"That is good, Captain," the colonel commended, then asked, "How do you personally feel about our presence in the Middle Kingdom?"

Captain Jovan looked perplexed as he replied, "Sir, I'm not quite sure I understand the question."

Brother Samuel cleared his throat and growled, "What's to understand, son? We want to know your personal feelings about patrolling in the Middle Kingdom!"

Captain Jovan answered reluctantly, "Your Majesty, I am only a short captain, and a young short captain at that. I just follow orders and draw my pay."

The colonel's voice boomed even louder than before as he asked, "Are you being impertinent, Captain?"

"No, sir, but I don't understand what my personal feelings have to do with me obeying orders," Jovan replied nervously.

Brother Samuel spoke in a soothing voice. "Young man, we are just curious, and the little assignment we have for you requires that our curiosity be fulfilled."

Jovan relaxed a bit as he answered, "Well, to be honest, I enjoy the patrols. The Land of—the Middle Kingdom is a beautiful place, except for the hadrac and orcs, of course, but most of the time we just ride up and down the roads, making them safe for the merchants. Our presence alone keeps most of the beasts at bay."

"And how do you feel about serving your country as a Royal Lancer?"

"It is what I've always wanted to be. My father, all his brothers, and my grandfather before them were all lancers. It is a great honor for me to serve. I only hope that I can live up to their example, sir."

Colonel Campbell let a genuine smile creep onto his face. "Oh yes, I remember your father and his brothers. I fought with them in the Shining Lands campaign. Your father was also a captain, if I remember correctly?"

Jovan replied, somewhat boastfully, "Yes, sir, he led the First Troop, First Company of the King's Own regiment."

The colonel stated, "Oh my, that is quite a distinction." Then he asked, disinterestedly, "How is your father?"

Jovan was a little confused as he thought, *Surely, the colonel knew what happened to the First of the First in the Shining Lands?* He then replied, "My father is dead, sir, along with all my uncles. They were all killed during that campaign."

A flash of recognition passed across the colonel's face, which he quickly hid, but not before Jovan noticed it and thought, *What is this all about? Are they playing games with me?* Jovan was not sure what to say, so he said nothing.

Brother Samuel gave the colonel a scolding look but changed it to a smile as he spoke to Jovan. "We are immensely proud to have an officer with such a prestigious pedigree serving in one of our most elite units. We have another question for you, Captain. You are aware of our distant cousins to the north and how they treat men?"

Jovan replied honestly, "Your Majesty, I have never been to the Three Sisters, but I have met their female warriors at the rendezvous point at Devil's Pass. They appear to be very competent soldiers, though I have never seen them in battle."

Colonel Campbell barked, "So you think it would be a good idea to allow our women to become soldiers also?"

Jovan was taken aback as he thought, *What kind of question is this? He had never once thought about women serving as soldiers. A thing like that had never happened in the Pact of Brothers. Women are meant to be mothers and to work in the fields and textile industries. Who would ever want a woman to ride into battle with him, or to share a fire with in the wilderness?*

Now Jovan was really confused by the two men standing in front of him as he responded defensively, "Sir, I only stated what I observed. I believe in the Holy Order and all its tenants. The role of women is clearly spelled out by the law, and as an officer in His Majesty's service, I am honor bound to uphold the law."

"So you would be opposed to a change in the natural order of things?" Brother Samuel said in a whisper.

Responding smartly, Captain Jovan said, "I trust my leaders, and again, I am honor bound to obey them, sire. I would be opposed to anything that would go against my duty to you and to the Holy Order."

The two men looked long and hard at Jovan, as if trying to see into his soul or at least to read his mind. Then Brother Samuel nodded to the colonel, who walked over to a map of the Westward that hung on the wall above a writing desk. "Come over here, Captain."

The colonel pointed to a spot on the map as Jovan moved to join him. "In two weeks, you will leave on patrol from Crome Castle with a full score of lancers. Your full squad will precede a full company of foot soldiers who should arrive in H'la four days after you."

The colonel drew an imaginary line up the Coast Road from Crome Castle to the crossroad town of H'la. "You will then be joined by both of the patrols that are already on station. That will give you sixty lancers and one hundred foot soldiers under your command."

Jovan could feel his stomach climbing up into his throat. His mind was reeling. They were giving him command of almost two full companies. That was a position meant for a major, or at least a full captain. What had he done to deserve so much responsibility? So he said, "Colonel, I am at a loss for words, and though I am greatly honored by your request, I am concerned about a possible breach of protocol and more than a little bewildered by what you want me to do."

The colonel stood fully erect and spoke. "Captain, first, I have made no request, I have given you an order. Second, I am not unaware of the possible breach of protocol, so the papers detailing your promotion to full captain are already in Major Smitt's hands and are waiting for you at Crome Castle. And third, I have not told you yet what we want you to do, only what you will do it with."

Brother Samuel asked Jovan another question. "Are you aware of the great queen prophecy?"

"Yes, I think I remember it." Jovan quoted the Holy Writ of the Pact of Brothers exactly as any nine-year-old student would. "A great king, a descendent of M'tin, will return and restore order to the Middle Kingdom, uniting the three kingdoms, and at the same time thwart the powers of darkness."

"Very good, Captain. Do you also know the time frame for the prophecy?" asked Brother Samuel.

Jovan replied, "I do not recall it, sir, only that it was a long time."

For some reason unknown to Jovan, there was anger in the king's voice as he growled, "Three hundred years, boy! And we are in the three hundredth year. In fact, it is one month from that exact day. In one month, this mysterious king is supposed to return to Queens Castle Home in the Midlands and be crowned as the supreme ruler of the Westward."

Now Jovan's mind was really plunged into confusion as he thought, *How could this be? Information like this should not be a secret. Everyone should know about it! It should be a time of celebration and rejoicing!* Then he asked, "Sire, this is wonderful news! Shouldn't we be preparing for this in some way?"

Colonel Campbell had moved to a chair and had sat down. He was breathing heavily; his face was flushed, and his hands shook. As he spoke, his voice cracked and seemed almost frail, but filled with anger. "Captain, why do you think you are here? You and your men are part of that preparation. We have other plans that do not concern you. We are sending a delegation to the Midlands to meet this new king, but we are also including measures to deal with other problems that may arise. We are sending forces to Port K'la and the Devil's Pass, but the force at H'la might be the most critical."

Brother Samuel took over and said, "That is where you come in, Captain Jovan. Your troops are a blocking force designed to stop others who would want to take advantage of the situation. There are many evil forces at work who would like to destroy this new king before he can consolidate his power."

Captain Jovan turned to the king and stammered, "We should send the entire army to the Midland to support the new king."

The colonel, who seemed to be getting angrier, spoke in a low, growly voice. "Because of our ongoing border war with the Ramaahian Empire, we don't dare move the army away from our southeast borders. No, the lancers and the northern border foot regiment can easily handle the situation as we see it."

Jovan thought about the conflict in the Impenetrable Mountains on the southern border. *The war has been going on since before the Shining Lands conflict. The mountain range that separates the Eastward from the Westward takes over ten days to cross and are so high the clouds cover the tops almost all the time. Only a small force can make their way through the mountains with enough supplies to survive.* Jovan had heard that in the past few years, the Ramaahians had been sending more and more troops, and no one knew how they were keeping them supplied. But even with this increased threat, the south did not seem to demand the attention of the entire army.

The colonel spoke again. "You, Captain Jovan, are to use your men to block the crossroads at H'la. You are to let no one pass, not anyone who does not carry a signed letter from His Majesty. No one is to come inland on the Queen's Highway, and by this, I mean *no one*, including soldiers from the Three Sisters."

Jovan's face must have shown the shock he felt as he thought, *Why would we have the desire or the right to stop Three Sisters troops from entering the Midlands?* because before he could say anything, the colonel continued.

He said, "We have already made arrangements with Their Royal Majesties of the Three Sisters. They have the signed documents they need, but things are not always as they seem. We have heard rumors that there is some discontent in our fair cousins' kingdom. Besides, they are women, and we have had our difficulties in the past in dealing with them. Do you understand your orders, Captain? No one without signed papers gets past H'la."

Jovan snapped to attention and saluted. "Yes, sir, no one is to be allowed to pass H'la without signed papers."

The colonel returned his salute, and as Jovan turned and began to walk away, the colonel added, "Captain, this order includes the seers too."

Jovan stopped dead in his tracks and turned his upper body to stare in disbelief at the pair of leaders, but he only replied with a weak, "Yes, sir."

* * *

Jovan walked briskly out of the palace in a daze. He made his way down the expansive stone steps to the street paved with baked bricks. His orders seemed to be contrary to every idea he had been raised with. The Three Sisters had been the Pact of Brothers' strongest ally for centuries, and the seers, well, they were seers. It was a seer that gave the original prophecy, and they had been advisers to kings from the creation of the Pact of Brothers over three hundred years ago. Why would the king want to keep those who had only helped the Pact of Brothers away from an event of this magnitude?

A voice called out, "Captain Jovan! Captain Jovan, where are you going?"

Jovan stopped and turned around. It was Sergeant Gallant. Jovan had been so lost in his thoughts that he walked right past the waiting sergeant.

The sergeant chuckled. "So what is our big secret mission that could only be found out in the secluded halls of the royal palace?"

"Sergeant Gallant, you should watch your mouth. Those rank insignia are not permanently attached to your shoulders," Jovan responded, half-smiling. "Let's go down to the Lance and Sword and I will fill you in."

* * *

The Lance and Sword was immaculately clean and orderly, like everything else in the capital. There were only three other patrons in the tavern, sitting around the cloth-covered tables. Young captain Jovan drank his second pint of cider ale, licked his lips, and frowned at the mug as he set it down on the table in front of him.

The sergeant smiled at the captain. "Once you get used to brewed wheat beer of H'la, this cider ale just doesn't seem to satisfy, does it?"

Jovan looked at him with the same frown. "Sergeant Gallant, you continue to misspeak. Alcohol is not allowed in the Holy Lands, nor are soldiers of the Pact of brothers allowed to drink it. You should be more careful with your tongue while you are in the capital."

"Yes, sir, I will watch what I say, but I quickly grow weary of all the rules. That was why I joined the lancers, because I knew that I would spend most of my time deployed away from the cities and their freaking laws."

Captain Jovan leaned back in his chair and made a sweeping motion with his hand. "I know what you are saying. The more time I spend out on patrol, the less I like being around all this. Well, Sergeant, we are both getting our wish. We are to take a full squad to H'la, where we will be joined by two more full squads and a company of foot soldiers."

The sergeant leaned forward in disbelief and concern. "And who is going to be our commanding officer?"

"He is a newly promoted full captain…with very little experience," Jovan replied with a smirk.

"Oh, great, a green-behind-the-ears know-it-all—just what we need going into a new assignment. Leave it to command to mess things up right from the beginning." Sergeant Gallant leaned back in his chair, disgusted.

Captain Jovan smiled back at him. "Well, you better get used to it. This new captain of yours has chosen you to be his new top sergeant, with all the extra work that goes along with it. And I am sure he will come up with all sorts of extra duty with two full companies under his command."

Sergeant Gallant looked quizzically at Jovan. "How would this new captain even know to pick me as his top sergeant if he was just assigned to this mission?" The sergeant stood up to protest, and then he realized the joke being played on him.

"Captain, you are a sly one. Congratulations! It could not have happened to a nicer guy, or a more deserving officer."

"Yeah, thanks a lot. Let us go pick up our supplies so we can leave early in the morning. We have a long, hard ride ahead of us."

CHAPTER 3

Daniel left the Body and Sole from a door in the rear. The bartender had become far more accommodating for some reason. Cautiously, he walked through the back alley; he knew his pursuers could be waiting for him anywhere. He decided he would take a roundabout path to the *Johansson's Pride*, and at the same time, he would see if he was being followed. He went up several dark streets, working his way to the other end of the bay. Daniel saw three or four shadows moving in the night but was unable to identify anyone.

If the old man were here, they could have run a "drive and trap" against one of the pursuers and reduce the odds a bit. But because he was alone, he would have to settle for trying to evade them.

Daniel shivered from the inside out. Rain was dripping from his hood as he slid from house to house on the back streets. He thought, *Give me a straight-up fight! This lurking around, people lying in wait, it's annoying.* Daniel tried to fight back memories of another time in the past when he first should have realized he was being pursued by unknown assailants, but they came rushing into his mind anyway.

* * *

He was only nine when he and his adoptive family came home from the festival in Karmac. They had been celebrating Flanderon's independence from the Ramaahian Empire. His stepdad had been an important official in Karmac, and the festival had gone on until almost dawn. When they approached their small farm, his father cautioned them to be quiet and slowed their pace. They were coming around from behind the barn when his father noticed the front door was open on the homestead.

Daniel was the eldest of the kids, so his father told him to take his two little sisters, Emmy and Kailyn, and his little brother, Martin, into their secret hiding place in the hay shed.

Daniel had gotten his siblings into the shed and was opening the trapdoor so they could crawl down the ladder into the spud cellar. Holding the trapdoor open with his left hand, he turned to help his sisters and brother into the hiding place with his right. But before they could enter, he stopped to watched as his father and mother approached the house. His heart leaped into his throat as four dark figures emerged from the open doorway. His father drew his sword as one of the dark men came toward him, but the dark man struck first, swinging his huge sword, cutting off his father's head. His mother dropped to her knees, screaming, as another dark figure swung a mace. He hit her in the head, knocking her over backward, her face smashed, with blood spraying all over. Daniel gasped and lost his footing and fell backward into the hidden cellar.

Daniel awoke with his head aching. He touched back of his head, and there was a large bump covered with a sticky liquid. He had no idea how long he had lain unconscious in the dark cellar. Daniel remembered seeing the trapdoor slam shut before he lost consciousness.

He stood up and searched with his hands for the ladder. Finding it, he slowly climbed up to the trapdoor. He was shaking with fear as he slowly pushed on the trapdoor, but it would not move. He started to panic, and his mind raced. Leverage, his dad had taught him about leverage, so he braced his back against the door and moved his feet up onto the top rung. Pushing with all his strength, he felt something shift and the door move a bit. He pushed harder, fear beginning to rage through his mind. Whatever was on the door slid off, and the door flew open.

As he put his hands down on the ground to climb out of the hole, he felt something cold and sticky. He lifted his left hand to look at what it was, and his mind lost complete control as he stared at the blood that covered it. By now he was totally consumed by fear. Getting to his feet, he looked around. He could see his brother and sisters lying in the straw covered with blood. His mind stopped working.

Daniel could not remember how long he wandered from body to body, pushing on them and yelling at them, trying to get them to move. Eventually, a friend of his father came by and found him curled up next to his mother, crying, with his father's head in his hands.

* * *

Daniel was startled to realize that he had stopped moving, having gotten caught up in his thoughts. He shook off the memories as he looked around to see if anyone was watching. With no one else around, he again started moving toward the south end of town.

He eventually found himself back at the wharf. Hiding behind some barrels and crates, he looked over the docks, found no one watching, and decided it was safe to look for Captain Short's brig.

Walking out onto the first pier, he could see a brig being loaded by several men. The brig had two stubby masts, hardly seeming to rise above the aftercastle; the ship itself was short and squatty, like a wood box with sloping sides. Lanterns were hanging from the yardarm, lighting the loading ramp and the upper deck. Daniel walked down the dilapidated pier, watching his footing, avoiding the holes and the broken boards. The worms and salt had chewed the wood up badly.

He could see no one watching as he approached the ship. All the men that he could see were working, and he could hear a man barking orders. As he approached, he saw a man dressed in a dark-blue overcoat yelling at the men as they loaded the boat. The man's voice was deep and gravelly, filling up the dark space around the pier. He had the type of voice that commanded respect.

His snow-white hair was pulled back in a long ponytail and hung down to the middle of his back. He was yelling orders to several deckhands who worked quickly and efficiently. This man was clearly the captain and cut quite a regal figure, appearing tall and slender.

Daniel walked up behind the man and cleared his throat. "Excuse me, sir, I am looking for Captain Short."

As the man turned around, Daniel was startled by what stood before him. The voice that came out of the man's mouth did not match the body that produced it. The man's forehead reached all the way to the crown of his head, but what hair he lacked on the top of his head was made up for by the eyebrows that protruded from his forehead like snow-covered bushes. The man's face was skinny with sharp cheekbones, which cut against his skin like a knife. His teeth looked like little yellow bits of corn, worn down to little nubs. The coat he wore was too big for his slender body. His shoulders were broad but slender, with toothpick arms and tiny hands.

As he spoke, he stepped off the box he had been standing on. The top of his head barely reached Daniel's shoulders. "I am Captain Short. What can I do for you?"

It took all of Daniel's effort to keep from laughing out loud—the irony was almost too much. He took a moment to recover from the shock caused by the man's apparent transformation. Catching himself, he replied, "I am looking for passage on your ship, Captain."

The captain only glanced at him as he answered Daniel, "I already have all the berths and cabins filled, but if you want, you can buy passage in the cargo hold." He turned to watch his men. Suddenly, he yelled out, "Pocksey, you dunderhead, those crates go in last! Now, put them down and finish loading those barrels of salted fish!"

As Daniel began to address Captain Short to discuss the accommodations, Pocksey let one of the barrels of fish slip, and it broke open on the dock, scattering in all directions. The smell was overpowering. Captain Short jumped back up on his crate, yelling, "Pocksey, what are you doing? Be more careful! That is our lunch you're scattering across the dock. Now, clean it up!"

Pocksey stood looking at the slimy fish scattered across the surface of the dock. He seemed lost and unsure of what to do as he said, "Captain, the barrel broke. What should I put these fish in?"

Captain Short sighed heavily. "You're useless, Pocksey, useless. If your father weren't my wife's brother, I would..." The captain lifted his hands up to his face and rubbed his eyes, shook his head, and let out a long breath. "Go get an empty barrel from the head of the pier. And be quick about it."

Daniel thought to himself, *Sleeping with the fish? I don't think so.* He then said, "Captain Short, I will need a private cabin, and I am willing to pay well."

Captain Short chuckled as he said, "Sonny, everyone pays. I already told you, they're all filled."

Daniel was not about to spend the next ten days living in the belly of this old scow with barrels of stinky salted fish. So he said, "Captain, it is important that I have a berth on this ship. I will not take no for an answer."

"Sonny, as I told the gentleman who came here earlier, I don't have any more cabins. They are all full. If you want to travel in a berth, you will have to wait for another ship."

Daniel stepped up next to the crate that Captain Short was standing on and growled, "None of the other ships are leaving for three or four days. They are all waiting out the storm. So I have no other choice. I need to leave on your ship."

"Then you will have to ride with the cargo," Captain Short replied without looking at Daniel.

With his left hand, Daniel slid a heavy pouch out of his pocket, and with his right, he grabbed ahold of the back of the captain's coat, picked him up, and turned him around. "Captain, I said no was not an acceptable answer." He raised his left hand up to the small man's face.

Captain Short flinched and raised his hands up to his own face. "Are you going to hit me like the other guy did?"

Daniel chuckled. "No. I am giving you eight gold pieces to compensate the people you are going to move to let me have a private cabin."

The captain's eyes lit up. "Well, that's a different story. The other guy just threatened to hurt me. I am sure that I will be able to find someone who will be glad to move."

Daniel smiled. "You don't understand. For eight coins, I'm taking the cabin I want."

"Yes, yes, of course. Help yourself," the captain replied.

Daniel stopped and then asked, "By the way, who was the other man that came earlier?"

Captain short thought for a moment and said, "He was a man much like you, a little taller, but not quite as big. He had dark skin and black hair."

"Did he give you a name?" Daniel asked.

The captain, wanting to get back to work, said curtly, "He didn't, and I didn't ask."

Daniel continued to probe. "And what cabin did he take?"

The captain turned away as he replied, "He is in the bow on the gun deck. Now please let me get back to work."

Daniel walked up the gangplank and headed for the stern. He knew the person whose cabin he would take would probably never see any of the gold coins he just gave the captain, but he also did not care.

His mind returned to the other late-arriving passenger. From Captain Short's description, the other man could be Count Valkar. If it was, Daniel was not worried. Valkar was a back-shooting, lie-in-wait assassin; he doubted that Valkar would ever confront him head-on.

* * *

Later that morning, the *Johansson's Pride* lifted anchor, raised sail, and headed out of port. Daniel walked out onto the poop deck, headed all the way to the stern to lean on the taffrail, and looked over the other passengers. He noticed two families with little kids and thought, *They must be going to Port Royal.* There were also two older couples and several individual males. The rest of the men on deck were seamen who worked aboard the ship. There appeared to be no sign of Count Valkar or a man who fit Captain Short's description.

As the ship cleared the outer seawall, Daniel turned to look to the northeast. Sure enough, the storm clouds were building, and it was looking to be a big one. As he looked to the south, the sky was clear and bright. Daniel wondered if they were going to be able to stay ahead of the storm.

Out of the corner of his eye, he caught sight of the man the captain had described—it was Count Valkar. He was just emerging from the bow companionway. Daniel stepped in close to a small dinghy that was housed on the starboard side and behind the mizzen rigging hanging down from the yard.

Daniel could see Valkar move all the way to the tip of the bow on the foredeck. The tall man leaned against the headrail and looked over the people milling around on the main deck. It was clear he was looking for someone, and that someone was probably Daniel. It seemed obvious that the man in the Body and Sole last night had been Valkar, and he had deduced that this was the only ship Daniel could leave port in. So Valkar had taken a chance and appropriated passage on the *Johansson's Pride*.

Daniel watched as Valkar milled around on the foredeck, talking to fellow passengers. Daniel thought, *There is no way I am sneaking around on this boat, trying to avoid this guy.* Daniel stepped out of the cover of the rigging and walked down the staircase to the main deck. Finding his way to the bow companionway, he went down to the gun deck to wait.

Eventually, Valkar sauntered down the stairwell with an older man. They were both laughing at a story the older man had been telling. Daniel, stepped out in front of the two men and said, "You're a long way from home, Valkar. What brings your sneak thief hide this far west?"

The older man who had been talking to Valkar looked at both big men and slowly slid down the passageway with his back against the wall.

Valkar smiled. "Manslayer, you have a nasty habit of avoiding the unfortunate situations that you get yourself into."

"No thanks to you, Count. It is a shame about your friend at the inn. You left him a little exposed."

"He knew the risks. Besides, he obviously was not meant to be in this business, so an early end to his career was probably the best for everyone."

"Nice, Valkar. That's some kind of loyalty you show to your friends."

"Friend! Manslayer, you are so simple. That man at the inn would try to kill me for the right price. There is no such thing as loyalty. There is only what one gets for what one does and who gets the most. What has your loyalty gotten you? What did you get out of your relationship with that old man before he was killed?"

The long knife that Daniel carried in his waist belt suddenly appeared in his left hand, and the tip of it rested against Valkar's belly.

With both hands, Valkar pulled his cape away from his sides. "I'm not armed, Manslayer, and I know you. You will not stick that ridiculously large blade into my belly. You are governed by an honor code that dictates what you will or will not do. On the other hand, I do not. But as you well know, I do have a system that I follow. So why do not you and I have an agreement that while we are on this boat, we pretend to get along? And we will continue our game at a later time."

Daniel's mild anger simmered beneath the surface. He knew if he let it slip just a little, he could plunge the razor-sharp blade hilt-deep into Valkar's belly. But he also knew that Valkar was right; he could not bring himself to kill a man who could not defend himself. Daniel slid the blade back into its sheath, grabbed Valkar by his lapels, tossed him to the floor, and stormed up the companionway.

Valkar rolled onto his back and watched Daniel go up the stairs, a wicked smile filling his face.

CHAPTER 4

"Mother, I can dress myself!" Alssa's face wrinkled in resentment as she pulled the dress from her mother's hands.

"I know you can, dear. But I also know if I were not here to watch over you, you would make the trip to L'ke L'fe dressed in chain mail and leathers," the first sister and queen mother scolded.

Alssa replied, "That is exactly what I should be wearing, not this frilly, lady-in-waiting peacock outfit. I am the future queen of the Three Sisters. I was born a warrior, not a maiden."

Alssa pulled the dress on over her head and turned so her mother could lace up the back. She lifted her long strawberry-blond hair off her shoulders and said, "You have been doting over me for two weeks now, pushing me and trying to make me into something I have never been. And now, to top it off, you want me to attend the rebirth of the Middle Kingdom dressed like a Pact of Brothers mistress."

"Alssa, watch your language! You should not talk about your cousins that way!" Ch'lene cried. "Their ways may be different from ours, but we are still family."

Ch'lene pulled hard on the laces, trying to draw together the eyelets on Alssa's upper back.

"Ouch!" Alssa rolled her shoulders in protest. "What are you trying to do, pull my chest apart?"

Giving one last hard pull, Ch'lene drew up the laces and tied them off. "Your chest and shoulders are getting bigger, my dear. You practice the sword and bow too much. Your waist is so tiny in comparison. I could hardly get the bodice tied off."

Turning to face her mother, Alssa put her hands on Ch'lene's cheeks, bent her head down, and kissed her mother on the end of her nose. "You have a lot of room to talk. I'm built just like you, and for the same reasons. You still practice more than I do."

Returning the kiss, Ch'lene said, "I do love the feeling of a stout longbow in my hands. But times have changed since your aunts and I fought all those wars. We no longer need to prepare constantly for war. With Cult Island secure and the last of the half-men hunted down and destroyed, we have only to worry about an occasional pirate. That was why we waited to have children. We wanted to turn over the kingdom to our heirs in a time of peace."

Alssa sat on the ornately hand-embroidered stool and looked at her reflection in the highly polished silver mirror. Brushing out her hair, she could see her gray-haired mother packing her leathers and chain mail in her trunk. She smiled to herself and thought, *Once a warrior, always a warrior.*

"Mother, have we heard any more rumors of the hadrac or goblins?" Alssa asked.

Ch'lene took the brush out of Alssa's hand and continued stroking her daughter's hair as she said, "There are so few goblins they need not be worried about. Besides, Count Gravelet would have sent word from the Gorge if there were a problem. As for the hadrac, I think our cousins in the south are making something from nothing to justify a larger military presence in the Middle Kingdom. Did I tell you that they are increasing the size of each lancer patrol to a full score, and instead of two patrols in-country at any one time, they want to make it to four? T'asha's scouts also say they are rotating new patrols in every two weeks. She says they have also established a garrison at L'ke L'fe."

Alssa's eyebrows rose, and she turned to face her mother as she exclaimed, "They have four patrols on the Coast Road and a garrison on the Queen's Highway?"

"I'm sure it is both," replied the queen.

Alssa got up and walked to the veranda. She pondered about the ramifications of the Pact of Brothers' increased presence in the Lands of Chaos as she thought, *Why would Brother Samuel take such drastic measures? All this intrigue and mystery is unsettling.*

Alssa looked out over Jukeele. The mud nesters were soaring and diving through the air, landing on the sheer cliffs on the other side of the river. The view from her palace bedroom overlooked the western portion of the city. From Alssa's vantage point, she could see down sheer cliffs one hundred feet to the rivers below. The maelstrom created by the joining of the north and south branches of the Twin Rivers was an amazing sight.

The two rivers and the dominant height of the land made this place perfect for establishing Jukeele as the capital city of the Three Sisters. For three hundred years, no army had been able to breach the fortress, though many had tried.

Her gaze passed over the old city. It had grown all the way to the cliff's edge and down the face of the cliff to just thirty feet above the water.

Over time, as the city grew, it became necessary to build bridges across the river in several places. These five bridges were made of ironwood from the South Barrier Islands, white marble from Alantha, and green jade from Ceraroma. Each bridge could have its center section lifted, making it impassable.

The new city quickly sprang up on the other side of the rivers. Walls had been erected around the new city over the last one hundred years, but houses and businesses were built outside of those walls even before they were done. The relative peace had emboldened the people to live outside the safety of the walls. The people's lack of concern for their own safety bothered Alssa.

Ch'lene's words cut into her train of thought. "His Holiness, Lord Samuel, sent a communiqué letting us know of his plans to station permanent garrisons in both H'la and L'ke L'fe."

Alssa raised her hand to her mouth "Oh my! That will cost the Pact of Brothers a fortune. Lord Samuel must be counting on a large monetary return to spend that much coin on troop deployment in the Lands of Chaos. The old tightwad must be having fits. He holds onto every coin as if it were his last."

Moving next to her daughter, Ch'lene wrapped her arms around Alssa's waist and said, "He is counting on an extremely big miracle, my dear. He is risking much hoping his financial gamble will pay off big. In this he plays the same game as we do. If the prophecy is fulfilled, an army will be needed, and cousin Samuel wants it to be his."

Spinning out of her mother's embrace, she put her hands on her hips and said, "That is exactly my point. Why do you want Cally and me to go to Queens Castle Home with only our royal house troops, dressed like couple of blossoming flowers? Would it not be better to march a legion of troops down with us?"

"Alssa, you forget, not everyone feels like we do about women's and men's roles. We are the only matriarchal kingdom in the known lands, and if it were not for the seers, most of the kingdoms of the Eastward would not even have recognized us." Ch'lene moved over to the hearth and turned to face her daughter. "A thousand women dressed in full battle armor may be seen as threatening, or even insulting, rather than impressive."

Alssa rose to her full height, feigned the motions of drawing a sword, thrusting it out in front of her, and said, "I know how to impress, and if that insults him, then so be it."

"You are certainly impressive, but I am not confident that would be the best approach. No, I think for now we will go with a softer, gentler approach. Later, we will show what women are truly capable of, both in battle and in royal court."

Alssa frowned and threw her hands in the air. "We are going to be deceitful and then hope we will have trust when the truth is known. If that is the case, you should send T'asha instead of Cally and me."

Without warning, dread came upon Alssa, filling her heart with darkness that chilled her to the bone. She looked at her mother in confusion and fear.

Alssa was hearing her mother speak, but the chill running through her was overpowering. "Mother, I'm…I'm…" A heaviness filled Alssa's heart, and her mind became cloudy. Her vision was filled with a black doom. She could feel her spirit tearing from her, drawn toward the darkness.

"Are you okay, my dear?"

Alssa shook her head, the emotional darkness lifting off her as quickly as it had come. "I'm okay."

"What was happening?"

"I don't know, but I think I'm fine now."

Her mother gave her a knowing smile and went to the window and closed it. "Things are changing, and you are so black-and-white, Alssa. Sometimes things have shades of gray. In this case, the trick is to keep men guessing, let them come to their own conclusions by assumption. After all, we are not responsible if those conclusions are wrong."

Alssa frowned at her mother.

Ch'lene spoke with firmness. "It is in these matters that I feel we could learn from our female cousins in the Pact of Brothers. They know how to get along with males in authority. In most other places, it is not acceptable for women to be as direct as men, at least not in public."

Alssa's indignation pushed away the remaining uneasiness she felt. "Mother, how can you talk like this? You have raised me to be honest in all things, and to be direct."

Her mother gave Alssa an encouraging smile. "Changing times require us to change with them. We can no longer stay apart from the other kingdoms. With the three hundredth year of the prophecy coming to an end, we face all sorts of new situations, and with them we must learn new things."

Alssa sashayed across the room; she spun around, causing the skirt to billow, at which moment she stopped abruptly and bowed. "And this is the new thing you want me to learn, how to flirt and curtsy?" Alssa then placed her hands together and set them against her cheek, smiled sweetly, and batted her eyelashes. "Or maybe I can learn to play the weak and timid fawning maid."

She then dropped to both knees and leaned over. "And then we can let the men do all the fighting. Maybe even let them rule over us, so we can bend our knee to their every whim."

"Alssa, that will be quite enough. You know that is not what I want, but we must be prepared to change in a great many areas." Ch'lene moved toward the door. "Finish getting ready and then come downstairs. I will send a servant to inform M'sillia and Cally that we are ready, and we will meet in the great hall. Hurry, it's almost time for you to leave."

Alssa watched her mother leave and then slumped into a chair. *Curse the dark lords! What is happening to me?* The cold feeling stilled lingered in the pit of her stomach. The truth was, she did not understand why her mother was so insistent on portraying things different from how they really are.

All her life she wanted to see things change in the Three Sisters. She did not like the idea of men being subservient to women any more than she liked the idea of women bowing down to men. *But how can I bring about such a drastic change?*

She found herself hoping the prophecies were true. Then the new king could lead the people into the new era. *Sometimes my own foolishness surprises me. It has been three hundred years since M'tin ran off with that farm girl and left the Middle Kingdom without a monarch.*

The ironic thing was that it was a woman, the great queen herself, that proclaimed that only M'tin's heir could sit on the throne as king and lord of the Western Lands. Alssa thought, *That was a foolish thing to do. The entire Middle Kingdom regressed into chaos. Man-orcs, hadrac, and goblins roaming around at will. Even the human inhabitants are of questionable reputation. Most of them are thieves and murderers!*

The door banged open, and Cally entered with a huge smile on her face. She ran over to her sister and knelt beside her.

"Don't you love these dresses?" Cally asked. "I think they are wonderful! I am so excited for this trip! Aren't you?"

Alssa smiled at her sister-cousin and thought, *What a joy and breath of fresh air she is to me! No matter what happens, she always makes me feel better.* "I was just thinking about that. Do you really believe in the prophecy?" Alssa asked.

"Of course I do," Cally replied, then asked, "What else would you want to believe in?"

"But the seer's foretelling was so long ago," Alssa said.

Cally giggled and pushed herself up and twirled around, admiring her reflection in the mirror.

"Cally, you're not listening. I am not confident that anything is going to happen. I cannot believe that after all this time, anyone will show up. All who have come before were proven by the seers to be impostors. Why do you think this time will be any different?"

Cally ran her fingers through Alssa's hair. "Because I have faith. We both must have faith."

"Faith in what?" Alssa asked. She stood up and walked to the mirror and sat down, then said, "The three-century-old uttering of an old hermit that no one had ever seen before and who spoke and was never heard from again?"

Cally stood up and went to Alssa's side, put her arms around her, and leaned a delicate chin on her shoulder. "You can't have faith in what you already know or in what you can already see. You can only have faith in what has not happened yet."

Cally stood up and spun around again, causing her dress to billow. With her ever-present smile, she continued, "What we are going to be a part of is incredible. Something no one has ever seen before. M'tin disappeared without a trace, and then a seer came and said that in three hundred years, order will be restored and a new ruler will return and prevent the release of the greatest evil the world has ever seen. You can only believe in something like that with faith."

Alssa blew out a heavy sigh and said, "That is my point, Cally. I don't know if I can believe like that. I'm not sure I have any faith."

Wrinkling her nose as if a bad smell had entered the room, Cally exhaled. "You're beginning to sound like T'asha."

Alssa stared at their reflection. Though the two of them and T'asha were not sisters by birth, only cousins, they sure looked alike, especially in the face. Cally's hair was lighter, though, and she was more petite. T'asha, on the other hand, was built just like Alssa, same height, same broad shoulders.

T'asha's hair was different, flaming red. But the biggest differences between T'asha and her sisters were her desires and motives. They seemed to be the opposite of Alssa's and Cally's.

Suddenly, the foreboding came over her again. The same feelings she had felt with her mother earlier. It was like she was about to lose something very dear to her but, at the same time, gain something.

"Alssa, what is troubling you?" Cally asked.

"I feel like…well, I don't know…like things are changing around us out of our control. At one moment I want the change because it feels right and good, and then the next moment it feels wrong and evil." Alssa shivered as a cold chill ran down her spine.

Cally hugged her close. Looking at her sister's contorted reflection in the mirror, she said, "You are changing, and it will not be long before our mothers hand over the crown to us. That is why we are going to L'ke L'fe and Queens Castle Home instead of them."

A knock came from the door.

"Who is it?" Alssa asked.

"It is Colleen and Carrie, Your Majesties. It is time. The queen mothers are in the great hall, waiting for you."

As the two personal bodyguards came into the room, Alssa smiled. Colleen and Carrie were identical twins, blond, six feet tall, and beautiful. They were now forty years old but could have passed for the same age as their charges.

They were two of the deadliest women in all the Three Sisters. Apart, they were unbeatable, but together they were instant death for anyone who challenged them.

Alssa and Cally had never known life without the twins. When they were children, they thought the tall blondes were playmates pulled out of an ancient story by their mothers. The twins were only nineteen when they were chosen and had spent their entire life protecting the future queens of the kingdom.

T'asha's bodyguard was chosen much the same way. But she had been accidentally killed while sparring with T'asha four years ago.

Alssa and Cally, along with their personal bodyguards, joined their mothers in the great hall. The four of them walked outside to the waiting carriage together.

The carriage was large, large enough to hold eight people. So large, in fact, it had to be pulled by six white draft horses. The carriage was made of solid oak and painted jade green. It had inlaid gold and silver on the trim and doors. The wheels were six feet high, and the driver rode out in the open on a seat mounted in front.

Alssa thought the carriage was too ostentatious. T'asha had said that if you wanted to be royalty, you had to act like royalty, and it was about time Alssa started acting like it. Of course, she would feel that way; T'asha's mother, T'nanta, was the only one of the triumvirates to use the coach regularly, or she was the only one until she died ten years ago. Alssa's and Cally's mothers had felt that it was not necessary to create such a show when everyone knew who they were anyway. After T'nanta had been killed in battle, the carriage only reminded them of their departed sister, so they quit using it altogether.

But now they agreed with T'asha, and they felt it was appropriate to use to travel to L'ke L'fe. Alssa did not agree but had given in after it was decided that she and Cally should take their own horses along. Alssa's secret plan was to change into her leathers as soon as they crossed North Pass into the Wasteland. Then she would ride her own horse the rest of the way to L'ke L'fe.

Ch'lene reminded her for the tenth time, "Alssa, you have plenty of time to reach L'ke L'fe, so enjoy the ride. We want you refreshed and relaxed when you arrive. Learn as much as you can, notice everything, and be sly but bold."

Alssa sighed and said, "I know, Mother. We have been over this and over this. I understand my role, and I will play it as you have instructed."

"It is just so important. We only have one opportunity to make a good impression. We must not waste it," Ch'lene encouraged.

"I am twenty-one years old, and I have been trained since birth for this." Patting her mother's hand, she encouraged her with a smile, "Mother, you have done a good job raising me." She then took M'sillia's hand also. "You both have. Cally and I will represent the Sisters well, so relax and trust in your efforts."

T'asha came running up to the carriage. "Alssa, Cally, I'm glad I caught you before you left. I wanted to wish you a safe journey and good luck in dealing with all those men."

Colleen and Carrie walked up to the carriage door and gave T'asha identical looks of mistrust and disrespect as they stepped up into the carriage to sit across from their charges. Alssa noticed a flash of hatred come upon T'asha's face; it quickly vanished as her ever-present half-grin, half-grimace returned. *Why does it always look like she has to work at smiling?* Alssa thought to herself. T'asha had always been jealous of the twins.

T'asha's smile vanished again when she heard marching feet and clanking horse hooves on the cobblestone street. Turning to Ch'lene with a glimmer of anger in her eyes, she protested, "I thought we had agreed that we would not send troops, that it would be enough to send only the four of them?"

M'sillia frowned at her redheaded niece-daughter. "We received more reports from the Holy Lancers in the last few days. Hadrac attacked a patrol at the south pass last week, and three of the lancers were killed."

T'asha's eyes searched for words, and her mouth oozed contempt. "So a few men fall in battle and we go into a panic. Would it not be better to show the new king that the Three Sisters are confident and unafraid of a few hadrac? That we are secure in our position as liberators of the Northern Lands?"

"I don't think sending House J'ta and House L'se royal guards is showing signs of panic. It is prudent. I know from the beginning you have felt a less-militant approach would work better, but with this latest news, it would be unwise for us not to provide proper escort," M'sillia encouraged.

Alssa was becoming more and more confused by T'asha's conduct. T'asha was the most militant of the three of them and never went anywhere without armor. She had even advocated for attacking Rodon. The Rodones mountain people had not been overly friendly over the years, but they were not friendly with anyone. Alssa believed that it came from living in land that was above ten thousand feet and covered with snow nine months out of the year. The Rodones had allied themselves with the original Three Sisters three hundred years ago to drive out the armies of the Lords of Chaos. It seemed to Alssa that the Rodones' unwillingness to embrace a matriarchal society was T'asha's reason for mistrust. So last year, T'asha had said they treated her with disrespect and contempt when she took the realm's yearly gifts of food, cloth, and iron to them during their feast of liberation.

Now, after all that aggression, she suddenly wanted Alssa and Cally to act like passive princesses.

I wonder what she is up too, Alssa thought.

"Thank you for your concern, sister, but I'm sure you would not like to venture into the Lands of Chaos without an escort, and neither would I," Alssa said as she searched T'asha's face for some sign of agreement.

T'asha took Alssa's hand and said, "Of course, of course. We would not want anything to happen to either of you, now, would we? How would I run things around here without the two of you?" Stepping up on the carriage rung, she clasped Cally's hand also. "Your safety is paramount. The three of us must rule like our mothers have in the past. Each of us should get what we deserve, and I know both of you will get what is coming to you: it is only justice." With that, T'asha stepped down and strode away.

The driver pulled the carriage in behind the formed troops as they marched out of the palace gate.

With a look of distaste, Colleen said, "Tibasha is such a presumptuous and conniving witch. She is up to something."

Cally and Alssa both looked at the bodyguard in surprise, but it was Cally who spoke for both. "Colleen, that's rude, and you know that you should use the honorific when saying her name. Besides, T'asha has been going through an extremely hard time this last little while." Shaking her head in thought, Cally continued, "Still, I wonder..."

Chapter 5

Megan sat on the sedan, looking out over the city, dressed in her robe and nightgown, the smell of peach blossoms wafting up from the trees below. Her attire was most inappropriate for the meeting she was about to have, but her plan required a totally different approach than normal, and the outcome was too important. So she had to be willing to sacrifice some dignity. She turned back to the city.

Jukeele was so lovely, especially when the trees were flowering, and from her room in the northern corner of the triangular palace, she overlooked the royal orchards. The first daughters of House K'jo had occupied this corner of the castle for seven generations, and if it were not for a foolish law, she would have been the eighth.

Megan loved the realm of the Three Sisters. She loved everything about it, from women having rule and authority, to the grace and elegance that having female leadership provided.

The Three Sisters was not afflicted with the rough, grotesque starkness that was common in patriarchal kingdoms. Their palaces were filled with dead animals and tapestries covered with scenes of bloody battles. *Men are such animals,* she thought to herself.

"Excuse me," a masculine voice came softly from behind her.

Ah, they are here, she thought. *Right on time.* She had told her administrative aide to show her guests in without announcing them. She ignored the voice and continued her thinking.

The palace of Jukeele also had trophies from hunting trips, but rather than butchering the poor animals, they kept them alive in large caged areas around the castle so everyone could enjoy them. Megan thought of the huge tapestry that hung on her sitting room wall. Its fine needlework depicted a great victory, but instead of blood-soaked plains and dying soldiers, it showed the grateful inhabitants of Cult Island being set free from their evil dark lord oppressors.

Looking out over the balcony, she marveled at the symmetry of the palace. The jade-green hue that colored its walls, and the white marble spires that capped the towers gave her goose bumps every time she looked upon the city.

"Excuse me?" the masculine voice came from behind her again, a little louder this time.

She smiled to herself and thought, *I think this pot needs to simmer a little more.* Megan went back to her musings.

The palace's design spoke of the need for a perfect balance of triumvirate rule, and so it had been built in the shape of an equilateral triangle. The shape reminded everyone of the equal authority that each of the sisters was supposed to share. She did not like to think about the way things had become under her cousins' rule but would rather think about the way it was intended to be by her greatest grandmothers when the kingdom began, and the way she hoped they would become again.

This time the voice was loud and angry. "See here, woman, this is an outrage. How dare you treat me with such insolence?"

Finally turning toward the voice, she flashed a mock smile of surprise. Rising slowly from the sedan, she walked gracefully toward the doorway of the balcony and looked over the five men standing in her sitting room.

The man standing in front was obviously the leader and the speaker, who was so angry. He was tall and lean, muscular without great bulk, quite handsome for an Eastward man. He was also obviously a dangerous man. The two men standing slightly behind and to each side of the speaker were studies in the absurd.

One was tall and ridiculously thin, the other was short, almost half the height of his companion, and rotund. In fact, he looked like a wine barrel with legs. The thought brought out a mischievous smile.

The remaining two oak trees standing in the back were obviously bodyguards—both were tall, well over six feet, with huge shoulders and bulging muscles. Megan thought, *So these are the famous Donnelly warriors the Ramaahians use in battle.*

Sweeping into the room with grace and dignity that did not match her attire, she stopped in front of her guests. Knowing full well who the delegation standing in front of her was, she purred, "I'm sorry, gentlemen. Who do I have the pleasure of addressing?"

With eyes ablaze and his voice just under control, the dangerous man spoke. "I am the Marquess Malasaad, Ramaahian ambassador. I will not tolerate this kind of breach of etiquette. I did not cross the entire known world to be ignored by a second-rate female official!"

Second-rate? We shall see. Megan flashed her most disarming smile. "Of course not, Ambassador Malasaad. Please accept my apology."

The marquess only nodded, with his eyes still ablaze.

Megan continued to smile as she asked, "And who else do we have with us today?"

The marquess scowled, gesturing first to the short fat man. "This is Baron Chalsmore, lord of Donnelly," he said, then turned to the thin man, "and this is Baron Dash, lord of Vickers."

Nodding in recognition to both men, Megan asked, "So you have come here to seek our help, and my job is to introduce you to our ways?" Megan infused as much contempt as possible into her voice.

"My lady M'gan, we are not here to discuss history, but the future, the future of both our great kingdoms," replied the marquess, his hawk face becoming ever redder as his anger grew.

"It's Megan." She spoke in a whisper.

"Pardon me?" Malasaad asked.

"I am not M'gan. That honorific is saved for the ruling sisters and their heirs. Though I am the head of House K'jo, I am not the ruling sister. That distinction belonged to my deceased sister, T'anta, and is now used by her lovely daughter, my niece T'asha. I am just Megan."

"I see," was the unsure reply.

"To the contrary, I am quite sure you do not see." The words reeked with sarcasm as they fell from Megan's tongue. She gracefully turned on her toes and walked across the room, her light garments flowing in the breeze she created. She stopped in front of a map displaying all the lands of the Three Sisters.

Pointing to the map, she said, "The Three Sisters' dominion is not limited to our own lands here on the mainland. We are also the protectorates of Styvow Plains on Cult Island, the Wasteland, and the Valley of the Three Brides to the south. In addition, the Rodones and Lystians both look to us as their allies and guardians." She pointed to the top of the map. "In the north, our mutual protection treaty with the Barbarian Kingdom is as strong as iron."

Striding back to the window, she pointed to the docks on the south side of the island, where a great many naval vessels, as well as merchant ships, stood at anchor. "Our navy has complete control of the Brigand Island Chain, the Pirates Channel, and the Seer Sea."

"But most importantly," Megan said, smiling slyly and pointing back to the bottom of the map, "our delightfully pious cousins rule with a holy zeal across the entire southern portion of the western lands."

The ambassador fidgeted in anger, grinding his teeth. "I am sure this is supposed to be very impressive, but what has it to do with our offer? Do you have any understanding of who and what is being offered to you?"

"I am well aware of the who and what, but I think, my honorable ambassador from the Ramaahian Empire, you are the one who is unaware."

The Ramaahian's hands trembled with rage, his normally dark complexion made even darker by hot blood. Slowly his years of diplomatic training won out. "Please do continue with your little story."

Megan smiled at him with anticipation. In fact, she almost beamed with joy. "Thank you. Let's see, where was I? Oh yes, I remember, I was going to explain what you were unaware of."

More smiles as Megan continued, "Thanks to you, our great queen was forced to finish what your forefathers had failed to do.

Led by her, our families destroyed the Alliance of Abomination and overcame the Lords of Chaos."

"Yes, that is true, but only after we defeated them and drove them from the Eastward," the tall Baron Dash interjected.

Ambassador Malasaad turned and fired off a look of withering chastisement that physically caused the baron to recoil.

Megan's eyes boiled with disdain, but the smile remained. "And again, thank you. Because you forced them into the west, but never truly defeated them, they had decades to rebuild. If not for the great queen and her children, the darkness that gripped the Westward would have poured around the Impenetrable Mountains and overrun the Eastward again and you would have been living under its oppression now."

Malasaad reached out in nervous agitation to the bronze sculpture that sat on a table beside him, but after rubbing it for a while, he looked at it for the first time. He pulled his hand away in shock as he realized it was of a scantily clad woman nursing a baby girl.

Recovering quickly, he said, "We are aware of the accomplishments of your famous queen, but that happened three hundred years ago. A lot of time has passed since then, and many things have changed. The exploits of a long-dead queen do not impress."

Megan moved away from the map and into the middle of the room. "Let me put it in terms a man like you would understand. We have not lost a war in three hundred years. In fact, in all that time, we have not even lost a major battle. Many people have underestimated us because we are women. This has proven to be unwise for them, and you would do well to learn from their mistakes."

Megan inched slowly toward the ambassador; though he was several inches taller than she, she dominated the room. When she was a foot away, she stopped, reached up, and pulled the tie string that held her robe closed. She allowed the robe to slide down her shoulders just a bit. Underneath, she was wearing a gossamer gown. The ambassador's eyes lost focus as he tried to keep his attention on her face. Failing miserably, he let his eyes wander.

Megan pulled the robe back up over her shoulders and tied off the cord, saying, "This is the one thing you must clearly see,

Ambassador. We are women. Our monarchs are women, our soldiers are women, our navy's sailors are women, and our royal representatives are women. This kingdom is a women's kingdom." With blinding speed, Megan grabbed the Ramaahian's wrist with her right hand, blocked his other arm with her left, spun him around, and pinned his hand between his shoulder blades. As she lifted her left hand up to his neck, the razor-sharp dagger snapped from her sleeve and came to rest against his throat.

His two bodyguards instinctively reached for their swords. Their hands remained empty. They had relinquished their weapons to gain entry into the castle. Both burly men then produced hidden knives from beneath their massive cloaks.

Turning Malasaad to face the bodyguards, Megan pulled gently on the blade, opening a small cut on his throat. "You see, Ambassador, you must never underestimate us because we are women. Now, tell your men to drop their weapons, or are you going to underestimate me again?"

"Drop your weapons, both of you," Malasaad ordered. Their knives clattered to the marble floor as Megan let the ambassador go. Taking out a white hand cloth, he wiped the blood from his neck. "I do not see the point of this little show of yours, Lady K'jo. We came here to negotiate an alliance with you, not to play games."

Megan touched the bloodied blade to the tip of her tongue and smiled wickedly. "That is the point, Ambassador: You came to us. You want an alliance with us. You want what we have, and I cannot, for the life of me, think of anything you have that we would want. Yet you come into my presence with your men carrying weapons they said they did not have. You act like I should bow down to you because you are a man and I am just a woman and that I should be delighted that you are willing to let us align ourselves with you. You would be better served to listen to my history lesson and learn what kind of allies you are soliciting."

The marquess, humbled but angry, stared at her for a long moment, then smiled with acquiescence. "Please continue." As

Megan turned toward the door, the marquess rubbed his throat, his eyes daring his companions to say anything. They did not.

* * *

Megan led the group out into the hallway and toward the queen's loggia, which overlooked the northwest side of the city. Walking with a little less swagger and a look of desire on his face, the Ramaahian ambassador remained silent as Megan showed him through the palace. For this, Megan was grateful. She hated this part of her responsibilities. She led them quickly through the House J'ta and House L'se portions of the castle, only briefly explaining the role the two other families played in the kingdom.

The rotund Baron Chalmer was a brooding little man who seemed to miss nothing. "Does the triumvirate still function as it once did?"

Megan wanted to lash out with her answer and rail against the injustice that had her trapped, but she could not. Instead, she willed the acid building in her stomach to settle down with thoughts of her dear, sweet T'asha sitting on the throne, and herself standing beside it, which always brought a smile to her lips, then said, "The original Three Sisters shared power and authority equally. Over the centuries, the family J'ta has become the senior house, but all things change with time and opportunity. Each of the families has its responsibilities and roles. Our triumvirate-based monarchy gives each family an equal say in each area, but the ruling sister of J'ta has the final word in all things."

Malasaad pulled on his goatee, smiled provocatively, and said, "Who is the head of House J'ta? And should I not be talking to her instead of you?"

Megan spun around, her hand rubbing the knife in her sleeve. Her forehead wrinkled, and her eyes simmered with rage. Leaving her hand in her sleeve, she again fought back the anger brewing in her. This time she was unable to keep the disdain from her words. "My dear marquess was not listening. The houses share authority equally, but we divide up responsibilities. Each house has areas of expertise and strength. It is the House K'jo's privilege to negotiate treaties and to introduce visiting representatives to our kingdom and its ways. To answer your first question, Ch'lene is queen mother, and Alssa is her heir. To answer the second, no!"

Megan noticed that the marquess's smile seemed to change, and his eyes rested on her for longer than normal. Megan thought, *What is he thinking?* Megan spun on her feet and walked on.

* * *

The little group of visitors and their guide had reached the queen's loggia. Walking out into the bright sunlight and crisp, clean air was refreshing and helped Megan regain her composure. She led them out to the edge, where the low marble wall stood two feet off the floor. When Baron Chalmer looked over, he gasped and staggered back, looking for a place to sit down.

They were standing at the edge of the loggia, ten stories off the ground. From this vantage point they could see that the triangular palace was placed in the center of the castle grounds. The castle was built in the shape of two equal-sided triangles lying in opposite directions, like a six-pointed star. In five of the valleys created by the star, there was a gate. The two gates on the north, the two gates to the south, all led down short sections of street to the bridges that spanned the Twin Rivers. The one to the east led directly into the merchant district of the city and the massive walls running across the neck.

Megan allowed them to take in the beauty of the palace and the jade city before she continued, "Jukeele is built upon Katan Hill, a large monolith rising out of the Twin Rivers, which run east to west around the city. After the river passes the city, it continues west, where it flows into the Seer Sea at the port of Safe Haven."

They all could clearly see two of the five roads that led out of the city. The city had grown huge and reflected the order and beauty of the Three Sisters. The image of the palace was the centerpiece of the realm's flag.

Megan gloried in telling this part of the story. "The original Three Sisters found Katan Hill when they led an army of one thousand survivors away from the ambush at Goblin Gorge. The orcs had built a small citadel on the summit. The sisters defeated the few orcs who defended it and made it their own for one last stand against the armies of darkness. The Lords of Chaos took six days to amass their army, and on the morning of the seventh, the sisters awoke to see an army of sixty thousand goblins, orcs, and the hadrac stretched out before them on all sides.

"With the river protecting the small army on three sides, the sisters had spent the six days building defenses on the east slope of the hill across the neck.

"The hadrac and orcs hate water, so the rivers offered some protection from them. But goblins are amphibians, so they tried to swim the river."

Baron Dash boasted, "We have not had those vile creatures in the Eastward for hundreds of years, but I seem to remember that they will not come into the open daylight."

As Megan turned away, she looked out across the plains and said, "That is an Eastward myth."

Megan continued, "As the battle raged, hadrac and orcs were stacked up as high as Giants Wall before the defenses on the east. The river carried the bodies of the goblins down to the sea at Safe Haven. Thousands upon thousands of the beasts died from the arrows, lances, and swords of the sisters' small army. The river ran red with blood, and after twelve days, only the Three Sisters and one hundred soldiers remained alive. All but a small portion of the army of the Lords of Chaos was destroyed. When the great queen arrived with her army, she used the Banisher on the remaining beasts and captured the four dark lords as they tried to flee."

Megan was always left in awe when she talked about her heritage and the exploits of her heroic forebearers. She continued, "From that time on, the Three Sisters were inseparable and shared all things equally. Out of this bond were formed the laws that have governed the Three Sisters for three hundred years." Megan folded her hands in front of her. "Let us go to the royal dining room and negotiate that alliance you so desperately want."

Megan herded the group down long hallways filled with tapestries, murals, and statues that depicted the grace, dignity, and power of the three great families that ruled the Three Sisters kingdom.

* * *

The shadows were on the opposite wall as Megan walked quickly back to her chambers, deep in thought. *That went better than I had anticipated. Men are so easy to manipulate.* Now, even though Alssa was getting ready to take power as the ruling sister of family J'ta, Megan could rest in the knowledge that T'asha would not be overlooked like she herself had been.

Megan knew that Alssa hated her and her niece T'asha, and if Alssa were left to take the throne, it would cause the family K'jo to continue to diminish. She could not let this happen. She knew that an alliance with the Ramaahian was risky, but she needed them, or at least their assassins, to deal with her nieces. Once that was done, she would deal with the Ramaahian's own demands as she saw fit.

She entered her chambers smiling. *I have succeeded. All my own suffering has been worth it.* She had known that she could never change it for herself, but she could change it for her dear T'asha, and now she had.

Megan was reclining in her sedan, reveling over the events of the day, when T'asha entered with a rush. Megan watched with pride. T'asha had such beauty and grace, most of the time.

T'asha stormed up to her aunt, and with a cultivated sweetness that could not mask the bitterness bound up in her heart, she addressed her. "How could you let them send an escort with Alssa and Cally?"

"T'asha, my sweet, it doesn't matter. We have planned well, and all is going better than we hoped."

"Megan, how can you say that? They needed to be alone on this trip."

Megan spoke calmly. "Who accompanies them is irrelevant. You don't really believe Alssa will fulfill the prophecy?" The last part dripped with sarcasm. Megan continued, "With them out of the way we can work out the rest of our plan."

T'asha screamed at her aunt as she stormed toward the door. "I was not consulted before the decision was made. You should have stopped them! Now Alssa and that sniveling little brat Cally will have two hundred and fifty of their best troops with them. Megan, you make me so mad I could just—"

She did not finish her curse as she ran into a serving maid who had entered through the door. The young girl was knocked back out the open door and across the hall, leaving her lying spread-eagle on the far side.

Megan ignored the maid as she chased her niece out the door. She was such a bright, strong-willed girl, but she just could not control her temper. Megan caught up to T'asha at the end of the hall.

She cooed softly, "T'asha, you must get control of yourself. If we are patient, we will accomplish our goals. Alssa's leaving is a great opportunity for you to visit and win the hearts of the influential ladies at court."

T'asha turned on her aunt and sneered. "Ladies! Ladies! Those old hags can hardly see beyond their own pompous noses. They will never change the law, and they cannot see that Alssa is too weak and stupid to rule properly." She turned and began to walk away.

Megan cooed again. "If we are patient and bide our time, all things will come to us."

T'asha was beside herself in rage and frustration. Turning quickly on her heels, she slapped Megan across the face, knocking her to one knee. She ranted, "Did your patience help you when my mother died? Did the court change the law so you could take your rightful place in the triumvirate? No! And that filthy bitch and her mother still hold all the power. Now she is on her way to fulfill the prophecy, and I have been left out again. What do you think will happen to you and me if that happens?"

Megan stood to her feet, wiping the blood from her lip. She whispered, "T'asha, you must control your tongue. Even you are not immune from the law. You can be tried for treason as well as anyone. If you are overheard, all will be lost."

T'asha barked back at her aunt, "If my prissy sister and her little tart reach Queens Castle Home, it will not matter what I say or do, will it?"

Megan's face lit up. "I have finished making arrangements today so that will not happen."

T'asha seemed not to hear her as she turned on her heels and waved her aunt away. "I have made my own arrangements. I will not be denied my rightful place as the ruler of the Three Sisters."

"Young lady, what have you done?"

Ignoring Megan's question, T'asha gave her aunt an order. "I am leaving for Castle Gorge. Tell Commander Nadja to assemble my royal guard and meet me at the east gate. I will not let what happened to you happen to me."

Chapter 6

The ship recoiled as the anchor struck the bottom of the bay, knocking Daniel to his knees. *Blast the captain, whoever told him he knew how to sail? A full fifteen days on this brig, curse the dark lords! I'm glad this is over,* Daniel thought.

Standing, he stretched his arms above his head to work out the kinks that had built up in his muscular shoulders on the long voyage. His hands rapped against the beams of the bulkhead. The bulkhead was less than two-and-half spans from the floor. Reaching down, he pulled on his leather trousers and tunic, picked up the sword and strapped it to the flat of his back, pulled the full-length cloak over his head, and stepped toward the door.

He had enough money from his last employer to be able to convince Captain Short to let him have private accommodations, but because of his size, even the private accommodations left him feeling cramped. Daniel was not used to being around people for any length of time. Trapped on board a cramped ship was extremely uncomfortable. He eagerly stepped into the doorway, anticipating the freedom that waited once he got ashore. His large frame easily filled the opening. Patiently, he waited for the other passengers to clear out of the narrow hallway.

He could hear the tiny Mrs. Grandview waddling up the passageway, her aged, grating voice nagging her husband. "Darnmoth, hurry, or we may get stuck on the same boat as that horrible man."

"What horrible man is that, dear?" droned Mr. Grandview.

"The big one." Mr. Tarbell's wife said he was a thief and a murderer.

"And how would Mrs. Tarbell know that?" Mr. Grandview asked.

"They were already on board when he arrived in the middle of the night," she stated. Then she asked, "Did you know that he's from the Barbarian Kingdom?"

"Corrine, I still have no idea whom you are talking about."

They were now passing in front of Daniel as she replied, "That great big man with the gold sword." When she turned to look up the stairs, her eyes met Daniel's. "Or I mean…oh, hello, mister, er… man…Daniel, is it?"

Daniel's lips formed a broad wicked smile, and he said, "Yes, it is. May I help you with your bags and lighten your load a little bit?"

Clutching her handbag tightly to her chest, she unfolded her hunched-over body and stood fully erect, only coming up to the bottom of Daniel's chest. She stuck out her jaw with a defiant scowl and said, "No! We don't need any of your help." Then she quickened her pace toward the steps.

While the last of the passengers went by, Daniel overheard Mrs. Grandview one more time. "That's him. I can't believe you brought me to this place with people like that. I told you that we shouldn't have come, not without the boys." She continued to scold her husband as her voice faded away.

Daniel followed the last man up the narrow stairs, his nose registering the stench for the last time. He stood a little less than two spans, making getting out of the short tight hatchway somewhat difficult.

When he emerged from the hatchway, he felt the hard rain on his face. Daniel liked the rain; it washed away the smell and made him feel clean. Walking across the deck, he could see the *Johansson*'s crew loading the last of the cargo into the transport boats that would take him and the other passengers to the shore.

Something bumped against his calf. Looking down, he saw the little Tarbell girls looking up at him. The taller one smiled and said, "Mister, can we stand next to you, so we don't get wet?"

Daniel thought, *Too late!* They were drenched, their hair matted to their heads, and their light linen cloaks hung uselessly from their skinny shoulders.

Frowning at them, he growled, "Where are your parents?"

The taller one responded, "Daddy's mad at the captain, and he is yelling at him. Mommy told us to go away."

The older one reached out and hugged his leg. "Besides, we like you, and there are mean people here who scare us."

He followed their stare to the tall man dressed in black, leaning against the rail. It was Valkar. Daniel made eye contact with him, and the count quickly looked away. This was the first chance Daniel had to see Valkar since the beginning of the voyage. Apparently, Valkar did not like the rain, because he stayed either in his own cabin or in the captain's cabin during the entire trip. Daniel guessed the Valkarian was going to wait until they reached the shore before he attempted to kill him.

Daniel thought he saw him get off the ship in Port Royal, but obviously not. Turning back to the girls and trying not to smile, he whispered, "Okay, you can stand here."

Both girls quickly moved under his cloak to get out of the rain.

The passengers were starting to board the transports. Nudging the two girls toward the gangplank, they got in line to wait their turn to board the cargo boats. Daniel took the time to survey the other deep-sea craft that had moored in Hogs Head Bay. There were other brigs, sloops, caravels, and one or two galleons. Many of them made the brig he was on show her age.

After a total of fifteen days on the *Johansson's Pride*, Daniel felt Johansson had little to be proud of.

The brig had tied off to one of the many mooring buoys located off the delta created by the Deep and Three Brides Rivers.

As he turned back to answer the tug on his cloak, Daniel noticed Valkar talking with Mrs. Grandview, helping her into one of the four other transport boats. He thought, *I'm glad she got her wish. I hope she doesn't get her fears.*

The girls cried out, "Mommy is waving for us to join her."

Daniel absently motioned for them to go. As he watched them run down the gangway, he looked out over the bay and the Sand Sea. He had overheard two of the crew say that Hogs Head Bay had at one time been a great seaport, with sailing vessels from all over the known world coming to trade and bring travelers and tribute to the great queen.

When he arrived at the bottom of the ramp, Daniel could hear the obnoxious Mr. Tarbell telling another man about Hogs Head Bay. He said, "Back when the great queen ruled, ships could sail into the bay all the way to J'ra at the mouth of the Three Brides River, or to K'la on the Deep River. Some of the smaller vessels could sail all the way to Queens Castle Home on the Deep River."

The other man looked at him in disbelief and said, "That's more than twelve days from the sea. How could they go that far inland?"

Looking smug, Mr. Tarbell lectured on, "That's why they call it the Deep River. That was three hundred seasons ago, and now the bay has silted up. The Sand Sea separates the bay from the ports by a half day's journey."

The harbormaster had finished collecting the fee for docking at the buoys from the captain. He now walked down the plank to the transport to collect the fees from the individual passengers.

He started with Mr. Tarbell. Mr. Tarbell's voice grew loud and defiant. "I don't see why I should have to pay. It cost us a small fortune to sail here in the first place! Go collect more money from the captain."

The harbormaster shrugged his shoulder, turned away from Tarbell, and continued collecting the toll from the rest of the passengers. Upon finishing, he returned to Mr. Tarbell, who was still ranting about the apparent extra charge.

The harbormaster spoke firmly. "Look, mister, you don't have to pay the fee." A victorious look came upon Mr. Tarbell's face. The harbormaster turned, picked up one of his little girls, and held her out over the low gunwale and continued, "You and your family can swim."

Daniel started to take a step toward the man when Mrs. Tarbell let out a scream. "Horace, quit being so miserly! Pay the fee and be done with it! We easily have enough money."

Mr. Tarbell turned on her and said, "Triana, shut up and stay out of this."

The little girl was kicking and screaming, "Daddy, don't let him throw me in the water!"

Reluctantly, Tarbell handed the harbormaster the coins. The little girl ran to her mother, sobbing.

Mr. Tarbell returned to the man he had been talking to and continued his story. Daniel shook his head and moved to the back of the transport to find a spot to sit on the soft cargo. He had hoped to get out of earshot of the history lesson, but there was not enough distance.

"These transports," Mr. Tarbell went on, "carry passengers up the little rivulets that make up the river delta. And it is only during high tide that the rivulets are deep enough for the loaded cargo boats to make their way up to the port towns."

The other man interjected, "You know, Horace, if you didn't want to pay the full fee, you could have had them drop you off at the beach and you could walk. They even have land guides to show you the way."

Tarbell snorted and said, "They're probably as big a thief as the harbormaster. Besides, it's most likely full of quicksand and sinkholes."

As the cargo boats continued to be loaded, Daniel took stock of his belongings. He had his bedroll and leather food sack draped across his right shoulder. His coin purse was safely hidden away along with the medallion under his silk undershirt. Hanging from his waist belt was his map case and his ivory-handled fighting knife, a gift from another grateful employer. In his carry bag, he had extra clothes, his mending kit, and a seeing glass. Looking up, he could see the sun peeking through the clouds. The rain had stopped, so he pulled the hood off and shook his head, his long hair swinging back and forth. As he tied his hair back, the two little Tarbell girls dragged their older brother over to him, saying, "Ask him to see it. Go ahead, ask."

The boy, maybe twelve seasons old, seemed reluctant and eager at the same time. Finally, he said, "Okay, okay, quit pushing me." He turned to Daniel. "They want me to ask you to let them see the sword. Can we?" he asked.

His broadsword was strapped on his back. Daniel wore an extralarge cloak, both for freedom of movement and to help hide the sword.

Much to their dismay, Daniel responded, "I don't think so, kids. A person should never draw his weapon unless he is going to use it."

As the kids walked away dejected, he thought on how others acted around the sword. Many saw it as an invitation to challenge him. In the beginning, he had let his enemies live, but it seemed they always came back for more. Now, he lived by one motto: "A dead enemy was no enemy at all."

By the time he had finished his thoughts, it was time to cast off from the brig and head toward shore. The six oarsmen pushed the boat away from the brig and began pulling hard against the oars. The boat struggled against the surf, rising and falling with each breaking wave. As they approached the mouth of a rivulet, the sea calmed and the waves turned to small swells that pushed them gently toward the beach. The rest of the passengers were talking quietly among themselves. Except Mr. Tarbell, of course; he was trying to engage the helmsman in conversation, and he said, "How long will it take us to reach J're?"

The helmsman responded sharply, "As long as it takes. Now, sit down with your family. I have no control over tide or wind." Tarbell stomped off to find someone else to talk at.

Daniel looked around, sizing up the rest of the people on the boat with him. Besides himself, there were nineteen other people on the boat, the navigator, the helmsman, six oarsmen, and two families.

The eight members of the boat crew were all big burly men. The oarsmen were giants but did not appear to be much smarter the then the oars they wielded. The navigator and helmsman appeared to be the oarsmen's match. All in all, none of them were a threat.

One of the families consisted of an older couple about forty seasons in age, and their three sons, all young men of little stature, whose movements showed their timidity and whose eyes were filled with fear. They also had a little girl several seasons younger than the boys.

The Tarbells, they were a young couple, the man being about twenty-nine seasons, and a complete ass; his wife, about twenty-seven, and quite comely. Their children consisted of a son about twelve seasons and two daughters, both younger than the boy. The boy was full of spit and vinegar, while the girls radiated wonder and amazement.

As the boat moved into the rivulet, the load on the oars increased dramatically and the six men had to fight hard against the stream's current. The helmsman called out to the oarsman, "Increase your strokes or we will be swept back into the swells!"

The boat sat so low in the water you could not see anything other than the sand on the shore and the large swells at the mouth of the river. There was no vegetation growing along the riverbanks.

"Increase the strokes! That's it, boys, pull, pull, pull!" the helmsman continued to cry.

Daniel reclined against some soft bales of cloth, watching the two girls, and he thought to himself, *What kind of fool would leave Port Royal with two little girls in tow and come to the Lands of Chaos?*

He remembered the conversation he overheard during the voyage between the two fathers. Tarbell had said, "The financial possibilities that await us on the mainland are going to make us rich men."

The older man countered, "A new start with the potential for greater liberty and even greater profits, now that is what I am looking for."

Daniel's thoughts continued, *Even more foolish, what kind of profit could an honest family man make in a place like the Lands of Chaos? A place filled with the dregs of civilized societies.*

In their conversation, they had mentioned that the time of the fulfillment of prophecy was at hand, and that things were changing.

More foolishness! Prophecies are just a bunch of useless words spouted by old men. In all of Daniel's travels, he had seen many things change, but always from bad to worse. Yeah, they were foolish, probably fatally foolish.

As the boat rounded a bend in the rivulet, the oarsmen lifted their oars from the water and secured them. The boat drifted toward a large pole protruding from the water in the middle of the stream. The pole was about twice as tall as Daniel. As the bow of the boat came alongside the pole, the navigator reached out and grabbed a floating ring that hung from it. The navigator quickly tied the lead rope to the ring and dropped it back in the water. As the passenger sat wondering what was happening, another cargo boat from the *Johansson's Pride* came around the bend in the river and coasted up to the pole in the same manner as they had. Their navigator tied off to the ring also. Both boats, caught by the current, drifted back toward the bay. As the lead ropes stretched tight, the boats banged into one another.

Daniel instinctively scanned the occupants of the other boat. The occupants were like those in his boat, eight crew members and ten passengers. There were no threats to be seen, so he relaxed and leaned back into the stern. He wondered where Valkar's boat was.

Then Tarbell asked the navigator, "Why have we stopped in the middle of the stream?"

The navigator replied, "The rivulets are too shallow this close to the bay, and we need to wait for the tide to begin rising before we can proceed farther."

"How long will that be?" whined Tarbell.

The navigator snorted, "I already told you I don't control the tide. Now go sit down."

With that, the navigator turned away from the father, pulled out his pipe, and began to talk with the navigator from the other boat.

The rain had let up, and the sun was shining through the sparse clouds. A slight breeze was blowing in off the bay. The boat was gently bobbing up and down in the current. It was quite comfortable and relaxing. The young children fell asleep on top of the cargo piled in the center of the craft. The ladies whispered to one another as the fathers twitched impatiently, waiting for the tide to rise. Slowly, slack started to appear in the lead ropes as the boats began to move forward. The tide was coming in. As the boats moved past the pole, the navigators reached out and unhooked the ropes.

The helmsman called out to the oarsmen, "Lower your oars and begin a ten-stroke pace!"

The boat quickly picked up speed, pushed along by both the oars and the incoming tide. They were easily moving twice as fast as they had been without the inrushing tide. The rest of the trip in from the sea seemed to go by amazingly fast. Somewhere along the way, the other transport had taken another rivulet, apparently headed for the Deep River port of K'la.

Daniel's craft was going to the Three Brides port of J're, where the passengers would debark and take the overland route on the Queen's Highway. He had no desire to go to K'la or to head inland on the Deep River aboard another ship. After fifteen days at sea on the *Johansson's Pride*, he realized the thought of spending more time on the water was most unpleasant.

By nightfall, they had reached their destination and docked at the old run-down piers of J're. After gathering his gear, he asked the helmsman, "Is there an inn in this town where I can get a room for the night?"

The helmsman replied, "None of us spend the night in this place. Better to spend it on the boat, safer and cleaner, but if you have to, the only inn is on the opposite side of the town square at the end of that road.

Daniel climbed up the ladder onto the dock. There were men loading wagons with the cargo that was in the transports. Daniel walked up to one of the teamsters and asked, "Where are these wagons headed?"

The teamster did not turn around but responded sarcastically, "There is only one direction to go from here, H'la and L'ke L'fe."

"Whose wagons are these?" Daniel asked.

"The owner of the inn the Hogs Delight," came the reply.

Daniel turned and headed into town. He could tell that J're had once been a busy and prosperous port, but now most of the buildings were falling apart or boarded up. The mud all but hid the cobblestone streets. He went into the only inn in the town and walked through the broken front door.

Hog's Delight seemed a fit name, for only a pig would stay in such a filthy place. Stepping through the trash lying on the floor, he walked over to the counter. A tall skinny man with long matted hair and yellow teeth was sitting behind the counter, aggressively chewing the meat off a large bone. The man's shirt at one time had been white but was now a grubby gray. The vest he wore was torn and tattered, and he had his bare feet up on the counter.

Daniel interrupted his revelry to ask, "Is the owner here?"

The man stuck out a greasy hand, grinned, and said, "He might be."

Daniel pulled a copper out of his pocket and tossed it into the skinny man's hand. The clerk set down the bone and wiped his hands on his shirt. Picking up the copper, he bit into it and pointed toward a door behind him. Daniel stepped around the counter and pushed the door open.

The owner screamed, "Tricket, what in the name of the dark lords are you doing? I told you not to let anything interrupt me!"

The room was full of smoke, and a familiar sweet odor filled the air—an odor Daniel had not smelled since leaving the Eastward. The large man looked like he was looking through a fog; his eyelids were heavy and swollen. Clearly, the man was using healer smoke for something other than healing.

Daniel addressed him, saying, "I saw your wagons, and I am looking for some work."

The owner waved for him to leave and said, "I don't need any drivers. I already have enough. And the same with loaders, two-man crews. They are all I need."

"I'm not a teamster," Daniel replied.

The stoned man did not seem to hear him but instead asked, "What I need is a sword-for-hire. Can you use a sword?"

Daniel smiled and said, "A little."

"Well, you're certainly big enough. Okay, I will pay you four coppers to ride with the wagons to H'la and one gold to go to L'ke L'fe."

Daniel scoffed at him. "Two silver to H'la and two gold to L'ke L'fe. Half in advance."

The owner protested loudly, "Are you trying to rob me before the wagons are even on the road? One silver now and another in H'la, and then the rest when you reach L'ke L'fe."

"Who else do you have to protect your cargo?" Daniel asked.

"The teamsters and Tricket," the owner replied.

Daniel replied with a chuckle, "You know the teamsters will run at the first sign of trouble, and if Tricket goes, I want double."

The owner smiled and said, "Okay, you're hired, and no Tricket. You will leave at first light."

Daniel responded quickly, saying, "I would rather leave tonight, as soon as the wagons are loaded."

"You make many demands for someone looking for work in an end-of-the-road town," the owner responded, then asked, "Who do you think you are?"

Daniel said confidently, "The man who is going to risk his life protecting your investment." Then he declared, "I am leaving tonight with or without your wagons."

The hazy-eyed man turned back around to breathe in more smoke as he waved Daniel out of the room and said, "Whatever you want. And good luck. You will need it."

Daniel did not move.

The owner turned around again and asked, "What?"

Daniel said, "The money."

"Hee hee, oh yeah." The owner chuckled as he reached into his money pouch and pulled out a silver coin and laid it on the table. "Orik, the lead teamster, will pay you the rest when you get to L'ke L'fe."

Daniel picked up the coin.

The owner yelled, "Tricket, get your scrawny butt in here!"

Daniel walked back outside. The two families that accompanied him in the transport were standing in front of the inn. The fathers were arguing with their wives. They were trying to convince them that staying inside, even in a place like the Hogs Delight, was better than having the children sleep out in the open. Daniel did not agree; he had been sleeping outside since he was very young. In fact, he could hardly remember ever living in a house, even after hooking up with Nathan.

Leaving the two families arguing on the street, he went back to the dock and found Orik and told him, "The inn owner has hired me to guard the wagons as you head east."

Orik replied, "It's about time! I guess he finally got tired of losing money to that band of thieves that work the Queen's Highway."

"Have you had much trouble in the past?" Daniel asked.

Orik scratched his beard and thought for a moment before responding, "We've lost two shipments in the last fortnight."

Daniel shook his head. "Have you tried to defend the wagons?"

"The first time it happened, old man Jagron—he was the previous wagon master—put up a fight, but the murdering scum killed him. When I took over as wagon master, I told the boys not to resist. We just stop the wagons and get down and walk away."

Daniel asked, "Do these highwaymen take the wagons?"

The lead teamster replied, "Nah, they just root through the cargo and take any expensive things they find. They then leave and we get back on the wagons and head on into H'la."

Daniel chuckled and said, "Seems like a nice arrangement."

Orik responded defensively, "Hey, listen, mister, we're teamsters, not soldiers or a sword-for-hire like you. We're not trained to fight. We just handle the oxen."

Daniel encouraged the wagon master, "Relax, Orik, I didn't mean you, I meant the thieves. They probably won't be happy if I'm there when they show up."

Orik smiled and said, "We'll be glad to have you along, but I still need to check with the owner."

* * *

After Orik checked in with the owner, they mounted the wagons. Daniel sat in the lead wagon with Orik as they headed down the Queen's Highway, looking for a dry place to camp.

Daniel asked Orik, “How many men are there in this gang of highwaymen?”

Orik scratched his beard again. “I don’t rightly know. I’ve seen five or six. There may be more hiding in the woods.”

Daniel snorted and thought, *Oh, that’s good. All I wanted was to have someone else pay my way into the interior, not get a battle with a gang of thieves.*

Chapter 7

Daniel stood staring into the darkness, a heavy, oppressive darkness. A darkness broken only by small shafts of moonlight reflecting off the steam rising from the flared nostrils of the horses standing before him. He could not make out the hooded faces of the riders, but it wasn't necessary; he already knew who they were.

Why did they hesitate this time? Always before, they had charged without warning. Had they grown as wary of him as they had been of the old man in that first encounter? However, this time there would be no old man. Daniel's heart ached as he thought of the man who had become his mentor after these same four riders murdered his adoptive parents.

The sound of stomping hooves disrupted his thoughts. The black battle horses thrashed the muddy ground, anticipating the charge. Their large hooves splashed mud to all sides. Slick ebony hair shone in the dim light. The sight was black upon black, drawing him into the darkness, pulling at his very soul, tearing him from the light.

The rider's power seemed to be growing; the presence of evil had never been so strong. It would be such an easy thing: walk down the dark road, embrace the comfortable cloak the blackness offered, the struggle would end, and he could breathe freely once again.

It wasn't the stomping horses that pulled him back from the abyss but the warmth of the blade strapped down the center of his back. It had begun to glow even before he began the chant. The four horsemen drew their weapons. Daniel threw back the hood of his cloak, and with his right hand, he grasped the hilt of the massive broadsword. His heart began to race even faster when he heard the metal blade sliding from the leather scabbard. Speaking in soft, rhythmic tones, he extended the sword in front of him. The sword burst into a flame, and the longer he spoke, the brighter it became, until it was one single source of light.

The four riders peeled off to attack him one at a time. The first rider bore down on Daniel, the steal tip of his lance growing larger and larger. At the last moment, Daniel stepped left, letting the lance slide under his right arm, trapping it between his large biceps and his immense chest. The black rider was dismounted as his horse galloped past. The dark-cloaked attacker struggled to his knees. Daniel took two strides toward his fallen enemy, lifted the giant blade in his left hand, and swung it down across the exposed neck. Blood squirted from the headless shoulders; the separated head splashed across the muddy ground.

The second rider's horse reared up as he spurred the steed toward Daniel. He lifted his jagged-edged black sword and charged. With his cloaked arm, he swung the steel death in a mighty sweeping motion. The blade clanged as it hit Daniel across the top of his back. The blade struck the chain mail armor and glanced off, but the strength of the blow rocked Daniel forward onto his knees. The rider turned his mount away from Daniel and raised his sword above his head for another swing. The horse spun back toward Daniel, exposing the rider's belly as he prepared for another strike. With both hands firmly gripped around the handle of his sword, Daniel swung upward with all his strength, catching the rider in the midsection, cleaving him in two, both halves dropping to the ground.

The third rider had held off his attack until Daniel's back was to him. Seeing his chance, he spurred his mount and charged. With unnatural power, he swung down with his mace, trying to crush Daniel's skull.

Daniel spun to the right and turned into the rider. The barbed orb on the end of the chain missed Daniel's head but caught his right shoulder, dislocating the joint, driving the chain mail through the skin and sending the barbs deep into the muscle. The flesh tore away as the rider jerked the mace loose. He swung it above his head for another blow.

With only his left hand, Daniel thrust the burning sword upward into the gap between the rider's codpiece and chest plate, separating the attacker from his horse and his life.

Daniel spun around, frantically looking to find the fourth rider, but he feared he was too slow. His fears were confirmed when he felt the hot, piercing sting of a black arrow enter his back and pass through to his chest. He looked down to see the flint-headed arrow protruding through his tunic; he sighed deeply, knowing he had failed again.

* * *

Daniel awoke holding his chest, breathing heavily, his body covered in sweat. He lay staring at the trees swaying in the breeze. Struggling to gather his wits, he searched his mind to remember where he was. Looking around, he saw the teamsters lying around the campfire. Slowly he remembered. Rising onto his elbow, he stirred the coals of the fire to awaken the flames and thought, *At least now when I wake up from the dream I'm not screaming.* The dream always left him cold and exhausted. Warming himself by the fire, he breathed hard, his hands shaking.

Although he had only seen the four riders the two times, once when his adoptive parents were killed, then again when he was twelve, he kept having the dreams. It was as if the four dark riders were able to find him in his sleep.

As Daniel packed up his kit, he continued to think about the dream. It always brought back memories of Nathan. Though he missed Nathan very much, the memories always gave him a warm feeling in his chest. Nathan had saved his life. It was Nathan who had rescued him from the four black horsemen when he was twelve. After that, the old man had taken him under his care.

At the age of ten, Daniel had run away from his father's friend who had found him the day they were murdered. Preferring to live on the streets of Karmac rather than put up with the beatings he regularly received at the man's hands.

At the age of eleven, he left the kingdom of Flanderon and traveled south to the Ramaahian Empire. He was still working his way south, trying to cross the Choson Mountains into the Valkarian frontier, when the black riders appeared. Nathan had rescued him and quickly headed him back into the Twelve Kingdoms, letting him know that little country of Valkar was not a good place to be.

Daniel threw a few sticks on the coals to restart the fire, buckled his waist belt, and strapped the scabbard across his back. He grabbed his leather bag and pulled out the oil-soaked wool rag and hung it on a branch. He then withdrew the sword from its scabbard. Taking the rag, he wiped the dew off the blade, turning it over repeatedly. He admired the shine on the blade; it never seemed to tarnish, nor did the blade ever get dull. That was the oddest part of the dream. The blade always burst into a flame in the dream, but never in real life. Sure, the blade would seem to glow at times, but it never ignited into a flame. Lifting the blade above his head, he slid it back into its home. Only after getting everything ready for his journey did he sit to eat the salted meat and dry cheese that made up his breakfast.

As he was wiping the crumbs from his beard and mustache, he noticed the teamsters starting to stir. Orik was the first to awake.

"Good morning, wagon master. Did you rest well?" Daniel asked.

"As well as any man can sleep on the cold, hard ground. I still do not understand why we had to leave the comfort of a warm bed to sleep outside. We didn't get more than a ninth trace last night," came the wagon master's disgruntled reply.

"I have a feeling that there is someone in town that is working with the highwaymen. Hopefully, by leaving in the middle of the night, we avoided being seen and we won't have any trouble on this trip."

As they were talking, they heard the unmistakable sounds of people. Standing up, they saw three little girls walking down the road, laughing and skipping, their parents and brothers following behind. It was the families from the *Johansson's Pride*. Daniel smiled as he watched the children pass. When the two mothers trudged by, he could see the black circles under their eyes. They obviously had not slept any better last night than they had on the voyage from Port Royal.

The two fathers passed, bringing up the rear. Mr. Tarbell stopped and asked the wagon master, "Can we purchase a ride on the wagons as far as H'la?"

Before Daniel could answer, Orik responded. "No, we do not take passengers, only cargo."

Tarbell pointed at Daniel and spit out, "Then why is this man riding with you?"

Orik responded, "I don't see what business that is of yours, but he has been paid as a sword-for-hire to protect the cargo."

Pointing at his fellow traveler, Tarbell boasted, "Landers and I can help protect your wagons if you need more protection."

Daniel smiled. Orik laughed aloud and said, "We do not need any more protection, little man. Be on your way, and try to keep up with your women."

Tarbell and Landers looked at each other and walked on down the road. Orik waited until the men had disappeared before speaking. "Those people don't belong in the Lands of Chaos. Nothing good will come to them here."

They finished cleaning up the camp. Out of habit, Daniel made sure no one would even be able to tell anyone had been there.

Orik was watching and said, "You are a very careful man."

The oxen walked at a steady pace toward the east. The mist was slowly burning away as the morning sun cast long beams through the trees. He could see why this place had the name of the Ebony Forest. The bark on the evergreen trees were as black as night. There was also scant underbrush, and he saw no sign of wild animals. That sent a warning bell off in his head as he thought, *There should be animals.*

The farther down the road they traveled, the more ominous the Ebony Forest became. The trees continued to get bigger, and the forest became denser. When the sun was straight over their heads, it was impossible to peer into the dense woods, and the trees were over forty spans high. The road cut through the forest like a canyon. By midafternoon, they heard people again. Daniel placed his right hand on the ivory handle of his fighting knife. As they rounded a slight bend in the road, he could see the two families. They were lying down alongside the road, and they looked worn-out, especially the children.

As the wagons passed, one of the older boys called out to them. "Yo, good sirs, how much farther is it to H'la?"

Orik replied, "H'la is a full three days from J're."

The two wives sighed heavily, turned to their husbands, and glared at them. The older man called out, "Would you not let us ride with you? Can you not see that our women and children are exhausted?"

Orik replied curtly, "No, you should go back to Jere, get back on the boat, and go home. Your kind doesn't belong in the Lands of Chaos."

Tarbell stood up quickly and yelled, "I don't see where that's any of your business! Who do you think you are, telling us what to do? We can go where we please, and if we want to live here, it is our business!"

Daniel challenged them, "You can also die here, you fool! This is no place for women and children. Listen to the man: go back to your home, at least for your children's sake."

As Orik whipped the oxen into motion, Tarbell made a derogatory gesture with his arms.

* * *

As the day wore on, the forest around Daniel and the wagons shouted with an eerie silence. There was no sound except for the creaking of the wagon wheels. Daniel saw no birds, no small woodland creatures. Daniel knew he should be able to hear sounds of the forest, and he wondered why he was not.

He had not heard anything this quiet since he had led a troop of mercenaries over the north end of the Impenetrable Mountains. It was bitter cold, and the snow was up to the belly of the horses. No creature was foolish enough to venture out in that kind of storm except man. Daniel thought, *I wonder what has driven these animals into hiding.*

Eventually, his mind wandered back to the two families. *Fools!* Traveling through the Lands of Chaos was dangerous enough, but to enter the Ebony Forest with women and children, with no weapons, and no escort? Complete foolishness!

Daniel would not have been opposed to letting them ride on the wagons, except for the Tarbell fellow, but it was not his decision. And if anything happened, he would have had to do all the work. They did not appear to be armed, and neither of them looked like they could use a weapon.

Now there was something strange also; they had boarded the *Johansson's Pride* in Port Royal, the biggest town on Cult Island. Most of the people of Port Royal were citizens of the Three Sisters, but it seemed from the look of the women that they were not. He had heard that Three Sisters women were all warriors and would only travel in armor. That was probably an exaggeration, but most exaggeration had their bases in truth.

These two women are not warriors, Daniel thought. Daniel was not sure where these families had come from, but he was sure of one thing about them: they were very foolish, maybe even fatally foolish.

On the next two nights, they camped as far off the road as possible, but still close enough to hear anyone or anything that might be on the road. Both days were uneventful, and they saw no one. At the end of the third day, right before dusk, they broke out of the forest and into open fields. About four hundred strides across the fields, he could see a wooden stockade built around a small town. Set up on the east ramparts was a half score of archers. Approaching cautiously, they hailed the guards at the gate.

The guards responded from behind the gate, "Who are you, and where are you from?"

Orik swore and said, "You orc-brained fool, we are the same people who come here every fortnight! There is nowhere else to be from on this road but J're. You blackhearted idiot, open the gate!"

Daniel could hear the bar being raised and the squeaking of the hinges as the gate was pushed open, but only wide enough for the wagons to pass through. The gate was quickly pulled closed, and the bar slammed down, locking out the outside world. The guards eyed them suspiciously as they headed for the town's blacksmith and the stables.

Reaching the center of the small town, Orik stopped the wagon to let Daniel get off.

Daniel asked, "What time will you want to leave in the morning?"

Orik smiled at him and with a laugh said, "Well, we will put the wagons in the stable tonight and then unload some cargo in the morning. But me and the boys will probably get a late start tomorrow."

Daniel knew what he meant; they were going to find a tavern to help relieve some of the stress from their trip. He himself needed to find a place to stay. "Orik, what inn do you and your men stay at while you're here?"

Orik's smile was filled with mischief as her replied, "Sonny, ain't nobody gonna let a teamster stay in their inn. We all sleep in the stable with the wagons, if we sleep at all!" With that, Orik snapped the whip and the oxen trudged on toward the stables.

Daniel stood in the dirt street alone, looking around. It appeared as if he had two choices, the Guest of H'la and the Boars Brisket. He chose the latter, the former being a little too nice for his taste; he headed for the common room of the Boars Brisket inn.

Most inns' common room served three functions in small towns. The first and most important was for eating. The second was greeting the inn's guests. The third was gathering for drinking and entertainment. However, there was an unofficial fourth function, fighting. It was not the favorite function of the innkeeper, but that did not seem to stop it from happening.

Daniel entered the inn and approached the bar; setting his bedroll on the floor, he looked for the innkeeper. He spied a large rotund man with greasy hands and a dirty apron setting plates of food on the table in front of some customers. The big waiter walked over to the counter and smiled a cheerful smile. He wiped some gravy off his hands onto his apron. Daniel was not sure which one got dirtier in the transaction.

The innkeeper asked, "What can I help you with? Room or board? Or maybe both?"

"I will need both," Daniel replied.

"That will be one silver for both. We will be serving meals until midnight, and you can eat anytime," the innkeeper said.

"How about a bath? Do you have a room for washing?" Daniel asked.

The innkeeper replied, "We can bring up a tub. Would you like warm water or cold? Cold is one copper, warm is four."

"I'll take the warm," Daniel said. Upon paying for his room and board, he asked for directions to his room.

"Your room is at the top of the stairs, third door on the right. The boys will bring up the tub and water in a bit."

Daniel bent down to pick up his bedroll, and his hood came off his head and exposed the hilt of the sword. The innkeeper lurched backward with a startled look of recognition on his face. Daniel glared back at the man and pulled the hood back over his head. As Daniel walked to the steps, the innkeeper watched with a look of concern in his eyes.

Daniel turned his head to go up the stairs and ran into a serving girl who was coming down. Daniel grabbed her waist to keep her from falling. She held onto his arm above the elbow, her small hands barely able to get a grip. He swung her around and set her feet on the step below.

"Excuse me." Daniel smiled.

The girl giggled. "Oh, that's all right."

As Daniel looked to go upstairs, the serving girl was watching him go, but it was not concern that filled her eyes.

CHAPTER 8

Daniel entered his room and pulled off his cloak and unbuckled his waist belt; he tossed them both on the bed. Daniel stretched to remove the scabbard that was strapped to his back. He laid the scabbard on the bed and withdrew the sword. He held the sword by the shank of the blade as he examined the markings on the pommel and the hilt. He wondered what it was that had the innkeeper concerned.

The blade had been with him since Nathan gave it to him seven seasons ago. In fact, it had never left his side, even for a moment. For six seasons, he had watched Nathan wield the blade in practice and in open battle.

Then one day, Nathan handed the sword to Daniel and spoke. "Son, I am returning this weapon to you, as our time together is coming to an end. Use it as I have taught you."

He wanted to ask Nathan what he meant by saying their time was coming to an end, but he knew it would be fruitless. It seemed that when he asked a question, Nathan would either ignore him, answer his question with a question, or give him an answer that made no sense.

He had once pressed Nathan about the markings and symbols on the sword. His mentor smiled and said, "That is a good question. Tell me, Daniel, where does the light go when darkness comes? And why do normally good people sometimes turn bad?"

Daniel answered him by saying, "The sun sets in the west and continues to roam in the ether until it again rises in the east. As for why good people go bad, I think people are neither good nor bad. They are just people, and people do whatever they want." Thinking that he had answered wisely, he beamed at Nathan.

Nathan frowned at him as he turned his head away. He said, "So it does, so it does."

Examining the markings and symbols again, he knew they meant something special, because of the way that people reacted when they saw them; he just did not know what it was. Taking his wool rag out of his leather pouch, he began rubbing down the blade. "Knock, knock." There was someone at the door.

He quietly stepped over to the door and asked, "Who is it?"

"It is the chambermaid, sir. I have brought up the tub for washing and the cloths for bathing," the soft, sweet voice from behind the door replied.

Daniel returned the sword to the scabbard and opened the door. The young woman he had run into on the stairs stood smiling brightly at him. She wore a serving wench's dress, cut low in the front to entice generous tips from the customers.

Two strong boys carrying a large wooden tub followed her into the room. The boys set the tub down and proceeded to bring in pots of hot water. The chambermaid busied herself in the corner, setting out the linen and sneaking glances at Daniel.

After the boys were done, they excused themselves and left. As Daniel pulled his silk undershirt over his head, he heard a sharp gasp from behind him; he grabbed his fighting knife off the bed as he quickly turned around. The chambermaid's face went from an appreciative smile to a look of fear.

Daniel stood erect, returned the knife to its sheath, and said, "I thought you had left."

The young girl's sly smile quickly returned as she moved closer to him and said, "No, sir, I stayed to see if there was anything else… I could do for you."

Daniel awkwardly replied as he backed away from her, "I believe I can do this myself."

"Are you sure?" she said sweetly as she again moved closer to him.

He went to take another step back and tripped over the wooden tub. As he lay half-in and half-out of the tub, the chambermaid bent over him, giggling. "It certainly looks to me like you could use my help."

Now embarrassed, he gently pushed the girl away, and as he stood back up, he said firmly, "I will not need your help, so you can go."

"Okay, I'm going, but my name is Cat, if you change your mind." She giggled as she slowly moved toward the door. She opened the door and turned around, took one last long look at him, and sighed. She then closed the door and left.

As Daniel removed the rest of his clothes and stepped into the, tub he thought, *Why do they do that? I said nothing to encourage her!*

After finishing bathing, he took a fresh set of clothes from his leather bag and set the dirty ones aside to be washed. Getting dressed, he went down to the common room to eat. A heavyset serving wench brought out large slices of roast, with potatoes and carrots in a thick stew. Sitting on a bench at a long wooden table, he dug into his first fresh-cooked meal in a long time. The few other men at the table were all dressed like him. They were wearing heavy woolen pants, wool shirts, leather boots, and a heavy cloak for a covering. Most wore hats that were now removed. All of them had a similar build to one another. One of the men was even a bit larger than Daniel himself. Looking at each of the men, he could see that they were all capable of taking care of themselves in a fight.

He doubted that any of the men wore chain mail with cotton tunic under their wool shirts or that they wore a silk undershirt like his. In Daniel's profession, protecting the rich from thieves and such, one was always careful and took every advantage that one could. Some had scorned his silk undershirt before and thought that it was a sign of weakness. What they did not understand was that when an arrow penetrated your chain mail, it would not be able to pierce the tightly woven silk. Sure, the arrow would still penetrate your body, but when it came time to remove it, all you had to do was give the shaft a hard pull and it would slide right out. The silk also slowed the bleeding, which was a particularly good thing; he knew this to be true because he had experienced it personally twice.

Judging his eating companions to be no immediate threat, he settled down to enjoy his food. During the meal, the inn continued to fill up until there was hardly enough room to stand.

Daniel had finished his meal and had moved to a chair that sat against the back wall next to the door to the kitchen. After the serving girls cleared away the remnants of the meal and all the patrons' tankards were full of ale, the innkeeper brought out his music pipe and began to play. It was easy to see why so many people came to this inn. Though the food was not that great and the surroundings were a little run-down, the innkeeper played a fine tune on the pipe.

It seemed that the innkeeper knew most of the popular dancing tunes. Daniel did not dance himself, but most of the other patrons did, and it was turning out to be an enjoyable evening. The little chambermaid came by twice and asked him to dance, which he declined. She always ended up dancing with someone else, but she never seemed to take her eyes off him.

Halfway through the evening, six men entered the inn together. They were all armed with swords and looked the type who knew how to use them. They had the attitude of men who liked to pick fights they could easily win. Purchasing strong drink, they began to search for a table at which to sit. Finding one they liked, between Daniel and the dance floor, they came over and intimidated the people sitting at it, forcing them to move. Daniel overheard parts of their conversation, something about making a great deal of money on this last deal and taking the time to enjoy some of the fruits of their labor, at which they all sneered and laughed.

He judged them to be petty thieves and marked them as needing to be watched. He would need to make sure they did not see the wagons leave tomorrow, but it looked like they would not be a threat tonight.

Around midnight, the innkeeper put away his pipes and, to the protest of the crowd, started urging the patrons to head home. The serving wenches took the men's arms and ushered them to the door, all the time giggling and laughing. Daniel started toward the stairs to head up to his room. As he turned the corner to climb the steps, he tripped over the little chambermaid, who was sitting on the steps. Falling on top of her, he caught himself with his hands on the step above her head. She giggled and wrapped her hands around his neck and her legs around his waist.

She smiled up at him and said, "You have been avoiding me all night, mister, but no more. I am not going to let you pass until you agree to let me take care of you."

Seeing that the girl was not going to take no for an answer, he reached down with both hands, shifted her around until she was cradled in his arms. She could not have weighed more than five stones. He bounded up the stairs two at a time, her ample breasts bouncing, and all the while she was giggling wildly.

Once he reached the top of the stairs, he headed for his room. The serving boys had pulled the washtub out into the hall and were emptying it with buckets. Daniel kicked open the door to his room and, in the same motion, dropped the chambermaid into the half-emptied tub. The young girl laughed as the water sloshed onto the floor. The front of her blouse needed adjustment, so she flirtatiously moved it around as she reached out with her right hand to Daniel. He smiled brightly at the girl and said, "Good night," and shut the door behind him.

The young girl let fly with a torrent of curses that should only be heard from the mouth of teamsters. Daniel shook his head as he thought. *I dislike girls who giggle.*

CHAPTER 9

T'asha had ridden hard to reach Castle in the Gorge in three days. Time was short, and she had to make sure that all was in place. Alssa would be crossing through North Pass this morning and would be supping in the Valley of Profit tonight.

Leaving her personal guard to set up camp in the valley beyond the gorge, she rode up to the fortress alone. The gate quickly opened to her as she galloped up the steep ramp and across the drawbridge. Count Gravelet was waiting for her on the steps of the keep. She looked up at the lascivious fat man leering at her from beneath his drooping brow. He was looking at her the way he always did, with pure lust. Though she hated it when men did that, she was glad he felt the way he did; it made it easier to manipulate him. But was that not the case with all men. At least the ones she dealt with, they all seemed driven by lust. She shivered as she thought about it. Yes, it was good; it made them easy to control.

Count Gravelet looked upon the object of his desire, taking in her beauty. She was tall and lean, leaner than he normally liked, but in her case, he would make an exception. Her long red hair cascaded down her shoulders to the middle of her back. She had a face filled with fine beauty, high cheekbones, slender nose, succulent lips, but her eyes were as hard as steel and cold as ice.

He knew that three years of campaigning on the Island of Kings had left her with great physical and inner strength. She could easily be stronger than her older, more self-righteous sister, Alssa. *Ah, Alssa, now there's a woman worth longing for,* he thought with regret. *But that would never happen. One must be content with what one has, for the time being, anyway.* He let his eyes wander down the rest of her hard body as he licked his lips.

T'asha shivered under the obese count's leers. The only thing that allowed her to endure this offense was her present goal of dealing with her sisters and the wonderful thought of this fat pig squirming on the end of her blade as he died.

"Your Majesty, how very nice to see you!" Count Gravelet oozed.

"Count Gravelet, it is always a pleasure to be with you," T'asha lied as she held her hand out for him to kiss. He grasped her hand firmly with his pudgy fingers and pulled her close to him.

Breathing heavily, he whispered, "I have made all the arrangements. Your personal army set out under the Black Mountains three days ago. They are now eagerly waiting in the Wasteland for your prize. Though not as eagerly as I await mine."

"Now, Count, you will get yours in time," T'asha replied, smiling wickedly. She abruptly pulled her hand away and quickly walked up the steps toward the massive doors. Without looking back, she said, "Bring Commander Westolve to the main hall so that the commander may lay out all the details of her plan to me."

Turning to go, Count Gravelet snorted as his lustful leer turned to anger. He resented the fact that his queen had so little confidence in his abilities and she spent most of what little time she resided here with Commander Westolve. You would think that Commander Westolve had come up with his plans and had enlisted their needed help. What a joke that would be! They would never deal with Westolve, especially knowing that Westolve was in the service of the Three Sisters. It was amazing that, even after ten generations, they still had strong hatred for the people who had hunted them almost to extinction and taken away their ancient tribal grounds.

The count had been so deep in thought he almost walked past Commander Westolve's quarters. As he faced the door, resentment weld up inside of him. Of all the things that bothered him, this one bothered him the most. T'asha seemed to genuinely care more for this young commander than she did for him. And what was worse, the commander knew it and took every opportunity to flaunt it in his face.

In his forefathers' day, this would have never happened. No one would have dared to mock a Gravelet, Count of Goblin Gorge, holder of the Pass of Death. Three hundred years ago, his honored ancestor had been stationed on this very spot. His orders had been to hold off the combined armies of goblins, orcs, and hadrac for as long as possible so that the original Three Sisters would have time to prepare their defenses on the Twin Rivers.

His distant grandfather had done just that. For five long days, he and the five hundred men with him held off the sixty-thousand-strong army of darkness. His troops had all been killed and then eaten, all except his grandfather. The beasts had been so impressed by the strength of the human's resistance that they had left his body intact and hung it spread-eagle on the huge rock that jutted out over the gorge as tribute to his strength.

Fortunately for Count Gravelet, his greatest grandmother had been with the Three Sisters and his family line had not been lost. As a reward for holding back the black torrent for so long, the Three Sisters had decreed that the Gravelet family would hold the gorge and rule over the renamed Goblin Valley for all time. So his family received the titles of Lord of the Valley of Three Brides and Count of Castle in the Gorge. During the entire three-hundred-year history of the Three Sisters, only the Gravelet province had been ruled by a male.

And now here he was, the Great Count Gravelet, reduced to an errand boy and sent to fetch the iron bitch. Angrily knocking on her door, he called out, "Commander Westolve, Princess T'asha is here and requests your presence in the main hall." The door burst open, revealing a sumptuous young woman dressed only in a nightshirt, her long black hair in disarray.

Commander Westolve said with excitement in her voice, "Her Majesty is here? Now?" As she caught herself, her joy turned to anger as she scolded the count, "Why was I not informed sooner?"

Gravelet smiled wickedly and responded, "The princess just now rode in, without escort. After I was told she was here, I greeted her and then came to inform you."

As the count talked, Commander Westolve stepped back into her room and began to dress. With her nightshirt pulled off, she turned back angrily toward the count.

"You are a lying pig. You would have known long before she reached the castle that she was on her way. You did not let me know so that you could meet her alone, in hopes of having her for yourself. You are so stupid. She has no use for a man of the likes of you."

The count stood with his mouth open, his fat lips quivering, as he watched the commander cover her nakedness. When Westolve saw his leer, she smiled. Westolve finished putting on her tunic, turned around, and spoke as she walked past him toward the door.

She said, "And neither do I."

It took Count Gravelet a few moments to take in all that had just happened. He had never realized how stunning Commander Westolve was—she was incredibly beautiful. Then her last comment registered in his mind, and in his anger, he said aloud, "These filthy wenches are driving me crazy! Maybe I should leave this male prison and join the Pact of Brothers. At least there a man can be a man and women like these are put in their place." Catching himself, he quickly looked around to make sure no one had heard him. Satisfied that no one had, he set his enormous frame in motion back toward the main hall.

* * *

Commander Westolve's face beamed with anticipation as she burst into the main hall. She walked briskly toward T'asha, bowing down on one knee. "My queen, my heart is your heart, my sword is your sword."

"Rise, Commander," T'asha replied as she stepped toward Commander Westolve and hugged her. "It is good to see you again. How have you been?"

"I am well. Are you going to be able to stay for a while?" the commander asked.

T'asha replied, "We will see. We need to watch over your plan very closely. Tell me how it is proceeding."

Westolve spit out the words, "The fat pig…"

T'asha scowled. "Commander, watch your tongue." Her scowl turned to a smile as she said mockingly, "You must not speak in such a way about the count. He is royalty, after all, and must be treated as such."

Commander Westolve asked, "And will we treat him as such at the right time?"

"Oh yes, most assuredly. When the time comes, he will be made to feel like the most prestigious of royalty," replied T'asha.

They both then laughed.

"Back to the situation at hand. How are your plans proceeding?" T'asha inquired.

"Count Gravelet…was able to convince our allies that the direct descendant of the females that all but exterminated their forebears will be traveling down the coast highway tomorrow. I placed our agents to watch them and to report back what happens. We will know the outcome very quickly so that you can be in place to take full advantage of the situation."

"Excellent work, Commander," T'asha praised, then said, "So we have days to wait. Let us retire to the royal suite and relax."

T'asha had a smug smile and Commander Westolve an eager grin as they bounded up the stairs.

Count Gravelet looked on with disgust and envy from the darkened alcove across the hall from the stairs. *So their plans are complete, and they do not include me*, he thought. *Well, we will see about that.*

* * *

Count Gravelet walked quickly through the doorway of the Bear and Lion Inn. He strode across the room without looking at anyone and into the back hallway. At the end of the hall, he opened the door and stepped into the sleeping area of the inn. It was time to use the secret that he had been holding until now. Having never trusted the Three Sisters troops for his protection, he had hired mercenaries and had kept them secret for such a time as this. Finding the captain's room, he knocked and opened the door.

Captain Kromsing yelled out, "Who in the name of the dark lords wishes to die so early in the morning?"

"Captain, it is time for you and your men to earn your money," the count replied.

A stout full-body girl wrapped in a bedsheet sat up in the bed next to the captain. She smiled sheepishly at the count as she hugged her bed partner. The count's anger surged to the surface.

"Get that whore out of here so we can talk!" commanded the count.

"Who does he think he is? I don't have to leave at the word of a fatso like this, do I?" the girl asked.

The count's anger turned to full rage, and as he began to shake, his belly bounced up and down. He screamed at her, "You dirty little tart! How dare you talk in such a tone to me? I will have you punished for this!"

The girl laughed at him as she walked defiantly by him to exit the door. Count Gravelet swung his fist at her to strike her, but she easily sidestepped the blow and skipped down the hall, laughing even louder.

The captain had gotten out of the bed and began to dress, so when the count turned back to face him, he was standing dressed, with a mocking grin on his face.

The captain asked, "Your Excellency, what can I do for you?"

"Why do you consort with the likes of that?" the count said with disgust.

Kromsing replied, "You hire me and my men and then have us sit around with nothing to do for months. I get bored, and she helps make life more interesting. Besides, I think you are not as immune to the charms of the likes of that as you would like to portray."

"Captain, you should learn your place!" the count growled.

Smiling, with his hand held out, the captain said, "My good count, I know my place, and it's at the end of your hand filled with gold. Now, what would you like me to do for your gold?"

"I need you to have all your men leave the city discreetly and then meet at the J'ta Falls tonight at dusk. You and I will leave together in an hour under the pretense that you are the new overseer for my farmland and stables."

"Before I send my men down into the Goblin Valley, I want to know where we are going and why," Kromsing stated.

The count explained, "We are traveling to L'ke L'fe, and you are to be my escort."

"If that is all, then why the secrets? And why us?" Kromsing asked. "Have Westolve's troops escort you."

"That, Captain, is none of your concern. I have been paying you too well and for too long for you to question my reasons. Be ready in an hour." The count turned and squeezed his way through the narrow door and into the hallway.

The mercenary captain thought to himself, *Something is not right here.* But then, his mind quickly turned to the gold that the count was paying, and he thought, *After all, this is why I got into this business—it pays so well.* He did not bother to think any further or to realize that his action was about to put him in direct conflict with the troops of the Three Sisters and, worse than that, in opposition to T'asha, the future queen.

CHAPTER 10

Daniel awoke before sunrise, dressed, and went downstairs to have breakfast. The innkeeper was not yet up, probably sleeping off last night's ale. The serving girls this morning were a different group, not quite as buxom or as pretty. The chambermaid was nowhere to be seen, which was just as well; he did not want to be bothered by her this morning.

After eating his breakfast, he walked out into the predawn morning. He stood on the bottom step leading down from the front door of the inn. Looking down the main street, he noticed a commotion at the west gate. Daniel thought, Should he go find Orik, the wagon master, or let him sleep a little longer after last night's drinking?

The commotion at the west gate grew louder. The guards were yelling at somebody outside the walls, and by the sound of it, the men on the outside were terribly upset.

"We are wounded, and one of us is dying!" they screamed.

The guards yelled back, "The gate will not be opened until full light! That's the law! You will just have to wait out there until then!"

As Daniel stood and watched, the chief constable walked out of the town keep and called out to his men, "What kind of commotion are you men causing this early in the morning?"

One of the guards replied, "There are men outside who want in, but we told them that the gates cannot be opened until full light. It's the law."

The constable bounded up the stairs and peered over the wall to see who was on the outside.

Turning sharply back toward his men, he barked orders at them. "Open the cursed gate! You bunch of hadrac-brained buffoons, they are obviously wounded! Are you going to leave them outside to die? Do you want me to get in trouble with the lancers by not helping travelers?"

Daniel watched as the guards swung the gate open and two men, both limping and bloody, entered, dragging a litter behind them. He instantly recognized the two men as the fathers of the families he had traveled with. Slowly he moved a little closer so that he might be able to hear the conversation between the constable and the men.

Talking hastily, Tarbell said, "We were set upon by thieves yesterday afternoon. Landers took an arrow in the leg, while I was hit in the head with a club. My eldest son there was run through the midsection with a sword when he tried to defend our women. They took our wives and the rest of our children and left us for dead. Landers saw them head in this direction. You had to have seen them! They would have passed through here last night. They had two women and six children with them. Constable, you must go after them immediately!"

The constable interrupted the jabbering man. "Sir, can you tell me how many attackers there were?"

"Six or eight, I think, all armed to the teeth," spit Landers out.

The constable shook his head and calmly said to the men, "A group of eight men. I should say we would have seen them, but only twelve people came through the gates last evening. Lord Galvan and his lady came in from the Holy Lands through the south gate. Three men came from the north, and three men came through the east, but they all came through separately. The only people to come through the west gate were the teamsters from H'la.

"As for chasing after them, my job is to protect this town and keep the peace inside these walls. If you want someone to chase after them, you can talk to the captain of the Holy Lancers when he gets here tomorrow."

"Tomorrow!" the fathers screamed in unison.

One of them continued, "Curse the dark lords, by tomorrow they will be long gone! Are you a spineless worm that would let innocent women and children remain in the hands of kidnappers?"

The constable glared at the man and reprimanded him with as much disgust in his voice as he could muster. "I am not the fool who brought his family into the Ebony Forest without any protection. And I will not become a bigger fool by sending my meager allotment of troops into hadrac-infested woods. You should have hired protection before you had the problem."

Turning away from the men, he noticed Daniel listening. He turned back toward the wounded men and said, "See that man over there? He is obviously the type who hires out his service for this sort of thing. Talk to him." He continued to walk away.

The two fathers looked up at Daniel.

The younger man recognized him and called out, "Constable, that man was on the road with us two days ago. He could be one of them!"

The constable came back and called Daniel over to him and asked, "Sir, these men say that you were on the road from J're with them two days ago. Is this true?"

Daniel stood his ground and thought, *Who does he think he is, commanding me to come to him?* He had begun turning to walk away when the constable ordered four of his guards to detain him. Daniel prepared to draw his sword and then thought better of it. After all, he was not involved in the kidnapping. Moving toward the constable, he noticed four archers up on the parapet, notching their arrows. Daniel thought, *If these men are experienced, then they are taking the proper precautions. If not, then they are scared, and that could be even more dangerous.*

As he stepped up to the constable, just out of sword reach, he asked, "What would you like?"

The constable addressed him. "Sir, these men were set upon by thieves while on the road west of here, and you came through the west gate last evening just before dark. They also say that you passed by them two days ago. Is this true?"

Daniel replied guardedly, "Yes, what you say is true."

"So you were on the road with them. Then it is possible that you may have been involved?" the constable inquired.

Daniel assumed a defensive posture and sneered his reply, "No, it is not possible for me to have been involved. I may be a great many things, but a common thief, I am not. Besides, I was riding on the wagon with the teamsters from J're."

The constable took a step back, looking intently at Daniel, then asked, "Are you armed?"

Armed! Daniel replied, "What do you take me for, the same kind of fool as these men? One does not enter the Lands of Chaos unarmed, nor does an intelligent man walk about the Ebony Forest as if he were walking the streets of St. Michaels Keep without a care in the world. Of course I am armed."

Daniel went on, "I arrived on the *Johansson's Pride* from Port Royal with those men four days ago. In J're, I hired out to protect cargo wagons, and then two days ago, around midafternoon, we passed these men on the Queen's Highway. They asked to accompany us on the wagon, but the wagon master refused them. We then arrived, as you know full well, last evening around dusk. I then purchased accommodations at the Boars Brisket and stayed there all night."

Tarbell had grown angry as Daniel had told his story, and he screeched out in anguish, "This man and the others on the wagons refused to help us! They must have had cohorts lying in wait for us."

The constable turned uncertainly back to Daniel and said with trepidation, "May I have your weapon, sir?"

Daniel snorted in disgust at Tarbell and Landers before saying, "Both of you know full well that I could not have laid an ambush for you. I have just spent seven days aboard ship with you. I was on the ship when you yourselves embarked from Port Royal, having spent the previous eight days coming from Brigand's Port. Fifteen days ago, I was in Staymos."

At this statement, the constable motioned for more guards to move in around Daniel. Now he was surrounded by more than ten armed men and half-dozen archers on the wall.

The constable commanded, "Give me your weapon."

With a puzzled look, Daniel responded, "Why? Is it not obvious that I had nothing to do with these men and their plight?"

The constable smiled and said, "Yes, this is true, but you yourself just said that you have come here from the Barbarian Kingdom, and we have had nothing but problems with the ilk that comes from there. Give me your weapon immediately."

Daniel lowered the hood of his cloak and reached up carefully to draw his sword. When he lifted it over his head, the constable took another step back, as all ten guards drew their swords. By instinct, Daniel dropped into a fighting stance, causing the guards to step back and raise their swords and the archers on the wall to draw back their bows.

The constable stared at Daniel's sword and said, "Be careful now, or you will force me to set my men upon you. Hand me your weapon hilt first."

Daniel looked around. He thought he might be able to handle the ten guards that had him surrounded, but the archers on the wall would be able to slay him before he could get away. Besides, he had done nothing. Reluctantly, he reversed the sword and handed it to the constable. As the constable reach out to take it from him, a sharp gasp escaped from the constable's mouth as he grabbed the hilt. After turning the sword over and over and closely examining the markings, he looked up at Daniel with a searching and unbelieving stare.

"Where would a man such as you get a sword with these markings? You are most certainly not a person of royal upbringing. So how would you end up with a sword with the markings of the queen's guard?"

The constable was talking absently, almost to himself. "Only a royal member of the Three Sisters or a member of the Holy Family from the Pact of Brothers would have a sword with markings such as this. This relief at the center of the handle, an engraving of a woman riding a Ptroc, is the emblem of the great queen herself. These other markings are from the Pact of Brothers and the Three Sisters." Turning to Daniel, he said, "This alone is enough for me to believe that you have been lying to me. You obviously are a thief!"

He turned to his guards. "Take him and lock him in the tower!"

The guards began to move in on Daniel. He stepped back from the first two men who were coming at him from opposite sides, grabbed them by the shoulders, and smashed their heads together. Daniel back-kicked the soldier lunging at him from behind, sending him sprawling into the dirt. He struck the guard rushing at him from the front up under the chin, knocking him unconscious. The remaining six men jumped on him as one, knocking him to the ground, and, after a lengthy wrestling match, subdued him.

The constable stood over Daniel and said, "You see, barbarian thief, you don't know whom you are dealing with."

They bound him hand and foot and carried him to the tower and locked him in the topmost room. The constable turned, called more guards to help those that had been hurt, and set them off in the direction of the healer.

Chapter 11

Alssa fumed as she sat in the opulently upholstered royal coach. Her eyes stared out over the Seer Sea and across the emptiness of the wave-covered sunken lava fields. She mulled over her feelings of anger and resentment toward her mother. Sitting next to her was Cally, her closest friend in the world and her "little sister" by triumvirate birth. Sitting across from them were their personal bodyguards, Colleen and Carrie. They were identical twins, totally trustworthy, and willing to give their lives in defense of Alssa and Cally.

She proclaimed to all in the coach, "Is it not bad enough that our mothers have made us ride in this ridiculous carriage? Did they also have to have us wear these dresses? We should be dressed in armor, leading this procession and riding our beautiful battle horses. Instead, Captain Brier gets the honor of leading the twelve score of royal guards, while we are trussed up like ladies going to a ball."

Alssa looked with envy at the twins, Colleen and Carrie, as they sat dressed in body armor. The twins became Alssa's and Cally's bodyguards when the girls were first born, and had been their constant companions ever since.

When traveling outside of the realm, no self-respecting soldier of the Three Sisters would be without their armor. She had planned to change into her leathers and armor and ride her horse after they had crossed North Pass, but Cally had insisted that they must stay dressed the way they were or their mothers would have their heads.

Alssa was glad that their mothers had insisted on Cally going with her instead of T'asha. Cally had always been a great friend and had continued to grow closer to her as they grew older. But T'asha was another story. They had all been remarkably close when they were little, running around the castle, pretending to fight goblins, hadrac, and any other form of evil their minds could think up. But when T'asha was ten seasons old, her mother had died in battle and her aunt Megan became the Third Sister. And though Megan could never rule, she took over the responsibility for T'asha's upbringing.

The change in T'asha was almost immediate. From that time on, she started treating both the other girls differently, but she was especially rude to Alssa. Slowly she turned into what she was today, a conniving, angry witch. Alssa hated having anything to do with her and avoided her whenever possible.

Cally cried out, "Alssa, look! Bottle fish playing in the sunken lava fields!"

Alssa pulled herself out of her thoughts and looked at what had made Cally so excited. She followed her pointing finger out over the black beach, past the lava outcroppings, to an open stretch of water. Her eyes saw what most people thought were only myths, giant fish with long bottle-shaped noses, leaping two or three spans into the air. They would do backflips and twist about in circles before slipping back under the water.

Alssa had seen them before when she had sailed to Seer Island. As the eldest of the Three Sisters, she had been taken there when she was twelve seasons. Along the way the court seer, who accompanied her, told her the story about the fish.

"They really aren't fish at all," he had said. "They breathe air and have live babies just like humans. They also have strong minds like men, but the bodies of fish."

She did not believe him at first, but after she had spent six months on Seer Island and learned more about the seers, she began to believe a great many things. The seers were well educated and understood things about the earth and sky, about things under the sea and on the ground. They even knew things about the stars and the unseen world. They had become the only men that Alssa fully respected and trusted. She came to understand why her mother treated them the way she did and why she let them have so much influence.

Cally was giggling with excitement as she stood up in the coach with her upper body hanging out the window. Her long blond hair was waving in the wind, and her light skin shone in the bright sun. She was such a delight to be around, always full of laughter and mischief. They had shared many young-girl adventures together. As the third sister, Cally was the youngest and had been exposed to less of the realities of ruling. Alssa was the first sister, the seventh great-granddaughter of N'ta, the oldest of the original Three Sisters. N'ta, K'jo, and L'se—those three names were embedded into her mind. The seers had drilled her on the stories about the original Three Sisters. They were the reason their domain existed, the reason the royal family was as it was, and the reason Cally, T'asha, and Alssa were sisters. The original Three Sisters were the eldest of the great queen's children and had led their troops up the Valley of the Three Brides River and across the Northern Barrier Mountains to liberate the Koazon Plain from the control of the dark lords. It had taken five seasons of fighting to drive the armies of evil off the plain, and another fifteen to drive them off the Brigand and Cult Islands. By the time they returned to Katan Hill, on the Twin Rivers, their children were grown women and a new city, Jukeele, had emerged where the Battle of Blood had been fought. They had become grandmothers, with their own daughters now having children of their own. So they asked their mother, the great queen, if they could rule under her in the lands they had liberated. With her approval they began to divide the land equally among themselves.

It was also at this time that the queen's youngest son, M'tin, disappeared. He was her seventh child and the designated heir to the great queen's throne. She had decided to make her youngest son the king of all the lands west of the Impenetrable Mountains. With her three daughters' holdings in the north and her first three sons having conquered the lands in the south, she gave direct control over the Middle Kingdom to M'tin. His disappearance led the three older sisters to think that one of them would be made queen when their mother passed away.

However, that was not to be. The great queen made a decree: only M'tin or his eldest heir could sit on the throne. That bit of foolishness had left the Middle Kingdom without a ruler for almost three hundred seasons. It also turned the queen's once-beautiful Middle Kingdom into the Lands of Chaos. M'tin never returned, nor had any of his heirs. Only impostors had ever tried to claim the throne, and the seers had exposed all of them as frauds.

After the upheaval caused by the great queen's departure from the Middle Kingdom for parts unknown and her leaving no heir, lawlessness consumed the Middle Kingdom. In the chaos created by her sentimental decree, the original Three Sisters banded together under the advice of the seers and created a triumvirate. All Three Sisters would rule as equals. It was also decided that the next generation of rulers would be each of their eldest daughters. If one of them died, their next older sister would take their place, but only in function, with no authority. The second and any subsequent daughters in the family would take positions of authority in government or the military, but they could never rule as one of the three. This process had worked for seven generations.

The official royal practice in rearing the next generation of rulers was to separate the three daughters from their natural siblings and raise the three of them from birth as sisters. Alssa, T'asha, and Cally were that seventh generation. The position of daughter of N'ta had gained more and more power over the generations, and the entire arrangement had become more and more political, which was the part she hated. Alssa would much rather lead a troop of horse soldiers into full battle than sit in the palace and talk politics. This was another reason she was glad that she and Cally were so close. Cally might be naive in her experiences in the world, but she was a genius when it came to understanding politics.

Suddenly, Alssa's thoughts were shattered by the sound of an arrow penetrating Colleen's shoulder armor. Alssa grabbed Cally and forced her onto the floor of the coach as two more arrows hit Colleen. Carrie pushed Alssa down on top of Cally and jumped on top of her. Alssa could hear the thudding sound of arrows hitting the carriage. She could also hear Captain Brier shouting orders for deployment. The archers quickly circled the carriage, and the pike-women set up a protective square around the archers. Though she could not see them, she knew what was happening with the rest of the company. The cavalry would be dispersing by squads of four to flush out the attackers. The heavily armed phalanx would be hoisting their lances and heading directly toward the enemy position, with the swordswomen deploying before them as skirmishers. With the deployment laid out in her head, Alssa thought about the direction the attack would be coming from. To their right was the Seer Sea; on the left was the empty black wasteland of the lava flows. Obviously, the attack was not coming from the direction they had just come. So that meant the attack was coming from Toller's Crag. Their options were to retreat toward the Valley of Profit or to fight through the riffraff that was apparently attacking them. With 240 fully equipped and trained soldiers, this should not be difficult.

Alssa started to rise, but Carrie's weight was fully on top of her. "Carrie, let me up!" Alssa cried.

There was no answer.

Alssa gave an order, "Carrie, I said let me up. I know you are trying to protect me, but I must get up to help in the battle."

There was still no answer.

Alssa felt something warm and sticky running down the small of her back. In panic, she pushed up with all her might. Carrie's body flopped onto the seat. As Alssa sat up, her gaze fell upon the arrow-riddled back of her personal bodyguard. Carrie had given her life in protecting her. Alssa's eyes began to tear up as she looked at the body of the woman who had been her constant companion since she had been born.

Cally climbed up off the floor, trembling in fear. When she saw the blood-covered bodies, she began to scream.

Alssa pulled her close and challenged her, "You must rise above this, Cally. You are a future ruler of the triumvirate and warrior of the Three Sisters. Now is not the time to grieve."

Cally sniffled and drew herself up and said, "I'm okay. Let's go."

The hail of arrows had decreased, so the troops were apparently having some effect against their attackers. They started to crawl out of the coach on the seaward side. With her foot, Alssa was trying to contact the ground, but instead it hit something soft. She looked down to see the body of a fallen archer. Finding a place to put her feet, she stood up and surveyed the scene. The ground was littered with bodies of pikewomen and archers, all of them. Four score of soldiers entirely wiped out. The bodies looked like pincushions. There were ten to fifteen arrows in each soldier.

Alssa thought to herself, *How many attackers are there if they can put up this much fire?*

Cally had finally extracted herself from the coach, and as she took in the carnage, she gasped in horror and asked, "Alssa, who could possibly be doing this?"

Alssa did not hear her as her eyes looked off into the distance toward the Wasteland. The ranks of the phalanx and swordswomen had been greatly reduced, but they were still holding their unseen attackers at bay.

"Where are the mounted troops?" Cally asked in despair.

Alssa was about to respond when nine mounted troopers rode up from the north at a full gallop. They had brought up her and Cally's battle horses.

Captain Brier shouted, "Both of you must mount up immediately!"

Alssa was about to make inquiries about the situation when another flight of arrows came soaring in upon them. Three of the arrows hit the captain in the chest and head, knocking her from her horse and killing her instantly.

Alssa was bending down to check on the fallen captain as Sergeant Sharon rode up to her and said, "Your Highness, we must get both of you to safety at once! Our way back to the Valley of Profit is already blocked. We must make for Toller's Crag!"

Alssa and Cally mounted quickly, and the ten of them headed south at a full gallop. Alssa looked back to see how the rest of the soldiers were doing. Even at the distance of three hundred paces, she could see the line of phalanx crumble as the last of the women fell to the unknown attackers' arrows. She could also make out the enemy horsemen circling to the north of the coach. They seemed to be riding what looked like small ponies that ran like a large dog.

As Alssa and her companions raced on, she looked back one more time to see the undistinguishable shapes of her attackers engulf the coach.

She thought to herself, *Who would be so bold as to attack the future rulers of the Three Sisters? Moreover, who could put together such a large force? They had attacked out of the east. How had they managed to cross the vast expanse of the Wasteland? And why are they stopping at the carriage instead of continuing their pursuit?*

Alssa pressed forward to catch up with Sergeant Sharon, who was leading their headlong flight. "Sergeant, how many attackers were deployed against us?" she asked.

"More than a thousand," came the sergeant's frightened reply.

Alssa looked at her sternly and spoke. "You must get ahold of yourself. You are a soldier in the service of the Three Sisters. Conduct yourself as such."

The sergeant just looked back at her with eyes filled with terror. This caught Alssa by surprise. What would cause an experienced soldier like Sergeant Sharon to act like this?

Alssa yelled at her and demanded, "Tell me who our attackers are. What kingdom are they from?"

Again, the sergeant did not respond but just looked at her with crippling fear in her eyes.

Alssa's anger was at the full as she screamed, "Sergeant, you will respond to me this instant, or I will bring this entire troop to a halt. Who are our attackers?"

With panic filling her voice, the sergeant responded, "Goblins, thousands of goblins."

CHAPTER 12

Captain Kromsing sat on a boulder, relaxing in the morning sun, eating his dried cheese and hard bread. This was not how he had hoped to make his way to the Midlands, and now he was saddled with the opulent count. He had only taken the job of protecting Count Gravelet because he needed a place to hang out away from spying eyes—and the money, of course. He had known going in that the count rarely left the castle, and he had relied on the count's distaste for Commander Westolve to keep him employed.

Now he sat in the middle of the Three Brides Valley, watching Count Gravelet's obese body try to negotiate the rocky hillside. When he had called a halt to his troops' march down the valley, he had picked this spot high above the K'jo Falls to eat his lunch on purpose, hoping that the fat count would not be able to get to him. For a full day now, he had been forced to listen to the count's constant whining and complaining. It was obvious he did not belong outside of the city walls.

Captain Kromsing found the count's struggles trying to climb up the steep slope quite humorous. When the count reached the top of the falls, he was wheezing heavily. Leaning against a rock, he swore at Captain Kromsing. "By the dark lords, why must you pick the most uncomfortable spots to rest?"

Kromsing just smiled and shrugged.

Gravelet continued to whine, "You are too cautious, Captain. All the goblins are on the other side of the Black Mountains. We have little to worry about here."

Kromsing replied, "My good count, the reason I am still alive is that I am cautious, and I take as few chances as possible. To camp on the main trail would be stupid. Evil comes in many forms, and often from where you least expect it. I prefer not to take chances. And how would you know where the goblins are?"

Ignoring his question, the count inquired, "When are we going to get moving again?"

"I sent scouts up ahead as far as the L'se Falls, and we are waiting for their return," Kromsing answered.

Gravelet shook his head and sighed. "I do not understand what you are so concerned about."

"Like I said, I am concerned about everything. Now, sit down and relax."

The sun had almost finished crossing the sky when they both heard horses approaching on the trail below. From his present position, Captain Kromsing could see the two men that he had posted on the trail as they stepped out and confronted the riders. It was his scouts returning. He had sent four out, and only two had returned. He made his way down to the trail. The two scouts were covered in sweat, dirt, and blood. One had an ax wound on his forearm.

"What has happened?" Kromsing inquired.

"We were set upon by hadrac well before we reached the falls. Machee and Robins were both killed outright. Smithy here was wounded when we ran into another group on the way back."

"How many hadrac did you see?"

"Forty or fifty in each group, sir."

Captain Kromsing queried, "Over one hundred hadrac between here and L'se Falls? Are you sure?"

"Well, I didn't have time to count exactly, but they were packed very tightly, marching up the valley trail."

Kromsing asked, "They're working their way up the valley toward us? What in the world is going on? The hadrac never come above the lower falls into goblin territory." Turning his head to look up at the count, he called out, "We need to turn around and go back."

Count Gravelet was sliding down the slope on his rear, but he had heard the captain's words. He said, "No! No! We cannot go back. We must go forward!"

Kromsing looked at him in frustration and said, "Count, we can't. There are over one hundred hadrac on the trail ahead of us, and they are on their way here!"

The count started to respond, "We cannot go back! T'asha and Commander Westolve are—"

Catching himself, he changed his story. "We must get to L'ke L'fe. That is our only option, and that is what I am paying you for!"

The captain looked at him suspiciously. "Do you know of another way out of this valley other than downriver into the Ebony Forest?"

"No, I do not," replied the count.

Kromsing grew impatient and asked, "Then what would you like to do?"

The count was exasperated and demanded, "We go forward. We cannot go back, so we trust our luck and go forward. Didn't I hire you to defend me and to fight off such threats as these?"

In response, Captain Kromsing pulled his sword from its scabbard and walked toward Smithy. Looking at the count, he said, "You want my thirty men to take on one hundred hadrac to get you to L'ke L'fe." He turned back to look at Smithy, whose eyes were filled with fear. "You're a good and faithful man, Smithy. I have enjoyed having you in the company, and it is an honor to help you to a better destination." Kromsing then thrust his sword quickly through Smithy's heart. The man dropped to the ground, dead.

Count Gravelet shrieked in horror. "What have you done? This man was hardly wounded and would not have been a hindrance to our travel! Why would you kill him?"

Reaching down, the captain rolled the body over onto its belly, then lifted its tunic to expose its bare back. The count dropped to his knees and began to retch. Huge pus-filled bumps ran in vertical ridges down its back, and tufts of featherlike hair grew out of each bump. His skin had turned yellowish brown, with big patches of it flaking off.

"You see, Count, Smithy had already started to turn. In just a few short hours, he would have been a hadrac, with no memory of us or his past, just a constant desire to kill and destroy. Do you still want to go forward and risk this?"

When the count pulled himself off the ground, his face was white and he was unable to respond. He had never seen the results of a hadrac ax wound. He stumbled for his words and began to plead. "I...don't...know what we can do. We cannot go back, and I do not want to go forward. Captain, what should we do?"

"I still don't understand why we can't go back," Kromsing said.

Count Gravelet seemed to struggle with information that Captain Kromsing did not have. Taking another look at Smithy's decaying body, he made his decision and said, "If we go back, T'asha will have all of us executed."

Kromsing looked at him in disbelief. "Why would the iron queen execute us? I thought you were her favorite?"

The count was sweating with fear. "Well, now that we left in the middle of the night, she will not believe she can trust me. In addition, because I know it was her that let the goblins begin to breed again in this valley, she will want to get rid of me. And because she knows you are with me, she will want you dead too."

Kromsing's face was contorted in horror as he yelled at the count, "The goblins are breeding again? What have you idiots done?" Turning to his men, he said, "Mount up! We are leaving now. Leave everything. We must flee!" Turning back to the count, he said, "Get on your horse. We must ride and ride, hard!" As the count mounted his horse, Kromsing rode up next to him.

"I am going to take you to a place that only a few people have ever heard of and only a select few have ever been. It's called the Thieves Tunnel, and I cannot let you see the route we take to get there. We will have to blindfold you and lead you into it."

"You will not blindfold me! I will not stand for it! Who do you think you are dealing with?" the count cried.

Kromsing growled, "At this point, I really don't care. Either you let me blindfold you or I will leave you here. You choose!"

The count quickly gave in, and they headed back up the valley.

CHAPTER 13

T'asha was going over the schedule in her head. So far, everything was going as planned. Alssa and Cally would have run into the waiting reception party in the Wasteland by now. Her own house troops were ready to play their part when she returned to Jukeele. T'asha smiled wickedly, a warm feeling coming over her. *And right now, Commander Westolve is dealing with that disgusting parasite Count Gravelet. Yes, everything is proceeding as planned.*

T'asha leaned back in the chair as she looked up the side of the steep hillside that extended above the castle. Her eyes stopped at the huge monolith that protruded over the valley. The monolith was the place that Gravelet's ancestor was strapped to by the dark lords' army. T'asha was disgusted. *The man loses the battle, and his male descendants are rewarded for it! Well, not anymore.*

A knock on the door pulled her from her pleasant thoughts. As she turned her head toward the door, she was about to tell them to go away when Commander Westolve pushed the door open and began to talk in a rush.

"Your Majesty, Count Gravelet is gone. I could not find him anywhere. One of my troopers saw him ride out late last night, but no one has seen him return."

T'asha flew out of her chair and screamed, "What! Why wasn't I informed?"

Commander Westolve flinched as T'asha drew near, and replied, "I just found out a few moments ago. He told the gate guard that he was going to inspect his personal landholdings and livestock. She did not think anything of it. He has often left in the middle of the night on such excursions, but usually with a woman. It was not until we reviewed all last night's reports that we realized that over thirty men slipped out in small groups. We think they might have been mercenaries."

T'asha's anger was rising as she asked sternly, "Commander, tell me, why were there mercenaries in the city in the first place?"

Commander Westolve was worried. T'asha was so unpredictable when she was angry. She cautiously said, "We think he had hired them for his personal bodyguard because he resented being protected by us. We really hadn't paid much attention to them. They have been living here for over six months and have not caused a bit of trouble."

T'asha turned away from Westolve as she said sarcastically, "Well, they are obviously looking to cause trouble now. You should know by now that men are always trouble."

Suddenly turning back to face the commander, she gave quick orders. "Send your entire garrison after them. Tell them to track him down and kill him."

"What about the men who are with him?" the commander asked.

Boring a hole through Westolve with her stare, she said, "Do you really need to ask? Kill them, kill them all!"

"Yes, ma'am," Westolve replied, then asked, "Do you still want to leave for Jukeele this afternoon?"

T'asha replied encouragingly, "Of course. There is no reason to change the plan. Your trained troops should have no problems dealing with the count and his mercenaries."

"Ma'am, I just want to make sure we are fully capable of accomplishing your desires with as little difficulty as possible."

"Oh, we will accomplish my desires, of that I am sure. Quickly, go and do as I have commanded, and then return to help me get dressed."

* * *

T'asha and Commander Westolve watched the troops march out the main gate and head south on the valley road to pursue Count Gravelet. They were about to ride out the gate themselves to join T'asha's house troops for the trip to Jukeele when a single trooper came galloping up to them. The trooper stopped next to Westolve and leaned in close to whisper into her ear.

T'asha watched as Westolve's face turned ashen and her shoulders slumped. Prodding her horse with her spurs, she moved next to Westolve and asked, "What has happened, Commander?"

Westolve turned in her saddle and responded, "They escaped, Your Majesty."

"Who escaped? What are you talking about?" T'asha demanded.

Westolve gulped and replied, "Alssa and Cally, they escaped the goblin attack."

"How could they possibly escape from the ambush we set up? There were to be over three thousand of those filthy lizards!" T'asha demanded indignantly.

Westolve replied, "My scouts are not sure how they escaped, but they are sure they did. They believe they made it to Toller's Crag."

"What about the goblins? What were they doing that let them get away?" T'asha asked.

"They pursued them, but they then stopped and returned to the ambush site."

"Why would they do that?" T'asha questioned.

Westolve responded reluctantly, "Well, the scout was pretty shaken up and somewhat incoherent, but what I got out of her was, the goblins had stopped to eat."

"Eat? Eat what?" T'asha demanded.

Commander Westolve shuddered and said, "Uhmmm…they ate the raw flesh off the bodies of our soldiers."

T'asha's face showed her disgust, not for the atrocities of the goblins, but at Westolve's statement of "Our soldiers." She said, "Commander, they were not *our* soldiers. They were in the service of a usurper. Keep that in mind. I am the one most qualified to rule, not her, and anyone who chooses otherwise deserves whatever fate befalls them."

Commander Westolve shuddered as she watched the hatred and contempt rise in T'asha. She said, "I know…or knew some of those people. Captain Briar and Sergeant Sharon are good friends of mine, and the thought of them being eaten by those beasts, it's…it's unbearable."

With disgust and contempt T'asha, declared, "Unbearable! Commander, what did you think was going to happen when we set this up? That the goblins were going to have them in for tea? Get ahold of yourself! We must now finish what we started. If Alssa and Cally have escaped our trap, they will head for Toller's Crag and then to Devil's Pass. If they escape the Wasteland, then we need to be waiting at the edge of the Ebony Forest on the other side of the pass. So let's proceed down the Valley of Brides and be waiting for them."

"Your Majesty," Westolve asked, "it is almost dark. We should wait for morning. Are you not afraid of what we have released by using the goblins?"

"No, I am not," T'asha replied, then said, "The sisters defeated the goblins before, and we will do it again. We will leave now! Send someone out to the valley beyond the gorge and tell Commander Nadja to bring my house guard forward. We will quickly catch up with your troops, and then together we will proceed to Devil's Pass."

Chapter 14

Daniel awoke in his cell with his wrist and ankles tied. He wondered how long he had lain unconscious after he landed headfirst when they tossed him in the cell. From his position on the floor, he could only see a sliver of sky, and it looked to be dusk. The rats had been crawling all over him until he sat up. He pulled with his hands and feet to see how tightly they had bound him. With his arms tied behind his back, he was probably not going to be able to get loose, so he sat to wait for someone to come and feed him.

While waiting for his keepers to appear, he began to think that coming to the mainland and the Lands of Chaos had not been the best idea. Before Nathan died, the old man had told Daniel to go to the Deep River headwaters, but Daniel could never see or understand the reason for it, so he did not. The Lands of Chaos were so scarcely populated there was little work for a man in his trade.

Daniel had spent his time instead hopping from island to island, sailing the eastern seas. He had grown weary of the sea and wanted to spend some time on solid ground. So he started traveling around most of the known world, all the time staying on the other side of the Impenetrable Mountains. He sold his unique abilities to the rich. He had become quite wealthy for an orphan. Then this yearning started inside of him, a desire to come to the Westward. A desire to be something more, to find himself, and something else; he just did not know what it was.

He was also amazed at how many people in the Westward recognized the sword. What had the constable called the flying reptile? A Ptroc? He had often wondered what the mythical creature was. No one had ever explained what the symbols and markings meant.

Daniel pictured the pommel of the sword in his mind.

The left handguard had the image of three soldiers with crosses on their tunics, riding horses, lances raised in the air. On the reverse side, the words *Tra suan sout*, in some language that Daniel did not know.

On the right handguard, there were three female warriors riding battle horses in full armor, with swords drawn. On its reverse side the words *Tra duan sout*, in apparently the same language.

In the middle of the handguard, on the side with the people, was the emblem of a crowned woman riding the Ptroc. And on the reverse, an open space that looked to have had an emblem in it but was now empty. The empty spot was there when he was given the sword, and he had always planned on putting something in it. He figured that the original marking had been there for something special. He was waiting for something special to happen to him.

With a rattle and a bang, the cell door burst open, and the constable strode in accompanied by sword-wielding guards.

Smiling down at him, the constable said, "What is your name, thief?"

Seeing no reason to not tell him, he replied, "Daniel."

"Well, Daniel, you are in luck. Tomorrow the Pact of Brothers Coast Road patrol will be stopping for a day of rest. I will turn you over to their captain, and he can decide what to do with you."

Daniel glared at him as he responded, "What right does the Pact of Brothers have to take prisoners in the Lands of Chaos?"

The constable gave him a questioning look, then laughed and said, "Ah, yes, barbarian, you probably don't know. The Holy Land sends patrols through every two weeks. They go as far north as Devil's Pass. Two of those patrols will rendezvous here tomorrow. That is two score of lancers, some of the best-fighting men in all the Twelve Kingdoms. They will find you and your sword most interesting, and I hope that I will find it most rewarding."

The constable continued to brag, "The Holy Land soldiers always pay with gold for everything, and that makes them welcome as far as I'm concerned. They don't get involved in local affairs, but most importantly, they keep the hadrac off the highways. Why, I even heard that the Three Sisters are sending the same type of patrols as far south as Toller's Crag, although I have never seen the wenches personally."

Daniel looked up at the constable and asked, "Why are the kingdoms to the north and south of the Lands of Chaos sending patrols into a place they have totally ignored for centuries? Are they making claims of lordship after all these years?"

The constable answered with a knowing smile on his face, "I have heard that it is because of prophecies about the return of the queen and the reemergence of the Lords of Chaos, but I don't believe any of that rubbish. I think they have finally come to their respective senses and realized what most of us common folk have always known. Seers are simply crazy old men who like to go around scaring people into taking care of them. Their prophecies are just stories they make up so people would feel like they need them."

Daniel smiled to himself and asked, "Have you ever met a real seer?"

The constable looked at him sternly, shrugged, and said, "No, I have not, and I have no desire to either. Nor do I have any desire to be ruled over by the whores from the north. I would much rather have the Pact of Brothers watching over me. In fact, that is why I am turning you over to them tomorrow. It never hurts to make friends with the future rulers."

The constable turned to leave and said, "Guards, untie the prisoner and give him food. He isn't going anywhere."

Daniel hid his excitement as the guards untied him and placed food on the floor. As he began to eat, he thought, *So I have until tomorrow to escape from this rathole.*

* * *

Having finished his meal, Daniel paced the cell, waiting for full darkness. Looking out the window, he saw that he was over ten spans in the air; there was no getting out that way. Even if he did survive the fall, the window dropped into the walled training grounds of the guards. Daniel hated heights, so not being able to go out the window was a good thing.

He looked over the town walls and across the four hundred paces of open ground that separated the town from the forest. He knew he needed a plan to escape his cell, escape from the tower, and get outside of the walls. He saw there was no moon tonight, so that would make it a little easier. If he could figure out a way to get out.

Daniel hoped he would be able to escape without hurting anyone. He had not done anything wrong, and killing someone would just make things worse. He totally understood why the constable would want to make friends of the Pact of Brothers soldiers, but he had no intentions of being here when they arrived.

He walked quietly over to the solid oak door. Leaning against it with his right ear, he listened intently for noise from the outer room. He heard only snoring. He examined the latch and the hinges; they were iron, which was good.

Pulling out one of his throwing knives from the lining of his boot, he cut the hem out of the front of his cotton tunic. He pulled the small waterproof leather sleeve from its hiding place and cut it open. The three round wax balls rolled out of the wax-coated paper and into his hand.

Breaking open the wax balls to expose the powder inside, he poured it onto the waxed paper. He then ran the thin blade of the throwing knife down the crack between the door and the sill. The blade stopped when it hit the metal hasp holding the lock. The blade had been forged with a narrow groove running opposite the sharp edge. With the blade pushed firmly against the metal hasp, he poured the powder off the paper, into the groove. He wiggled the knife gently, and the powder slowly moved down the groove and onto the iron hasp.

For some reason that Daniel did not know, the powder always clung to iron. Now came the dangerous part; he only needed a few drops of water. The guards had taken away his watercup, so he would have to use his own saliva, letting a line of drool flow from his mouth into the groove on the knife. The spittle dripped down the groove. He quickly pulled his face away and flattened against the wall.

There was a sudden bright flash as the water hit the powder, followed by a hissing sound, and then nothing. Counting to twenty, Daniel moved in front of the door and kicked it open with his foot. The latch had been eaten in half. He said a silent thank-you to the seers for the powder. Surveying the room, he found the lone guard blinking his eyes in disbelief. In two quick steps, Daniel grabbed the guard around the neck with one arm and squeezed until the guard dropped to the floor, unconscious.

Again, he looked around the room, finding his cloak and leather bag, which he put on. He figured the sword was with the constable, so he headed down the stairs. The stairs wrapped around the interior of the outside wall of the tower. Passing the third floor, he could see into the soldiers' barracks. They looked to be sound asleep.

Continuing down the stairs to the second floor, he passed the mess and kitchen. The cook had been busy preparing bread for the morning. He silently stepped into the room and carefully picked up a couple of fresh loaves and stuck them in his leather pouch. Moving back into the stairwell, he descended to the main floor. He could see the door to the street and freedom. But he needed to find the sword; there was no way he was leaving without it. Opposite the exterior door was the door into what Daniel thought had to be the constable's office.

Opening the door very slowly, he eased into the room. There were no windows to the outside, so the room was black as coal.

Calling out quietly, he said the words the old man had taught him. "By the light, all darkness is dispelled. By the light, all is made right."

Dimly at first, because he was not holding it, the sword began to glow in the darkness. It was lying on the constable's desk. Daniel had started to step toward it when he heard a noise coming from behind a door on the other side of the room. He effortlessly stepped behind a large fireplace hearth. The sword was now shining brightly as the door slowly swung open.

The constable stared in disbelief and exclaimed, "What in the name of the Lords of Chaos is this witchcraft?"

As the constable reached out to touch the sword, the light quickly faded from the blade.

Daniel had not wasted any time as the constable was looking at the blade; he had moved in behind the light-blinded man. He placed the tip of his throwing knife against the constable's back. Daniel whispered, "Constable, do not move or call out. I have no wish to harm you or anyone else."

Pushing the constable down into his chair, he bound him to it with a set of binding ropes hanging from the wall. He gagged him with a cloth designed for that purpose, which was hanging next to the rope. Replacing his ivory-handled knife in its sheath and picking up his sword, he then turned to leave. Upon his reaching the door, a sudden urge that seemed to come from outside of him overcame his better judgment. He turned and faced the constable and uttered: "By the light, all darkness is dispelled. By the light, all is made right."

This time the blade burst into a bright glow. The constable's eyes filled with terror as he tried to turn away from the light.

Daniel said to him, "You have no idea whom you are dealing with."

As Daniel made his escape from the town, he thought to himself, *I wish I knew whom he was dealing with.*

Chapter 15

Alssa and Cally sat in a run-down tavern in Toller's Gulch, drinking ale and discussing their predicament. They had escaped from the goblins not because of their cunning or the speed of their horses but because goblins ate their victims warm.

The fate of her fallen royal guards sent waves of grief rippling through Alssa's body. They had been the best of her kingdom's military, and she knew every one of them by name. Now there were only eight left. She began to sob uncontrollably as their faces flashed through her mind. What hurt the most was the loss of Colleen and Carrie. How could she and Cally go on without their wisdom and support?

Cally reached over, held her hand gently, and whispered encouragement to her. "I am so sorry, sister. I know that this must be so hard for you, but it is not your fault. Who would have thought that we would be set upon by goblins? It is only because of Sergeant Sharon's training that any of us escaped at all. With the number of attackers, each trooper fought like ten. The losses the goblins sustained must have been enormous."

Completely baffled by the attack, Alssa was angry. Not since the time of the Lords of Chaos and the Battle of Blood had goblins massed in such quantities. With this many assembled, it could only mean one thing: their population was growing again, and someone, or something, had united the different tribes. Usually, intertribal fighting kept their populations low. Goblins would eat anything they had freshly killed, including one another. It had taken something immensely powerful to unite them.

This morning, Alssa had sent out six scouts, two to the north, two the south, and two to the east. They had brought back the news she had expected at the cost of two more of their own to goblin arrows. The goblins had Toller's Crag surrounded. She had informed the townspeople of the situation, and she knew she could count on them to fight. They really had no choice; if the goblins broke into the gully, they would be overrun and there would be no survivors. They understood that the green beast had to be held at bay. Fortunately, that would not be hard, considering the location of the town and the population.

Toller's Crag was formed by an underground stream that had eaten the soft limestone away and left a gully over three hundred feet deep. The north and south sides of the gulch were made of granite, so they had formed tall steep ridges or extended crags that towered above the surrounding plains. The original founder of the town had discovered the short tunnels, which were the only way in and out of the gully. The closest forest was a full trace away, so the residents built all their homes out of the native stone, thus no wood to burn.

Best of all, there were only two ways into the gully, one from the north and one from the south, both on the Coast Road. These entrances were easily guarded. Wisely, the first arrivals to the gully built the roads so they had to pass through the short tunnels. They had built iron gates across the openings. At first, the gates were built to make it easy to collect the toll for passing through the gulch. Now they served a greater purpose of keeping out goblins.

There was no way around the gulch to the east. The Wasteland was impassable, and there was no water. To the west the gully ran up to the edge of the Seer Sea. If the goblins wanted to attack from that direction, they would have to swim through the surf under the watchful eyes of the town's archers.

To travel from North Pass in the north to Devil's Pass in the south would take days at a steady pace, and there were only two sources of water in the entire distance, the Fountain of Life that flew out of the ground in Toller's Crag, and the Green River that flew through the Valley of Profit in the north. Blocking off the Coast Road as it entered the gully had been very profitable for the townspeople, and they were not about to give that up to a bunch of cave-dwelling cannibals.

Also in the townspeople's favor was the very nature of the Wasteland. Black volcanic rock, no trees, no shade, no water, and that was the one thing that really had Alssa confused. Goblins liked damp, moist caves, so why were they attacking in one of the most inhospitable places in the known world?

The townspeople knew that they could hold out for weeks and that the goblins would have to leave to get water. However, Alssa and Cally did not have weeks. They needed to be in Queens Castle Home in a fortnight, and they were still three traces away. They had planned to travel south on the Coast Road to H'la, then head east on the Queen's Highway to L'ke L'fe, and then finally on to Queens Castle Home. That plan was going to have to change.

Sergeant Sharon walked up and handed Alssa the list of the remaining troops and their equipment. It was a short list. They were now down to six soldiers; with Cally and herself, that made eight. They had lost their royal coach and the two supply wagons. The supply wagons that held her and Cally's armor, weapons, and all the company's food. And they had hardly any money and no extra horses.

Along with trying to reach their destination, they also needed to try to get word back to the Three Sisters. The goblins were breeding again, and something had united the tribes. Fortunately, T'asha would be able to deal with this new problem. But how they were going to accomplish all this while trapped in this gully, she did not know. Alssa could not think of a solution to their problem.

As she sat and thought, an old bagger dressed in rags came up asking for food. She only had what was in front of her, so she handed him what remained on her plate. Digging in with great gusto, he quickly made short work of what was left.

He smiled a toothless grin at her and said, "I cannot pay you money for the food, but I can give you a poem as thanks."

She replied, "That wouldn't be necessary. You are quite welcome."

"I insist. After all, I am not a beggar," came the reply.

Alssa smiled and said, "If you must, go ahead."

The beggar began, "The light shines in the darkness, revealing the way into the deep. The fountain flows from the deep, leading the way into the light. The deep leads the way to the light."

With that, he turned and walked away, shoulders held back and head held high, apparently with the sense that he had easily covered the cost of the food.

Cally laughed aloud and asked, "Sister, did you get proper compensation for your meal?"

Alssa replied, "I am not sure. If I did not know better, I would think he might have been a seer."

Cally turned and watched the beggar disappear down the road and said, "Do you think he was trying to tell you something important?"

As Alssa and Cally pondered over the poem, a young barmaid brought Alssa another mug of ale and busied herself with wiping off the table and collecting the dishes. Alssa turned to Sergeant Sharon and asked her to go get the rest of the troop.

As Sharon saluted and turned to go, her robe flung open and her green-and-gold tunic with the Three Sisters double triangle flashed in front of the barmaid. The young girl let out a short gasp of recognition.

Alssa looked up at her and asked, "What is it, girl?"

The barmaid stuttered, "I am…well, you are from…from…?"

Frustrated with the girl's lack of confidence, Alssa barked at her, "Get your senses about you, girl! There is no reason for you to be acting like some Holy Land prissy. What is your name?"

She sheepishly responded, "My name is Lynnday."

Alssa hated to see women act like timid, domesticated animals and could not understand why they allowed themselves to become that way. She spoke to the girl sternly. "Listen, young lady, you have nothing to fear from us. Speak boldly."

Lynnday asked, "Aren't you warriors from the Three Sisters?"

"Yes, that is true," Alssa replied.

The young girl's expression was a combination of excitement, fear, and admiration. Gathering her courage, she asked them, "I would like to go with you when you leave, if I could."

"I don't see that we are going anywhere. Unless you know another way out of here besides the Coast Road?"

"Well, I do, but…," the young girl stuttered.

"But what?" Cally pressed.

The girl said, "There is a way, the Fountain of Life."

"An old beggar mentioned it just a few moments ago. Is that not the name of the stream that flows through the valley?" Cally asked.

Lynnday replied, "Yes and no."

Alssa was growing more frustrated with the girl, so she asked, "Yes and no? Either it is or it is not. Make sense, girl!"

Lynnday explained, "Well, that is the name most people call it, but the real name of the stream is Travelers' Hope. The Fountain of Life is where it emerges from the ground."

"The beggar told us a poem about the fountain and light emerging from the deep. Have you heard the poem before?" Alssa asked.

Lynnday replied, "No, I have never heard that poem, but I can take you to the Fountain of Life."

"What good would that do us? We need to escape from the gulch, not get water," Cally interjected.

The young girl blushed and giggled when she realized she knew something that the great warriors from the Three Sisters did not. She said, "Ma'am, the fountain flows out of the side of the cavern in a waterfall about ten spans off the valley floor. There is a small cave behind the waterfall that leads to a cavern from which the water flows. I have been in it many times with my…ah…male friend. Anyway, I've been inside of it."

Alssa was still unconvinced and asked, "I still don't see what good this will do us?"

Lynnday continued, "I have been told by people who have explored the caves many times that the cavern leads to tunnels that go for miles. Those tunnels have many exits out into the wilderness on the other side of the Black Mountains. I myself have never gone there to explore, so I have never been in the tunnels."

"Why would you go there if not to explore?" Cally asked innocently.

The girl replied reluctantly, "Well, I…um, I go there with a… friend, to be alone."

Alssa recognized the girl's plight and stepped in to rescue her by asking, "Has your friend…been through the tunnels?"

"Yes, many times," Lynnday replied thankfully.

Cally asked, "Do you think he would be willing to help us?"

"I believe he would," the girl replied and then asked excitedly, "Would you like me to go get him?"

Alssa replied cautiously, "Yes, but do not tell him who we are or where we are from. Some men are not comfortable with helping us."

As she watched the girl run off, Sergeant Sharon came up with the remainder of the troop.

Alssa removed a gem-studded gold bracelet from her wrist and looked at it longingly. It had been a gift from her mother when she had left for Seer Island.

She gave orders to Sharon as she handed her the bracelet. "Sergeant, take this bracelet, and the horses, and sell them. Then go purchase supplies and women's common traveling clothes for you and the rest of the troop. Also, pack up your armor, uniforms, and weapons, except knifes, and take them all to the head of the canyon and wait for us, and be quiet about it. We don't want anyone to know what we are doing."

The sergeant looked at her in disgust and asked, "But, Your Highness, why would you want us to do that? How will we defend ourselves? Why do you want us to look like a—"

"Like what, Sergeant?" Alssa asked to stop her question. Then she said, "Whoever has sent those goblins after us is looking for warriors from the Three Sisters, not a bunch of peasant women traveling through the Lands of Chaos. Now, get moving, and be quick about it!"

The sergeant walked away like she was heading for a funeral.

Cally turned to her sister and asked worriedly, "Do you think this is wise, Alssa? Can we trust someone we don't know? Can we trust someone from Toller's Gulch?"

The look on Alssa's face spoke agreement, but she said, "I don't see that we have a choice. We know that we have over a thousand goblins waiting on the road for us, so we cannot get out of here that way, and we know that we cannot wait for the goblins to go away. So we will choose the only option we have left, no matter how much we dislike it."

After some time, the young serving girl came back with a big strong lad. He swaggered with pride as he walked, his sword swaying gently at his side.

"I told you he would want to do it!" the girl gushed as she mooned over her handsome friend. "His name is Grayson. Isn't he wonderful?"

Grayson asked much too confidently, "So you ladies want to leave Toller's Crag without being seen? Now, why would such beautiful women want to sneak out of our lovely little sanctuary?"

Alssa looked at him coyly, batted her eyes, and replied, "We need to get to the Holy Land. Can you guide us through the caverns? We can pay you."

The young man's pride was probably enough to get him to do it for free, but the gold would ensure the deal. The famous Toller's Gulch greed quickly came out as the young man chuckled and asked, "How much?"

Knowing her sister was far too free with the coin, Cally interjected quickly, "Two pieces of gold now and five more if we succeed."

"Ten now and fifteen later," the young man bargained back.

Cally cried, "Thief! Four and eight!"

"Five and ten," he said with a sly smile.

"Deal, but you provide your own supplies." Cally held out her hand to seal the deal, not realizing her miscue.

Grayson took her hand reluctantly and gave a quizzical look at the barmaid. "Pay me and I will go get everything ready and meet you at the head of the canyon." He held out his other hand for payment.

Cally counted out the four coins and dropped it in his hand. He then turned and, without saying a word, walked off. Alssa and Cally gathered up their belongings, said goodbye to the barmaid, and headed for the head of the canyon.

As they walked, Alssa asked, "You usually drive a harder bargain when negotiating. Why did you let him go so high?"

Cally replied knowingly, "Because he thought we were just foolish women looking to sneak away. If he had known that it was us that the goblins were after, he would have asked for fifty coins in advance."

When they reached the spring, Sergeant Sharon and the troopers were in their new civilian clothes. Alssa could tell that her soldiers were quite uncomfortable with their new attire. Nevertheless, she had to admit, they all looked nice; in fact, if they were in a civilized country, they would likely have to beat the men away with a club.

This was an area that she never had been able to understand in men. These women had changed nothing but there outside appearance, yet men would now howl like wolves chasing their prey in their pursuit to be with any one of them. But put them back in uniform and the men shy away. And men say women are finicky! As she surveyed the group again, she was pleased they would now appear as a group of ladies trekking through the wilderness, and having a male guide would only add to that ruse.

The trooper Sergeant Sharon had posted to watch the trail signaled them that someone was coming. Grayson, the barmaid, and two other men came walking up the trail totally unaware they were being watched by trained eyes. Immediately, Alssa was defensive and asked, "Why have you brought extra men along without telling us?"

Grayson replied, "There are places in the cavern where we will need to have more help. In addition, both of these men also know their way through the tunnels." Then he introduced them, "This is Jamison and Pater. They are brothers."

Feeling a little better but still suspicious, Alssa assented to their help.

Grayson led them up a narrow trail hewn out of the stone by hand. From a distance, it blended very naturally with the solid rock around it. Slowly they worked their way behind the falls created by the spring. Once they were totally shielded by the wall of water, the small entrance to the cave could be clearly seen. It had once been an exit for the falls. The new exit was two spans above the cave entrance and quite a bit bigger than the old one. The hole for the entrance was above their heads; each person had to be lifted to the opening. There was only room enough to squeeze one person through at a time, so they had to hand their packs up one at a time. As they crawled on all fours through the narrow entrance, it curved upward and to the left before leveling out. It then turned straight up for one and a half spans. They boosted one another out of the hole and found themselves inside a huge cavern.

Looking around, they realized that it should be complete darkness, but there was a strange green glow coming from the rocks.

Alssa reached down and touched the rock and found that it was some form of illuminous algae. It was bright enough so that they could see the full size of the chamber. It was easily six spans high and twice that in width. From where she was standing, she was unable to see the back of the cavern. The Fountain of Life was flowing almost through the center. It seemed to just flow right into solid rock as it left the cavern to later emerge in Toller's Crag.

After everyone was out of the narrow tunnel, Grayson took out a long piece of rope and, with the two other men, began to tie it around the waist of each of the women. He placed Jamison in the center of the line and Pater at the end. He took the lead position.

Alssa silently made sure that Cally took up the rear of the line, and Sergeant Sharon the middle behind Lynnday and Jamison. This was a new and uncomfortable position for the Three Sisters warriors to find themselves in.

The men also took way too much time and liberty in putting the ropes around them. They said nothing; the troop played their role as peasant women, as she had ordered. This was fortunate for the men. If they tried what they did at any other time, they would find a short knife in their ribs.

The group began to move out, walking toward the back of the cavern. Everything was damp, and the air was chilly. Water dripped from the ceiling at regular intervals and made pools in any depression. The illuminous algae covered everything that did not have standing water on it, making walking difficult. They slipped and slid, pulling one another down, bruising their arms and legs. The men easily fell as many times as the women did.

The ceiling would climb out of sight and then drop down to just above their heads. It took all the rest of the afternoon to reach the back of the cavern, or at least that was what Alssa estimated; there was really no way to tell.

Their small group approached what looked to be a dark hole about two spans high. They had passed similar openings that led out in different directions, but Grayson never bothered even to look at them. When they asked him about them, he grunted and kept walking. He definitely knew where he wanted to go, Alssa hoped; it was also where she wanted to go. Grayson stopped and took three stick and tar torches out of his pack. He lit them and handed them to the other two men.

He turned to the group and said, "From here we enter the stream. It is totally dark without the torches. Follow the men in front of you exactly. Step where they step. There are many deep pools, so stay alert."

As they began to slosh through the water, Sergeant Sharon called out, "Your Maj—Alssa, I have a question."

Alssa responded, "Yes, Sharon, what is it?"

"This cave is dark, damp, and cold, right?" Sharon asked.

"Yes," came the curt reply.

"And I believe we have been heading the same direction the entire time," Sharon continued.

Alssa said, "Yes, we have been going east the whole time."

Sharon asked, "And that would be toward the Goblin Valley?"

"That is correct," Alssa answered, then asked, "Why?"

"Don't goblins live in cold, dark, damp caves?" came Sharon's question.

Grayson laughed aloud. "You don't have to be concerned about scary goblins, little lady. There aren't any within three days' walk of here."

Sergeant Sharon shivered and picked up her vigilance.

CHAPTER 16

The sun was just setting over the Ebony Forest as Jovan led his score of lancers and their accompanying healer through the gates of H'la. The morning was fresh and clean, a beautiful day to be alive, especially when one was in hadrac country. Their ride north had been uneventful. There had been no sign of the evil beasts on the Coast Road during the entire four-day trip. On the way they had passed half a dozen individuals, most of whom were probably of ill repute, but they had paid them no heed. They were not bothering anyone, and he did not have any reports of recent thefts.

What was strange was the total lack of any sign of hadrac. At night, one usually heard them moving about in the woods. For the last six months, Jovan had led his patrol up the Coast Road, and they could always hear one or two hadrac lurking around the edge of the camp at night. The hadrac would not come close to the campfire. However, this time he had not seen or heard one, nor had they received any reports of hadrac activity.

What was even stranger was, when they had crossed the Deep River at the mouth of the Orc Gorge, they saw no sign of the disgusting creatures that the gorge was named for. Every other time he had passed by, he had seen them clinging to the sheer rock walls of the canyon, waiting to ambush any unsuspecting ships that might be traveling up the river.

Jovan had been past the mouth of the gorge four times, and he had counted over a hundred of them on each occasion. But this time there were none to be seen. All this seemed odd to him. Not that he was not grateful for the peace; it just gave him a bad feeling.

Jovan dismounted in front of the stables and gave orders to Sergeant Gallant. "Dismount the troops and stable the horses. Prepare the men to bed down for the night in the stable loft."

The sergeant turned to face Captain Jovan and asked, "Sir, what of the healer? Where shall I put her?"

"Sergeant, you know healers as well as I do. She will find her own place to roost. You need not concern yourself with her. Look to the needs of the troop."

One of the younger troopers interrupted the sergeant's reply. "May we partake in some local female entertainment before we call it a night?"

Captain Jovan gave the trooper a withering look as he addressed Sergeant Gallant and said, "Each squad may share two flagons of ale after they have eaten, but no more than two."

The sergeant turned to go.

"Sergeant?" Captain Jovan called him back.

"Yes, Captain," came the reply.

The captain scolded with his mouth as well as his eyes. "We will not have a repeat of the last time we were here!" The captain continued, "Send the men to the Boars Brisket for their fun and…" Then he raised his voice a little so that the troops could hear him. "I will accept no excuses this time!"

Sergeant Gallant snapped to attention and shouted, "There will be no trouble! I will see to that personally. Where will the captain be when I make the day's end report?"

"I will be at the Guest of H'la if you need me," the captain replied as he walked away.

He could hear Sergeant Gallant unleash a threatening torrent of oaths against any man that so much as moved a toe out of line tonight.

Jovan thought back to six weeks ago, when they had last been here. The men had just come south from the Black Mountains and Devil's Pass, where they had run into a large group of twenty hadrac. Though they were outnumbered, the troop showed itself well, dispatching all but three of the loathsome beasts before they could escape into the night. Two of his men had been killed outright in the fight, and a third had been gravely wounded by the ax-wielding hadrac. The wounded man had begged his fellows to perform the ritual on him before the curse took effect.

Healers had not started accompanying the patrols, and they were a full week away from H'la, so they gave into their fellow trooper's pleas and began their return patrol. The outcome of that skirmish convinced the high command to start sending healers with the patrols.

But that did not help them back then, so when they had arrived in H'la with only seven troopers, the local constable was shocked to hear not only that three soldiers were killed but also that a score of hadrac was bunched up together. The hadrac normally ran in small packs of six to eight, not in large groups, and they had never organized an attack on trained troops, at least not since the Lords of Chaos.

The constable had been right; it was very unusual for the hadrac to bunch up, but with the southern portion of the Ebony Forest seemingly devoid of hadrac, the unusual was becoming the norm. Something was happening, something big; the problem was, Captain Jovan could not figure out what it was. Some speculated that the Lords of Chaos were loose from the Island of Exile, but he knew that was not true. His superiors would tell him if something as catastrophic as that had happened, wouldn't they?

He shook his thoughts from his head and entered the Guest of H'la. The caretaker quickly confronted him. "So you dare to come back to the scene of your crimes? Are you and your villainous horse soldiers going to ransack my inn a second time?"

Jovan drew his sword and stuck the tip under the man's chin as he said with venom, "If you ever refer to a trooper of the Holy Lancers as a villain again, I will cut out your tongue and feed it to you!"

The innkeeper began to apologize, but the captain cut him off and said, "Get me some of your wife's fine cooking before I answer her prayers and remove your ability to yell at her."

The innkeeper stumbled over a chair as he backpedaled away from the officer's sword.

Jovan sat down as he thought, *The innkeeper's attitude is understandable, but no officer in the Holy Lancers could let anybody talk in that manner about the troops under his command!*

The captain looked around the large common room. The owner had fixed the chairs and tables since his men had busted up the inn. It had happened the night the troop returned from losing three of their comrades. The men were shaken up bad by the size of the hadrac attack and by having to relieve their comrade of future suffering. They had all been quite morose on the ride back from Devil's Pass.

By the time they had reached H'la, their black mood had intensified. The troop chose the Guest of H'la because it was quiet, and they just wanted to drink and forget. Unfortunately, one of the other patrons was already drunk and began asking question as to why they were all in such a bad mood. The troop had tried to ignore him and focus on their drinks.

When he persisted to pester them, they told him the story and they asked him to leave it alone. The foolish patron began to taunt them about how he always thought that Holy Lancers were invincible, but if they could not protect their own, how could they keep the Coast Road free and the people along it safe?

When the soldier told the man to leave before he started something that he could not finish, the innkeeper came out and yelled at the troopers to pay their bill and leave. With that, the troopers' self-restraint snapped and they began to take out their frustration and anger out on the inn and its patrons.

Nobody was hurt badly, but by the time he and Sergeant Gallant got the men under control, the common room was a mess. Jovan ordered his men to the stables and then paid for the damaged furniture. He gave the innkeeper three solid gold sovereigns for his discomfort. The innkeeper was just as rude then as he had been today.

The innkeeper's wife appeared with the food. She was a heavyset, jovial woman who adored men in uniform, and she was especially fond of Captain Jovan. She stood with her mouth slightly open, her eyes glazed over, waiting for the captain to taste her specialty. He forked a slab of roast into his mouth and began to chew. With his mouth still half-full, he exclaimed, "Mrs. Granderfield, this is the most delicious roast you have ever served! I do believe that I will ask for seconds right now and avoid the rush."

Mrs. Granderfield beamed, blushed, and giggled as she scurried back to the kitchen to fetch the handsome captain another serving of her best dish. She had prepared it today knowing that a patrol change was due, and she had hoped it would be Jovan's.

She giggled again as she made her way back toward her favorite customer with another heaping plate.

He had just finished his first plate when Sergeant Gallant came rushing through the front door. Jovan sighed heavily, leaned back into his chair, and asked, "Sergeant, has something happened at the Boars Brisket?"

Sergeant Gallant replied, "No, sir. The constable sent me to find you. He asked that you come to the north gate at once, before things get out of hand."

Standing up, he began to walk toward the door. Mrs. Granderfield saw that he was leaving, so she scolded him sweetly. "Captain, how dare you leave without finishing your supper!"

Smiling mischievously at her, he replied, "Ma'am, only duty would pull me away from so magnificent a meal and such a gracious host. I promise to return and finish what I have started and to say good night."

The innkeeper's wife almost fainted as she swooned heavily into a chair, batting her eyelids and giggling.

As they walked swiftly away from the inn, the sergeant chuckled as he asked the captain, "Pardon me, but what was that, sir?"

The captain smiled and said, "One day, Sergeant, when you are a grown-up, you will learn that being a gentleman has more uses than just impressing young women."

They could hear shouts coming from the direction of the north gate. When they rounded the corner of the dirt street, they were confronted with the entire lancer troop arranged in a semicircle, swords drawn, staring down the constable and his guards. In between the two groups, lying on the ground, was a man dressed in a Holy Lancers blue tunic.

The captain and sergeant dashed into the middle of the circle. Sergeant Gallant knelt beside the man and immediately turned his head in revulsion. The man's face was one big open sore, with pus running from every opening.

He looked up at Jovan and said, "It's private Jansen from Captain Clark's troop. He has been wounded by a hadrac's ax."

Composing himself, Jovan turned to his men and gave them orders. "You men, calm down and get in rank."

As they formed up, he called Corporal Taas to come forward and asked, "Corporal, what is the meaning of this undisciplined display?"

Corporal Taas replied tentatively, "Sir, that soldier is from Captain Clark's troop, who we were supposed to meet tonight. Trooper Coombs and some of the other men had come here to await their arrival. When Trooper Jansen came to the gate, these buffoons wouldn't let him in." Glaring at the constable, he continued, "Even though these are obviously hadrac wounds. These ignorant fools were afraid that he had the plague and were not going to let us attend to him."

Jovan said gently, "Corporal, mind your tongue. Now back in rank with you."

As he turned and approached the constable, he motioned with his hands to Sergeant Gallant. Gallant passed the orders onto the rest of the troop with the same hand signals. The troop slowly deployed into preassigned positions around the constable's men.

While this was happening, Captain Jovan spoke to the constable. "Sir, it can be easily seen that this man is a soldier of the Pact of Brothers. As an officer of the Holy Lancers, I take charge of and full responsibility for this trooper."

The constable, looking shaken and perplexed, wanted desperately to conform to the captain's wishes, but he was also accountable to the townspeople. And even though he was not sure what was wrong with the man, he was not about to let some half-dead, plague-infested corpse infect his town. Working up the courage, he said, "Captain, I should throw this man out of the gate right now, but if you agree to take him outside of the town, I will let you have him."

The captain gave more hand signals to Sergeant Gallant and replied, "Constable, have you never seen the effects of a wound from a hadrac's ax? This man must be taken to the healer at once!"

Again, Jovan gave hand signals to the sergeant, and four men stepped forward and picked up the wounded soldier. At the same time, the remaining sixteen members of the troop drew their swords. Looking around in dismay, the constable realized that while he was talking, his men had been surrounded.

As the guards began to draw their weapons, Captain Jovan called out, "Constable, control your men! There is no need for bloodshed tonight."

With another hand signal, the entire troop began to back away from the constable and his guards.

Following Captain Jovan's orders, Sergeant Gallant and the four soldiers found the healer standing on the parapet overlooking the east gate, gazing into the dark forest.

Sergeant Gallant called out to her, "Healer, we have a gravely wounded man down here. Come down and attend to him. He has received a hadrac wound, and he looks to be quite far along in the transformation."

"How far along has his symptoms progressed?" she crackled.

"His hands, feet, and face are swollen and seeping with pus, and he can hardly breathe," Sergeant Gallant said.

Not taking her gaze away from the east, she responded, "Why have you bothered me with this? You know as well as I that he is too far along to be helped. Perform the ceremony yourself and be done with it."

Sergeant Gallant leaped up four or five steps and yelled at the woman, "Healer, you will come down at once! The captain has commanded you to try to heal this man, and so you will, whether you want to or not!"

The woman slowly descended the stairs as if she were not the least bit concerned about the soldier. As she passed Sergeant Gallant, she looked through him and through the wall he stood next to and said to herself, "The light passes through the darkness, and the darkness can do nothing to stop it."

When she finally reached the wounded man, she put her hands into the fold of her robes and produced a flask of liquid. She poured it on his face, hands, and feet and muttered to herself about the waste of valuable medicine on someone it could not help. As she began to stand up, Captain Jovan and the rest of the troop arrived.

Looking at the poor man, Captain Jovan addressed the crone. "Healer, I am not interested in him walking. I need his thoughts. I need to know what happened to him and the rest of his troop."

The healer leered up at him and said, "This man is too far gone into the transformation. Most of his mind has already been captivated by the madness. You should set him free and be done with it."

Captain Jovan responded impatiently, "Something odd is happening in these forests, and I must find out what it is. This man has encountered hadrac in the north that apparently has wiped out the rest of his troop. We saw no sign of hadrac in the south. We must know why. Now do it!"

The healer pulled out more potions and began to chant. As they began to take effect, the soldier's eyes seemed to clear of the madness, and he asked for water. Sergeant Gallant brought a flask of water to the captain. Jovan held the flask up to the man's lips, and the soldier drank greedily.

Holding him in his arms, Jovan looked compassionately at him and asked, "Jensen, can you understand me?"

Jensen replied weakly, "Yes."

"What happened to you and the rest of your troop?"

Jensen's eyes closed as he began to talk. "We had just finished our patrol to Devil's Pass and had camped for the night. All through the night we heard hadrac..." *Cough cough.* "Moving through the forest. Two hours before light, they attacked, hundreds of them. The captain..." *Cough cough.* "Had expected it, so we were already mounted when it began. We broke out of the trap and reached the Sandhurst slide when we ran into hundreds more. They surrounded us again.

"The captain told me to hold back and, when I saw an opening, to break away and warn everyone on the Coast Road that the hadrac were organized and on the move. We charged three times, killing scores of them on each charge, but they just kept coming. It was as if unseen forces drove them. At some point in the last charge, I was knocked unconscious.

"When I woke up, all my friends were dead, everyone but me. The hadrac were gone..." *Cough cough.* "And they had not taken any bodies. They just left us lying. They killed all the horses also, so I started walking. I knew I was wounded and only had a short time. I'm afraid I'm too late."

A look of terror crept into his eyes as he begged, "Captain, don't let me turn. I know I've gone too long without a healer. Please, Captain, don't let it go on any longer!"

A tear came to the captain's eye as he turned to look at the healer.

The healer looked at him with an indifferent stare of inevitability and said, "I told you before, he is too far gone. The turning will be completed by morning."

The captain looked at Sergeant Gallant and ordered, "Sergeant, prepare Trooper Jensen for the freeing and turn him over to the healer." Turning to the healer, he said, "And you will do your job and perform the ritual. That is the other reason you are here."

The healer looked at Jovan as if he had said nothing, but she did move over by Sergeant Gallant to wait.

Looking down at the wounded man, Jovan watched as the trooper's eyes clouded over and his skin transformed. Captain Jovan turned away with resignation and disapproval. He started walking toward the constable's office. It was always hard to lose a trooper, but he hated the freeing ceremony. He knew it was necessary, but he still hated it. If they did not do it, trooper Jensen would become a hadrac by morning.

Jovan thought, *Curse the hadrac! Curse the Lords of Chaos for creating them! When would this evil come to an end? If only the prophecy were true and the queen's heir would return to restore light to this land.*

CHAPTER 17

Daniel had walked all night after escaping from H'la. He had stayed away from the main road and found game trails that paralleled the Queen's Highway, knowing that the north-south Coast Road was patrolled by the Holy Lancers. The constable would pursue him east, if he pursued at all. He seemed like the type of man that would act tough behind strong walls but would lose heart if he was out in the open. What would be more likely would be for the constable to inform the Coast Road patrol, which could be worse for Daniel.

The predicament he found himself in was to either stay off the main road and avoid other people or make better time and risk contact. This morning he intended on going back out to the highway. The forest was so dense that unless he found a trail, it would be impossible to get back to the road. He was north of the road, looking for a trail heading south, when he came into a small clearing.

The sight that greeted him was beyond his comprehension. There were so many bodies filling the clearing it was hard to tell how many. Body parts were lying everywhere—arms, legs, and hands. Daniel had seen the carnage of war many number of times, and it was never pretty. Then his eyes caught sight of some colorful cloth. As he moved the body of a man, he found a woman under it; she was quite dead. Her hands were tied up, and her clothing was torn off her body. That was strange, he thought. This carnage was obviously caused by hadrac, but hadrac would not bother with women, nor would they tie someone up. Then he found another female body in the same condition right down to the bonds on her wrist.

As he looked at the women, he realized that they were the two women that were on the ship with him. It was Mrs. Tarbell and her friend. Only the face of one man was in a condition that he could tell who it was. It was one of the six men he had seen at the Boars Brisket. If the women were here, then the children must have been also. He was able to find all the males' body parts, even the little boys', but could not find any sign of the girls. He slowly began to look outside the clearing for tracks. As he used a circular search pattern, it did not take him long to find the signs he was looking for.

The girls had crawled through the underbrush on their hands and knees for a long time. It was almost three hundred spans before they came upon a game trail and began to follow it. Daniel was not sure if he should continue looking for them. It depended on when the girls escaped; if it was during the hadrac attack, then he was wasting his time. No living being could lose a hadrac if he had one's sent. Their sense of smell was better than dogs' and even pigs'.

However, if they took off before the hadrac attack, then they might still be alive. But he still was not sure he should go look for them. After all, he was probably being pursued himself.

Thoughts like this did not stay long in his head. He could never leave the little girls no matter how slim their chance of survival was. Now, if it were the girls' fathers lost in the Ebony Forest, he would walk away; the fools would deserve whatever happened to them. But the idea of three little girls lost in this horrible place was more than he could take. He would continue to look.

After an hour and a half of tracking the girls, he came upon the hadrac. They were milling around on the trail, sniffing the air and ground like they were looking for something. It was obvious that they had stumbled upon the girls' scent trail. Also obvious was that they did not know he was here. There were only six of them, so he seized upon the opportunity and drew the sword.

Sneaking in close from downwind, he started the prayer to ignite the sword and leaped into the middle of the trail and sliced the head off two of the hadrac before the rest knew he was there.

One of the four who remained stepped forward and swung his ax in a wide arc at Daniel's head. Daniel easily ducked underneath the ugly weapon and thrust his sword into the beast's belly. As he withdrew the blade, the hadrac wailed in pain and fell to his knees. As the evil animal began to fall over, he disappeared. The others looked at where their comrade had fallen in disbelief. Daniel took full advantage of the opportunity and dispatched them in quick order.

As Daniel stood on the trail, blood dripping from his blade, the dead hadrac bodies all dissolved in front of his eyes.

This was new. He had never had this happen before. Always before, the bodies just lay where they died; they did not disappear. As Daniel pondered what he just saw, he heard a soft rustling sound coming from the bushes. Moving to the edge of the trail, he peered into a thick thornbush, and sure enough, there were the three girls, holding one another in one another's arms. Trying to smile, he asked, "Are you all right?"

With a small, squeaky voice, the oldest one responded, "Are the monsters gone? Where are our mommies? We're hungry! Do you have anything to eat? Melissa's scared, but Beth and I aren't. I'm Saaraha! Who are you? Are the monsters gone? We knew they would not find us. We always win when we play the hiding game with the other kids. Where are the mean, ugly men who took us away from our daddies? Are the mon—"

Daniel interrupted her and said, "Okay! Okay! Yes, the monsters are gone, and I do have something for you to eat." Reaching into the bush, he pulled out the littlest one and set her on the ground. As he turned to help the other two, they came scampering out from under the bush on their own.

Standing, smiling at him, Saaraha blurted out, "See, Beth and I are the best hiders! We can get in and out of anywhere. Where are our mommies? Didn't we see you before? Melissa needs to go potty. Are you alone? Who helped you scare the monsters away? Do you have any fo…mmm…?"

Daniel held his hand gently to her mouth to get her to stop talking.

"Listen to me, don't talk. There might be more had—monsters about." Daniel reached into his leather bag and pulled out a loaf of bread, broke it into three pieces, and handed one piece to each of the girls. They grabbed it quickly and shoved it into their mouths and barely chewed it before they swallowed. Daniel had begun to think about what to do when Saaraha pulled on his sleeve. He turned to face her and said, "Yes?"

Saaraha just mumbled, "Mm…mm…mm."

"What do you want?" Daniel asked.

"Mm…mm…mm."

Daniel smiled and said, "Oh yeah. You can talk."

"Mister, can we have more food? We're still hungry. What is your name? Where are our mommies?"

Daniel handed out more food to the girls as he said, "Your mommies…well…they…ah…they are…well…" He did not know what to say. How could he tell them what had happened? So he decided to ask them what they knew instead. "Saaraha, when was the last time you saw your mommies?"

Saaraha answered, "They were with those mean men, who tied them up. They tied us up too, but Melissa and Beth cried a lot because it hurt their hands. I didn't cry at all. They untied us and made us sit in between our mommies."

"When did you sneak away to hide?" Daniel asked.

Saaraha responded, "When the mean men tore our mommies' clothes, we hid behind a tree. The men made our mommies scream. Beth's mommy told us to run away, so we did. We crawled until we found the path, and then we ran for a long time. But then we got scared, so we hid in the thornbush. We thought the monsters were our mommies, but then we smelled them, and then we knew they were monsters."

Daniel comforted them, "You girls are really brave, and I am going to need you to be even braver. I am sure there are more monsters in the forest, so we must be really quiet and not talk. We are going to go back to the road and see if we can find some more people who can help you, okay?"

Now Daniel needed to figure out what he was going to do with three girls and how he was going to keep from getting caught.

Chapter 18

In the late morning, Captain Jovan met Sergeant Gallant at the stable and said, "Assemble the troops and draw rations! We are not going to continue the patrol. Instead, we are going to return to the Pact of Brothers and report what has been happening. I'm going to check on the constable."

While the troop was assembling, Jovan headed for the constable's office to see if there had been any other reports of the hadrac activity and to talk about lasts night's altercation. The constable was not in his office; he had not been there last night either. One of the constable's men told Captain Jovan that he would find the constable drinking at the Boars Brisket.

When the constable saw Jovan approaching, he pulled back into the corner where he had been hiding. Jovan respected his uncomfortable position. After all, an outsider, in force of arms, had upstaged him.

"Good morning, Constable," Jovan said politely as he pulled up a chair and sat down next to him. "I am sorry about the unfortunate confrontation last night, but it was necessary. Trooper Jensen had been wounded by a hadrac ax, and well, you know what that means. The healer performed the freeing last night, so all is well," he added, only half-lying.

"Captain, I know how you Holy lander deal with people who have been wounded fighting hadrac, and I don't hold with any of it," spit out the constable. He chugged down a long drink of his ale and continued, "I have heard of many men who received hadrac wounds, and some did die, but most recovered with no side effects."

The captain half-chuckled and half-cursed as he said, "Were you there to see these men wounded, or were you just told about it?"

The constable pulled a little deeper into his corner and did not respond.

"As I thought." Then the captain continued to press, "Have you received any word about the hadrac activity since the Twenty-First Lancers left her two weeks ago?"

The constable glared at him and gloated, "No, not a single report of hadrac. In fact, the only travelers came through the night before last."

"Who were they?" Captain Jovan asked.

The constable hesitated, then he said, "The Lord G'laven and his lady. They are staying at the Guest of H'la."

Jovan responded, "Yes, I saw their carriage when I arrived."

"Then there were the six individual men, all of whom left early in the morning when the gate was opened," the constable continued as if not hearing the captain. "There were also the usual cargo wagons. Then yesterday morning, three men came in, saying they had been set upon by thieves, but they were on the Queen's Highway, coming in from J're."

"That's all in two weeks? Doesn't that seem strange? Isn't there usually far more traffic than that during this season?" Jovan asked, a bit astounded.

"Yes, but…," the constable started to say, then stopped.

Captain Jovan sensed that the constable was holding something back, so he asked, "Is there anything else that may have seemed out of place?"

The constable's doubts must have been showing on his face, because the captain continued to question even harder, "What is it? What are you not telling me?"

The constable paused, then related the events from the previous morning involving the three wounded men, leaving out the part about the thief.

Captain Jovan asked, "Do you know where these three men are?"

"Yes, they are with the town's Healer. One of them was gravely wounded and still might not make it," the constable replied as he waved toward the stables.

As Jovan turned to leave, he looked back sternly at the constable and said, "You will keep me informed of the comings and goings of any visitors or if any more unusual things happen, won't you?"

The constable nodded reluctantly as he ordered more ale and crawled farther into his corner.

Captain Jovan found the abode of the healer tucked behind the stables against the outside wall of the town. It was well separated from all the other residences, which seemed to be normal occurrence with healers. As he knocked on the door, he thought, *Why are healers so strange? Every one of them seems to be so reclusive, mysterious, and old, although, I'm not sure about the old part.*

He was incredibly good with faces; if he saw someone, he had always been able to remember them when he saw them again. Now, as he thought about it, he had never really seen the face of a healer. In fact, he could not even recall the face of the one traveling with the troop now. He did not think he would be able to pick her out of a group of women, at least not without her distinctive purple cloak. They always went about with their cowls pulled up over their heads. He had only seen their eyes, and they seemed to be filled with knowledge, aged wisdom, and malice.

Yes, it was malice that he noticed most of all. They seemed to dislike everyone, as if they were living in a separate world, where they knew what was important and no one else did.

The door opened, and a purple-cloaked healer stood before him. He stared intently, but as hard as he tried, he could not make out any features of her face, only her eyes. It really was not that he could not see her; she was right there in front of him. It was more like, as soon as the image appeared in his mind, he would instantly forget what he was looking at, while he was looking at it.

The healer cleared her throat. "What is it that you want, Holy lander?"

Jovan realized he was staring and quickly looked away and stammered, "Ah…yes, I…was…ah…"

"Yes?" she asked as she smiled fiendishly.

Regaining his composure, Captain Jovan stiffened his back and barked out, "I am here to speak to the three men who came in with wounds yesterday."

"Yes," she responded absently as she turned and walked away.

He stared at the blazing sun symbol on the back of her purple cloak. He was not sure if she wanted him to follow her. As she passed through the doorway, she rotated her head slowly and extended her bony finger toward him and motioned for him to follow.

She led him to a large room with six beds, three on each side of the room. Other than oil lamps hanging from the log rafters and the beds, there was no other furniture in the room. The floors appeared to be polished and were immaculately clean. He turned to thank the healer, but she was gone.

Jovan introduced himself to the three men and asked them to tell him their story. As he listened to the details of the attack, he knew it had not been hadrac. Everything they said lined up with the constable's story until they reached the part about the thief's arrest.

Jovan interrupted them. "Who is this man you claim the constable arrested?"

Two of them began to speak at the same time. Finally, Tarbell let the older man continue. He explained about the arrest and the fight with the guards.

Tarbell interjected, "And he didn't even arrest him for kidnapping our families. He arrested him for having that sword."

Landers chuckled aloud. "You know what that incompetent constable did? He let that murdering thief escape, the very same day he locked him in the tower."

The older man chimed in, "I heard that not only did the thief escape, but he was also able to steal back all his weapons, including the sword, right from under the constable's nose!"

"That sword must have been worth a year's wages," Landers added.

Jovan asked, "Were you able to get a close look at it?"

"I did!" the severely wounded young man gasped out. "I was lying on the ground when the constable set it down during the fight."

"What made it so special?" the captain asked.

"It was a large broadsword with a handle with inlaid jewels," Landers added excitedly.

Captain Jovan smirked and said, "That doesn't seem very unique."

Landers blurted out defensively, "Like I said, it had jewels in the handle along with a carving of female and male soldiers and a woman riding on a strange-looking bird."

Jovan quickly stood up; without saying goodbye, he turned and walked briskly for the door. As he pushed it open, he knocked over the healer, who must have been leaning against it. He apologized as he helped her up, but she did not seem to even notice him.

She just muttered under her breath, "The light is still weak. The darkness will gather quickly." Then she turned and walked down the hall away from him.

The captain went out the front door, headed back to find the constable. Shaking his head, he thought, *Healers are surely the strangest people.*

The constable was still at the Boars Brisket, and still drinking, when Jovan found him for the second time. He was quite drunk and could barely talk.

The captain question him, "Why did you not tell me about the thief and the sword?"

Lifting his heavy eyes away from the flagon of ale, he spoke with slurred speech. "You want to know why I did not tell you about a man who appears out of the darkness, who can chew through solid iron, and who has a sword that burns with fire? Because I no longer believe that he was even here. I have decided that it was just a nightmare. That's why."

As the constable said this, Jovan's face turned from a look of disgust to one of shock and fear. With great anticipation, he asked, "Did you actually see the sword light up? Was he holding it when it happened? Did you get a close look at the marking on the hilt?"

The constable laughed drunkenly and then started coughing out a reply. *Cough, cough.* "Oh yes! He was holding it when it burst into a bright light as bright as a flame!" *Cough, cough.* "It scared me to death. I thought he was going to kill me!"

Jovan asked, "What about the markings? Did you see the markings?"

The constable's eyes were filled with fear as he replied, "When I took it away from him, I examined it. You were on it, along with two of your brothers. There were also three of the armored whores from the north, and the witch queen herself riding on one of her winged lizards."

At the last statement, Captain Jovan grabbed the constable by the front of his ale-stained tunic and lifted him off his bench. Anger burned deep in the captain's eyes as he pulled the constable up to his face. Speaking in a deadly tone, he said, "You wretched little coward, you hide behind your little walls while real men protect you! You cannot even hold on to a single man, and you dare to insult the greatest ruler to have ever lived? Then you curse the very kingdoms that keep the Lords of Chaos bound on their filthy island! I should kill you for your insolence, you sniffling parasite!" With that, the captain threw the man to the floor and stormed out of the inn.

The troop was assembled in front of the stable when Captain Jovan walked hurriedly up to Sergeant Gallant and said, "Sergeant, get Corporal Taas and three other troopers up here immediately."

The men came jogging up, leading their mounts. "Yes, sir," Corporal Taas said as he saluted the captain.

Captain Jovan looked adamantly at the corporal and said, "I want you to take your squad south to Crome Castle and report all the things that have happened here and my recommendation that the commander send three entire companies to be stationed in H'la. And that it would be best to start patrolling from here. Tell them that everything has changed and, most importantly, that the Banisher has returned."

Corporal Taas looked at Sergeant Gallant, then at the other men, and then back at Captain Jovan. He then said, "I don't understand, sir. Who is the Banisher?"

Jovan responded sternly, "Corporal, you do not need to understand, you need to obey. Leave now." As the troopers mounted, Jovan added, "And, Corporal, it is absolutely critical that one of you get through to Crome Castle."

"Yes, sir!" the corporal replied. The four troopers put spurs to the horses and rode out the south gate at a gallop.

Jovan ordered the rest of the troop mounted and led them at a trot through the east gate and up the Queen's Highway.

Sergeant Gallant rode up beside him and asked, "Captain, why are we heading east? First, you said we wear going to deal with the hadrac that we heard are massing in the north. You then changed your mind and said we were going back south to Crome Castle. Now we are headed for L'ke L'fe. What is going on, sir?"

The captain responded excitedly, saying, "Curse the hadrac! They are not important. The sword of light has returned, and it is in the hands of a common thief!" For emphasis, he spurred his horse and led the troop down the highway at a canter.

CHAPTER 19

Alssa was following the young man that they had hired to lead them through the tunnels as they entered another large open cavern. They were still all tied together at the waist. They emerged from the tunnel one by one as Grayson called them to a stop.

Alssa called out, "Why are we stopping?"

The men did not answer but instead untied the ropes from themselves and then placed the torches in carved-out slots in the cave wall. They then drew their swords and held them up toward the women and commanded them to sit down.

The young serving wench cried out, "Grayson, what are you doing?"

He yelled at Lynnday, "Shut up!" He then looked at all the women and said, "Do you think we are stupid? We know who you are." Pointing at Alssa, he continued, "You're one of the wench queens from the Three Sisters, and the rest of you are her armored whores."

"Grayson, please don't do this!" cried his girlfriend.

He yelled again at Lynnday, "I told you to shut up!" With a wicked smirk, he said to Alssa, "Now, Queenie, we know that you are rich, and yet you tried to pay us almost nothing to get you away from the goblins. This is just another example of women from the Three Sisters taking advantage of men. Well, not this time. This time the men are going to take advantage of you!" He laughed evilly and said, "And get a little revenge in the process."

He stepped forward toward Cally, holding the sword in her face. He quickly cut the rope from around her waist. Smiling lustfully, he said, "We will start with you."

All the women jumped to their feet as Alssa cried out, "Don't touch her, you pig, or I will cut your heart out!"

Grayson grabbed Cally's wrist as he said, "We'll see who does the cutting!"

He pulled her close to him and smashed his mouth onto hers. Wrapping his arms around her, he was starting to tear at her dress when he suddenly stiffened and fell, dragging her to the ground. Alssa was moving to grab him when she saw the black goblin arrow protruding from his back.

Sergeant Sharon knocked Lynnday down as the rest of the warrior women dropped to the ground. The remaining two men had their backs to the goblins and did not realize what had happened until it was too late. Arrows flew from the other side of the cavern, knocking both men to the ground.

The warrior women scrambled on their bellies to their packs to retrieve their weapons, including their bow and arrows.

Cally rolled Grayson off her, picked up his sword, and stepped out to meet two goblins who were rushing at them. She was able to kill them both as they crossed the stream. Taking a defiant stance, she was ready to die protecting the others. Three more goblins rushed at her, and as they entered the stream, a flight of arrows whizzed past her and struck them in the face.

Alssa called out orders. "Sergeant Sharon, get us out of here. The rest of you, pick up your stuff and follow her!"

She grabbed Cally by the back of her torn dress, pulled her away from the stream, and said, "Get going, Cally."

Alssa had turned to follow when she noticed Lynnday kneeling next to her dead boyfriend. She said, "Lynnday, come on, we have to go. There will be more goblins!"

Lynnday could not move, frozen by fear and grief. Alssa reached down, grabbed her by the arm, and pulled her up to her feet. Turning her around, Alssa pulled her face close and said, "Run and don't look back."

Alssa followed Lynnday through the opening that Sergeant Sharon had chosen. Arrows bounced off the rock walls around her as she entered the tunnel. She pulled four arrows from the quiver, stepped around the corner, dropped to one knee, took aim, and launched the shafts in rapid succession. The sound of four solid, meaty thumbs rewarded her efforts. Rising quickly, she followed the other women through the black passageway.

They rushed through the darkness, having left the torches in the cavern. Sergeant Sharon kept pushing on more by instinct than on knowledge or sight. They ran through the maze of tunnels, twisting and turning in different direction, everyone following the person in front of them. Sergeant Sharon kept the pace fast, seeming to know where she was going.

Alssa stayed in the rearguard position. It was quite some time before she heard any noise from behind them. When she reached the end of a straight section of tunnel, she stopped, turned, dropped to a knee, and let an arrow fly in the darkness. She did this as she reached each new turn in the passageway, and about half of the time, she was rewarded with a goblin scream.

She quickly ran out of her own arrows, so she started having each of the trooper's hand back their arrows to her. The longer they ran, the more often she kept running out of arrows. She could not be sure of how many were following them.

Running through a long section of tunnel, Alssa stopped and sent a barrage of iron-tipped shafts toward their pursuers. Reaching back into her quiver, her hand coming back empty, she cursed, "Damn!" She then called out, "Do any of you have any more arrows?"

The reply came back unanimous: "All out!"

She called out to the sergeant, "I think this would be a good time to find an exit from this hellhole!"

Sergeant Sharon's response was caught in her throat as she burst into the intense brilliance of the noonday sun. While she was running through the tunnels, she thought she could feel cool, fresh air; it had paid off. It had led her to an opening in the tunnels.

As the rest of them tumbled out of the cave opening, some stumbled and fell to their knees; others grasped the trees that lined the path. Alssa emerged from the cave last, casting a weary look back into the darkness. She then spoke to Sergeant Sharon. “Sergeant, take stock of what we have and redistribute the weapons and the food.” The problem Alssa now faced was to figure out where they were.

CHAPTER 20

A scout came galloping up to Captain Jovan and excitedly proclaimed, "We found something, sir! We have fresh sign and a good set of tracks. It looks like there was a small battle. We also found children."

"How far?" Jovan asked.

The lancer replied, "About half an hour."

Jovan ordered Sergeant Gallant to send four troopers ahead to help secure the site and prepare for the search. As Jovan rode next to Gallant, the sergeant shared his thoughts. "So this stranger was part of the kidnapping?"

"It sure appears that way," Jovan replied.

The sergeant asked, "Is this why we are leaving the highway unguarded?"

Jovan said, "No, Sergeant, it is not. We are now pursuing something far more threatening than hadrac."

"What could be more of a threat than the hadrac getting organized and attacking in large numbers?" the sergeant asked.

Jovan questioned him, "Do you remember the stories of how the great queen defeated the Lords of Chaos and banished them to the Island of Exile?"

"Yes, of course. All children in the Holy Lands grow up with that story as one of their favorites," Gallant replied.

"And do you remember what she used to accomplish that great task?"

"Yes. The story goes that she wielded a great sword that burned with an unquenchable fire, and with it she defeated the great giant ogres that defended the evil lords. Then with its power, she bound the lords in their own darkness and led them as blind men to their present prison. But my instructor on Testros said that the story is only a legend. Made up to bring honor to the Pact of Brothers' mother. He said the truth was that the three brothers overcame the dark lords. That was why they lived on the Island of Exile in our kingdom. He said that the brothers were the only ones with the power, and will, to keep them bound up."

With a look of frustration and a little anger, Captain Jovan asked, "Sergeant, did you ever serve your twelve days on the Island of Exile?"

After a long pause, Sergeant Gallant responded, "No, of course not. You know that honor is reserved for officers only."

"I am sorry, Sergeant, I forgot," Jovan apologized. He then continued, "Well, if you ever had, you would not be as confident in your instructor's words. That place is the most evil and vile place I have ever been. It makes the Ebony Forest feel as peaceful as St. Michaels Keep. It is most unnerving. There is no way you cannot come away from there a changed man. It is also the reason that those officers assigned to patrol the Lands of Chaos are only those that have served a week on the Island of Exile. We have felt the evil and known its horror. So we are extremely diligent to seek out and destroy it when we find it. But we also know that we cannot possibly overcome it on our own strength."

"Why?" the sergeant asked. Then he said, "I don't understand."

"Again, if you had been to the island, you would know that it is not by the strength of common men that those vile and disgusting creatures stay bound. How do you think it is that they still live after three hundred years?" Jovan asked.

"I think that…well, I don't really know," came the reluctant reply.

Comforting Gallant, Jovan said, "Never mind. It isn't something easy to comprehend." He then explained, "Let me describe to you the insidious blackness that is the Island of Exile. When you first arrive in the area of the island, you are greeted by the combined fleet of the twelve nations. No ship can get within twelve leagues of the island without being spotted by a patrol craft. By the time you reach six leagues, the fleet is upon you, and if you do not have a seer aboard, they'll sink you on the spot. It is not until you reach three leagues that you start into the mist that surrounds the island. After you travel two more leagues and you re-emerge from the mist, you're able to see the dormant volcano that rises from the sea.

There are no beaches, no trees, no grass, no vegetation of any kind, just solid rock jutting from the sea like a giant cone. The only way onto the island is by docking at one of the twelve piers that are spaced evenly around the circumference of the volcano, one pier for each of the twelve nations."

Sergeant Gallant interrupted and asked, "Why are there twelve different piers? That seems like a waste!"

Jovan replied, "The seers do not allow the arriving guards to interact with guards from the other nations. Twelve different piers allow each nation to disembark their guards from their ships without contacting anyone else."

Jovan continued his story. "When I went for my tour, there were six of us from the brothers, all skilled archers and swordsmen. As we approached the pier, we could see three of our comrades manning the rampart that protected the dock. They had their bows strung, arrows notched, and I swear the look in their eyes communicated that they were ready to kill us.

"Our seer called out to them, and they let us dock. I began to fear at that point, but I tell you, Sergeant, the fear I would come to know later that week set my course for the rest of my life."

Jovan stared off into the forest for a few moments before he continued, "When we disembarked from the boat, three of our company relieved the guards on the pier, who quickly climbed aboard the boat and would not come off again no matter how we urged them. Our seer instructed the three new guards that they were to kill instantly anyone who set foot on the pier unaccompanied by a seer, including the three men who just boarded the boat."

"Sergeant, we had be given these same instructions by the commandant on Testros before we left, but when the seer gave those orders, it became reality and all six of us knew that we would follow our instructions or die trying.

"We then left our three companions, and with the seer leading the way, we began our long ascent up the side of the volcano. It was exactly 1,500 steps with no break. I do not believe I have ever been as tired as that day. The closer we got to the rim, the harder it was to walk. I felt like I was carrying a five-stone pack. We inquired of the seer why we felt the way we did. He replied, 'It is the burden of evil that you feel.'"

The captain shivered as he thought back to that day, and said, "I am not sure even today, if I know what he meant, but I sure understood the feeling, because when we left that place twelve days later, I felt like I lost twice that much in weight.

"Once we reached the rim, we came upon a guard tower with three more of our fellow brothers. The look on their face was surely the look of death as they peered down the shaft of the arrows pointed at our hearts. Again, the seer rescued us by speaking out. We expected to be able to talk to the soldiers we were replacing. We wanted to ask them a few questions and have them share their experience, to prepare us for the coming twelve days. But instead, they just started down the steps, and they only stopped because their seer instructed them to. They still would not talk to us. So we gave up and took our gear into the tower."

Sergeant Gallant interjected, "I don't understand. Why would trained soldiers, and officers at that, act in that manner?"

Jovan looked at the sergeant with understanding eyes and said, "I can identify with your confusion. We felt the same way when we first arrived. The place was sparkling clean, not a speck of dirt or dust, nothing out of place.

"The guard tower was elevated above the rim of the volcano and cantilevered over the pit. It allowed us to see down into its depths. However, when we first arrived, we could not. There was a swirling black mist that covered the crater floor.

"We could see across the crater, about 450 paces. The towers on our right and left were about 120 paces away. All the other towers had three guards and a seer, with all of them looking at us. The air above the rim was clean and clear. The little shack had a deck that ran around its entire circumference. In 40 paces, you could walk all the way around it.

"The view out over the ocean was amazing. You could see out to the mist a league away. I quickly noticed that the nature of the rim of the crater made it impossible to walk to any of the other towers. We were completely isolated from one another. Eighty-four people on a small island and no way to contact anybody else but our own company.

"Our seer then joined us as the previous tenants made their way down the mountain. He instructed us on how the next twelve days would go. Every hour of the day, one of us would stand watch over the stairs leading up from the pier. At dusk we would stand watch as one of the other nations rotated their guards off the island like we had done this morning. Then at noon each day, the two of us who were not watching the staircase would stand watch as one set of two guards from a different nation would descend into the crater.

"Our job was to watch for any odd behavior in the two soldiers being lowered in the wicker baskets. Our turn would come on the last day of our twelve-day tour. He told us that this was the case for all the other nations. You only went down to feed the dark lords once and only on the last day. Then the seer revealed what we were guarding against. We were not keeping the lords from escaping. They could not break the bonds that held them. And if they did, we would not be able to stop them anyway.

"I had quickly asked, 'Then what are we doing here?'

"The seer replied, 'The dark lords can only break free with help from mortal men and your true task is to make sure that never happens.'

"Sergeant, what the seer told us next set a sober tone for the rest of our twelve days. Our job while we were there was to execute any soldier that acted like they were under the influence of the dark lords, including our own.

"And we were to kill anyone, without question, who approached us unaccompanied by a seer. There were never any exceptions, and no seer would bring anyone here for twelve more days, so we were to shoot on sight anyone who approached the guard tower."

"My god, Captain, are you serious? What happened?" Sergeant Gallant asked excitedly.

"Those first eleven days were uneventful.

"On our twelfth day, Gerard and I were selected to descend in the basket to feed the captives. I was terrified. At noon we walked out onto the deck and loaded the food into the basket. I could see the other nations' soldiers watching us, bows in hand, ready to strike us dead if we succumbed to the influence of the darkness.

"The seer gave us a prayer that we were to say repeatedly, the entire time we were in the crater. As we got into the basket, all twelve of the seers stood on the edge of their decks, raised their hands into the sky, and began to pray in a language I could not understand. Just like the previous eleven days, the swirling mist disappeared and we could again see the bottom of the crater. As Gerard and I lowered ourselves into the giant hole, we could feel the subtle probing fingers of the dark lords' thoughts. We both prayed louder.

"Sergeant, I am not sure I can accurately tell you what happen next, but it was like a war in my mind, and I feared for my sanity. Darkness would flood into my thoughts, and I could hear voices and what felt like icy hands pulling at me, begging me to come and set them free. I prayed harder and louder. I do not know if I saw or felt what was happening. I do not think my eyes were open, but somehow, I managed to deposit the food, and in my next conscious thought, I was standing in the basket and Gerard was walking toward me with his eyes all clouded over and a look of extreme pleasure on his face.

"I asked him what was happening, but all he did was smile wider and move closer to me. When he climbed into the basket, he grabbed me around the throat and began to choke me. Now, I am a stone and half heavier and quite a bit stronger than Gerard. I had beaten him at hand-to-hand fighting many times during our training, but this time he had unnatural strength.

"I was almost ready to pass out as twenty-two arrows came whizzing in from the towers above us. One of them hit me in the shoulder and another tore into my thigh, but the rest of them riddled Gerard's body, he went limp and fell to the bottom of the basket. I collapsed, as my strength was gone.

"The seer and my fellow officer hoisted me up as I had neither the strength nor the will to move. As I ascended, a wave of hatred washed over me, but it was not just for me—it came from below. The Lords of Chaos hatred is for all humans. They hate us in ways that we will never understand.

"It totally consumes them. It almost consumed me that day. I do not remember anything that happened after that until we were eight leagues away from the island.

"Sergeant, I know their hatred, I know their loathing, and it is not the hand of man that keeps the dark lords bound on the Island of Exile. It is the great and mystical power that the great queen wielded back on the day she bound the evil lords to the island.

"From what I have been told, the power she used is tied in some way, to the sword of light. And now a common criminal has unknowingly returned the sword to this place at this time as the prophecy is to be fulfilled. I wonder how it came into his possession?"

"Probably stole it," Sergeant Gallant speculated.

Jovan spoke to himself more than to Sergeant Gallant. "I guess the leaders of the Pact of Brothers were wrong. All this time, they thought that the seers had the sword. Now it turns up back where it belongs in the hands of a thief." Turning to the sergeant, he said, "Let's be off. We must find this thief and recover the sword."

Chapter 21

Daniel had spent most of the afternoon looking for a trail that would lead him and the three girls back to the Queen's Highway. He wanted to avoid the site of the hadrac attack on the kidnappers. Daniel did not want the girls to see what had happened to their mothers; he still had not told them and did not intend to. He would let someone else do the telling.

Finally, finding a trail that headed south, he took it. It did not take them long before they were overlooking the Queen's Highway. He could hear men talking and moving around back down the road toward the massacre site. Daniel hid the girls in a thick bush. He told them that they were playing a hiding game and that they should stay as quiet as possible.

Slowly he worked his way down to the edge of the road. From there he could see who it was that was making all the noise. He was not surprised to find that it was a troop of Holy Lancers. This was the break he needed. He would be able to leave the girls on the road for the troopers to find, and he could be on his way.

He walked back down the road to where he had left the girls. When he got back to them, Melissa was sobbing, and Saaraha was encouraging her to be quiet.

Daniel asked as he sat down beside them, "What is wrong with Melissa? Was I gone too long?

Saaraha replied, "No, I told her that I thought monsters are coming."

"Monsters! Why do you think that monsters are coming?" Daniel asked.

"I don't know. I can just tell," Saaraha said.

Daniel stood up and said, "Well, let's have a look around and see if you are right."

Leading the girls toward the road, he was very unconcerned about the monsters on the Queen's Highway; hadrac just did not come around during the daylight. He was encouraging the girls that everything was all right when he heard footfalls and low growls and grunts.

The sounds were distinctly bestial, but that did not make sense, and they were not the sound of hadrac.

"Curse the dark lords!" Daniel swore, and said, "Girls, quickly, let's get back into the trees and hide again!"

Saaraha stopped, turned around, and asked, "What's the matter, mister? Are there monsters coming?"

Grabbing her by the hand and pulling her quickly along behind him, he responded, "Yes, there is, and we have to hide quickly so they will not find us."

Getting the girls hidden, he eased back out of the hiding place and into a position to watch the road. He was right; they were not the hadrac. They were orcs! They came by him, walking casually, sniffing the air. Fortunately, orcs did not have the same sense of smell as hadrac.

There were at least thirty of them walking down the road toward the lancers. This would not be good; his only hope of getting rid of the girls safely was to leave them for the troopers.

Now the lancers were going to end up fighting a superior force, while dismounted and caught off guard.

He had to act and act quickly, or else, he would be stuck with three little girls in monster-infested woods. Daniel could see only one way out of this situation.

* * *

Jovan sat on a big rock by his horse and listened to Sergeant Gallant give his report. "We found two groups of hadrac tracks leading away from the massacre site. The main body of about twenty came back this way, crossed the road, and continued to head south. Another group of six, which seemed to be searching for something, went to the north."

"How about the children? Were there any sign of them?" Jovan asked.

Gallant seemed lost in his retelling of what he saw. "I'm sure that the two women are the ones the men who were with the H'la healers described to you."

"And the children?" Jovan asked again.

Gallant continued as if not hearing the captain's question, "The site is horrible. Blood everywhere. Clearly, the women were being violated when the hadrac attacked."

Captain Jovan spoke loudly and sharply to the sergeant as he asked a third time, "What about children? Were there any children?"

The sergeant replied reluctantly, "Sir? There were what looked to be two young boys. Remember, the bodies were hacked into pieces. We could not find any young girls, only the two women. Maybe the kidnappers disposed of the girls earlier. These men who took these women appeared to be interested in only one thing, and they seem to have been in the middle of that when the hadrac attacked.

Jovan snapped at the sergeant as he said, "I heard you the first time. Are you sure there was no sign of the little girls?"

Sergeant Gallant responded sheepishly, "It's hard to tell, Captain. We did find what might be a set of tracks of another human heading north. The tracker says that he is sure it is a human who knows how to cover his trail well. But that doesn't make any sense. If a human thought he was being followed by hadrac, it would be useless to cover your trail. Hadrac don't use sight to find their pray, they use smell." Then he asked, "What would you like to do now, sir, follow the main group going south or the small party heading north?"

"Neither, Sergeant. We must continue looking for the thief," came the captain's reply.

Gallant protested, "But why? If he had been involved with the kidnapping would he not have been here with the dead? Isn't it our responsibility to hunt down these beasts and destroy them?"

"Sergeant, we have been over this before. Did you find the sword?"

The sergeant shook his head no.

Jovan continued, "Then he was not there. The thief was our prey when we left H'la, and he still is our prey now. This changes nothing."

Sergeant Gallant was about to object again when the sound of metal clanging against metal interrupted him.

* * *

Turning toward the girls, Daniel told Saaraha, "Don't move until you hear the monsters leave and other people coming by on the road. Those men will be soldiers who will help you. You must run to the road and make enough noise for them to hear you. Saaraha, do you understand me?"

"Yes," she replied but then asked, "Why can't you stay here with us? We don't want to be alone."

Daniel reassured them that it would be okay. He made his way back to the road. He waited for the ugly beasts to pass before sneaking out behind the two orcs that were trailing the main body. The closest orc fell dead immediately, cleaved in half by Daniel's heavy blade.

The second, larger orc reacted quickly and attacked. Daniel was able to block the blows rained down upon him for a moment, but then his grip on the sword was broken and it fell from his hand. Stepping in close and with great strength, he grabbed the orc around the waist, used a cross-body throw, and tossed the heavy animal to the ground. Pulling his fighting knife from the scabbard, he thrust it under its rib cage, where its heart should have been. The beast howled in pain and delight as he clenched Daniel's wrist.

It took a moment for Daniel to realize what was happening. He was attempting to keep Daniel from escaping until his fellows could return. This was very un-orc-like. It was showing way too much intelligence for a normal orc. Using his free hand, Daniel reach down to his boot, pulled out one of the throwing knives, and stabbed the monster through the eye.

Quickly returning the knives to their scabbards, he picked up his sword and cut off the beast's head. Daniel looked up the road to see if the rest of the orcs were coming back. Sure enough, the first one was just rounding the bend in the road. Daniel waited until he was confident that the beast had seen him. He started off at a dead run, up the road, in the direction the orcs had come. Away from the girls and the lancers.

He could hear the guttural yell of the orc calling for the attention of the rest of the group. Risking one last look back to make sure they were following him, he dashed into the woods on the first trail he found heading north.

* * *

Jovan quickly had the lancers remount and gallop down the road toward the noise of battle. The lead trooper rounded the bend in the road as the last orc disappeared into the woods. As the lancer approached the spot on the road where the orcs had died, his horse began to buck wildly, throwing him off and onto the road. Sergeant Gallant and Captain Jovan rode up just as the corporal was getting up.

"Are you all right, trooper?" Sergeant Gallant said with a chuckle.

"Yes, sir, I am quite all right," the trooper replied, "but I seem to be covered with orc blood, which explains why my horse acted up."

Surveying the blood on the road, Captain Jovan queried, "With the amount of blood that has been spilled, there is no way these orcs could have lived, and so where are the bodies?"

"We know that orcs don't carry off their dead, so they must have lived," responded Sergeant Gallant. Captain Jovan gave Gallant a disbelieving look.

The trooper walked up the road toward where the orcs had turned into the woods. When he returned, he informed Jovan,

"There is no blood trail. Whatever was killed here didn't run off, nor was it dragged off. It is as if they disappeared. Should we go after the survivors, sir? They must be chasing someone."

Captain Jovan had begun to give orders to pursue the orcs when he heard a small, scared voice from the forest on the north side of the road. He asked Sergeant Gallant, "Did you hear something?"

Gallant replied, "Yes, sir, I did."

Jovan gave orders to his men. "Spread out and search one hundred strides into the woods."

The soldiers dispersed into the woods in pairs. Quickly the source of the noise was found; it was the three little girls. The troopers carried them out of the woods kicking and screaming.

Saaraha was yelling, "Put us down! We aren't babies! We can walk by ourselves!"

The soldiers brought them to Captain Jovan, who had dismounted. Getting down on one knee to be face-to-face with the tallest one, he asked, "Who are you?"

Saaraha's excitement and fear came out in her voice. "My name is Saaraha, and these are Beth and Melissa. We were lost when we ran away from the monsters, but then the man from the boat found us and brought us here. He was nice, but he had to leave to scare away the other monsters. And we still don't—"

Captain Jovan interrupted, "Slow down. How did you three girls get out here in the forest?"

"We were taken by big scary men with our mommies. When we stopped to eat, Beth's mommy told us to run and hide, so we did. Do you know where our mommies are?"

Jovan avoided her question and asked his own. "Saaraha, this man from the boat who you said saved you from the monsters, where did he go?"

"I told you, he left to scare away the new monsters who came. He told us that you would come after he scared them away and that we were to run out here and make a lot of noise."

"How did the man scare away the monsters?"

"I don't know. I guess with his sword. He's really big."

"Did you see the sword? Did you see him use it?"

"Yes! Well, no. I mean, yes, well saw it on the boat. My brother wanted to play with it, but the man wouldn't let him, but he let me look at it and touch it. Do you know where our mommies are?"

Captain Jovan did not know what to say, so he said nothing. The girls began to sob.

Up to this point, one would have never known that the healer rode with the troop, but she stepped forward and said sternly, "I will take care of the girls." She turned about on her heals, covered the girls with her purple cloak, and walked away.

"Captain, this is getting stranger and stranger!" an exasperated Sergeant Gallant exclaimed. "First, we end our patrol to chase after a glowing sword. Now three girls appear alone in the middle of the Ebony Forest and the old hag starts acting like some kind of doting grandmother."

Jovan answered, "I can't explain the healer, but I believe the rest is clear. The girls belong to the two dead women in the woods back there. The thief escaped from the hadrac with the girls and then brought them to the road to leave for us. What I don't understand is this thief's actions. Why would he care about these girls? And how did he catch up with them in the first place?"

Captain Jovan wandered off in thought, trying to figure out this situation. Sergeant Gallant was at somewhat of a loss on what to do. His captain was ignoring their prime responsibility, which was killing the hadrac and orcs. Instead, he seemed fixated upon this thief and his sword.

CHAPTER 22

T'asha paced back and forth, moving from the doorway on the north side of the keep to the window overlooking the south side. From each position, she could see down the slope at the roads that led up to Devil's Pass. The look on her face was not one of pleasure.

Her officer sat around a table on the west side of the great room, trying ridiculously hard not to catch her attention. None of them dared to go anywhere near her, especially when she was in one of her frustration-induced rages. They all had seen her quick temper before, but that was not what scared them the most—it was her seemingly perverse delight in striking people while in a rage.

When they first arrived at Devil's Pass to await Alssa and Cally, T'asha bubbled with excitement and giddy anticipation of revenge, but now after two days of waiting, her excitement had faded, along with her patience.

T'asha addressed Commander Westolve. "Have your scouts returned from Toller's Crag?"

Westolve replied timidly, "Only the one, Your Majesty. The rest were all killed by the goblins before they could reach the town."

"Did you send more troops to replace the ones that were lost?" T'asha asked.

Westolve started to answer, "I have not—"

T'asha spun around, fists clenched at her side. "What? I clearly gave orders to you to find out if Alssa and Cally are still in the town!"

Commander Westolve flinched, as did her fellow officers at the table. She said, "Your Majesty, it is futile to send more troops. The goblins have the town completely surrounded."

T'asha's gaze pierced through the commander, causing her to squirm. "If you are unwilling to send more troops, how do you plan to find out if they are still there? Maybe you should go this time. With your leadership, your squad might get through."

T'asha smiled and turned away from Commander Westolve and walked back to the door. Westolve stood stunned and unable to move or talk. Commander Nadja intervened and said, "Majesty, if we cannot get in, then they most certainly cannot get out."

T'asha turned around slowly, her frustration clear on her face. "So you agree with Westolve that my orders can be disobeyed at will?"

"No, Your Majesty, but I can see when a situation has changed to create greater opportunities." Nadja smiled at Westolve.

"My patience is thin, Nadja. Get on with it," T'asha demanded.

"Let's let the goblins finish them off and we can go to L'ke L'fe to await the new king." Nadja's sureness of her idea produced another smile for Commander Westolve.

T'asha noticed and was not happy with their banding together to resist her. She smiled wickedly as she said, "Commander Westolve, you will take your company to L'ke L'fe and prepare for my arrival and deal with any problems that arise. However, you will leave twenty troopers here to make sure Alssa and Cally don't escape."

"Your Majesty, that would be a death sentence to leave them here alone. They will be trapped between the goblins and the hadrac," Westolve pleaded.

T'asha smiled slyly. "In that case, we won't leave them here alone. Commander Nadja will stay with them."

Nadja's face filled with panic as her eyes entreated Westolve for help. Commander Westolve began to object. "Is it really necessary to leave anyone in such an exposed position? We should keep our forces consolidated to combat any threats we might encounter."

What little patience T'asha possessed disappeared as she screamed at her two commanders. "Maybe I should leave the two of you here alone! And then you can whine and cry on each other's shoulders like a couple of quivering maids!"

She turned to leave, then stopped. Turning around slowly, she smiled at the two of them. "Nadja, your troops will come with me back to Jukeele, but you will stay here. Maybe you will learn something about loyalty. Commander Westolve, you will leave your second-in-command along with twenty soldiers here, and you will take the rest of your troops to L'ke L'fe."

Commander Westolve began to object again, but T'asha ignored her and walked out the door. Westolve turned to Nadja, who was staring at her dumbfounded, and whispered, "What is going on? She has changed!"

Nadja rose from her chair and walked to the door to see if T'asha was gone. Turning to face the rest of the officers, she addressed them. "You heard Her Majesty. Let's get everyone ready to go. You move out in one hour!"

As they hustled out the door, Nadja addressed Westolve as she moved to stand by the fireplace. "Maurice, you should watch your tongue in front of others."

"Yes, you're right," Westolve agreed but then asked, "How long has she been like this?"

Nadja looked at her quizzically and asked, "What do you mean?"

Westolve wasn't sure how to respond, so she said, "I don't know. She seems angrier, meaner. I have not been around her for a couple of months, not since we finalized this plan. I understand why she has the feelings she has toward her sisters, but…"

Nadja turned around, interrupted Westolve, and spit out, "Those two are not her sisters. They are just cousins. I'm her real sister!"

Commander Westolve took a step back and said, "I know that, Nadja, but you must admit that she is acting a little strange?"

Nadja stormed out the door, yelling back at Commander Westolve, "You just look after yourself and obey your orders!"

Westolve sat down facing the fire and lowered her head into her hands. With a deep sigh, she said to herself, "What have we done?"

Chapter 23

Alssa and her small band had escaped from the goblins who had attacked them in the tunnels. They now had to decide what they were going to do. Should they go west to the coast highway or go south and east through the Ebony Forest?

Sergeant Sharon was first to voice her opinion. "We have lost a lot of time, and Your Majesties need to be in L'ke L'fe in four days. I say we press through the forest. Going all the way out to the highway will force us to go to H'la before we can turn east."

Cally countered, "This area of the forest is still goblin territory. I say we head to the highway."

Sergeant Sharon argued, "How many lizards can there be? Most of them have to be in the Wasteland, looking for us."

Alssa spoke up and said, "You both have good points, but I believe we are better to play it safe and be late than to tempt fate in the Ebony Forest. We will head to the coast highway."

As they set out on the river trail, Alssa took the lead, with Sergeant Sharon bringing up the rear. They walked for two hours, making good time. Sergeant Sharon caught up with the group when they stopped to rest. She pointed up on the hill to the north and said, "Do you see that open area up there? That's the Sandhurst slide. It is a rally point, and often the Pact of Lancers use it as an encampment area. Considering our lack of arrows, I think we should make our way up there to see if anyone is home, and maybe we can accompany them to H'la."

Alssa frowned. "I would rather walk a hundred miles than go begging a ride from the Pact of Brothers."

Sergeant Sharon looked to Cally for some support.

Cally shrugged her shoulders but said, "Sister, she might be right. In the last few days, we have lost over two hundred troopers. I think we should take help from wherever we can find it."

Alssa gave her sister a sour look and said, "All right, we will go to Sandhurst and see if the lancers are there, but we do not tell them everything that has happened."

Sergeant Sharon's fatigue and frustration started to show as she said, "What should we tell them?"

"Just let me do the talking. I will tell them that we were attacked by goblins, but not how many or where."

It took the small group another half an hour to reach the slide area. As they approached, Lynnday cried out, "What is that awful smell?"

The answer appeared quickly as they moved out of the trees and walked into the open. There were bodies of humans and hadrac scattered over the entire area. Lynnday started screaming, but that quickly turned to retching; she had never been exposed to the gruesome carnage of a battle. The sights and smells overwhelmed her.

As they looked over the carnage Cally asked, "Do you see anything odd here?"

"You mean, besides the ten-to-one kill ratio of hadrac to lancers?" Sergeant Sharon asked.

Cally shook her head. "The lancers certainly acquitted themselves. There must be close to two hundred dead hadrac and I only count fifteen Pact of Brothers, but that is not what I was looking at. A number of the lancers were killed by arrows, but the hadrac don't use bows, only axes."

Sergeant Sharon reached down and pulled one of the arrows out of a dead lancer. "These are goblin arrows!" she exclaimed, then said, "Goblins and hadrac working together? This can't be good."

Alssa turned to Corporal Raskis. "Take Trooper Stims and follow the tracks of the victor. See which direction they head. The rest of you gather up as many goblin arrows as you can find. At least we will be able to use our bows now." Alssa motioned to Cally. "Can you help Lynnday? Take her back to the stream and clean her up."

It did not take long for the two scouts to return. Corporal Raskis saluted as she approached. "Your Majesty, the tracks lead to the coast highway, and it looks like they head down the road toward H'la."

Sergeant Sharon and the rest of the small band had finished gathering all the arrows they could find. Sharon had heard the scout's report, so she said, "I think that settles it. We must go back the way we came and then head south and east through the forest."

Alssa nodded in agreement and said, "I am afraid you are right, Sergeant. When Cally and Lynnday return, we will retrace our steps and look for a ford to cross the river."

Upon Cally and Lynnday's return, Lynnday appeared to be more upset than before. She was arguing with Cally in a hysterical voice. "I want to go back to Toller's Crag! I don't want to go with you. You must take me back to my home!"

Cally was gentle but firm with her as she said, "We cannot. We would never make it back, not with all the goblins."

Lynnday turned to face Alssa and demanded, "You must take me back. I want to go home, please!"

Alssa stood up from the log she was sitting on. "I am afraid Cally is right. We would never make it through, and even if we could, we cannot spare the time." Motioning to the rest of the group, she stood up and started walking back up the trail they came down. "Let's get moving. I want to be across the river by tomorrow morning."

That night, they camped just one mile up the river from the cave they had escaped from early the previous morning.

When they awoke, Lynnday was gone. Sergeant Sharon set out to find her tracks; the rest of them broke camp and prepared to look for a ford to cross the river.

Sergeant Sharon returned with not-so-surprising news. Sharon said, "She went the wrong way. She is headed upriver, not down. We will easily catch her in a short time."

Alssa exhaled forcefully and said, "Not if someone or something finds her first. Let's get moving."

Unfortunately, they both proved to be right; they caught up with her in half an hour, and she had met something. A wolf had ripped her throat out.

Sergeant Sharon pointed out, "There are goblin tracks all around the body, but they did not eat her. I wonder why."

"Let us not stay to find out. We need to get across the river." Alssa was going to say more, but she stopped talking when the sound of a howling wolf sent shivers up their spines.

Chapter 24

Daniel had spent the entire night on the move, trying to avoid the few man-orcs who had successfully followed him to the north side of the Three Brides River. He was tired to the point of exhaustion and was having a difficult time keeping his eyes open.

Sometime during the night, he remembered passing a waterfall as he climbed his way eastward up the valley. It was not until dawn that he had reached the ford that he was now surveying. Finding an excellent hiding spot, Daniel had been watching it for more than an hour and nothing, not even an animal, had used the crossing. As his eyes searched intently for movement in the woods on the far side of the river, he rested his head on his forearm and closed his eyes, saying to himself, "I will rest only for a moment, then I will cross the river and keep moving."

Daniel awoke with a start. He had been unable to stay awake after so many hours of physical exertion. As he cleared his mind of sleep, he looked around, trying to remember where he was and what he had been doing. He was wet from head to toe; it must have started raining while he slept. His mind raced as he tried to regain a grip on his situation. He ran through the events of the last two days that had brought him to his hiding place above the ford.

Daniel looked up into the sky. The sun was straight above his head. He thought to himself, *Midday, and it was only dawn when I fell asleep. Six hours lost!* Where were the man-orcs? he wondered. Had they closed the gap he had worked so hard to create the night before, or had they given up the chase?

As he worried about his situation, he began to wonder what sound had awakened him. Then he heard it again, the unmistakable snorting of orcs. They had indeed closed the gap. They appeared one by one from the woods into the clearing next to the crossing. He counted twenty-one of them as they milled about. They appeared to be trying to decide whether to cross the river or go east along this side.

Daniel's scent trail must have been washed away by the rain—at least he hoped so. Maybe his luck was changing. His hope grew as a fight broke out between two of the bigger ones. Daniel could tell that they disagreed on what they should do.

The largest one, the one he had named Kroll, after a big ugly prison guard he had encountered while residing in the Eastern Islands, swung his ax and sliced off the other's arm. The argument seemed to be settled; they would go the direction Kroll wanted to, and Daniel hoped it would be west.

Unfortunately, his luck had not changed. Fifteen of them followed Kroll across the ford and into the woods in the direction Daniel himself needed to go. The remaining five helped One-Arm off the ground, and they headed east along the river.

Daniel sat in his hiding place, waiting for the orcs to get far enough away from the ford so that he would not run into them after crossing the river.

As he was crawling out of his concealed resting place, he heard noises coming down the path from the north. Pulling back into his hiding place, he waited. Whoever it was, they were not orcs. Suddenly, a woman dressed in peasant garb emerged from the woods. She was quickly followed by a line of women similarly dressed. They crossed the ford and entered the woods.

Daniel had spent ten minutes, waiting and contemplating who they could be, when four large black wolves burst into the clearing. The wolves were held in check by twelve goblins. They, too, quickly crossed the river.

He had heard that goblins and wolves shared a bond. The goblins seemed to be able to get the wolves to work with them without any kind of coercion or verbal commands. Maybe they worked so well together because of their shared fondness of human flesh. Whatever the reason, the eight women who had just passed by were now surrounded by two of the worst forms of evil.

Man-orcs in front of them and goblins behind them—their fate was assuredly sealed. Daniel did not think they would be able to handle one of the enemies, let alone two.

The presence of goblins and man-orcs together convinced Daniel to change his plans. Instead of crossing at the ford, he would stay on the north side of the river and look for another crossing farther east.

Daniel crawled from his hiding place and started along the same path as One-Arm and his few companions had taken.

He had only walked for about five minutes before that same annoying voice came back to let him know that he had made the wrong decision. He now had to decide whether to argue with himself for another five minutes and then turn around and go back to help the women or to just turn around now and get it over with.

In the past, he would have argued so he would be able to tell himself, "I told you so," if things didn't turn out. But this time he was having none of that. He turned around and headed out at a trot. It only took him a couple of minutes to reach the ford he had spent so much time watching.

After crossing the river, he began look for a sign. That did not take long either. To his trained eye, the trail the three groups were leaving looked like the Queen's Highway.

As Daniel continued on the trail south, he noticed the man-orcs were beginning to disperse to find his nonexistent trail. This made things worse for the women. Now, instead of possibly bypassing the orcs as a group, they were sure to run into one or two of them in the forest. Though it would be purely accidental, the outcome would be the same. The man-orcs would raise the call and all of them would converge on the women in a bloodlust. As he continued to follow the women, he thought, *Orcs tend to get crazy when they are thwarted from their desires, and my ability to lose them must be driving them into an absolute rage. I had better hurry.*

CHAPTER 25

From the look on her face, Alssa knew the news that Sergeant Sharon had to tell her could not be good. "What is it, Sergeant?"

"Your Majesty, it appears that we have stumbled onto the trail of a large group of orcs."

"What do you mean it *appears*? Are they orcs or not?" Alssa asked.

The sergeant explained, "When we first crossed their trail, the footprints made me think it might be a large group of men, but the gait is all wrong. They do not walk like men but like beasts. And now they are beginning to disperse as if they are looking for something. As you know, when orcs separate, they all have to give homage to their leader." Pointing to the ground, Sergeant Sharon indicated a group of tracks where the ground was all pawed up. "This is clearly a homage site."

"But you said they were dispersing. Isn't this a good thing?" Alssa questioned.

The sergeant shook her head no and said, "Not in this case. Like I said, they are dispersing to look for something, and that will only increase our chances of running into one of them."

"Should we set a course around them?" Alssa asked.

Sergeant Sharon cautioned, "We certainly can, but it will cost us time, and you need to be at Queens Castle Home in three days. And we still have the goblins behind us."

"We will not make it at all if we get trapped between orcs and goblins," Alssa declared.

Sergeant Sharon thought for a few moments, then replied, "There are legends that say there are trails that cross the Troll Hills from the west and lead out into the Midland Plains. These orcs seem to be steering south, so if we travel east, we can look for another trail, and when we find it, we will be moving toward L'ke L'fe."

Their conversation was suddenly cut short by the howling of wolves.

"Your Highness, the goblins have caught our scent again. We must move quickly!" Sergeant Sharon encouraged.

The eight women quickly headed east.

CHAPTER 26

Two hours at a hard pace had still not caught Daniel up with the women or the goblins that followed them. It was clear that these women were not just peasants. They had taken an easterly course that would turn them away from the direction the man-orcs had taken and, by so doing, had probably staved off an early demise. But soon the man-orcs would realize they had lost his trail, and they would turn around and come back.

The women would soon be in the troll hills. Would they turn south or try to cross them? Daniel did not think the man-orcs would venture onto the Midland Plains, so if the women crossed them, they might get away. With four more hours until nightfall, he hoped he would be able to catch the goblins in daylight.

After another half an hour of hard pursuit, Daniel slowed and began to wonder what in the world he was doing. He was supposed to be heading for L'ke L'fe and beyond. Instead, he had chased after, and found, the three kidnapped little girls, leaving them for the troop of Holy Lancers who had stumbled onto his trail.

He delt with the hadrac that had been after the girls. But then they had run into the man-orcs, who had chased him all the way here. Now these women had come into the fray. Why could he not just mind his own business and stick to what he had started out to do? This seemed to happen to him all the time.

Daniel thought about his chosen profession of a hired protector. The rich always felt that someone was trying to do them in, so they paid handsomely to anyone who could keep them safe. Daniel's problem was that there always seemed to be an innocent woman or child whose presence messed with the simplicity of his life.

From the very beginning, he could never bring himself to inflict pain and suffering on the innocent. If not for that hindrance, he would have been an extraordinarily rich man by now.

That aside, he still did not understand why he had to always go out of his way to help complete strangers. Although he thought, *Several of the women who had crossed the stream were quite attractive, and it might be worth my while to help them out of this fatal jam they have put themselves in.* He picked up his pace to a trot.

In the next hour he had made up half the distance. By nightfall he would catch them. Hopefully, he would be in time.

Chapter 27

Alssa's hairs stood up on the back of her neck, telling her that the goblins had closed the gap. Sergeant Sharon deployed the troops in a defensive circle, with Alssa and Cally in the middle. They both hated the idea of being protected, but they also knew the necessity of it.

Dusk was just beginning when Sergeant Sharon saw movement in the trees. She thought, *The goblins are being a lot more cautious than usual. Their normal practice is to just charge in without planning.* As the goblins moved closer, Sergeant Sharon realize that they were not goblins at all but men; she could tell by their walk. Sergeant Sharon called out, "Stop and be recognized."

"Stand down and we will come into the camp," came the reply.

Sergeant Sharon commanded, "Don't approach until you identify yourself."

"We are pursuing a man. Let us approach and see if he is among you," the voice asked.

Alssa called back, "There are no men here, but we are well armed. Step forward so that we might see who you are."

Sergeant Sharon began to relax her guard.

As the man began to step out of the trees, the ladies could tell, even in the failing light, the hideousness of the man-orcs' faces.

As a loud crash came from behind them, they recognized what they now faced. Half the troop turned to face the new threat. Eight of the man-orcs had sneaked around behind them; now they were surrounded.

As the eight man-orcs rushed them, three arrows erupted from their bows, taking down the first three. Again, their bows strained and released shafts of death, dropping three more.

The remaining two orcs were upon the troopers before they could notch a third arrow. Dropping their bows, they drew their swords. But two of the troopers fell to the orcs' onslaught. Alssa and Cally rushed to the remaining troopers' side and hacked down the orcs in midstride.

When the two troopers fell, the remaining man-orcs attacked from the other direction. Sergeant Sharon and her two troopers let their arrows fly; all struck home, but that still left five of the nightmares to deal with.

These man-orcs were half again the size of normal orcs, making them five stones heavier than the women they now attacked. As the two groups crashed into one another, Sergeant Sharon went down with a nasty gash on her right thigh. The two troopers straddled their fallen leader and were able to kill two of the orcs. By the time Alssa and her group got back to Sergeant Sharon, both troopers were also severely wounded. Alssa and Cally drove the remaining three orcs off, and they ran back to the tree line.

Alssa and Cally knelt beside the sergeant just as a barrage of goblin arrows raced in from the far side of the clearing, killing, instantly, the two remaining troopers. Alssa and Cally helped Sergeant Sharon to her feet. The three stood with their backs to each other, waiting for the next attack. As they looked on in horror, four wolves emerged from the trees, followed by their goblin handlers.

Cally cried out, "What do we do now?"

With determination and resolve, Alssa replied, "We die well and take as many of these lizards with us as we can."

As they watched the goblins approach, the remaining man-orcs began to re-emerge from the trees. The three ladies braced themselves as Sergeant Sharon smirked and said, "Nine-to-one odd, just that the way I like it."

Suddenly, a bright light appeared behind the goblins, followed by a bloodcurdling lizard scream. The flaming light cleaved the first goblin in two, and before the goblins could recover, three more fell to the burning blade. The women were momentarily frozen in awe as they watched the large dark figure hew its way through goblins and wolves.

The circle of evil that surrounded the figure was made up of snarling, snapping, blood-crazed wolves and howling, drooling, lizard-skinned goblins. The dark figure continued to slaughter goblin and wolf a like.

Alssa, Cally, and Sergeant Sharon only recovered just in time to meet the onrushing man-orcs. The Three Sisters soldiers were hard-pressed, only killing the last one after they had received several wounds. The mysterious newcomer had dispatched all the goblins and wolves. He was cleaning off his sword with a rag as he walked toward them.

Letting her age show, Cally ran to Daniel and jumped up and wrapped her arms around his neck and kissed him. She giggled in relief and awe over their deliverer.

Alssa, helping Sergeant Sharon, walked slowly over to Daniel and Cally and said, "You will have to forgive my little sister. This is the closest she has ever come to dying, and her manners are suffering because of it."

Daniel lifted Cally off him and set her down on her feet.

Alssa continued, "My name is Alssa, and these are Sharon and Cally. We are most grateful for your assistance. As you can well see, we were most inconvenienced by our attackers, and your appearance made a difficult task much more manageable."

Daniel laughed out loud, saying, "Assistance! I believe you were about to be slaughtered to a man, or woman, in this case."

Alssa scowled at him and retorted, "We are quite capable of taking care of ourselves, and we did not ask for your help."

As Daniel turned to walk away, he mumbled, "Sure, lady, if that's what gets you through the day." Daniel did not need some prideful woman giving him a hard time.

Surveying the clearing, now covered with goblin blood but no goblin bodies, Daniel thought, *These women are obviously not peasants as their attire appears. The body armor that shimmers from under Sharon's cut and torn blouses also testify to that. The one called Alssa has the look of authority. All three of them carry themselves with a military posture. They also are handling the carnage around them too well for them to be peasants. All this could only mean one thing. These are soldiers of the Three Sisters.*

Daniel decided to cut through their ruse and get right to the point. "From what I see, you might be right. That makes me wonder, What are soldiers of the Three Sisters doing this far south in the middle of the Ebony Forest? And why are they being pursued by goblins?"

Cally blurted out, "We were set upon by these creatures while coming down the coast highway. Our company was quite large when we set out. We have lost many friends to these beasts."

Sergeant Sharon declared, "We have dealt out more death than we have taken. Five to one, I would say." Grief gripped her voice as she continued, "But they…they just kept coming. It seemed like an unending stream of them."

Cally boasted, "There were thousands of them to start with, but our archers and swordsmen cut them down like wheat."

Alssa glared at her sister as she calmly said, "Cally! Calm yourself. You allow yourself to get too excited and you tend to exaggerate."

Cally stopped but returned Alssa's stare with a hurt look.

A look that did not go unnoticed by Daniel. He thought, *She said "our archers and footmen," a lot of them, gold body armor… I think there is more here than they are willing to tell.*

Daniel asked, "Your soldier is badly wounded. Would you like me to take a look at her?"

Sarcasm dripped from her voice as Alssa said, "Are you also a healer as well as a warrior?"

Daniel looked at her with distaste. He was beginning to not like this woman very much. Ignoring Alssa, he bent down to look at the gash on Sharon's thigh. Reaching into his bag, he pulled out a bag of tobacco weed and rosemary mixed with seaweed. He placed a generous amount on a small piece of cloth and added some water from a waterskin. He lifted Sharon's skirt to reveal one of chain mail. As he slowly pushed it up out of the way, he felt the point of a knife on his stomach.

Sharon smiled harshly and said, "Be very careful where you put your hands, warrior."

Daniel slowly pushed the knife away from his side and replied, "Maybe you should adjust your own clothing." He poured water on the wound and cleaned it out very carefully. He took a needle and a length of dried animal gut from his pouch along with a leather strap. He said to Sharon, "You might want to bite down on something while I do this." He quickly sewed up the wound. Finally, he took the poultice and laid it on her thigh and tied it in place with the leather strap.

While Daniel was working on Sergeant Sharon, Alssa and Cally were burying their fallen comrades.

They decided to have a cold camp and to move on at first light. Daniel took the first watch. The moon was full, so Daniel's trained eyes had no problem seeing. Daniel sat wondering what course of action to take in the morning. Should he stay with the women or continue moving east? He felt he should stay with them until they reach some form of civilization. But he also felt this overpowering desire to move on. The pressure that had started him on his journey to the highlands had only grown stronger with each passing day. In his final decision, as always, he would stay with the women until they were safe.

He just started to grow tired when he saw Alssa moving through the trees toward him. Again, he was reminded that she was no ordinary farm girl.

He had seen her before he heard her; she was moving through the trees so quietly. Her fluid movement reminded him of the stealthy jungle cats of Donley-Vickers.

The extent of her military training was obvious. But she also had a natural grace that reflected great agility and coordination. On top of that, she was beautiful.

She and her sister had transformed from poorly dressed peasant girls into stunningly beautiful women when they had changed into their armor. It was then that Daniel realized the entire troop had dressed in disguise.

It was midnight, so it was time for her to relieve him. When she approached close enough, he whispered her name, "Alssa."

She let out a loud gasp, and her sword flashed into her hand. He knew she still could not see him, so he decided to have a little fun with her. Though she called out his name, he let her walk past him. Quietly he moved behind her and tapped her on the shoulder. Alssa stepped back into him, grabbed his wrist, and threw him over her shoulder and onto the ground, ending up with her sword point on his neck.

He cried out, "It's me, Daniel. Put your weapon away."

"You startled me!" she said, gasping, and then more sternly said, "What is wrong with you? Do you think because I am a woman, I can be teased and played with?"

As Daniel got off the ground, he did not know what to say, so he just shrugged and dusted himself off. This made her furious with him, thinking he was ignoring her. She rammed her sword back into its scabbard as she angrily said, "I'm here to relieve you so you can get in bed…or whatever you want."

Daniel turned and began walking back to the camp.

Alssa bit her lip in anger and thought, *Men, they are all the same. Not until they have been shown, do they take women seriously, and then they act like wounded puppies. This man appears to be no different from the rest. Still, he can sure handle himself in a fight.* She found herself watching his backside as he disappeared into the trees. She was startled and disgusted with herself as she sat down.

After a short while, her thoughts returned to Daniel and his smooth skin and large muscular shoulders. She smiled as she thought of the way he had easily held Cally off the ground. She was angry at herself for how she felt when Cally had kissed him and how she wished it had been her instead. How would it feel to have his strong arms wrapped about her waist and the firmness of his chest pressing against hers?

Alssa was shocked by her own thoughts. She cursed silently, *Stupid men! May the queen take them all! How silly of me to think such things.* Alssa settled down to watch but spent most of her time fighting off thoughts of Daniel.

The next morning, before first light, they set off to the east.

CHAPTER 28

Jovan continued to press his troops forward. Darkness was falling, and he wanted to find an open field to camp for the night. Being trapped inside the dense forest was not an option he wanted to exercise. They had been following the thief's trail for two days and were not getting any closer. Sergeant Gallant worked his way up to Captain Jovan.

Sergeant Gallant asked, "Captain, how is this possible? We are mounted, and this thief is on foot, but we seem to be falling farther behind."

The captain replied, "I think you are right, Sergeant. His endurance is amazing."

The sergeant went on, "Have you also noticed his woodcraft? I do not think I have seen the like."

Captain Jovan agreed, "His abilities make it awfully hard to track him. Even with as many troops as we have, we have trouble acquiring his trail."

The sergeant went on some more. "I don't get it, Captain. Why would a common thief possess skill such as this?"

The captain curtly replied, "I don't know."

"And why would he stop to help those little girls like he did?" the sergeant asked.

Somewhat exasperated, Jovan said, "It is unusual."

The sergeant clearly did not know when to quit, as he asked, "Do you really think that he attacked those man-orcs so we would be warned about their presence? Why would he do that?"

Frustrated with the situation and the sergeant's barrage of questions, Jovan responded in anger, "I do not know the answers, but I do know that if we don't catch him, we will never know them. Let's put more effort into tracking and less into talking?"

* * *

As the captain rode away, Sergeant Gallant thought, *This situation must be getting to him. I have never seen him respond with such anger.*

Sergeant Gallant looked around at the troops; they were spread out way too far to offer mutual protection. But it was necessary to keep from losing the trail completely. Still, he worried about being attacked in this situation. If the attacking force was large enough, they would be wiped out without much of a fight.

As he tried to figure out how to create better security for the hundredth time, Corporal Blain rode up and said, "Sergeant, we've found something out on the left flank."

"Take me to it, Corporal," the sergeant replied.

Sergeant Gallant followed Corporal Blain for about a quarter of a mile to a battle site. Dismounting, he surveyed the carnage before him; it looked like a large battle had taken place. Upon further investigation, it was clear several humans had fought off both man-orcs and what must have been goblins, because of the dead wolves; there were twenty of the beasts and five graves.

The corporal asked, "What do you think happened?"

"I'm not sure, Corporal Blain. I've never seen anything like this. It looks like four humans survived this holocaust and headed south. But how could four people fight off a combined attack from goblins and man-orcs?"

Captain Jovan rode up out of the woods and asked, "Sergeant Gallant, what do we have here?"

The sergeant replied, "It looks like a small band of humans battled orcs and goblins. There are five graves over by that big tree, and we are stacking the orc bodies on the other side of the meadow so we can burn them before we leave."

"Sergeant, we will not be burning the bodies. We don't want to attract any attention. I don't see any goblins. Why do you think there were any here?"

Sergeant Gallant pointed to a dark mound over next to the orc bodies. "There were four dead wolves on the opposite side of the meadow from the orcs, but no goblins. It's real strange, Captain. I don't understand it."

Captain Jovan stood up erect in the saddle and said, "He was here! Did you say there are five graves?"

"Yes, sir," the sergeant replied.

The captain ordered, "Detail some men to dig up the bodies."

Sergeant Gallant looked at Jovan in horror. "Excuse me, Captain, did you say you wanted us to dig up the bodies?"

The captain explained, "Sergeant, don't you see? The thief took part in this battle. That's why there are no goblin bodies, and they were killed by him. We need to see if he escaped with the victors or was killed."

The sergeant protested, "But, Captain, it's wrong to dig up the remains of the dead. It will bring a curse down on us for sure."

"The dark lords take your curse, we must hazard all to catch this thief! If they buried him, they might have put the sword in the grave with him. Finding the sword is the only thing that matters. Now, get some men on it!"

The captain began to ride away as Sergeant Gallant walked reluctantly to dig up the dead. Captain Jovan turned in his saddle and asked, "Sergeant, have you sent men to find out what direction the survivors took when they left?"

"Yes, sir. I told them to follow the trail for one league and then come back."

* * *

Corporal Blain walked quickly up to Captain Jovan and Sergeant Gallant as they sat under a tree, waiting for the scouts to return. "Sirs, you both better come and look at what we have found."

They both stood up as Gallant asked, "Did you find the sword, Corporal?"

The corporal replied, "There are swords, but not one like you described, sir."

Jovan questioned, "Does any of the bodies look like it could be the man we are looking for?"

The corporal answered, "Sir, the bodies in the graves are not men."

Sergeant Gallant frowned and asked, "Are you saying that the beasts have buried some of their dead?"

Corporal Blain replied, "No, sir, the bodies are women."

Gallant shook his head. "Women? Women, out here in the middle of this dreadful place? This is getting stranger and stranger."

"Sergeant, it gets stranger than that," Corporal Blain said as he reached down and grabbed the edge of the blanket he used to cover the bodies. He lifted it up for the officers to see. Both Jovan and Gallant swore at the same time. "By the dark lords, what evil goes on here?" They were looking at two of the women clothed in Three Sisters armor.

Jovan was lost in thought while Sergeant Gallant examined the bodies more closely.

Sergeant Gallant looked up at his captain. "Sir, these are not just Three Sisters common troops, they are soldiers of the royal house, personal troops to one of the queens."

Jovan still looked like he was talking to himself when he answered Sergeant Gallant, "That would make sense, Sergeant. The Three Sisters would be sending some member of the royal family to meet the returning heir of M'tin. However, why would they be this deep in the forest instead of on the coast highway? And why would they have such a small escort?"

As they talked, the scouts rode up and reported, "Sir, we followed the track straight east. It looks like they are going to cross the troll hills and make for the midland plains. I would guess they are going to L'ke L'fe."

Jovan nodded and said, "I think you are right." Turning to Sergeant Gallant, he said, "Let us get mounted up. We will ride back to the Queen's Highway and make for L'ke L'fe. I need to talk this over with Major Losguard, the commander of the garrison stationed there."

Looking wide-eyed at his commander, Sergeant Gallant asked, "We are going to stop our pursuit of the sword? I thought that was the most important thing?"

Jovan replied, "Sergeant, if the Three Sisters are somehow involved in this, I am not going to be the one who gets us in a conflict with them. I will let that dubious honor fall to someone with greater rank than me."

Chapter 29

Long before the sun rose, Daniel had reconnoitered the surrounding area and assured himself that they had killed all the goblins and man-orcs the day before. He had ended his search on the edge of the small clearing they camped in. He sat down with his back to a big tree. He was trying to decide what to do, whether to leave the ladies and be on his way. They had, after all, made it noticeably clear that they did not need or want him around. Although he thought it was more for show and the benefit of their own pride. With only three of them left, all of them wounded, and one of them severely, it would be difficult for them to make it by themselves.

Still, his weird desire to go into the interior was always present; all these delays had not diminished the pressure he felt. Daniel did not know why there was such a strong urge to go east. He just felt compelled to be somewhere east on the Queen's Highway.

It was not really his decision, anyway; if they did not want him along, they would make it clear to him. He heard a sound from behind him, and slowly he turned onto his knees. As he eased himself to a standing position, he was able to see Cally walking casually through the trees. He gave out a low whistle so as not to startle her.

When she looked up, her face lit up as she saw Daniel. She quickly ran over to him and hugged him and said, "I wanted to thank you again for yesterday. You saved our lives by showing up when you did."

"I'm not sure your companions feel the same way," Daniel replied.

"Sergeant Sharon is like that with everyone. And my sister... well, my sister is kind of standoffish toward most men she li—well, toward most men."

Seeing her discomfort, Daniel changed the subject. "Where are you heading? And why are there so few of you in your party?"

Cally answered, "We started out with troops to protect us, but we were attacked by a whole army of goblins. It was horrible!"

As she thought about Carrie and Colleen, she began to cry. Daniel reached out to put his hand on her shoulder, and she just fell into his arms. She stayed there until she finished telling him the whole story except for the part about them being the heirs of the Three Sisters thrown. Sliding her arm around his waist and looking up at him with her eyes filled with infatuation, she said, "And that was when you appeared."

Daniel was extremely uncomfortable, so he gently removed her arms from around his waist, and he held her wrist and created some space between them. Hoping to distract her, he asked, "Where were you going?"

Smiling coyly at him, she replied, "We are headed to L'ke L'fe and then to Queens Castle Home."

He asked, "Why there?"

Cally explained, "We are going to watch the celebration of the fulfillment of the M'tin prophecy. All the royalty from every nation will be there. The leaders of the Pact of Brothers, even the leaders of the Eastern Kingdoms, will be there. Most of the seers and healers should be there too."

Daniel asked, "You all actually believe that a person is going to show up and say, 'Hi, everyone, I am your new king'? How do you even know if there is an heir?"

Cally countered, "The seers all believe his heir will come back. The healers have been looking for him for over 120 years. The prophecy says that when the darkness returns, the heir will come. As we have seen from the last few days, the darkness is certainly returning."

Slowly the other members of their party arose; they all began to pick up camp and prepared to leave. They headed out for the Troll Hills that lay between them and the Midland Plains.

Heading straight east, Daniel and the women started to climb the Troll Hills without incident. At noon they arrived on the ridge and they began to see hadrac and orc sign everywhere. They could easily see that they were on the edge of the Ebony Forest. The trees were of many different species here, and they were not quite as dense. There was a lot more underbrush and many kinds of flowers. They were leaving the darkness of the Ebony Forest and were emerging into some woods with far more life in it.

Daniel brought the group to a halt at some stone outcroppings. Looking around, he found a shallow cave. Turning to Alssa, he said, "The three of you can stay here, and I will scout to the south toward the Queen's Highway and see if we can get around these beasts."

Alssa stood defiant. "Why should you be the one to go? We are both fully capable to look around the area."

Daniel sighed. "Listen, lady. Someone needs to stay with Sergeant Sharon. She cannot keep up if I need to move quickly. And even you have to admit that my woodcraft is a lot better than yours."

To Daniel's surprise, Alssa did not continue to argue; she only turned and walked away.

Daniel spent two hours walking south, and the orc sign were more numerous. There were two or three times that he saw them moving in large groups through the trees. He was still quite some distance from the highway when he decided that this direction was not the way to go.

Turning around and heading north, he walked quickly but quietly. Suddenly, he sensed someone watching him. Slowly turning, his eyes alert for any movement, he searched the forest but saw nothing.

All the way back to the little cave, he was sure someone was following him, but no matter how many times he checked his back trail, he did not see anything but trees moving in the breeze.

Coming up over the small rise that marked the south edge of the rock outcropping, he stopped dead in his tracks; between him and the cave stood twenty hadrac. Dropping onto the ground, he crawled on his belly to several large boulders that were forty strides from the cave.

The hadrac action revealed to Daniel that they had not found the women, but they were milling around, looking for something. What should he do, stay put or rush them while their guard was down?

The hadrac made up his mind for him; one of them climbed up the rocks that shielded the cave mouth. As the hadrac reached the top, he turned to call out but instead tumbled forward, with two arrows sticking out of his back. The remaining beasts turned, watched the body bounce off the rocks and land at their feet. They howled as one as they ran toward the rocks. Daniel drew the sword and started the chant as he ran down the slight slope. He could see Alssa and Cally on top of the rocks with their bows, firing black shafts down into the mass of hadrac.

They never saw Daniel coming; he slew four of them before they even noticed that he was there. By the time they turned around, he dispatched two more. Once they turned their attention to him, the girls started hitting home.

In the course of just a few minutes, all twenty of them were dead. Daniel bent over, put his hands on his knees, and tried to catch his breath. Alssa and Cally came down the hidden trail to join him.

After Cally counted the bodies, there were nine with arrows sticking out of them; she said, "I still do not understand why they disappear like that when you kill them with the sword."

"I don't either," Daniel replied, then he said, "It never happened until I came here. Of course, I never battled hadrac and orcs until I came here."

Alssa cut in, "We better get moving. There are bound to be more of them."

As if on cue, a large group of man-orcs came loping down the road. The four in the lead did not stop but just charged at the humans standing in front of them.

Daniel ignited the sword and rushed out to meet them. Both Alssa and Cally drew back on their bows and let fly at the two man-orcs on the outside. Daniel jumped into the air and thrust his flaming sword down into the chest of the man-orc on the right. Landing on his right foot, he pivoted back to his left. Twisting his torso around hard and swinging the huge broadsword with all his might. He cut the last beast clean in two at the waist. Daniel retreated to Cally and Alssa.

The remaining group of man-orcs stopped as they watched the two animals that Daniel killed disappear before their eyes.

Daniel and the girls stood mystified. They were outnumbered ten-to-one.

Cally spoke for all three of them. "What are they doing? Why don't they attack?"

Daniel started to talk, but Alssa cut him off. "Quiet! They're talking."

It was true; they were speaking in common speech. The man-orc who appeared to be the leader was urging the others, "Get your ugly carcasses moving!"

A brave orc turned to face the speaker and said, "Whipmaster, the bodies of those killed by the burning blade disappeared. It is the Banisher."

The whipmaster snarled back and said, "And you have goblin spittle for brains! Attack, attack now!"

To accentuate the point, he lashed out with his whip, laying a large wound open on the chest of the brave orc who spoke out. This got the rest of them moving; however, they moved forward with great caution.

Alssa and Cally drew back on their bows and let fly with the black goblin shafts.

Alssa cried out, "Daniel, there are too many of them! We don't have nearly enough arrows."

Daniel planted his feet and turned toward the girls. "Get Sergeant Sharon and run! I will hold them off as long as I can."

Cally cried out, "No, we will not leave you! Come with us."

Daniel swore, "By the dark lords, we cannot leave Sergeant Sharon, and we will not outrun them with her. You must go now."

Alssa said, "He is right, Cally. We must go!"

The two ladies let go three more arrows apiece and then ran up to the cave to get Sergeant Sharon. Daniel turned to face his doom.

They did not appear any more eager than before to face the flaming sword. The whipmaster continued to bellow at his charges and put to the whip anyone who held back. Daniel knew he would not live through this mess, but he also knew if he fought well, he could hold the horde back for some time.

The air was dead calm; Daniel could smell the foul beasts that were moving to encircle him. Out of the corner of his eye, he could see the trees stirring, or more precisely, one tree moving. At first, only the branches moved, then it appeared to walk; the tree moved up behind the orcs. Daniel blinked his eyes and thought, *What is happening? Am I hallucinating?*

Then it was too late to worry about it; the beasts were upon him. Daniel started the sword chant once again, calling on the light as Nathan had taught him, adding the next verse that he never used before:

The darkness is dispelled by the light,
By the light all is made right.
With the light that dwells within,
I will fight this fight and win.

Suddenly, the sword took on a new intensity, a pure flame that burned blue. As Daniel looked up to battle the man-orcs, it was as if they were moving like drunkards, their every response slow and predictable. Daniel cut through the first wave of attackers like a hot knife through lard, six of the beasts disappearing into thin air before they hit the ground.

As Daniel sliced through two orcs in the second wave, he took a sword blow to his upper back. The blade did not penetrate his chain mail armor, but the stroke was strong enough to knock him two his knees. Instead of trying to stop himself, he let the force of the blow propel him into a forward roll, coming out of it on his feet. Unfortunately, he ended up surrounded by eight orcs. He raised the blade above his head. Somehow, he could feel energy flowing through him and into the blade. It shone more brilliant than ever before. The orcs recoiled, blinded by its brightness; even the whipmaster lost his speech for a moment. Only for a moment, the large beast raised his whip above his head, preparing to beat the rest into attacking Daniel. Suddenly, the whipmaster flew off the ground and went hurling into the boulders. His head cracked open, and his back snapped in half.

Daniel could not believe his eyes, as one after another the snarling, screaming beast went flying into the boulders to join their leader.

He was only able to kill two more before the small remainder ran off in the direction they had come. Daniel watched them leave and then turned to look at the broken bodies at the base of the boulders. Fifteen man-orcs lay dead and mangled. But how had it happened? Had the power of the sword grown again? Since he came to the Middle Kingdom, the sword had been changing, changing in ways that Daniel did not understand.

Daniel scratched his head in wonder as he turned to go after Alssa and Cally. His motion stopped as he staggered backward, raising his sword out in front of him.

Before him stood, a man, or at least it looked somewhat like a man; the creature was easily three times Daniel's height, six spans at least. Its head was huge, set above massive shoulders that held arms like the limbs of a giant oak. The arms hung down to its knees. At the end of the arms hung the largest hands Daniel had ever seen, hands that had six fingers. Each finger was as long as a short sword, but thicker than Daniel's forearms. The head and hands were overly large, even for the giant body that they were attached to; it had wrinkled skin, like the bark of a tree, and every part of its body had moss-like hair growing from it.

The legs of the giant were in proportion to its arms, long and thick, which ended in enormous feet, equal companions to the hands. Its skin was a greenish brown, but the color seemed to change as Daniel looked at it.

Daniel did not know what to do. He looked up into the massive face towering above him, into eyes that were dark brown and had whorls like that of a knot in wood.

Daniel called out weakly, "I have no wish to fight you, but I will if you force me."

There was a deep creaking sound, low and strong, like the timbers of a ship in a heavy gale. The sound grew louder and louder, until it sounded like thick tree limbs breaking in the wind. The giant before him began to shake, every part of its body convulsing in tremors.

Daniel thought, *Could this thing be laughing at me?* Daniel was perplexed and angry, so he said, "Are you mocking me?" Daniel called out defiantly, "Fight me or kill me, but don't mock me."

This only made the thing convulse harder, so hard, in fact, that it fell backward onto the ground. The force of the fall caused the ground to shake. The giant was now in a sitting position, its arms stretched out in front, almost touching its toes.

Daniel did not know what to do. He was too exhausted to do anything but sit down in the same position as the giant. They both looked at each other, the giant laughing, and Daniel breathing hard.

Chapter 30

Count Valkar walked slowly down the gangplank of the *Deep River Queen*, the small dirty single-mast scow he had booked passage on from K'la. The winds were contrary, so the trip took longer than expected.

Valkar scanned the city. The grandeur and elegance that had once graced L'ke L'fe had long since passed away. Most of the city stood abandoned. The decay of centuries evident wherever one looked. The rooflines swayed down like the back of an old horse; many gave way to the weight of last winters snow, and from the look of them, many more would give way in the next winter.

The tall count turned and began walking up the street toward the center of town. The cobblestones were broken and ragged, with many of the stones missing. The sewer gutter that ran down the center of the street was open; the flat stones that made up the cap had been stolen and used elsewhere. The gutter itself ran over with dirt and waste, the stench almost unbearable.

The loss of the shipping business had ruined L'ke L'fe's economy, and most of the buildings had their windows and doors boarded over with decking from salvaged vessels. A great number of buildings looked like they were the city's source of firewood. Stripped clean of trim, sash, steps, and timbers, with only the stones remaining, falling in on themselves with their supports removed.

There were no people on this end of town. The only sound Count Valkar could hear was the slow creaking of wagon wheels carrying the cargo from the *Deep River Queen.*

Valkar hoped the ship's delay had not cost him the chance to get ahead of Manslayer. L'ke L'fe was the perfect place to ambush the sword-for-hire. What Manslayer had said was not totally true; Valkar would certainly stand up to most men and take them on in an even fight. But Manslayer was not most men. Valkar took pride in his abilities but also took pride in his common sense. He knew there was no way he could beat Manslayer in a fair fight, so why try? It was more important to avenge his brother and live than to just avenge his brother.

He knew the type of people who inhabited towns like this; they only cared about themselves and would not be concerned about a stranger's death. In fact, this place reeked of death. Valkar could feel it. He had heard that the Middle Kingdom had become a haunt of thieves and murderers, but he would not have guessed that it had fallen into such chaos.

The Holy Lancers must have their hands full with the orcs and hadrac and had no time to deal with this human scum. They must be leaving that up to the local constables, who, it appeared, must also be corrupt. A smile came across Valkar's lips as he thought, *Yes, this is a perfect place to wait for Manslayer, and this time my crossbow will not miss.*

By the time Valkar found the center of town, he had come to another revelation: L'ke L'fe was crawling with Ramaahian spies. He had spotted many who he knew personally and many more who he could tell by the way they acted they were spies. They were dressed like the locals, and some as travelers, but they carried themselves in way that the trained eye could tell was not that of common folk.

He had chosen a tavern to ask a few questions and was about to enter when he saw the marquess Malasaad sitting at a table in the corner with some men who were obviously Ramaahian nobility.

What in the name of Valkira is he doing here? Valkar new the marquess personally; they had met before. However, they were not friends. In fact, Valkar would like to see his small nation remove itself from the empire.

Although Valkar believed that Valkarians were a better, more noble people than the rest of the nations in the Eastward, he still believed those nations served a place and purpose in an ordered society. Malasaad and the rest of the ruling class in the empire considered all other nations fit only for bondage or worse.

Valkar felt their ambitions and beliefs moved them too close to those of the Lords of Chaos. Though Valkar's gods were stern and demanding, they were not nearly as evil as the dark lords.

Still, the marquess might be a good source of information. Therefore, Valkar walked over to the corner table and, with a short bow, addressed Malasaad. "Your Excellency, how surprising to find you in this part of the world and in the company of such noble men." Valkar turned to the two other men sitting at the table and, with a twisted smile, said, "Ah, let's see, what do we have here? A couple of barons from Donnelly and Vickers, I would wager."

Glancing out of the corner of his eyes, Valkar frowned and said, "And the lumbering oaks standing behind me must be two of your renowned mindless warriors from Isle of Donnelly-Derdain."

Turning back to the marquess, he said, "I see we have every nation in the empire represented, except Valkar. No, wait, I am Valkarian. I guess we are all here."

Forcefully, Valkar asked, "And what is that we are here for, Malasaad? What is it that brings you to this remote, backward place?"

Malasaad waved his bodyguards away and sneered. "So, Valkar, Manslayer led you to the end of the world and you still have not been able to kill him. How long has it been, five years? For so long you have been trying to avenge the death of your brother. You Valkarians take this honor thing way too far. Tell me, Valkar, what honor lies in being continually embarrassed by this no-account thief?"

Valkar's hands shook and his eyes drilled holes into the marquess's face as he said, "An honor someone of your ilk would never understand."

The marquess laughed. "You should spend more time ruling your kingdom and less time defending your honor, or you may have no kingdom to rule."

"Is that a threat?" Valkar asked.

"No threat. I am just telling you the way it is. Times have changed, the empire has changed, and it will no longer be held back by the limited vision of the confederated kingdoms. The empire is removing the bonds that have held it captive and kept it from its rightful position of ruling all the Eastward. Soon all lands in the east will be a part of the empire, and nothing will be able to come against us, not even this silly prophecy and its dubious heir."

So that was it; the emperor had finally been convinced that the prophecy might be true, and must be taking steps to prevent it. Valkar thought, *What a load of ox beast droppings!* Then he said, So you think I am wasting my time hunting down a murderer, yet you are sitting here in a filthy, run-down tavern, in the middle of an abandoned and cursed land, waiting for the mythical return of a king. You are the pathetic one, Malasaad. The emperor picked the right mook to greet the new king."

The marquess stood up with such force his chair crashed into the wall, his sword leaping into his hand. Both of the marquess's bodyguards rushed forward and grabbed Valkar by the arms. With the tip of his sword pressed against Valkar's chest, Malasaad mocked Valkar. "You and your puny country are insignificant in the plans of the empire. Your family has restricted the emperor and his desires with your cowardice for too long. One less Valkarian will only make the empire stronger."

Baron Chalsmore stood up hurriedly, wringing his hands. "Marquess, you must not do this. We cannot expose ourselves so soon."

Malasaad chuckled and said, "No one would miss this cur."

"But his murder would draw attention. He is of no account to us. Just send him on his way and be done with him," Baron Dash interjected nervously.

Malasaad spoke to Count Valkar. "I happen to know that you and your fellow assassins have been ordered by the emperor to kill the princesses of House J'te and House L'se from the Three Sisters, but instead you are still pursuing Manslayer. Who is the pathetic one? The emperor will not tolerate your disobedience." Nodding to the Donnelly soldiers, he said, "Throw him out in the street, and be rough about it." Speaking to Valkar, he said, "Stay out of my way and out of my business, Valkarian."

Valkar ended up in a heap, thrown against the building opposite of the tavern. The two Donnelly warriors had taken turns smashing his face with their giant fist and kicking his ribs with their armored boots.

Rising from the broken cobblestones, he spit out the blood that flowed from his mouth and nose. Every breath he took sent a stabbing pain up his side. Valkar knew his ribs were broken. He stumbled down the street, looking for an inn and someone to help him as he thought, *I have received no command to assassinate the future queens of the Three Sisters. What is going on here? This must be why there are so many assassins here all waiting for the princesses to show up.* Finding an inn, he made his way to the front desk to get a room and rest.

CHAPTER 31

As Daniel stood in disbelief and wonder at the seated giant, a different sound began to emerge, a sound like the soft rustle of the breeze blowing through the leaves. At first, Daniel could not make out what it said, but slowly he began to hear what he thought were words. The words where long, stretched out, and each syllable had other sounds mixed in, the sharp, clear sound of instruments. The notes of the music wrapped themselves around each word.

The music was complex; Daniel could hear flutes, harps, and the soft tapping of drums and cymbals. The sound was so soothing that he lowered his sword and stared entranced at the thing sitting before him.

Suddenly, he could understand the behemoth's words as it said, "We have been watching you, Lightbearer, and you are truly strong and courageous. The mighty relic you wield testifies of your virtue and promise. I have been sent to see you safely through our forest."

Daniel was stunned, his mind spinning like a top. The sounds were so beautifully melodic, and it filled him with peace. "Who are you? What are you? Why are you here? Why did you help me?"

The monster treelike being sitting before him began to chuckle, a chuckle that resonated through the forest around him. "Ha, ha, ha, you ask many questions, Lightbearer." The being rose to its feet/roots and then bowed toward Daniel. "I am Oaklawn, son of Oakglade, servant of the most majestic queen of light." As Oaklawn spoke, he transformed into a giant oak tree.

Daniel took two steps back, not sure that he was conscious. He thought, *Maybe I'm dreaming, or maybe I'm dead. This cannot be real!* Daniel turned around quickly as he heard another voice.

"Daniel, are you okay?" Cally called out as she ran up to hug him.

Daniel hugged her back. "I'm fine. Are you guys all right?"

Alssa came walking up with Sergeant Sharon leaning on her shoulder. "We are fine. Whom were you talking to?"

Daniel started to point toward Oaklawn, but he was still an oak tree. "I'm not sure. I think I was hallucinating."

Cally and Alssa gave Daniel a funny look. Cally started to speak, but the booming sound of laughing drums interrupted her.

"Ho, ho, ho, you are not seeing things, Lightbearer. I am still here!" The oak tree morphed back into its manlike appearance.

Alssa's sword leaped into her hand. "Daniel, look out! You don't know what you are dealing with!"

Daniel gave her a quizzical look. "I know, but he was about to tell me when you showed up." Daniel turned to face Oaklawn and gestured to the three women. "Oaklawn, these are Alssa, Cally, and Sergeant Sharon. Ladies, this Oaklawn, son of Oakglade."

The giant bowed to the three women. "I recognize two of you. You both dwell in radiance. The light runs in your blood. Though, in the third, I see no light in your veins, I distinctly smell the odor of courage and sacrifice."

Daniel smiled at Oaklawn's perceptiveness. "You speak kindly for a…ahm what are you?"

"I can tell you what he is," Alssa barked. "He's a troll!"

"I am honored that you know what I am, daughter of light." The troll tipped his head.

Alssa spit out, "Don't be! I intended no honor in my remark."

Cally frowned at her sister but said to the troll, "My sister means no disrespect with her words, noble Oaklawn."

Alssa growled at Cally, "Sister, don't apologize for me and don't speak for me! I have no reason to show respect for a troll, and every reason to mistrust one."

Oaklawn stood erect and made a whistling sound. "Why, daughter of light, are you filled with such darkness for the humble servants of the queen of light?"

Alssa did not answer; she just turned and helped Sergeant Sharon sit down against the rocks. Cally watched her sister, then turned back to Daniel and the troll. "Again, I regret my sister's actions. She had a tragic experience with some trolls up in the Rodones highlands."

Daniel liked the Rodones and had been to their high mountain country a few times in the last few years. "I didn't know there were trolls in Rodon."

Oaklawn laughed again. "Lightbearer, there are trolls everywhere! But we prefer to keep to ourselves."

Alssa snorted in disgust.

Cally quickly started talking before Alssa could say anything. "We had taken a company of troopers up into the highlands to help the Rodones with a large group of Ramaahian pirates. The pirates lived in a secluded inlet on the north coast. We surprised them early one morning, and they fled into the mountains. They hid in a cave up above the snow line, and as we prepared to extract them by force, they suddenly burst out of the cave on their own. They quickly surrendered to us and begged for our protection.

"Alssa and I rode up to the cave's mouth, but the horses refused to go in. We dismounted and entered; the smell of rotting flesh almost overcame us."

Alssa was standing next to Cally, her face twisted in anger as she listened to the story. Oaklawn had sat back down and transformed halfway between the form of a man and a large tree.

Cally continued, "The cave was large, over ten spans high. Bones were strewn all over the floor, human bones. We could see no one, so we turned to go. Suddenly, I was lifted off the ground, caught in a viselike grip of fingers made of stone.

"I dangled four spans in the air as the stone hand turned me around so that I was looking at the wall of the cave. Slowly a face appeared, and then the body. It was a cave troll."

"Oh, that is not good. Of all the trolls, rock trolls have suffered the worst at the hands of humans. But they would not have dared hurt you. Even a slow-witted rock troll would have seen the light in your veins," Oaklawn interjected as he shook his massive head.

Cally nodded. "No, the cave troll did not try to hurt me, but unfortunately, that didn't stop the tragedy from happening. We had riding with us Prince Johann, son of the king and heir to the Rodones throne. He had followed us into the cave, and when he saw me trapped in the hands of a cave troll, he took it upon himself to try to free me. The troll tried to turn away, covering me with his body. The prince hit the troll several times with his sword with little effect.

"The troll reached back and pushed him away. Unfortunately, the prince tripped over a large rock and hit his head, killing him."

Oaklawn moaned a moan that made the trees shake. "That is sad, so sad. Was the prince close to the daughter of light?"

Cally glanced at Alssa, who had returned to looking after Sergeant Sharon. "Yes, they were engaged to be married. It would be the marriage that would unite Rodon and Lystia with the Three Sisters forever."

Oaklawn transformed into a willow. "Ooh, poor daughter of light. The grief you must bear, my soul weeps for you."

Alssa spun around. "I don't want your sympathy, troll."

Cally continued the story. "When the prince fell, a number of Rodones soldiers saw part of what happened, and they demanded the death of the troll. In Alssa's grief and anger, she relented to the Rodones and killed the troll."

At this, Oaklawn stood back up and howled. "Oh, darkness, darkness, darkness erodes the light! My sorrow is even greater for you, daughter of light. Oh, curse the darkness!"

"Stupid trolls! What was I supposed to do? The Rodones would have rebelled if something weren't done." Alssa was not really talking to anyone; she was looking up into the tops of the trees. But Daniel was sure he saw a tear run down her face when she said, "Stupid man, why did he have to try and be a hero?"

Cally moved over to Alssa's side to comfort her. Daniel wished he could do that, but the whole situation had made him uncomfortable. So instead, he turned to Oaklawn and asked, "What is the difference between cave trolls and forest trolls?"

Oaklawn sighed deeply, causing a symphony of sorrowful sounds to resonate through the forest around them. Then he said, "Lightbearer, first, they are not cave trolls, they are rock trolls. You use words that describe the region we inhabit. All trolls of light prefer to be known by the nature of their organic power. I am a tree troll, not a forest troll.

"The troll that daughter of light spoke of is a rock troll. There are water trolls, sand trolls. Trolls live for many of your lifetimes. I was born before the time of the queen of light, and my father was here when the dark lords brought chaos to the land.

"You must understand that the light created all things. Thus, all things created have the power of the light. The light created us trolls to husband its creation."

Daniel was not sure he understood what Oaklawn was talking about, but what he did know was that most of the tales he had heard about trolls were negative. All that he was hearing here now was new to him, so he asked, "Oaklawn, are there other types of trolls, evil trolls?"

The troll started to shake with anger as he said, "You speak things you should not speak. Those things you speak of are abominations that have left their former estate to take the form of evil beasts, corrupted by darkness. They have no place in the world of light." Oaklawn stopped talking and transformed into a towering oak tree.

Daniel looked at him and shrugged, then turned around to talk to Alssa and Cally and asked, "Are you guys okay?"

As Alssa regained her composure, she replied, "I'm okay, but I will be better when we get away from this troll."

As if on cue, Oaklawn transformed back into his manlike form and, for a troll, spoke very quickly. "My siblings say that a great evil is moving toward us. We must leave here at once."

Alssa stood erect and announced, "I will not travel with a troll. I would rather face a hundred orcs!"

Cally was starting to get angry at her sister and said, "Alssa, you are being rude. Oaklawn has done nothing to you, and he saved Daniel's life. I think he deserves more respect than you are giving him."

Alssa replied bitterly, "I have no respect for trolls. They have their own agenda, which you cannot trust. They only come around when they feel like it. They are undependable, unpredictable, and untrustworthy. We are better off without them."

Oaklawn sighed a reply. "The daughter of light is correct. We do not serve men, we serve the light, and we must be faithful to the light. Therefore, there have been times when men have felt we were not faithful to them, but at this time, we both are serving the light. We must go. The evil draws closer, and it is very dark."

Cally and Daniel stared at Alssa without saying anything.

Alssa said sarcastically, "What? Must I repeat myself? I have already told you how I feel. We go our own way."

Suddenly, Oaklawn reached down, scooped up Sergeant Sharon, and cradled her in his arms.

"What do you think you are doing? Put her down! I order it." Alssa's face was crimson, her sword leaping back into her hand.

"Daughter of light, it is too late." The troll's head motioned down the trail. "The evil is here. We must flee!"

The four humans looked up the trail, and to their horror, their eyes beheld the evil Oaklawn warned them about.

The man-orcs filled the trail, tightly packed in the front. Hadrac followed the orcs, grunting and growling, swinging their giant axes above their heads. Daniel could hear wolves snarling in the woods on either side of the trail, which could only mean goblins.

However, the giant beast that followed behind the orcs sent shivers of fear down the humans' spines. It was as if they emerged from Daniel's imagination, giant, filthy, muscle-bound monsters. They were swinging giant clubs that were as big as tree limbs. Daniel could sense something else about them, but he could not quite get ahold of what it was. Daniel looked up at Oaklawn and asked, "Are those what I think they are?"

"Yes, Lightbearer, ogres."

CHAPTER 32

Commander Westolve and her depleted company had ridden hard all through the previous night and into the morning. Their horses were completely exhausted, as were all the troopers. She could hardly keep herself in the saddle in her weary state.

Westolve's mind was churning over the events of the last few days. In her admiration of T'asha's strength, she had not realized the horror of what they were doing. Allowing the goblins to reproduce at such a prolific rate had been a great risk. And now it seemed to be shortsighted. How could they possibly believe that the goblins would honor their side of the deal? Especially a deal with the women of the Three Sisters.

T'asha was going to return to Jukeele by herself to execute the second half of her plan. Westolve questioned whether T'asha would even make it back to the capital city with the goblins loose. How could they be so shortsighted?

On top of all that, T'asha had left orders for her blood sister, Nadja, to stay at Devil's Pass with just a small force to prevent Alssa and Cally from crossing through into the Middle Kingdom. If the goblins instead crossed over the pass, Nadja and her troops would surely all be killed. It sent a shiver up Westolve's back with the revelation of what T'asha was becoming. Her queen ordered her to get to L'ke L'fe as quickly as possible to prepare for the arrival of the Three Sisters entire army and to deal with Alssa and Cally if they made it that far.

Lieutenant Palin rode up next to her and said, "Ma'am, the troops cannot go on much longer. They are falling asleep in the saddle. If we run into any more opposition, they will not be able to put up much of a fight in their fatigued state."

The lieutenant's comments pulled Westolve from her thoughts. She snapped a sharp response at the lieutenant. "The troops are fine. I think it is you who is tired and are using the troops as an excuse."

Lieutenant Palin's face blanched white in disbelief, then slowly turned red in anger as she said, "Commander Westolve, I take offense at that accusation. I am only looking out for the welfare of the troops!"

Commander Westolve sat up straight in her saddle. Lieutenant Palin's rebuke shook her from her dark mood, and she thought, *I am lashing out like T'asha.* Her shoulders slumped as she realized how much she was acting like her queen.

Two years ago, she joined T'asha's house guard and was given her special assignment at Castle in the Gorge. She had been a young lieutenant then. She had been serving in Alssa's house guard, moving quickly through the ranks. It was after meeting the famous twins Colleen and Carrie that she knew what she wanted to be, the personal bodyguard to one of the future queens. It did not take her long to recognize that the twins were not going anywhere and that she would never be able to take their place. She intentionally pursued service with House K'jo as T'asha's personal guard.

She made captain almost immediately and was placed in charge of the company of swords. It was then she discovered there was a vast difference between serving the House N'ta and House K'jo. At first, she had attributed the difference to House N'ta having a ruling queen and House K'jo's queen having died.

After some time, though, she came to understand there was resentment and animosity between the houses because the law forbade Megan from becoming queen. It was not long before she came to agree with House K'jo, and she had developed a strong sympathy for T'asha's and Megan's plight.

Even though she never observed Alssa or Cally show any disrespect toward T'asha, she felt T'asha was justified in her feelings.

That sympathy turned into feelings of love. And now she realized it was that loved that blinded her to T'asha's transformation. She could now plainly see the consequences of that animosity; she was struck with grief. She groaned deeply and bent forward in the saddle.

Lieutenant Palin misread the action for exhaustion and said, "Commander, even you are falling asleep. We must stop and let the troops rest."

Westolve turned to look at the young lieutenant, and with a weak smile she said, "You are right, of course. Why don't you ride down the line and let everyone know that we will be stopping at the next opportunity?"

When the lieutenant returned, Commander Westolve again apologized for snapping at her. "Thank you, Lieutenant, for doing your job. We will be stopping soon. If I remember correctly, the Oschner farmstead is just up ahead. We will come to a sharp bend in the road, and then we will be upon it. They have a water well and probably some fodder for the horses we can purchase. You will like this place. They are really nice people, very hospitable, and Mrs. Oschner makes wonderful pies."

The lieutenant rubbed her belly and said, "That sounds delicious."

Sure enough, after they rounded the bend, the farmstead came into view. But it was not what Commander Westolve remembered. It had never been a fancy home, just a nice, sturdy cottage with a privy, a smokehouse, a small storage shed, and a barn. But now the outbuildings were all falling over, and the cottage was sagging in the middle. The door was torn off the hinges, and the windows were gone.

Lieutenant Palin exhaled hard and commented, "Looks like there will be no pie tonight."

Westolve was disappointed and concerned, so she said, "I know that there has been a lot of orc and hadrac activity, but I didn't think it was bad enough to produce this. We are not that far from H'la and the Holy Lancers. I cannot believe they are not protecting settlements this close to H'la. Lieutenant, we will only rest for fifteen minutes. Now, I want to be in H'la before nightfall."

The lieutenant had turned her horse to leave when Westolve added, "And, Lieutenant, post pickets, I am not at all comfortable with this situation."

Palin saluted and said, "Yes, ma'am."

After resting for fifteen minutes, Westolve had them all back in the saddle, and they covered the last few miles to H'la quickly. Upon arriving at the gate, they were greeted with suspicion by the town's guards. And even though the guards opened the gate without question, their looks made it clear they were not as welcome as Westolve felt they should be.

H'la was built astride the crossroads of the Queen's Highway that ran east and west, and the Coast Road that ran north and south. The Queen's Highway was the main street, and most of the businesses were built along it. Westolve led her company off the Coast Road onto the Queen's Highway, heading west.

Arriving in front of the Inn of H'la, she turned to Lieutenant Palin and ordered, "Take the company out the west gate. There will be a big open field where you can set up camp. We will rest here for two days before we move on to L'ke L'fe. Use the script to purchase any supplies we need."

Westolve dismounted and handed her reins to a trooper who would look after her mount. As the company moved off, she looked around. Up the street a ways was the Boars Brisket, which she remembered from her childhood.

She had been through H'la many times when she was young. Her mother would take her to the Pact of Brothers to see family. As they traveled through the Middle Kingdom, they would stop and stay in H'la. It had always seemed like a grand adventure back then.

The Three Sisters and the Holy Lands were so modern, clean, and safe, as opposed to the Middle Kingdom, which was old, dark, and dangerous. They would never have any trouble on those trips, but she always imagined fighting orcs and thieves as they traveled. In her imagination, she was always the heroine. Wielding a broadsword, she would vanquish the beast one by one, saving her mother and the guards from the dark evil.

A smile came to Westolve's lips as she thought of the past, but it was quickly replaced by grimace of pain. Now that she was battling the beasts for real, it was not a grand adventure. Instead it had become a series of terrifying encounters that cost the lives of people she cared about.

She shook off her feeling and entered the inn. Stopping for a moment before sitting down to let her eyes adjust to the bright light. After looking around, she was surprised to see eight officers of the Pact of Brothers sitting at two tables in the corner. While moving to an open table, she thought, *Why are there eight officers here? Normally, a lancer patrol only has one officer. So even if both patrols were here at the same time, there would only be two officers.* Then she noticed the uniforms of the two groups were different from each other. Yes, the close table were officers of the Holy Lancers, but the other table were infantry. With eight officers that would mean that there were at least two full companies with over two hundred men. *Why?* she mused.

The serving girl interrupted her thoughts. "What would you like to eat, ma'am?"

Westolve looked up at the girl without seeing her. Her thoughts were on the men at the other tables. She absently responded, "Whatever your main dish is will be fine."

The girl made no move to leave but just looked at the commander.

Annoyed, Westolve questioned, "What is it, girl? Speak up!"

With a small step back, the girl replied, "Well, ma'am, the owner says we have to make all Three Sisters customers pay in advance."

Westolve looked at her in disbelief as she pulled some script from her tunic pocket. "I find this offensive, but if that is what he wishes…" She held out the script to the girl, but the girl did not take it.

As she pushed the script toward the girl again, the serving maid said, "I'm so sorry, ma'am, but he said we can only accept gold or silver, no script."

Westolve's anger began to rise. "You are saying that he will not accept the queen's script? Go tell him I want to talk to him."

The girl's eyes had filled with fear as she curtsied and hurried out of the room. No sooner had she left than Lieutenant Palin rushed hurriedly through the door. Her paced slowed as she noticed the Pact of Brothers officers.

Not taking her eyes off the two tables, she spoke quietly to Commander Westolve. "Ma'am, the western field is filled with Pact of Brothers soldiers, nearly two hundred of them. We will have to find somewhere else to camp."

Westolve was not surprised, but she was curious. Standing, she walked toward the two tables. Looking at the men, she found it hard to pick out who was the senior officer. The Pact of Brothers officers wore so much embellishment on their uniforms it was hard to tell one rank from the other. As she began to speak, all the men quickly glanced at the man with bushy sideburns and gold epaulets on both shoulders. That would mean he was a major.

Westolve gave him a sharp nod. "Major, I am Commander Westolve of House K'jo's royal guard. And the personal attaché to Her Royal Highness Princess T'asha K'jo."

The major acknowledged her with a nod, but he did not rise to greet her as he should. And instead of a formal response, he said, "First, I am a lieutenant colonel, and second, you are a long way from home, Commander. What are you doing this far south in our territory?"

Westolve was shocked by the lieutenant colonel's lack of military protocol as well as his claim that the Middle Kingdom was the Pact of Brothers territory. She responded strongly, "I am on the queen's business. Am I to understand by your statement that Brother Samuel now claims the Middle Kingdom as part of the Pact of Brothers Kingdom?"

The colonel chuckled. "Commander, I am sure you are aware that the Pact of Brothers have kept the peace in the Middle Kingdom for over a hundred years. Our possession of this land is not in question but a fact of history. So I think it would be best if you and your women return to the Wasteland to play at soldiering."

Lieutenant Palin blurted out, "You will speak to the commander with respect, you arrogant—"

Commander Westolve interrupted Lieutenant Palin before she could finish. "That will be enough, Lieutenant! You may return to the troops and move them to the east of the town."

The colonel spoke out quickly. "No! You cannot go to the east. No one is allowed east on the Queen's Highway without the permission of Brother Samuel. So unless you have a letter from the Crown stating such, you cannot go east!"

Lieutenant Palin stopped on her way to the door and turned abruptly. "Who does this man think he is ordering you about?"

But Commander Westolve spoke to her in her most foreboding voice. "Lieutenant Palin, I gave you an order. Do not make me repeat it."

Lieutenant Palin spun back around and stomped her boot prints into the floor on her way to the door, but she did not leave.

Westolve smiled, looking at the colonel first, and then panning around to the rest of the officers. She reached into her tunic pocket and pulled out some folded papers.

T'asha had given her the papers at Devil's Pass before she left. The letter made no sense to her then, but now it did. T'asha must have an agreement with Lord Samuel to keep Alssa and Cally away from L'ke L'fe. Westolve shook her head at the thought of how many layers of deception T'asha had created in her quest to destroy the other members of the triumvirate.

Westolve slowly unfolded the thick expensive paper that held Brother Samuel's signature and the writ of permission to proceed east on the Queen's Highway. With a smile, she handed it to the lieutenant colonel and said, "You will see that I do have the necessary permission."

The lieutenant colonel stood up as he read the paper. The disbelief on his face quickly faded into a knowing smirk. He gave her a short bow and said, "I am Lieutenant Colonel Barnes, and I am sorry for the confusion and my lack of decorum, Commander Westolve. You may move your troops east of the town at your convenience. If you or your troops are in need of anything else, please do not hesitate to let me know."

"Thank you, Colonel." Without turning to look, she said, "Lieutenant Palin, please move the troops to the east of H'la. Keep them close to the walls and make sure they know not to venture into the forest alone." Then addressing the lieutenant colonel, she said, "Thank you, Lieutenant Colonel Barnes. I believe we have everything we need."

With a smile, he responded, "Will you be staying here in the inn tonight?"

"No, I will be sleeping with my troops," she replied. She frowned just a bit as she remembered that the Pact of Brothers liked to keep an obvious distance between their officers and enlisted troops.

She noticed the look of disapproval on the lieutenant colonel's face as she turned to return to her table. As she approached the table, there was a man standing between her and her chair, so she asked, "Excuse me, sir?"

With impatience in his voice, he said, "I am the owner, and my serving girl said you wanted to talk to me?"

Westolve asked, "Yes, your girl said that you would not accept the queen's script. Is that true?"

Glancing at Lieutenant Colonel Barnes, the owner responded loudly, "This is the Middle Kingdom, and we hold our allegiance to the Pact of Brothers, not you or your kind."

Westolve was about to respond when Colonel Barnes intervened. "Commander, please excuse this simple man's rudeness. He is only a peasant and does not realize who he is addressing." Turning to the owner of the inn, he said, "You will be most happy to accept any form of payment that the commander offers, wouldn't you?"

The innkeeper shuffled his feet in resignation, but anger mixed with fear covered his face. "Colonel, I cannot use their worthless paper in trade with other business owners, and you know it."

Lieutenant Colonel Barnes shook his head and said, "Nevertheless, you will take the script of our ally and the brothers will make it good in gold."

Shocked at the colonel's offer, he blurted out, "Well, okay, but I don't like doing business with these women in any case."

As the innkeeper walked away, the colonel said, "I am sorry for his behavior. It will not happen again, and if you have any more problems like this with other businesses, I will be happy to speak with them also."

Westolve nodded a thank-you and sat down.

All during the meal, she struggled to put what had just transpired into the big picture. The lieutenant colonel is obviously aware to some degree of what was transpiring with T'asha's plan. Referring to as an ally after he had seen the letter from Lord Samuel confirmed that there was a commitment between the two leaders. The only reason to close the Queen's Highway would be to stop Alssa and Cally from reaching L'ke L'fe. This made Westolve even more uncomfortable with T'asha's plan. The Pact of Brothers would only involve themselves if they saw an opportunity of a large reward. How far were T'asha and Megan willing to go in their quest for power and control?

Finishing her meal, she arose and dropped a plentiful amount of script on the table. She nodded at the other officers as she walked out the door, taking a deep breath to clear her head. She was still wrestling with the information as she walked toward the east gate. She could only come up with two clear thoughts. First, she felt dirty on the inside with all that had transpired around her, and second, she would lead her company away from H'la at first light.

CHAPTER 33

Oaklawn led them north back the way the three of them had just come. As they ran, Daniel could hear trees breaking and orcs screaming. The crashing sound was behind them and on both sides. He could sense the trolls and ogres; he could tell they were out there moving. His senses were keener than they had ever been. He could even feel the animals that were fleeing from the evil beasts. Then suddenly, all the sensations stopped.

Daniel came to a dead stop, and he asked, "Oaklawn, what just happened? It's as if all living things just disappeared."

Oaklawn stopped next to Daniel and transformed again, but this time he was pure white, white like the bark of a birch tree, only instead of leaves his extremities emitted light. In fact, his entire body glowed.

Oaklawn replied, "Lightbearer, we have entered the crook."

Daniel looked around. The forest seemed to change. The trees were magnificent. Instead of the ebony color of the forest they just left, there were many different species. The trees were old, but vibrant and full of life.

Daniel asked, "What difference does 'entering the crook' make?"

Oaklawn explained, "Few humans even know the crook exists, and most of them would be unable to enter it even if they tried. The Ebony Forest is at its densest here, and the area is warded against evil. Even the ogres with their dark powers are unable to penetrate the ward."

Daniel did not know if he believed in an invisible shield that prevented people from moving through the forest, but it sure felt different. The forest was so dense it was hard to see the trail. The forest canopy completely blocked out the sky, but the trees seemed to produce a light of their own. If their pursuers continued, they would be hard-pressed to find them—the forest was so close. It seemed to Daniel that they might have problems finding their own way out. The branches blocked their path until they touched them, and then they moved out of the way.

Daniel was sure their progress was slowed considerably. By the end of the day, he figured they were no more than a few thousand paces beyond where they entered. He had started looking for a place to stop for the night when they broke out into a clearing, and to his amazement, there was what looked like a building in the middle of it.

Daniel stared at the small building, but it was not a building at all; it was something formed out of trees and plants. There was an entry on the short side of the structure, and on the long side it had three openings that looked like windows. The openings shimmered in different colors.

On one end of the canopy of branches, there sat a chimneylike growth. On the other was a steeple fashioned out of branches from a tree Daniel had never seen before.

Daniel's amazement turned into perplexity. How could this structure be here? They were deep in the Ebony Forest, an area controlled by the hadrac. The hadrac never left anything made by human hands remain standing. They would dig and pry and pound until every stone or piece of wood was removed. Then they would cart the stones away, and in a short time, you would not be able to tell that humans had even been there. Even the towers and forts that the queen erected in the Ebony Forest had been torn down. So how did this structure escape their attention?

Daniel voiced his opinion. "How can this place be here?" Cally laughed aloud.

Sergeant Sharon moaned out a painful laugh.

And Alssa snorted in contempt.

"What have I said that is so funny?" Daniel questioned.

Alssa spit out, "Your ignorance amazes me. You have never heard of the abbey of light or of the power that dwells here?"

"No," Daniel responded.

Alssa turned her back on him and walked to the opening that would be a door on a normal building.

Cally stepped toward him and leaned in close. "Don't pay any attention to her. She is always like this when she comes here."

As they both followed Sergeant Sharon into the chapel, the growth blocking the entry swung away on its own so they could pass through.

The abbey was unoccupied and held no furnishings. Daniel had expected to find a dirt floor, but instead the floor was of wood planks, but the planks were not planking at all. The floor had no marks from human tools, and somehow, it appeared to be alive.

As Daniel looked around, he asked, "This structure, how can it exist?"

Then he looked at the window openings from the inside; they were actually pictures, like you would find in the stained glass window, but there was no glass.

Daniel shook his head in bewilderment as he asked, "What is this place? It looks like an abbey, but it looks and feels alive."

Daniel walked over to one of the windows and reached out to touch the image, but his hand passed right through it and the picture disappeared. He quickly pulled his hand back, and the picture reappeared.

Daniel turned around in circles, looking at all the windows opening with shimmering pictures. Looking up at the ceiling, he noticed it was made from living plants and trees. It left him speechless. Unable to think of anything to say, he stared at Alssa and thought, *This place is almost as beautiful as you.*

Alssa stared back and then asked sarcastically, "You really haven't heard of this place?"

"No," Daniel responded weakly.

Alssa responded derisively, "If you knew anything about the history of this land. you would know about this abbey."

Daniel ignored her tone and said, "I had heard of places like this in some wild tales, but I thought it was a myth, just like the stories about the trolls."

Alssa retorted, "Well, they aren't myths, as you can plainly see."

Daniel asked, stammering, "How was this place made? Who made it? When was it made and why?"

All three of the ladies were looking past him to the entry. Oaklawn was bent over, looking in at them, with his head filling the entire opening. It looked like he was grinning, if it were possible for a tree to grin.

Daniel looked at the ladies, pointed at Oaklawn, and said, "Him?"

All three nodded in unison.

Oaklawn let out a hearty laugh and said, "I told you that I am a young troll, but very old by human standards. The queen of light asked me to make it for her youngest son. Daniel, this is what tree trolls do. We husband the light's creation. The light has given us the ability to create the most beautiful things. This is not one of them. It is not a natural from. But I serve the light, and the queen did ask nicely."

Daniel's head was spinning. So many new things were happening all around him. He thought, *Is this why Nathan encouraged me to come here?*

"Daniel, come here," Cally said, pulling him out of his confused stupor.

She said, "The story of this place can be seen in the shimmering windows. Each panel tells a different event. It starts here with the original Three Sisters on horseback. Three hundred years ago, they left the Middle Kingdom with the blessing of their mother, the great queen, she was depicted sitting on a throne. The sisters had asked permission to rid the Northern Lands of the dark evil."

"Who is the man walking away from them?"

"That is their little brother, M'tin. He disappeared after the queen decreed that he would be her heir to the throne."

Daniel commented, "I have heard some part of this. He marries a common farm girl, against the will of his mother, and they run away together."

"Well…that is not quite accurate, or at least that is not the story the windows tell. This next window shows what happened."

It was a picture of the three warrior women with many soldiers standing around a post with empty manacles hanging from it.

"The Three Sisters had caught up with M'tin and the girl on this very spot. They confronted him and put the girl in irons, planning to take them both back to Queens Castle Home. In the night, M'tin and the girl escaped, and they fled through the Ebony Forest and into the Goblin Valley. The next morning, the Three Sisters set out to look for them but never found them. For three weeks they searched. They could only assume that the goblins had caught them."

"But no one knew for sure," Alssa whispered dejectedly.

"What did the sisters do?" Daniel asked.

Cally continued as they moved down to the next window. This one had a picture of the Twin Rivers, but instead of blue for the water, it was red. Standing on the volcanic rock were the sisters, each with tears flowing down their faces, and all around them lay the corpse of humans, hadrac, orcs, and goblins.

Cally said, "This one depicts the Battle of Blood on the Twin Rivers."

"Where the greatest army of evil was ever assembled," Alssa boasted.

"That part of the story is well-known," retorted Daniel.

Cally looked crossly at both of them and then directed their attention to the next panel. This one showed the sisters in caves, slaughtering goblins.

Cally continued, "After the Battle of Blood, the sisters turned their attention solely on the goblins. In their anger over the loss of their brother. they hunted the goblins into near extinction. Only at the end did L'se overcome her grief and convince her older sisters to stop before they became like the very enemy they were trying to destroy. They relented and let a handful of goblins live."

Angrily, Alssa said, "Yes, and we almost paid for it with our lives just a few days ago. The goblins have started reproducing in greater numbers, apparently, right under Count Gravelet's nose."

Thinking Alssa was going to launch into another diatribe, Cally quickly explained the last window. "This window is the most important. The Three Sisters met their future husbands and came back here. The great queen had Oaklawn build this abbey, and they were married. They did this as a tribute to M'tin and to covenant together to keep the family name intact."

"This is why we women control the Three Sisters and men take the women's name, to continue the queen's heritage and to try to return a male heir to the throne of the Middle Kingdom."

Looking closely at the next window, Daniel asked, "Why are the three waterfalls of the Goblin Valley included with the chapel wedding scene?"

Smiling, Cally cooed, "That is why this one is so important. The sisters were married, and as they left with their grooms, each one of them stopped at one of the falls, starting with the eldest to the youngest, as they worked their way up the valley. They then spent their first night together under the stars, with the falling water serenading them. That was how the falls were named. It was like having a wedding veil provided by nature. Isn't that romantic, Daniel?"

"Yeah, real romantic! Cally, sometimes your youth reveals your foolishness. The way you carry on about such things! Marriage is important, but it isn't like...well, I don't know what it isn't like, but I'm sure it's not what you think it is."

The frustration and resentment poured out of Alssa as her voice cracked and tears welled up in her eyes. She turned on her heels and stormed out the entrance.

Daniel watched her rush out.

Bewildered, he said, "Wow! I guess marriage is a subject she does not enjoy talking about?"

"Unfortunately, you're right," Cally replied. Then she continued, "It was not always this way. Alssa has been betrothed two different times. We have already told you about the first one. The last man was much older than her, and not from the Three Sisters. We all thought he was a rogue, but she would not listen. When he left her standing alone at the altar, she became angry and bitter.

"We thought she was getting better when we sailed up to the Brigand Islands to deal with the pirates. We hoped it would give her something to take her mind off him, but it only allowed her to bury her pain deeper. She took her bitterness and anger out on the pirates. I do not think they will ever forget her. She was quite ruthless! It left them in great fear.

"Now she avoids men and has little patience with me or anyone else who talks about them in a positive way."

"That explains why she treats me the way she does. You can tell her she need not worry about fending me off. I am not the least bit interested in her," Daniel lied.

The truth was that he admired her greatly. She was everything he admired in a person—strong, straightforward, honest, and she did not snivel and whine during hardship. There was no giggling either; that was a real plus. The fact that she was also strikingly beautiful had not escaped his notice either.

Up to this point in his life he had not allowed himself to become overly involved with any one woman. However, he had never met one like Alssa before. It was just as well; there was no hope that she might feel the same way about him.

CHAPTER 34

After riding for two days, Captain Jovan was sitting in front of the stable in H'la as Sergeant Gallant walked up. "Well, Sergeant Gallant, what can you tell me this morning?" he asked with great frustration in his voice.

Sergeant Gallant responded reluctantly, "Captain, the situation is as confusing as it was last night. I talked to Lieutenant Colonel Barnes's orderly, and he said that you will have to wait for your opportunity to meet with the lieutenant colonel and that the lieutenant colonel is terribly busy setting up the defense of H'la. Something the major felt should have already been done before he got here, but because of incompetence and disobedience, it was not. The orderly's words, not mine, sir."

Captain Jovan stood up and said, "What is the lieutenant colonel thinking? He doesn't know anything yet. We are the only lancers in-country, and he refuses to talk to me? We are wasting time! I am going over there myself and demand he meet with me."

Jovan and his small troop had lodged in between the stables and the healer's hovel. Jovan dusted himself off, washed his face in the horse trough, and marched down the dusty road to the Guest of H'la. The town was full of so many people. And that did not count all the soldiers from the Pact of Brothers. Just a few short days ago, when he was here, the town was almost empty.

Jovan arrived at the front door of the inn and was greeted by a big burly infantry sergeant who was immaculately dressed and spotlessly clean. The sergeant said nothing, but Jovan could see the look of disgust on his face. Jovan went to go in the door, and the sergeant said, “Sorry, sir, no one goes in unannounced. Could you please wait here?”

“What? This is an inn, and I am going in to eat. Why would you need to announce me?” Jovan asked.

The sergeant moved between him and the door. “Again, I am sorry, but these are Lieutenant Colonel Barnes’s orders. Please wait here.”

The sergeant was only gone for a few moments, and when he returned, he closed the door firmly behind him and said, “The lieutenant colonel says you can go to the Boars Brisket if you want to eat.”

As Jovan stepped toward the door, he said, “Then I would like to see the lieutenant colonel myself.”

The sergeant reached out and grabbed Jovan by the arm to stop him. Jovan slapped the sergeant’s arm down and barked, “How dare you lay a hand on an officer! You will accompany me in to see the lieutenant colonel, and I will report your conduct to him.”

With that, the sergeant took a step back and motioned for Jovan to go through the door, and he followed. The lieutenant colonel and several other officers were standing around a table with a map laid out between them. As he approached, the lieutenant colonel looked up, ignored Jovan, and addressed the sergeant. “I said I did not want to be disturbed! Why is this man in here?”

“Lieutenant Colonel Barnes, the captain insisted he be allowed in even after I informed him that he was to go to the Boars Brisket,” replied the sergeant crisply.

The lieutenant colonel turned his eyes on Jovan, looking him up and down, noticing Jovan’s disheveled appearance. A deep frown came across his face as he said, “Captain, what possible justification could you have for appearing in public in such a state?”

Jovan was stunned as he replied, “Lieutenant Colonel Barnes, I have been in the field for two weeks, and this last week, we have been battling man-orcs, goblins, and hadrac as we pursued a thief who has the sword of light.”

The lieutenant colonel scoffed and chided Jovan, "Are you not the Captain Jovan who was supposed to have greeted me when I arrived and was responsible for arranging the defenses of the H'la crossroads? Why were you not here when I arrived?"

Jovan shook his head in disbelief and responded, "Sir, I sent word back to Major Smitt about what I found when I arrived and what I was going to do."

The lieutenant colonel smiled arrogantly as he said, "Your Corporal Taas arrived just as Major Smitt and his entire command were leaving. I met with your corporal, and he told me your wild story about the hadrac organizing and the mysterious actions of the orcs. It sounded as preposterous then as your story does now. These ignorant beasts haven't the intelligence to build a fire. I hardly think they could organize into an army. You are a young captain. In fact, in my considered opinion, you are too young to be a captain at all. You obviously are overwrought and exaggerating."

Jovan half-pleaded, "What about the sword, sir? The return of the Banisher? It is back in the Middle Kingdom. I have spent many days chasing the man who has it."

Lieutenant Colonel Barnes smiled at all the officers standing around the table as he said, "Ah, yes, the mysterious, magical sword. Your Corporal Taas told us about that also. Am I to understand that you completely disobeyed your orders to establish a defensive position here in H'la to chase after this mythical weapon?"

"It is not mythical, Lieutenant Colonel. I have seen what it can do!" exclaimed Jovan.

The lieutenant colonel asked with derision, "You have seen the sword yourself being used? Why, then, did you not apprehend the user?"

"I have not seen the sword," Jovan replied, "but I have seen what it does to those that it is used upon."

The lieutenant colonel shook his head and said, "You haven't even seen this weapon and yet you believe it has special powers? Pray tell, what have you seen it do that is so amazing?"

"The victims, their bodies vanish. Their spilled blood remains, but the bodies disappear," Jovan responded adamantly.

The lieutenant colonel as well as the rest of the officers around the table looked at him in disbelief, and then one by one, they began to chuckle. The lieutenant colonel laughed out right, then scoffed at Jovan. "Disappeared, disappeared! This has to be the most outrageous excuse I have ever heard to justify blatant disobedience and dereliction of duty. I should court-martial you right here, right now. What do you take me for, a complete fool?

"I can see now why His Holy Majesty had Colonel Campbell and the entire command reassigned. He has clearly lacked discipline and has allowed his entire unit to become sloppy. The Holy Lancers have spent too many years in this backwater place, and it has resulted in poor leadership."

Jovan replied defensively, "Colonel Campbell and the First of the First have been the premier fighting division for the Pact of Brothers for generations. That is why they were assigned to keep the peace in the Middle Kingdom. I take offense at what you say, sir."

Lieutenant Colonel Barnes recoiled at the strength of Jovan's response, his face became flush, and he said, "Why, you insignificant little upstart! How dare you challenge me! I have spent the last ten years battling the Ramaahians in the Impenetrable Mountains. I know what fighting is about, and it is not riding up and down the highway, looking for a few stupid beasts that hardly bother anyone. No, Captain, a real fighting force is here now, and we will make quick work of these *monsters* of yours, and we will not need any magic sword to do it!"

Jovan was shocked by where the conversation had gone and was perplexed by the lieutenant colonel's attitude and tried to change the direction by asking, "Sir, you said that the First of the First has been reassigned. Do you know where they were sent?"

The lieutenant colonel replied with contempt in his voice, "I do not know, and I do not care, but I do know that I will bring order and discipline back to this place. The same as I did in the Impenetrable Mountains."

The lieutenant colonel was almost talking to himself as he stood, staring up at the ceiling. "I brought those Ramaahians to their knees and have kept them at bay for years. I will do the same here."

Looking back at Jovan, he said, "And we will start with you. Sergeant, take this man out and execute him!"

The heads of everyone around the table popped up, including that of Captain Jovan, who yelled, "What!"

One of the senior officers, also a captain, spoke up. "Sir, are you sure you want to do that? We would need to have a trial."

"Why?" barked the lieutenant colonel. "He has already admitted to all of us that he disobeyed his orders and followed after who knows what kind of foolishness. Beside, a court-martial board would be made up of senior officers who are all standing here right now, and all of you heard him tell his ridiculous story. It is clear the man is not of sound mind. No, I say we execute him. Sergeant, take him out and dispose of him!"

Jovan could not believe what he was hearing. He looked at the sergeant, whose eyes were pleading with the officers around the table for help.

Seeing no response, he weakly said, "Yes, sir."

He gently placed his hand on Jovan's shoulder, saying, "Let's go."

As they turned to leave, another one of the officers, an infantry major, spoke up and said, "Lieutenant Colonel Barnes, may I make an observation into this situation?"

Impatiently the lieutenant colonel replied, "If you must."

The major continued, "I understand your dissatisfaction with this officer's behavior and the need to set an example, but I think there may be a more effective way to send a message than just having the man executed out of hand."

The lieutenant colonel, growing more impatient, replied, "And in what way would you suggest doing that?"

The major explained, "We should have a trial. Like you said, we have the necessary officers to convene one. All the evidence can be presented so that everyone who hears what happens will know that you were justified in your actions. It will send a clear message to all the other officers and troopers that they need to follow your orders."

The infantry officer ended with, "Which would most certainly establish that you are in charge."

Lieutenant Colonel Barnes smiled brightly and said, “Thank you, Major, that is an excellent idea. Please, go set this up. We will have the trial first thing tomorrow morning. I want this man dead by noon.”

CHAPTER 35

Commander Westolve and her remaining company finally reached L'ke L'fe. The road had been hazardous; three times, they fought off hadrac and orcs, each time losing more troops. She had started this campaign with 120 troopers, and she left Devil's Pass with only 93, and now she was down to 82. What made the losses sting the most was, she was not sure why she was here. Did T'asha really expect her to kill Alssa and Cally in cold blood? There was no way she could do that; on that, she had already made her mind up. She would detain them and wait for T'asha to return.

For now, she needed to make arrangements for her women and their horses. Westolve decided to find the garrison commander of the Holy Lancers. They had been patrolling in this area for a long time, so they would know best where to find accommodations.

Maurice did not share the disdain for the Pact of Brothers like her fellow officers. She felt that all soldiers served their leaders in much the same way. It was not that she liked or disliked men; she felt people were people and all should be treated with respect if they deserved it.

They rode down the Queen's Highway through the center of town, but they did not find the Holy Lancers Barracks until they reached the far side.

Dismounting, she walked up the wide stairs to the garrison commanders headquarters. Walking through the door, Maurice entered the room greeted by a disbelieving stare. The corporal sitting at a small desk asked, "May I help you, miss?"

Maurice could not believe her ears; this man would not dare address a male officer from another kingdom so casually.

She replied sternly, "I am an officer of the Three Sisters. Therefore, it is Commander Westolve to you. Corporal, you will let your commander know that I am here, now!"

The corporal rose slowly and stepped into the next room.

* * *

Westolve stood in the waiting room for some time before the corporal returned to speak to her. "Major Losguard will see you now."

He motioned her to the door from which he had just emerged. The room she entered was not much bigger than the waiting room. It was dominated by a desk that was oversize for the room. The man behind the desk sat in a large chair that he filled to overflowing. His hair was white and unkempt, and his beard matched his hair. His uniform was overly ornate, which Westolve knew was the custom of the Pact of Brothers. He did not smile at her; instead, he looked at her with disdain.

He asked, "What can I do for you, young lady?"

Commander Westolve frowned and said, "Major Losguard, I am an officer in the royal guard of the Three Sisters, and I expect to be treated as such."

Major Losguard moved things around on his desk, acting like he did not hear Commander Westolve, but before she could speak again, he said quietly, "I have no concern for how you expect to be treated. You will find that things here in the middle territories are different from up north. Your people have no authority here, so do not be trying anything."

Westolve responded, "Major, I have no intensions of trying anything. We are here for the same reason you are, the return of the king. I was only stopping in to pay my respects and to see if you knew of a place for my company to find lodging."

The chubby major rose suddenly, and it was all Westolve could do not to laugh aloud. Losguard only stood a span and half high, a full head shorter than Westolve. He was a big round sphere with a small round white sphere on top of it. When he started yelling, Westolve lost it completely and started laughing.

"You filthy wench, I am here because this land belongs to the Pact of Brothers. We are the stewards of the Middle Kingdom. If the heir returns, he will have to work with us to establish his rule. Furthermore, I am not interested in your respects, and I am even less interested where you and your whores stay." Yelling through the door, he called out, "Corporal, come in here and show this woman out!"

Westolve's desire for civility quickly disappeared. She wanted to respond, but she knew there was nothing she could do about his insolence at this time, so she turned and marched out the door before the corporal could come in to remove her.

Returning to her troops, she had them mount up, and they went to the other end of town and commandeered a large old inn. She was tired of dealing with people who showed no respect, so when the proprietor of the inn treated her rudely, she had him and all his guests thrown into the street. Now she just needed to wait; hopefully, T'asha would return before Alssa and Cally arrived.

Chapter 36

The five of them emerged from the crook into the edge of the Midland Plains by the same rock outcropping where they had battled the hadrac. Their wounds had been healed, and a week's rest had them well-fed and re-energized. But their hopes of reaching L'ke L'fe before the prophecy date were lost. They had needed the time to heal, but it was way more than they had planned.

For six days they rested by the abbey. Oaklawn had been content with sitting around and telling them stories from centuries past. He had let them sleep most of the day and lie around eating and drinking during the remainder. Daniel was never sure of where Oaklawn obtained all the food and wine, but they never ran out. Then, on the seventh day, Oaklawn took a harsh tone and insisted that they leave the crook immediately. He all but forced them out onto the path and hurried them along with great haste.

As they passed the outcropping by the little cave, they could see the orc bodies that Oaklawn had thrown against the rocks the week before. As Daniel was about to ask the obvious question, Oaklawn spoke first.

The giant tree troll said in a whisper, "You must be very quiet. The enemy is still close at hand."

Daniel quietly asked his question, "How is this possible? The blood is still fresh, and the bodies are not bloated. It has been seven days. They should be stinking something fierce. The woodland animals should have carried them away by now!"

Alssa spoke up and asked, "Well, troll, do you have an explanation for this?"

Oaklawn did not respond but signaled for everyone to be quiet. It was then that they could all hear orcs moving along the path they had just walked down on. The humans scampered up the rocks into the little cave, and Oaklawn transformed into an oak tree, blending seamlessly into the surrounding forest.

The orcs entered the clearing in front of the rocks and started milling around, looking at the dead bodies of their fellow orcs. Because they could understand their speech, they knew that this group were man-orcs and were much smarter than regular orcs. The beasts were arguing among themselves on what they should do. In common tongue, but with lots of guttural sounds and hissing, they said, "We should flee. I do not want to battle an old tree troll with such great strength."

Another added, "To die at the hands of our long natural enemy would be an honor rewarded by the dark lords themselves, but it is dying from the flames of the Banisher that I fear. I say we find more of our kind before we continue to look for them."

The one who appeared to want to be the leader spoke up with what sounded like forced courage. "The humans were clearly wounded when they left the battle. We could see their blood trail and smell their fear of death. We must look for them!"

Though he did not seem any more eager than the rest of them to face the sword and Oaklawn again when he said, "We will split into two groups, one will go back the way we came and look for their hiding place. The other will head deeper into the forest."

Then he said something that astonished Daniel. "Remember, they are wounded and have only a part of one day's head start. If we push hard, we will find them, and our reward will be great!" With that, the herd broke up and went their different ways.

The four humans crawled out of the cave and down the rocks into the clearing and stood staring at Oaklawn as he transformed from a tree back to his troll from.

"Why do you look at me so?" he sang.

Cally spoke first. "Those orcs acted like they had just lost our trail today, not a week ago. They still think we are wounded."

Alssa said tersely, "Nothing makes sense here. Fresh blood, no scavengers, orcs who act like they haven't been looking for us for days? Troll, what is going on?"

To Daniel Oaklawn appeared flustered or at least Daniel thought he did, but how can you tell with a tree?

Oaklawn sang a heavy sigh, "Not everything that is in the light appears the same in the day. I have been around for many of your centuries, and I do not understand how it happens, but when you are in the light, things are not what they seem. We were only in the light of the crook for a few of your minutes. You only think we were there for days."

Daniel scoffed, "That cannot be so." He pulled up his shirt to reveal his smooth, muscular belly. "I had an orc sword wound on my stomach. It shows no sign, not even a scar." He lifted Alssa's shoulder armor. "And her wound was deep but now healed completely."

As he reached for Sergeant Sharon's skirt to show Oaklawn, she said, "Watch it, Manslayer."

"Oh, sorry," he said sheepishly, but then continued, "Even the sergeant's leg wound from before is completely healed with no scar. How is that possible? Are you saying we were healed in minutes?"

"I did not say you were healed in minutes." Oaklawn sang out another heavy sigh. "I said we were only in the light of the crook for minutes. What happens when you are in the light is one thing and it is another thing in the day. No one can tell, for the light does what it wills and those that walk in the light cannot always understand it."

With that, Oaklawn turned around and headed east through the trees toward the Midland Plains. The four humans took a moment to take in the scene around them one more time, gave one another a look of confusion and disbelief, then hurried to catch up to the fast-moving tree troll.

* * *

They walked for the rest of the afternoon until dusk. Which put them at the edge of the forest and the Midland Plains.

Oaklawn stopped and said, "This is as far as I can go."

Cally was surprised and upset. "You are not going to go with us? I thought you believed it the Lightbearer and the sword talisman? What about the return of the king?"

"Oh, I do, I do," Oaklawn sang, "but even in the few short years I have been in the light, I have learned that the light does not force us into our destiny. We still get to choose. And not all creatures choose to follow the light, even those of prophecy."

Cally motioned at Daniel, "You said that he was the Lightbearer. Do you not want to help him to sit on the thrown and defeat the coming darkness?

Daniel jumped into the conversation, "Cally, wait just a minute, I am not the Lightbearer regardless of what this tree says, and am certainly not a king, and I have no desire to sit on any thrown."

Cally turned on him, eyes ablaze with frustration, anger, and dismay.

Oaklawn's deep voice rumbled out a song, "Not all creatures can be depended upon to walk in their destiny, least of all human ones." Then with a graceful turn and a deep laugh that sounded like happy tumbling boulders, he strode back into the forest and was gone.

Cally began to cry and lashed out at Daniel, "Why are you such a selfish man? You have driven him away with your unwillingness to be who you are supposed to be."

Daniel, as always when a woman began to cry, was unable to think of anything to say. In his discomfort, he turned to look at Alssa.

Alssa smiled, shrugged her shoulders, and said, "Hey, don't look at me. I agree that you are selfish and running from your destiny." Turning toward Cally she continued, "But I am also glad the troll is gone. It just goes to prove once again that you cannot trust trolls. Besides, we will not need his protection once we enter onto the plains."

Sergeant Sharon Cleared her throat to gain the others' attention and said, "Your Majesties, if we will be safe when we get out of the forest, then we should get moving before we camp for the night."

* * *

Oaklawn stood upon a ridge, watching as the four humans walked out onto the plains. He spoke with a low hum of the tree troll dialect. "Truly, the Lightbearers have returned! Let us hope that they find their true purpose before it is too late. Let us be about helping in the way that we can."

The forest around came alive with the sounds of mournful songs of many tree trolls as they transformed from tree to troll.

No orcs, hadrac, or goblins living had ever heard such a terrifying sound, and the ones on the ridge were no exception. They stood frozen, listening to the song of the trees filled with fear. Their leader called out to them, "Quickly, we must leave this place and return to the master and tell the master what we have seen." The other beasts were unsure of what he was talking about, but they all agreed they wanted to run away. Fortunately for the four humans out on the plains, none of the dark beasts would make it off the ridge alive.

* * *

The next morning, Daniel stood on the crest of a low hill, looking out over the Rolling Plains. The Midlands were not as flat as their name seemed to imply. Looking at it from a distance, one would realize it looked relatively flat, but once you started moving across it you discovered that the land was made up of swells and troughs. The swells ran west to east, and they seemed to move across the plains like waves of the ocean.

The big difference was the grass; it was as tall as them in the troughs but grew shorter on the crests. As Daniel surveyed the plains, he spotted what looked like a dark smudge out in the middle, miles away to the southeast.

Cally cautiously walked up beside Daniel and stood for a moment, looking out over the plains, then finally said, “I am sorry about what I said last night. I did not mean it.”

Daniel did not turn to look at her but continued to stare straight ahead and responded, “Don’t worry about it.”

Fidgeting nervously, Cally pressed on, “I guess I am confused and a little scared. I do not understand how we could have only been at the abbey for a few minutes when we all remember sleeping each night and that all our wounds were healed. That is impossible, right?”

Daniel finally turned to face her and said, “I don’t understand either. But then there are a whole lot of things happening lately that I do not understand. Like trees walking and talking. Man-orcs, how by the cursed darkness orcs learned how to speak common speech. My sword now bursts into flame when I wield it, and those, I slay with it disappear. It never did that before I arrived in this cursed land.”

He then looked forcefully at Cally and said, “And to top all of that, I am traveling through the most dangerous place in the known lands with two important officers of the Three Sisters. Who believed—wrongly, by the way—that I am the fulfillment of a three-hundred-year-old prophecy. Yeah, I would say there is a lot I don’t understand.”

Chapter 37

Captain Jovan had been led back to the stable by the infantry sergeant, who said he was commanded to stay with him. He was not sure what to do. This whole situation was crazy, and Lieutenant Colonel Barnes seemed to be the craziest part of it. What military leader would just suddenly say, "Execute the man," and then order a court-martial hearing? It was true that Jovan did disobey orders, but the opposite was true of for the dereliction of duty charge. Was it not his duty to retrieve the sword of power, and did that not justify him disobeying the orders given to him weeks before by people hundreds of leagues away from the situation?

As he was stewing over the situation, he did not notice the infantry major walk in the stable until Sergeant Gallant yelled, "Attention!"

All the troopers in the room jumped up and saluted, including Jovan.

The major motioned for them all to sit down and said, "Relax, men. Go back to what you were doing."

Walking over to Jovan and the infantry sergeant, the major made a request. "Would the two of you join me outside, please?"

Once they were alone, Jovan quickly said, "Sir, I don't understand. I am not making up a story. I can prove it."

The major interrupted Jovan and sharply said, "Stop talking, Captain. I am not here to talk about your defense. In fact, from my perspective, you look guilty, which you probably are. But again, I am not here for any of that. I am here to see that justice is done or at least has the opportunity to be done. If you go to trial tomorrow, you will hang at noon—there is no question of that. I have been with Lieutenant Colonel Barnes now for two years, and once he has decided something, he will not turn aside from his goal." The major stopped talking and just stared off toward the east.

After a few minutes, Jovan asked, "Then why have you come to see me, sir?"

The major replied, "I am going to make you an offer, Captain, that I hope you will not refuse." He pointed to the infantry Sergeant as he continued, "You are going to kidnap Sergeant Black here and escape. Then after a day or so, you are going to let him go. You will then go your own way. I do not care where, except not back to the Pact of Brothers. This way, Sergeant Black will only suffer a reprimand and I will avoid having to sit on a court-martial board that can only end in a travesty of justice."

Jovan shook his head in disbelief and said, "This is not right. It is not fair. I cannot believe this is happening."

The major put his hand on Jovan's shoulder and tried to comfort him. "Sometimes life is like that, but when you are left with so few choices, which all of them are bad, choose the one that lets you live to fight another day."

Jovan looked toward the stables and asked, "What about the rest of my troop, sir? What will happen to them?"

The major responded quickly, "They are to be broken up and reassigned to separate units. Lieutenant Colonel Barnes said he didn't want the bad seeds all together."

Jovan did not think he could feel worse than he did a few minutes ago, but he was wrong. He looked at the major and said, "Can I have some time to think about it, sir?"

"I am not sure what there is to think about, but yes, you can. Just make sure you decide and are gone before tomorrow morning, for both of our sakes," the major said as he motioned for Sergeant Black to follow him.

Jovan went back into the stable and told his men what was happening, not leaving out any details. To a man they said they would rather go with him than stay, even after he told them that if they went with him, they could never go home.

When Sergeant Black returned, they "escaped" through the east gate that had been left open and unguarded. They headed south on the coast highway until they reached the Orc Gorge, where they turned east on the river road toward L'ke L'fe.

CHAPTER 38

Daniel's small group headed out toward the black smudge that sat so far out in the distance. They had been walking for more than an hour, and as they got closer, the black smudge turned into a circle of huge rocks jutting from the ground. The rocks sat on top of one another, almost like they had been placed there by a giant hand.

It was not for another hour before they were close enough to see them clearly, and it was at that time that they realized how large the stones were. They had been hewn out of a much larger rock formation. The lines were too straight to be natural.

As they crested another ridge, they stopped to take in the sight. The stones had been arranged in a circle around a giant tor that rose twenty spans in the air. Some of the stones stood on end and were about four spans high. A few of them looked like they had been knocked over.

Turning to look north, Daniel could see the ground they had crossed undulated, much like giant rollers on the sea. They would walk up one side of the land wave, then slowly over the rounded crest, and then down the other side to end up in the wave's trough.

When down in the bottom of the troughs, they could only see the wave in front and behind them. The grass grew taller in the trough bottoms, rising above their heads in many places. When they looked from side to side, they could see the swells curved slowly like a half-moon. Their vision was blocked after only a few hundred spans. It was like that the entire time as they crossed the plain.

As they topped the next rise, Cally turned to look behind them. Calling to the others, she pointed and said, "I think someone is coming."

The other three stopped and looked back. They could see a small dust cloud about three miles away. Daniel scanned the horizon, looking for more dust clouds, hoping it was the wind stirring up the dust. The air was hot, and still, no such luck.

Cally commented again, "Now it's gone."

When Daniel looked back again, the cloud was gone. As he started to say what he thought it might be, Alssa spoke up. "We are all tired, and it is hot as a furnace out here on the plains. We might be seeing things."

"Let's pick up the pace just in case," Daniel encouraged as he headed them toward the tor again. "I would rather we be in those rocks if someone is coming."

As they crested the next ridge, they turned to look again; they only saw the ever-present heat waves. Just as they began to leave the crest, Sergeant Sharon stumbled in a prairie badger hole, twisted her ankle, and fell. Daniel and Alssa stopped to help her up, and Cally glanced behind them again and exclaimed, "See, there it is again!"

And sure enough, as they all turned to look, the little cloud was back, but much closer. Alssa put Sergeant Sharon's arm over her shoulder, wrapped her arm around the sergeant's waist, and said, "We had better hurry and get to those rocks before whoever is making that dust gets here!"

Cally moved to the sergeant's other side and said, "Here, let me help. We will be able to move much faster."

As the women moved down the slope, Daniel stayed on the ridge to watch the dust cloud. It disappeared again, but after a minute, it reappeared and then disappeared again. Reaching into his travel bag, he pulled out his looking glass and pointed where the dust had last appeared. This time when the cloud appeared, Daniel was shaken by what he saw. He quickly returned the looking glass in the bag and turned and ran down the hill. As he caught up to the women, he exhorted them, "The dust is being created by about thirty people on horseback, and they are moving fast. Let's hurry!"

They still had two more ridges to cross before they would reach the tor. Daniel thought they would make it, but just when they topped the last ridge, they could see that the tor sat on the top of the ridge and the area around the rocks had been flattened out. This place had obviously been made by someone or something.

Daniel looked back to see that the riders were only four ridges away. Turning to the ladies, he said, "Why don't the three of you take the bows and find a spot where you can be hidden but still shoot from? We will not be able to intimidate them with our numbers, but we might be able to surprise them."

Sergeant Sharon spoke up. "Why do you assume they will be enemies?"

"Because we have not run into too many friends out here, and I would rather be overly cautious than dead. Also, these are humans, so we need be prepared," Daniel answered.

"Why do you think they could only be humans?" Cally asked.

Daniel responded, "One reason, I have never heard of dark beasts using a horse for anything but food."

Daniel turned toward the riders as the they descended into a trough and said, "Second, I do not think they are pursing us. In fact, I doubt they even know we are here."

"Then why are we hiding?" Cally questioned.

Alssa answered her, "Because, as Daniel said, better safe than sorry. Besides, what kind of people would be out here in the middle of nowhere at the far end of the Rolling Plains?"

"We're out here!" Cally retorted. She nocked an arrow in her bow and slid in behind one of the big slabs of rock to hide. The other two women quickly followed.

Daniel hid in a cluster of rocks that would leave him unseen until the riders were right on top of him. He was not sure what they could do when they were so grossly outnumbered. As he continued his thoughts, the first riders stopped in front of him. Daniel looked up at the rider, and a flash of recognition went through his mind. The rider stared back at him with a look of "Do I know you?" on his face.

The rider leaned out to get a closer look at Daniel and, with a startled voice, said, "Manslayer? Daniel Manslayer!"

The rider's face was familiar, but when Daniel heard his voice, he recognized it immediately. Only one man had that voice; it was quite unique, almost feminine, but with strong masculine overtones. Daniel stepped out from behind the rock and greeted the rider, "Eric Kromsing!"

Kromsing dismounted and stepped over to Daniel, holding out his hand. Daniel obliged, and they shook hands firmly, and Kromsing pulled Daniel in close and gave him a hardy hug.

Kromsing asked first, "What in the name of the light are you doing out here in the middle of this endless plains? You are the last person I would have thought I would run into in this wilderness!"

"I can say the same to you," Daniel said with a big smile as he looked at the rest of the riders that were with Kromsing. He continued, "It is good to see you again, though. It looks like you have changed your line of work again?"

Kromsing looked back at his men, smiled, and said, "I just saw how much money you make in your line of work and decided I would join you, but you know me, I had to go bigger, so I formed a company. And here we are!"

Kromsing gave orders to his men. "Dismount and give the horses a rest. We might as well eat while we are at it. Strip down the horses and set up camp." Turning back to Daniel, he asked, "What are you doing all alone out here? I see no horse, I see no client, and you are miles from any form of civilization. This is not like you. Has something happened?"

Daniel shuffled his feet as he searched for an answer that would not be a total lie. Just then, a short fat man waddled around the rocks they were standing by. He was huffing and puffing, his face red and covered in sweat. The man had on fine clothes that were caked with dirt. In Daniel's mind he was a man who did not belong with the people he rode with. He was about to speak again when the fat man interrupted.

He said, "Kromsing, why have we stopped in this horrible place? There is no shade, no water, nothing but dust and more dust!"

At that moment, he noticed Daniel. "Who is this? Another one of your thieving friends?"

Daniel chuckled and asked, "Your client, Eric?"

Kromsing nodded and said, "Now, Count, just relax and find a place to rest. It wasn't a half-hour ago that you were complaining about having to ride forever. Go lie down in the shade of a rock."

The count was about to start into another one of his tirades when Alssa stepped out of her hiding place and challenged the count. "Count Gravelet, you petulant little man, what are you doing here? You are supposed to be at Castle in the Gorge."

The count spun around to see what woman would speak to him in such a way. When he saw who it was, his mouth fell open and he froze in place. Daniel thought he looked like a man who did not know whether to shit himself or run away. The count did neither; instead, he dropped a knee and lowered his head, which surprised Daniel, but not as much as when he heard Eric say, "Your Majesty."

Daniel looked up at Alssa and mouthed, "Your Majesty?" Alssa smiled at his shock and discomfort.

Alssa walked between the two kneeling men and commanded, "Tobias, get off the ground. I hate to see a royal groveling." Turning to Eric, she said, "And who do we have here?" As Eric began to stand, Alssa reached out and touched him on the shoulder, saying, "I didn't tell you to rise." Eric dropped back to one knee as Alssa continued. "My guess is that you are a mercenary, seeing that you are friends with the Manslayer. What are you doing out here so far from home with my wayward count?"

Eric began to answer, but Alssa shushed him. "No, let me guess. The count has hired you as his personal bodyguard even though he has an entire company of Three Sisters troops at his disposal back home? Of course, those troops answer to Commander Westolve, who is the personal favorite of my sister Asha, which explains why he has you."

"Your Majesty?" Count Gravelet tried to interrupt.

"Quite, Tobias! I will get back to you in a bit." Alssa walked around Eric with her hand running around his shoulders. "Yes, I believe you are a mercenary, a bit handsome for a mercenary, but a mercenary nonetheless. You must be from the Eastward, much like your friend here." She pointed at Daniel. "They do grow them big over there."

Daniel stared at Alssa and thought, *What in the world is this? She has not acted like this before, but if she really is a royal, maybe she has been acting the whole time?*

Alssa gave Daniel a mischievous smile. "Surprised, Daniel? All this time you have been wandering through the wilderness and you never realized that you were with two of the future queens of the Three Sisters?"

Daniel shrugged and said, "Makes me think I should have continued heading east instead of getting involved in other people's problems."

Alssa feigned shock. "Oh, that hurts. I thought you liked being with us?"

Daniel began to respond, "Now that I know you're royals, I am positive I should have minded my own—"

Gravelet interrupted in a panic by saying to Alssa, "Wait, do you mean both of you are here?" The count started to tremble uncontrollably.

At that moment, Cally and Sergeant Sharon stepped out from their hiding places, and Cally spoke. "Daniel, you do not really mean that, do you?"

Count Gravelet gasped out, "Oh, this is bad. This is really bad! What have we done?"

Alssa turned to the count and asked, "What are you babbling about?"

The count just continued to groan and mumble under his breath. Cally moved to Daniel's side as Alssa grabbed Gravelet by the shoulders and shook him, saying, "Speak plainly, man. What is wrong with you?"

He looked at her with horror on his face and said, "If both of you are here, then she is free to work the rest of her plan. Oh my, this is bad!"

Alssa was getting frustrated and spoke angrily. "What plan? What are you talking about?"

As the count looked back and forth from Alssa to Cally, the horror on his face was replaced by fear. He slowly said, "We or she thought if the goblins became a threat again, more authority would be placed in her hands instead of yours, her being in charge of the military,"

"Are you talking about T'asha?" Cally asked.

"Yes," responded the count meekly.

Alssa's anger was not just frustration now as she said, "You're saying that T'asha ordered you to let the goblins breed uncontrolled again?"

Shaking, Gravelet squeaked out, "Yes, but the plan was that when you encountered them in the Wasteland you would turn back and return to Jukeele. Why did you not go back?"

Cally yelled, "We were attack by thousands of goblins! We could not go back! All but a few of our troops were killed and eaten. The goblins had no intentions of letting us get away."

"She is going to go back to Jukeele, and you will not be there to stop her," the count said.

"Stop her? Stop her from doing what?" Alssa demanded.

"If T'asha believes you are dead, then she will try to take the throne!" Gravelet sniveled.

Alssa snarled, "That is ridiculous! For her to ascend to the throne, our mothers would have to be—"

"Dead!" Cally exclaimed. "She would never do that. She may be a little jealous and covetous of Alssa, but she would never do harm to the queens. I cannot believe that!"

Gravelet liked the focus off himself and more on T'asha. So he cautioned, "I would not be too certain of that, my queen. It appears that her goal was not just to usurp you but to kill you."

"Why should we believe you?" Cally retorted. "You have already admitted that you chose to neglect your sworn duty to control the goblin population. Of all people, you know better than anyone that the goblins would never have anything to do with a woman from the Three Sisters." Cally drew her sword and stepped toward the count. "The goblins would only work with men, and that means you!"

Stepping back in fear, the count stammered, "No, it was T'asha. She brought her entire house guard with her to the Castle in the Gorge. She then traveled with them to Devil's Pass to make sure you were dead. After that, she returned to Jukeele."

Cally cried, "You lie!" She raised her sword to strike him.

The fat count was now terrified and begged, "No, please, Your Majesty, I am not lying!"

"He isn't lying," Eric said as he rose off the ground. "At least not entirely."

Alssa spoke soothingly to Cally. "Let us hear this out. Lest we compound our errors by acting rashly." Turning to Eric, she asked, "What do you know, mercenary?"

Eric rubbed the beard on his chin and said, "Where to start?"

"Start with why you and this liar are together," spit out Cally. "Why can we trust you any more than we can trust him?"

Eric smiled and said, "You can't, but you should. The count hired me, or us." Eric motioned toward his men, who had stopped setting up the camp to watch what was happening. "He hired us about six months ago to provide security for him and his personal landholdings. Although riding around the countryside, watching your subjects laboring in his fields didn't require much work on our part."

Both Alssa and Cally glared at the count, who seemed to shrink up under their stares.

Eric continued, "Then a few days ago, the count busted into my headquarters and informed me that we had to all leave immediately. This was the same day that Princess T'asha arrived and secluded herself with Commander Westolve."

Alssa interrupted, "T'asha was as at Castle in the Gorge? Were her troops with her?"

Eric shrugged his shoulders and said, "I didn't know if they were there when we left that night, but when we reached the second falls, we ran into hadrac. I was going to turn us around and head us back to the castle when the count informed me that we could not go back. Because T'asha would send Westolve to find us and have us killed.

Killed because we were with him. That was when he told me about the goblins."

Cally, somewhat calmed down, asked, "How, then, if you were trapped between those two forces, were you able to escape?"

"Well," Eric replied while stroking his beard, "we used another way out of the Three Brides Valley."

"Another way!" Alssa exclaimed. "There is no other way. The Black Mountains to the north and west are impassable, and the seer's wards will not let you pass over the south ridges, unless the wards have failed?"

Kromsing responded, "You are right, of course. Those ways are all impassable, and the wards are still in place."

Cally asked, "Then how were you able to get out of the valley and out onto the plains?"

Eric replied, "We used the Thieves Tunnel."

"Thieves Tunnel? I have never heard of it," stated Alssa.

"Few have. It really isn't a tunnel. It is a series of long twists and turns through the wards that you can pass through," Eric said.

"How is that possible?" asked Cally.

With a smile Eric replied, "I am not sure, but it exists."

Alssa asked, "You're telling me that hadrac, orcs, and goblins could come out onto the plains without anyone knowing about it?"

"The tunnel only lets humans through. Dark beast cannot pass through it," answered Eric.

Cally spoke up again. "Let's go back to Gravelet's statements about T'asha and her house guard. What do you know?"

Eric said, "They did pass us as we were traveling to the tunnel, but they were not looking for anyone. They were moving way too fast. We hardly had time to hide. They never knew we were watching. It took us quite some time to find the entrance to the tunnel. We found it just as T'asha and her troops returned, going back up the valley."

Cally looked concerned and said, "Sister, what do you think she is up to?"

Alssa shook her head and said, "Nothing good."

Cally asked, "What do you think we should do?"

"One of us needs to go home and see what kind of trouble she is causing," Alssa said.

Cally quickly responded, "I agree. I will leave before dusk."

Alssa looked surprised and said, "You? Why you? I think it should be me. After all, I am the eldest sister."

Cally glanced at Daniel and said, "Yes, that is true, but that is also the reason you should stay here. You are the one who should greet the returning king."

Alssa also glanced at Daniel. "I am not sure that that is going to turn out like we thought. I don't see that it matters much which one of us is here."

Cally argued, "Sister you know how important this is. We must follow through on our duties, and this duty falls on you as the eldest."

CHAPTER 39

Cally and the Count left for Jukeele that evening. Eric had sent his second-in-command and two other men with her to help with protection and to keep an eye on Count Gravelet while Cally traveled back to the capital.

The rest of them were going to continue to L'ke L'fe and then to Queens Castle Home. As they rode, Eric asked Daniel, "How did you end up working for the princess?"

Daniel replied, "I am not working for them."

"What? You're kidding, right? Why are you providing them protection, then?" Eric asked.

"Believe me, Eric, these women do not need my protection." Daniel proceeded to tell Eric the entire story of how he had come upon Alssa and Cally.

When he was done, Eric asked, "So you really didn't know they were the princesses of the Three Sisters?"

"I knew they were part of the royal troops, because of their armor, but they never let on about being royalty. How was I supposed to know? I have never been to the Three Sisters other than sitting on a ship in one of their harbors," Daniel countered.

"You couldn't tell from their looks? There are not that many women that are as beautiful as those two and the other sister, T'asha. They are all three stunningly gorgeous. The three of them are famous for their beauty, and everyone knows it," Eric chided.

Daniel looked at Eric with distaste and said, "We have known each other for a number of years, Eric, and you know that I would never be interested in a royal. I do not believe in that kind of crap. People chosen by the gods to rule over others? Give me a break! From what I have seen, rulers take what they can and then justify it by declaring they have special privilege granted by some divine power."

"Daniel, you are so naive and simplistic. Why do you think that you get to decide the way the world should be? Do you think you are right and everyone else is wrong?" Eric asked with a hint of frustration in his voice.

Daniel replied with resolve, "I don't think I am always right. I just don't like others thinking that they can rule over me without my say-so. As far as my interest in those two princesses, it doesn't exist. I have no desire to live in a so-called civilized nation. Too many people, too many rules, and too many people trying to tell me how I should live." Daniel looked toward Alssa, who was riding ahead of them, and said, "This is why I came to the Lands of Chaos. Few people, no rules, and no royals."

Eric laughed. "That is ironic. You came here to escape it and you end up frolicking through the forest with two of the most powerful rulers in the known world. Now that sounds like destiny to me!"

"Don't you start on that nonsense! I am nobody's king," Daniel declared as he spurred his horse away from Eric.

Eric yelled back at him, "I said destiny! I didn't say you were a king, yet!"

* * *

Later in the day, Daniel rode up beside Alssa and asked, "Are you okay, Your Majesty?"

Alssa turned and glared at him and sternly said, "Why are you so darn obstinate? I am fine, and please do not call me Your Majesty. You are not one of my subjects."

Daniel shied his horse away a bit as he responded, "I am not trying to be obstinate. But I was surprised that you are a queen."

Alssa corrected him, "I *will* be a queen. My mother is the queen. Why are you surprised? Did I not act queenly enough for you? Not smart enough? Not strong enough? Or just not pretty enough!"

Daniel held up his hands and said, "Who's being obstinate now? I only asked if you were okay. I don't want to fight with you."

Alssa stared at him for a long moment, then said, "I am sorry, Daniel. I am worried about Cally, our mothers, and what T'asha is up to in Jukeele." She paused for another long moment, then continued, "To answer your simple question, no, I am not okay."

"I can understand that, and I want you to know that I am here for you." Daniel paused and thought, *Why did I just say that? I am not here for her? I need to start thinking before I speak!* He quickly changed the subject. "I wanted to ask about the wards that you talked about that are in the Troll Hills?"

Alssa said, "I really do not know that much about them other than where they are and what they do. What would you like to know?"

"Let's start with what they do," Daniel said.

Alssa thought for a moment, "The simplest answer is, evil cannot pass through them."

Daniel said with a smile, "Humans are evil, we're human, but we went through them."

"Thanks," Alssa said kiddingly but then continued, "There are different kinds of wards. All block evil, but in different ways. The wards that are set up in the Northern Hills block all but simple animals. Not even humans can pass through. Except Kromsing's Thieves Tunnel, which I did not know about. Apparently, it will let a human pass. The wards that run down the western troll hills will let any human through. Which was us when we left Oaklawn."

Daniel shook his head in disbelief and asked, "Then what about the crook? What was that all about?"

"The wards that block movement into the crook are special."

Alssa paused. She had a far-off look in her eyes as she said, "I knew that not all humans could enter the crook. But I did not know that it was so few of us. My sisters and I only went there with our mothers, so I guess our family is special."

"If that's so, then why was I able to pass through them?" Daniel asked skeptically.

"Like I said, I really do not know that much about them. But the troll did call you the Lightbearer, so maybe you are special too."

Daniel looked at her sternly as he said, "I am not special, believe me."

Alssa's horse skittered away, and she reined her back in and said, "I am not sure you know who or what you are."

Daniel chose to ignore her and pressed her more about the wards. "But who made them? And how? And why do they work? Do you know how many there are?"

Alssa replied, "I do not know those answers. I do know that they have been there for hundreds of years. Many people speculate that it was the great queen who set them in place. The say that she erected them so that M'tin or his heir would have something to come back to."

Daniel thought for a moment, then said, "That seems like a long shot. You say it has been three hundred years and no heir. But you believe that no orc has been able to enter the plains in all that time."

Alssa responded and said, "You have experienced the Ebony Forest for yourself. Imagine what this place would be like if hose horrible beasts could get out of their confinement."

At that moment, Sergeant Sharon rode up and asked, "Your Majesty, may I speak with you?"

Alssa gave Daniel a knowing smile and replied to the sergeant, "Yes, you may. Daniel, will you please excuse us?"

After Alssa and the sergeant rode away, Daniel said aloud, "I do think you are beautiful!" Then to himself he said, "And strong, and smart!" He quickly looked around to see who was listening, and thought, *I really need to start thinking before I speak.*

CHAPTER 40

Jovan and his fellow escapees approached L'ke L'fe by the Deep River Road instead of the Queen's Highway. Jovan had been right; there was almost no traffic on the road between K'la and L'ke L'fe. They set up a camp on the edge of town in the forest alongside the river.

Jovan had been surprised when Sergeant Black said he was not going back. Instead, he was going to stay with them. The sergeant had said that Major Stone had warned him that he could not guarantee how Lieutenant Colonel Barnes would respond. Major Stone let him have his choice. Jovan could see that Sergeant Gallant was happy that the infantry sergeant was staying. The two acted like brothers right from their first meeting.

Jovan left the two of them in charge as he slipped into town to see who was all there. On the way he had stolen some close off a clothesline and had changed out of his uniform. His thoughts returned to what had happened in H'la. He could not comprehend the unjust turn of events that had befallen him and his troops. He and his family had been Loyal to the Crown through many generations. In fact, he could not remember any of the male members of his family who had not served in the military, and most of them had given their lives in the line of duty. He was not sure what he was going to do now. He had never done anything but serve in the military. He had never wanted to do anything else. The more he thought about it, the more his anger and frustration grew.

He arrived at the edge of town, so he stopped to get his head right, and then he slipped quietly into the first bar he found. As his eyes adjusted to the darkness, he was shocked to see a Three Sisters officer with her head lying on the table. The table was tucked away in a dark corner.

He stepped to the bar and ordered an ale and kept an eye on the Three Sisters officer. He saw her lift her head a couple of times and wave at the bartender. On the third time she slurred out a yell that sounded something like, "Where's my dwink…I…I ordered dwink?"

Jovan looked at the bartender, who made no move to get her a drink. Jovan asked him, "Has she had too much so you don't want to give her any more?"

"No, she can drink as much as she wants. I don't care," the bartender responded angrily "She hasn't paid me for the first two, and I don't want to try to collect it from her. She's a mean drunk. She has been in before. Plus, she only pays with script, not gold. I just hope she leaves peacefully."

Jovan pulled a silver coin out of his pouch and set it on the counter and said, "Here, give me two more ales. This should be enough to pay for mine and hers."

The bartender smiled and quickly snatched up the coin and said, "This is more than enough. Do you want your change?"

"No, you keep it for your troubles," Jovan replied as he picked up the ales.

"Thank you," the bartender replied and then warned him, "I would be careful, if I were you. I don't think she likes men."

Jovan walked over to the officer's table and looked her over. He recognized the shoulder epaulets as the rank of commander. He thought, *Now, that is odd, a Three Sisters officer with this high a rank, publicly intoxicated.* He studied her more closely; he realized that she was wearing a royal house guard uniform, like the ones they had found in the graves in the Ebony Forest. He sat down next to her as she lifted her head off the table.

He smiled at her and said, "Hello."

She looked at him through bloodshot, blurry eyes and, with slurred speech, stated, "I dwink alone."

Jovan chuckled and said, "You don't have anything to drink."

She looked at the two mugs in front of him and asked, "Aren't those mine?"

"No, these are mine, but I will give you one if you tell me who you are?" Jovan offered.

She tried to stand and salute as she said, "Commander Westlo—"

She fell back in her chair but continued talking. "Formally of House K'jo royal guard, but now sent away to this disgusting place for disobeying an order and dereliction of duty."

Well, that is interesting, Jovan thought, then said, "I know the feeling. I have suffered somewhat of the same fate."

She shook her head no and waved him away as she said, "You don't understand. I was T'asha's favorite. I was special to her. She loved me, and I loved her." She smiled at Jovan as she patted him on the leg and said in a whisper, "We were lovers."

She reached out, grabbed one of the mugs, chugged it down, and let out a loud belch. As she wiped off her mouth with her sleeve, she cried, "But then I ruined it because I would not send my troopers to die for nothing!"

Jovan shook his head and said comfortingly, "I don't know, but not being willing to send your men, or women to die for nothing doesn't sound like that bad a thing to me."

She reached out to him again, but this time she grabbed the front of his shirt and pulled him close to her, so their faces were almost touching, and said, "Oh, it gets worse! Now she wants me to kill her sisters, and I know I can't do it. I just can't. She will never want me again. I am such a failure." With that she fell headfirst into his lap and passed out.

Jovan sat there holding her face in his hands, trying to think of what he should do with her. He could not leave her here. There was no telling what someone might do to her. He thought, *She must be here with her unit. A full commander would not be alone.* He did not want to take her into town. Jovan knew there was a Pact of Brothers garrison in L'ke L'fe. He was not sure if they had received word of his escape yet; he hoped not. But he also did not know Major Losguard. It was just not worth the risk. So he carried her back to his camp.

Jovan had let Commander Westolve sleep for a couple of hours. When she woke up, he had Sergeant Black give her coffee until she was sober. He and all his men stayed in their tents until the commander left. He had given Sergeant Black instructions to escort her back into town or wherever she wanted to go. He also asked the sergeant to pass by the Holy Lancers Barracks to see if he could find anything out about their situation.

While Sergeant Black was doing that chore, Jovan spent his time trying to come up with a strategy of what he and his men were going to do with themselves.

* * *

When Sergeant Black returned, Jovan asked to be debriefed immediately. "Were you able to get Commander Westolve back to her camp successfully?"

"Yes, and it was interesting," Sergeant Black replied. "I don't think she remembers anything about what happened, or else she doesn't want to remember it. After we got there, she inquired who I was and what unit I was with."

Concerned Jovan asked, "And what did you tell her?"

"The truth, that I was Sergeant Black with the Fifty-First Infantry Regiment out of H'la. It looked like there were only about eighty troopers in the camp. That doesn't seem like a large-enough unit for a commander to be leading."

"She did say that she had lost a lot of her unit in a battle," Jovan commented.

Sergeant Black held up a bag and said, "She offered me some dinner, but I told her I had to get back. So she had a junior officer give me a bag of provision."

Jovan took the bag and handed it to Sergeant Gallant and congratulated the sergeant. "Good work! We can always use more provisions. Did you find anything out about the garrison stationed here?"

"I did. I walked into town and past the garrison headquarters. It looked like no one was around, so I went in the building. It was empty, and it looked like they left in a hurry. A few papers scattered on the floor. The furnishings were still there. I went back outside and into some of the businesses and asked if they knew what happened to the garrison. The owner of the bakery said he was a friend of Major Losguard. He said he always came in for his pastry, which are delicious, by the way. Anyway, the baker said that Losguard told him that he had been ordered to leave immediately and he was to be transferred to the Shining Lands."

Jovan said to himself, "The lancers transferred to the Shining Lands. That is strange. The Shining Lands are peaceful. Why would you send your most experienced and decorated unit to such an out-of-the-way posting?" Looking up, he said, "Sorry, Sergeant. Good job of reconnoitering."

Turning to Sergeant Gallant, Jovan ordered, "Tell the men they can go into the town, a couple at a time. Have them look for different clothes. Also, they can have a drink, one drink each! Caution them to be careful and watch what they say. We do not want to announce our presence."

Sergeant Gallant saluted and said, "Yes, sir." And turned to leave.

Jovan called him back and said, "Sergeant, let's not salute, and drop the 'Yes, sir,' if you would, please." Then realization hit him. "Sorry, I suppose I need to stop ordering you about and start making requests instead. And no more *sergeant*. What is your first name?"

Sergeant Gallant got a distressful look on his face. "I think I would prefer to be called Gallant. I would like to keep my first name to myself, if that would be all right with you, sir…or Jovan."

Jovan smiled. "That would be great! And how about Mr. DeRoan for me? Would that make you more comfortable?"

"Yes, yes, it would, sir…or Mr. DeRoan, much more comfortable."

As his men left him, Jovan turned his mind back to figuring out what they were going to do for the future and tried not to think of the injustice of it all.

Chapter 41

After another day, Daniel, Alssa, and Eric rode into L'ke L'fe, having left Sergeant Sharon and Eric's mercenaries to set up camp north of the town.

They stopped at the first inn on the north end of town. Alssa led them into the common room. It was early morning, so the room was empty, except for a man sweeping the floor by the counter, a serving girl, and a very tall skinny man sitting at the corner table. When the serving girl saw her, she let out a loud squeak and ran out of the room.

Daniel and Eric looked at each other and sat down at the closest table. Alssa approached the man at the counter and asked, "Are you the owner?"

The man looked up from the floor with a start and said, "Yes, I am. What can I do for you?"

"May I ask, have you seen any Three Sisters soldiers in town? They would be dressed like me."

The owner took a step back from her with fear and anger in his eyes and responded, "Yes, there is a group of them camped west of the town." He quickly asked, "Are there more of you coming?"

"Why would you be worried about that?" Alssa asked.

He looked around as if looking for help, stuck out his chin defiantly, and said, "Those that are here are rowdy and cause trouble with the townsfolk. They drink too much."

Alssa did not believe what he was saying. She was confident no Three Sisters officer would let her women act in such a way. But she needed information, so she encouraged him. "I can assure you, that kind of behavior will not be tolerated any longer, and I apologize for any inappropriate behavior my troopers may have had before my arrival."

The owner looked at her askew and asked, "Your troopers? Who are you?"

Alssa switched to her command voice and said, "I am Alssa Martina Ann J'ta, daughter of Ch'lene Fernande Rose J'ta, the ruling queen mother of the Three Sisters."

The owner's response was not what Alssa expected as he laughed out loud and said, "Yeah right, and I am His Majesty Brother Samuel, Lord of the Pact of Brothers." With that he went back to his sweeping, laughing loudly.

Alssa was not sure what to do but resigned herself to going and sitting down next to Daniel and Eric. As she sat down, the tall skinny man from the corner table walked over to them and stared at her for a long moment.

Looking up at him, she said, "Can I help you?"

The man seemed startled by her words. He shook his head no and ran up the staircase, taking two steps at a time.

Daniel chuckled. "Wow, you are generating all sorts of interesting responses this morning."

Alssa laid her hands palms down on the table and declared, "Don't start with me, Daniel."

Daniel held up both hands in mock defense, but Eric spoke up quickly. "Don't let it bother you, Alssa. This is the Middle Kingdom. They haven't delt with royalty for three hundred years. They're all like Daniel. They have no king yet."

Daniel responded this time, "Don't you start with me, Kromsing."

"You two need to get a grip on your emotions. You're both way too tense," Eric said as he looked around for the serving girl.

"And what would you suggest we do to relieve our tension? It's a bit early to start drinking, even for Manslayer," Alssa said, getting a barb in.

Daniel started to respond, but Eric cut him off again. "I could suggest something, but you both just might take turns killing me. So I will keep my suggestion to myself for the time being."

Alssa smirked. "That is wise, Kromsing."

As Daniel started to speak again, the serving girl appeared behind him and said, "Can I get you something?"

Alssa responded, "We would like whatever you are serving for breakfast and three glasses of milk."

The girl walked away as Kromsing and Daniel mouthed *milk* to each other. Alssa saw them and said, "What, you guys don't drink milk?"

Daniel snorted, "Not since I was eleven."

They only had to wait a short time for the food and the milk. They did not talk too much during breakfast. The food was really good, and all three were quite hungry.

As they finished their plates, three men came walking down the stairs. The man leading them was tall and had dark-red complexion; he was followed by the tall skinny man they had seen earlier, and a third man who could only be described as a wine barrel with legs.

The owner came from behind the counter and rushed up to the dark man, asking him if he needed anything. The dark man ignored the owner as he shoved him out of the way with one arm. All the time never taking his eyes off Alssa.

The leader walked up to the table, dropped to one knee, took Alssa's hand, kissed it, and said, "Your Royal Highness, I am very surprised to see you here."

Alssa rose out of her chair, bowed to the man, and said, "Thank you. Who do I have the pleasure of addressing?"

"I am sorry, Your Majesty. My manners escape me because of your beauty," the dark man replied.

Daniel grunted and said, "Oh, the crap is flowing now."

The dark man continued as if Daniel had said nothing, "I am the Marquess Malasaad of the Ramaahian Empire."

Alssa responded using her command voice again, "And who are these two distinguished gentlemen with you?"

Both men stepped out from behind the marquess, beaming bright smiles. The tall skinny one said, "I am Baron Dash, Lord of Vickers."

The barrel quickly followed with, "I am Baron Chalsmore, Lord of Donnelly, and may I say it is an honor and a delight to finally meet you!" The baron took a step toward Alssa, but the marquess stepped in front of him and cut him off.

Everyone just stared at one another for a long moment, until Daniel said with mocking derision in his voice, "Isn't this nice? Royalty from all over the known world. All gathered right here in this little village. Way out here in the middle of nowhere."

Daniel pushed his chair away from the table and stood up. Turning to face the three men, he went to attention. Bowing mockingly, he said, "I am Daniel Manslayer, protector of the rich, vanquisher of evil. From Flanders and all points east." Pointing to Eric, he continued, "This is Captain Kromsing, bard, tailor, mercenary captain, and to be honest, I do not know where he is from."

In unison, Alssa and Eric scolded, "Daniel! That will be quite enough."

He gave a hurt look at both of his friends and then said, "Yeah, way more than enough." And stormed out the door.

Alssa looked at Eric and motioned with her head toward the door. Eric got up out of his chair and hurried after Daniel.

The marquess asked, "You are traveling in the company of Manslayer? An odd choice for the future queen of the Westward."

Alssa thought, *He is familiar with Daniel. That is interesting. What kind of game is he playing at? He obviously knows who I am. Why would he call me the future queen of the Westward?* She said, "You are mistaken. I am the future queen of the Three Sisters. The Westward is not our domain."

The marquess laughed and asked, "Where is your other sister? You did not venture into these wild lands alone, I hope?"

Alssa sensed something odd and replied, "No, of course I am not alone. My troops are massed just north of town, and my sisters are in Jukeele." All the while thinking to herself, *How could he know that Cally was with me?*

The marquess's smile was predatory as he said, "We did meet one of your commanders the other day. Did she precede you here?"

Alssa responded coyly, "Which one would that be? I have so many."

Looking at the two other men as if to seek confirmation, he said, "I believe it was Commander Westolve, if I remember correctly. She was quite into her cups when she was here. Not very talkative, but a bit sad, I do believe."

This was unbelievable to her. When Alssa had met Commander Westolve, she had been a young lieutenant, serving in the House J'ta royal guard. She had then transferred to House K'jo, hoping to be T'asha's personal protector. She became one of T'asha's most senior officers. Alssa knew that serving in T'asha's personal company could be hard duty, but to be drunk in public, Alssa did not think so.

Alssa bowed to the three men as she said, "It has been a pleasure to meet you. We should dine together some evening while we are all here." Then she started for the door.

The marquess called after her, "I look forward to that. I hope you are still available when the time arrives." Then he cautioned, "Be careful out there, Your Majesty."

* * *

Jovan had decided that they would move their camp farther out of town. One of his scouts had found a cave high up on the side of a solitary mountain. It was about five miles east of L'ke L'fe.

The men were all packed up and he was leading them through town when he saw two men and a woman standing in the middle of the road. The woman was wearing a Three Sisters uniform just like the ones the soldiers had on in the graves they had dug up in the forest.

Jovan pointed them out to Gallant and said, "Does that uniform look familiar to you?"

"It does. I wonder if she was part of the group that escaped that day," Gallant answered.

"Let's go ask her," Jovan said.

* * *

Commander Westolve was tired of sitting around, tired of being in the tents, and tired of getting drunk. She had been in L'ke L'fe for over a week, and nothing had happened. She had no word from T'asha. If her morale were low, her trooper's morale would be even lower. Because of that, she decided to move the entire unit into the old Pact of Brothers garrison house. No one had shown up to replace Major Losguard and his men, so it was just sitting vacant.

As they rode through town, she could see a large number of men on horses gathered around three people standing in the street. One of the people was a woman wearing a uniform of the House J'ta royal guard.

She was not sure what was going on, but something looked wrong. She called for her first squad to join her. They rode forward at a trot.

* * *

As Alssa left the inn, she could see Daniel and Eric on the other side of the road. Waving to them, she started to cross the cobblestone street. Both Daniel and Eric stepped out into the road to meet her.

Eric had calmed Daniel down and was just going to tell Alssa what they had decided to do next when a large group of men rode up to them.

The man who was leading them stopped and asked Alssa, "Excuse me, ma'am, but were you in the north end of the Ebony Forest a few days ago?"

Alssa was taken aback by the question. How would this man even begin to know that? Except for beasts and the troll, they had been alone. So she responded with, "Who are you? And why would you want to know?

Jovan was unsure of how to proceed but thought the truth was the simplest. He said, “I and my men were lancers for the Pact of Brothers. We were patrolling up there when we came upon the sight of a battle. Dead man-orcs, some wolves, and oddly enough, five partially buried women. Some of which were wearing that same uniform as you. We knew someone had survived, because of the buried bodies.”

“I still don’t see why you would care if I were there or not. What business is it of yours?” Alssa asked.

“Well, we were trailing a man who had escaped from the jail in H’la. There were reports that he was carrying a unique sword that could not have belonged to a thief such as him. His trail led to your battle site. And if it was your battle site, I was wondering if you might have seen him.”

Jovan had just finished talking, and it became quiet. Sergeant Black noticed Commander Westolve and four of her troopers coming up the road at a trot. He quickly moved up by Jovan and Daniel to let Jovan know.

They all heard the swish and thud of a crossbow bolt, and Sergeant Black was knocked forward off his horse. The men with Jovan began searching for where the bolt came from.

Daniel drew the sword and stepped in front of Alssa.

Eric dropped down low, looking at the rooftops for the shooter.

Commander Westolve, being close enough to see that it was Princess Alssa, spurred her horse and charged forward, yelling to her troops, “It’s the princess Alssa! We must get her.”

Jovan’s mind raced as he heard the commander’s yell and saw the sword in Daniel’s hand. Should he protect the princess? Because he knew Westolve’s orders. Or capture Daniel and the sword? Having the sword would redeem him and his men.

As he was about to make his decision, another bolt came flying in, hitting Daniel’s left shoulder and deflecting into his head. The blow spun Daniel around, knocking him to the ground. The sword flew out of Daniel’s hand and clanged on the cobblestones.

Four more bolts came flying in, all four aimed at the princess. Three missed, but one bounced off her armor with a clang and knocked her to the ground. That made up his mind for him. He ordered some of his men to block Westolve and her troopers from getting to the princess. Then he jumped from his horse and instructed men to put Daniel into his saddle and to get him out of town.

He helped the princess off the ground and led her to three horses that were tied up on the edge of the street. He then helped her mount and grabbed a horse for himself. Yelling to his men, they all departed the town, heading east.

Commander Westolve was about to give chase when she noticed that it was Sergeant Black on the ground with a crossbow bolt sticking out of his back. She stopped and dismounted to check on him. He was still alive. She ordered her troopers to carry him into the garrison headquarters. Then she sent another trooper to get the healer who traveled with them.

As she stood there looking east at the fading dust cloud, she kicked the ground in frustration and the sword went spinning away. Picking it up, she recognized it immediately. Turning it over in her hand, she was amazed that it matched the stories she had been told.

Valkar came walking up to her, carrying a crossbow. He pointed the crossbow at her and said, "I will take that, if you please."

Westolve had not started the day in a good mood, and it had become worse. She thought, *This fool of a man has picked a bad time to challenge me!* She motioned to her four troopers, and they lowered their lances, tips aimed at Valkar's chest. She then said, "I suggest you lower your weapon, sir."

Looking at the four lances, Count Valkar lowered his crossbow and said, "That sword is my prize. I have been chasing Manslayer across the known lands for five years. I finally had him, and then all of you show up. But I hit him this time. I am sure of that. That sword belongs to me."

Commander Westolve looked at Count Valkar and said to her troops, "Arrest this man for attempted murder. Lock him up in the Pact of Brothers garrison jail."

Count Valkar struggled with the women who were dragging him away. He cried out, "You don't know what you have there! That sword is special, and it's mine by right!"

Commander Westolve smiled as she thought, *That is where you are wrong, mister. I know what I have here. I have a way back into my queen's good graces, and hopefully into her heart.*

CHAPTER 42

One of the scouts Commander Westolve had sent out on the day she saw Alssa burst into her new office in the garrison building.

"You found them?" she said to the panting scout.

"No, ma'am. I was posted to the west on the Queen's Highway, halfway between H'la and L'ke L'fe."

"Okay, what is happening out there that has you barging into my office unannounced?" she questioned, half-scolding.

The scout inhaled deeply and said, "The Pact of Brothers infantry company that was in H'la is marching this way, and T'asha is with them."

"You're sure it was T'asha?" Westolve asked with too much excitement.

"Yes, ma'am, royal dress and flaming red hair. It was her for sure," the scout replied.

The commander got up and started pacing around the room, then she asked the scout, "How many Three Sisters troops were with her?"

The scout said, "Not many, less than one hundred, but they were her royal house guard."

"Is someone still observing them?" the commander asked.

"Sergeant Goins and three more troopers. She was going to be sending back a messenger with any new reports."

"Thank you, Trooper. Go get yourself cleaned up, get some hot food, and then report back to Sergeant Goins," Commander

Westolve said warmly. "And please send the lieutenant in when you leave."

Commander Westolve and the lieutenant made plans for T'asha's arrival.

* * *

It was abundantly clear that T'asha was not happy when she arrived. Commander Westolve had set up a greeting for her. She had her troopers line up on the road to receive the princess. T'asha ordered Westolve to dismiss them all and commanded that she would meet with the commander's senior officers one by one and that Commander Westolve would be last. As Westolve was getting ready to dismiss the troopers, T'asha also informed her that she would have to stop squatting in the garrison house. The Pact of Brothers infantry colonel wanted his property back.

Commander Westolve had set up rooms for T'asha in the nicest inn in L'ke L'fe. When Westolve entered the big rectangular room on the second floor of the inn, it was obvious that T'asha's mood had become worse.

T'asha greeter her. "Maurice, please explain your actions since you left Devil's Pass."

Westolve thought, *This is not good. T'asha only uses my first name when she is really happy or really mad. What should I tell her? How much does she already know? How much did my senior officers divulge?*

"I am waiting, Commander," T'asha demanded.

Seeing Daniel's sword lying on the side table, she found an answer that might save her yet. She pointed at the sword and said, "It had been uneventful until the man wielding this sword came to town. There was confrontation between the man with the sword and a group of men on horseback. I took a squad and charged into the melee. I rescued a Pact of Brothers infantry sergeant but was only able to capture one person, an attempted murderer. But as you can see, I did obtain the Sword of Power."

The commander's color drained from her face as T'asha said, "That is an interesting perspective, Maurice. The story I have constructed from what your officers have told me seems a little more eventful."

Commander Westolve cried, "Your Majesty, you must understand, the task you gave me was—"

T'asha stood up and interrupted her. "Was what, Commander? Too difficult? You had two simple tasks, prepare for my arrival and deal with my sisters if they made it to L'ke L'fe. You failed at both. On top of that, you failed to notice that the town was crawling with Ramaahian assassins, that an entire company of disgraced lancers was camped just outside of town, who clearly were in league with my sister! And worst of all, you let her escape."

Pleading, Commander Westolve said, "What about the sword and the attempted murderer?"

T'asha walked over to the sword and picked it up, brandished it in front of her and then threw it on the table, and said, "This is obviously a copy. Why else would a vagabond thief have it? The lieutenant Colonel from H'la says that this disgraced lancer, this Captain Jovan, was spreading wild stories to make up for his disobedience and his dereliction of duty."

Westolve implored T'asha, "But all the old stories we were told in school, it fits the description."

"The operative word being *stories*, and that is just what all this is." T'asha reached out and pushed the sword. "Just a story. Much like the story you have been telling me about your failure to obey my orders."

"But what about the murderer?" the commander begged.

"Ah, yes, the horrible villain you apprehended." T'asha called out to her orderly, "Please bring the count in here."

In a few moments, the man Commander Westolve arrested walked into the room. He had a broad smile on his face and no shackles on his wrists.

Westolve turned quickly to face T'asha to say something, but T'asha started talking first. "Commander, I would like you to meet Count Valkar, fourth in line to the throne of Valkaria."

The count could hardly take his eyes off the sword as he asked, "How may I be of service, Your Majesty?"

Commander Westolve could not believe her bad luck. She had arrested a royal and accused him of attempted murder. She just dropped her chin to her chest, expecting the worst.

"The count believes that this sword belongs to him," T'asha said with a wicked smile. "It seems he has been pursuing this Daniel Manslayer. I like that name very much. The count has been pursuing him for the last five years. The count says that every time he gets close, someone, or something, gets in the way. Like you did the other day."

T'asha sat back down and leaned back in her chair and continued, "The count believes like you that the sword has some special power. He says he has seen this Manslayer in battle before. He says that it gives the wielder an almost-magical advantage in a fight and that this Manslayer has used it that way."

Count Valkar interjected, "It does, Your Majesty. I have seen where he has been outnumbered ten to one and emerged without a scratch."

Commander Westolve was grasping at straws when she said, "I don't know anything about that. I was only going by the design of the sword. I have a hard time believing anyone can win with ten-to-one odds."

T'asha waved her hand at the both of them and said, "I am not really concerned about what you or the count believe. I am really only concerned on whether this Manslayer and my sister believe it. We may have an opportunity here."

T'asha stood back up and reached out and touched the commander on the shoulder. With a pleasant, comforting tone, she said, "Maurice, I would like you to take your command and scour the land east of here and find my sister." T'asha patted the commander on the shoulder, which made the commander flinch. T'asha continued, "I have ordered you company to be brought up to full strength. I want you to leave tomorrow morning."

Westolve could not believe her ears; she was not going to be sacked but instead was given her full command back. She got up to leave and said, "Thank you, Your Majesty. I won't let you down."

T'asha had begun to address the count but stopped and said to Westolve instead, "Maurice, please don't come back without my sister."

As the commander left the room, she heard T'asha respond to something the count had said, "No, the sword stays where it is at, but wouldn't you rather have the Manslayer?"

CHAPTER 43

Daniel's shoulder and face were bruised by the crossbow bolt, and he had a throbbing headache. But worse than those wounds were the loss of the sword. He had been heavily dazed by the shock of the bolt, so he did not remember most of the trip to the cave they were in now. He sat up on the rock he had been reclining on to regain his bearings. He wobbled a bit when he stood up and walked over to join the others. They were discussing the incident in the street.

Alssa was questioning Jovan, "How did you know what Commander Westolve was thinking?"

Jovan was reluctant to tell the whole story, so he said, "I overheard the commander say she had been ordered by her queen to kill you and your sister. I had no idea who you were until the crossbow bolts started flying. I then heard the commander order her troops to get you. I figured I was going to have to pick a side sooner or later, so I picked yours."

Daniel spoke up and said, "I am glad you did!"

Jovan gave Daniel a distrustful look and said, "I really do not care what you think, thief. You are probably the cause of all this, anyway."

Daniel frowned, with a puzzled look on his face, and said, "I don't know how you came to that conclusion, Captain, but it is the wrong one. I have done a great many things in my short life, and I can assure you that being a thief is not one of them."

Jovan smirked and turned his attention back to Alssa and said, "Like I was saying when the crossbow bolts started flying at you, I decided to intervene."

Daniel did not like being dismissed by the captain, so he commented loudly, "Like I was saying, I think you have misread the situation. Those crossbow bolts were meant for me."

Jovan countered, "I don't think so. After the second one hit you, the next four were clearly aimed at the princess."

Alssa gave Daniel a questioning glance. "Why would anyone be looking to kill you, especially trained assassins?" She then continued, "I do not like what Captain Jovan is saying, but I think he is correct."

Daniel gave her a hurt stare and asked, "What, you don't think I could have made powerful enemies?" He then boasted, "Listen, Your Highness, I have traveled more of this world than you, and I have made my share of enemies. I am really good at what I do, and that has angered a lot of powerful people."

Kromsing interrupted, "You two need to stop your bickering. You are all correct in your assumptions, but incorrect in your final analysis. Most of the bolts were aimed at the princess, by Ramaahian assassins, but those that killed Sergeant Black and wounded Daniel were fired by Count Valkar. I know, because I wasn't the target, so I was able to see the shooters. I could only identify one of them by name, and that was the count, but the others were all Ramaahians."

Alssa, not wanting to give in so quickly, asked, "How do you guys know this Count Valkar?"

Eric looked at Daniel, and Daniel nodded for him to go ahead and tell the story. Eric said, "Count Valkar's vendetta against Daniel is infamous in the Eastward. Five years ago, Daniel killed Valkar's brother, one of the heirs to the Valkarian throne. Valkar swore vengeance and has been chasing Daniel ever since. That was why Daniel fled to the Westward, at least that is what Daniel believes."

Daniel was going to object to Eric's last statement but thought the better of it. Instead, he said, "We must get my sword back."

Jovan looked at Alssa and Kromsing and then challenged Daniel by saying, "Your sword? What would a thief be doing carrying the

Sword of Power? How did you end up with it? And whom did you steal it from in the first place?"

Daniel turned to face Jovan, and with anger rising in his voice, he snarled, "Listen closely, soldier boy. Open your mind and pull that uptight military stick out of your ass. I am not a thief, and if you call me that one more time, I will show you what I am and why I have it."

Kromsing stepped in between the two men and said, "Daniel is right, we do need to get the sword back."

Alssa agreed but added, "We must also find my sister and deal with her."

"We do not need to find your sister. She is in L'ke L'fe," Jovan announced as he glared at Daniel. "She came a few days after we left. The sword and your sister are both in the same place, the Royal Inn, right in the middle of L'ke L'fe."

"How can you know that?" Alssa asked.

"I left two men in town to keep an eye on things. While snooping around, they found out that Sergeant Black did not die of his wounds. My boys were able to make contact with him, and he gave them the information."

Daniel rubbed his hands together and said, "All right, let's make a plan."

CHAPTER 44

Daniel, along with Alssa and Kromsing, crept closer to the back of the Royal Inn. The windows were dark and shuttered. Daniel thought, *That's just the way it should be. It is much too early in the morning for anyone to be up. This is way too easy. I don't like it.*

They had positioned Captain Jovan and his men in the woods east of town, and the day before, Kromsing told his mercenaries to wander into town in ones and twos during the daylight hours.

They had come up with this plan two days ago. It seemed like a good idea at that time, but Daniel had a nagging tug pulling at him from deep inside his mind. He was not worried about the plan, but the people involved in it concerned him.

The goal was to recover the sword and take T'asha captive. T'asha was probably the more important of the two tasks. But in Daniel's mind, getting his sword back was an overwhelming desire. He was amazed at how much he had become attached to it. It had not left his side since Nathan gave it to him, at least not until he came to this accursed land. He was always fond of it, but he assumed that was because it had been a gift. But something was changing. In the last two weeks, the sword was becoming more a part of him. With it not in his possession, he could feel it calling to him.

He disagreed with Alssa and Cally, who said that his possession of the sword meant he was the promised king. Nor did he agree with Oaklawn, who kept saying that he was a Lightbearer, whatever that meant.

What he knew was that he was an orphan raised for a few years by a nice family in Flanderon and that they had all been killed by bandits. And then a kind strange old man took him in and taught him how to survive, and he too had been killed. He knew that everyone he had ever become close to ended up dead. He was confident that he was not a royal heir; he was just a very unlucky person when it came to relationships. He could not allow himself to get too close to anyone ever again.

"What are you looking at?" Alssa asked.

Daniel was startled from his thoughts. He quickly realized that he had been staring at Alssa. He continued to stare, not knowing what to say.

"What!" Alssa glared.

"Nothing! I…I was just thinking about our plan," Daniel lied. He was glad the darkness was covering up his embarrassment.

Alssa shrugged and said, "I don't think you need to worry. T'asha tends to be overconfident in her own plans. She will never expect us to try something like this. She won't be ready for us." Alssa put her hand on Daniel's shoulder and said, "It's going to work."

Daniel was not worried, at least not about their plan; he had been doing this kind of stuff his whole life. But he was concerned for Alssa, or more accurately, about his feelings for her.

They moved past the last house that sat behind the inn. T'asha's headquarters was a two-story building built of stone with a slate roof. There was an outside stone staircase attached to the back of the inn that led up to the second-floor back hallway. One of Jovan's troopers had scouted out the building earlier. He reported that the back of the inn was only guarded by one person on the outside and one person at the top of the stairs on the inside.

Alssa and Daniel watched as Kromsing easily sneaked up on the sentry and choked her unconscious, she had been asleep. The two of them then followed Kromsing up the stairs. To their surprise, the door was not locked, and when they slowly opened the door, there was no second guard.

Working their way down the hall to the fourth door on the left, Daniel motioned them to a halt. Kromsing continued past the door and on down the hallway to the top of the inside staircase. Daniel and Alssa watched as Kromsing peeked over the rail and then returned to them.

In a whisper, Kromsing reported, "There is a guard at the base of the steps, but she is sitting in a chair and looks like she might be asleep."

Alssa's face contorted in a quizzical look as she spoke softly. "That's odd. Both guards asleep and the door unlocked. This feels wrong."

Daniel's lips formed a half smile. "You want to walk away now? We are already inside. Besides, you're the one who said we had nothing to worry about."

He placed his hand on the door latch and pushed it down with his thumb; this door was not locked either. The door easily swung open, with only a slight squeak. They entered the room slowly one at a time. Daniel scanned the room, looking for his sword, while Alssa silently stepped to the edge of the bed. She withdrew her knife from its scabbard on her hip with her right hand, and with her left she covered T'asha's mouth.

T'asha's eyes flashed open at the touch. She began to squirm and kick until she felt the sharp edge of Alssa's blade against her throat.

"Sit up," Alssa ordered.

T'asha recovered her composure quickly and sat up in the bed. Looking from Daniel to Kromsing, contempt filling her voice, she said, "So, big sister, I see you have stooped to the level of thieving men, sneaking around in the night, executing people in their sleep."

Kromsing grinned and gave Daniel a what-who-me look. Daniel smiled back the same look. He walked over to the bed, wrapped his huge left hand around her neck, and squeezed so she could not speak. Picking her up out of the bed, he stood her on her feet.

He pointed his finger in her face and said, "Don't scream or I will snap your neck."

He let a little pressure off her throat and motioned for Kromsing to tie her hands behind her back.

T'asha smiled wickedly at Daniel and turned her eyes to see Alssa and said, "I can see why you like this one, big sister. He's a wild beast of a man."

Alssa turned her face away as she began to blush but responded harshly, "T'asha, shut up!" and then questioned, "What have you done with the sword?"

Ignoring Alssa, T'asha turned her eyes back to Daniel and asked, "So, Daniel Manslayer, personal bodyguard to the rich and nefarious, how does it feel to be just a common thief and have turned the head of the most powerful female in the known lands?"

Daniel's eyes darted to Alssa, but her face was turned away.

T'asha laughed wickedly. "You didn't even know? Typical male, always two steps behind."

Kromsing twisted the ropes tighter on her wrist, causing her to wince.

Alssa turned around and grabbed her sister by the shoulders and demanded, "Where is the sword?"

T'asha growled her response, "I sent it away! Back to Jukeele to our dear, sweet mothers. Or should I say to *your* dear, sweet mothers? Since mine is dead."

Talking way too loudly, Alssa said, "You're lying! You would never let it out of your control. Where is it?"

T'asha smirked and laughed. "You are coming off way too desperate, my dear big sister. Your newfound male lover has lost his toy, and you so much want to get it back for him. You are so pathetic!"

Alssa's hand moved so fast it surprised her. She slapped her sister with such force it knocked T'asha to her knees. Standing over her, she commanded, "Stop your stupid taunting and tell me where the sword is!"

T'asha struggled to her feet. She smiled at Alssa, with blood on her teeth. Spitting on the floor, she said, "That's new! I like it. You have always been such an annoying proper bitch. Never losing your temper, always under control. This is more like the person who I knew you really were. Wouldn't Mommy be proud of her little princess now, all out of control and angry?"

Alssa raised her hand to hit her sister again, but T'asha stood defiant and taunted, "It feels good, doesn't it? Go ahead, hit me again. It would do you good."

Alssa turned away, but T'asha continued, "I can feel the rage inside of you, the pent-up, desperate anger of a spoiled child. You're so used to getting your own way, no one ever telling you no. You have had everything you ever wanted handed to you. Your every whim catered to by your precious mother."

T'asha pointed at Daniel, spit out blood again, and said, "And now you have the man you always wanted right in front of you, and you don't even realize it. You have been so naive and vain that you have never really known what you really wanted."

Alssa spun around and yelled, "As opposed to you? Megan gave you everything! She never disciplined you for your evil behavior, and now it has brought you to this!"

Kromsing looked at Daniel with worry in his eyes, so Daniel spoke up and said, "Alssa, quiet down. Someone will hear. Let's just go."

Neither Alssa nor T'asha was listening. T'asha laughed wickedly and said, "That is where you are so wrong. Megan taught me all I needed to know and trained me how to get it. She raised me to know that everything that was withheld unjustly from her would be mine and that you and Cally would serve me as your queen once your mothers were gone. She trained me to be the only rightful queen of the Three Sisters."

Alssa glared at T'asha in disbelief, unable to speak.

Daniel had had enough; he pulled a cloth gag out of his belt and stuffed it in T'asha's mouth and tied it off tightly around the back of her head. He led her by the elbow toward the door, following Kromsing, who was opening it. Kromsing checked to make sure no one was in the hall.

Alssa recovered from her shock and moved quickly to join the others. Daniel turned to go back down the hall the way they had come, but Alssa called softly, "Wait, Daniel, we must have the sword."

Alssa pulled her knife out again and held it up to T'sha's face as she said, "You're right, Little Sister, this does feel good." Resting the razor-sharp edge against T'asha's cheek, she continued, "You know I cannot kill you, but if you do not tell me where the sword is, I will slice up your perfect little face."

For the first time, T'asha seemed knocked off balance, but only for a moment. She shook her head in a motion to undo the gag, so Daniel did. T'asha breathed in heavily and said, "All right, all right, your worthless hunk of metal is in the room at the far end of the hall."

Daniel retied the gag, and the four them crept down the long hall. He grew more nervous as it seemed odd that the guard at the bottom of the steps had not heard them arguing. When they passed the staircase opening, the guard was gone. Daniel thought, *Alssa must be right. T'asha must be way overconfident to have such lax security.*

They reached the end of the hall, and Alssa went to open the door slowly, but it was locked. Daniel handed T'asha's elbow over to Kromsing and pulled his knife out of his boot; kneeling before the lock, he quickly picked it and the door swung open on its own.

The room was a large rectangle with a big solid table in the middle and a narrow side table against the wall opposite the door they entered. There was a desk table in one corner. The wall across from them had windows overlooking the main street. There was a door set in each end wall, and both were closed.

A little moonlight was coming in from the outside, enough to see that Daniel's sword was not on the big table or on the side table between the two windows. Kromsing and Daniel each went to the doors on the end walls and opened them. They led to short hallways that were empty. They closed the doors and turned towards T'asha.

Alssa grabbed the gag and pulled it roughly from T'asha's mouth. "I am tired of your games! Where is it?" she demanded.

T'asha looked at Alssa sheepishly. "Honestly, it was lying on the big table when I went to bed last night. Maybe someone stole it."

Kromsing was looking frantically from Daniel and back at Alssa and said, "We are running out of time. We need to go now."

Daniel was getting worried. He could feel that the sword was near, but the nagging voice in the back of his mind was telling him something was not right. He said, "The sword is close, but we are in real danger."

Kromsing started for the door to the main hallway when Alssa said, "Let's leave from a different way."

They had only taken a few steps when T'asha stopped and proclaimed, "I don't think you will be going anywhere." She then spun around twice and said, "The light is blind, but the darkness sees us free, so in the darkness let us be."

The moonlight coming in through the windows went dark. Daniel could see nothing. Then he heard all three doors open and footsteps of people coming in. And as suddenly as the moonlight had disappeared, it reappeared. They had been joined by ten of T'asha's royal guards. Looking at the big mirror hung between the two windows, Daniel saw that T'asha was free of her bonds.

Daniel took two strong steps toward one of the doors, hoping to bull his way through, but Count Valkar was blocking the way and he was holding the sword of light in his right hand.

"Going somewhere, Manslayer?" Count Valkar laughed.

Before the three of them could recover, the guards grabbed them and confiscated their weapons.

T'asha took control immediately. Pointing at Kromsing, she ordered, "Bind his hands and gag his mouth so that the seer cannot do any of his simple magic tricks."

Daniel did a double take at Kromsing and said, "Eric, what is she talking about?"

T'asha chuckled. "You never knew? All this time your mercenary friend has been hanging around, coming in and out of your life, and you never knew he was a seer? Their order has been watching you from the beginning, keeping their eye on you, their precious Manchild. You never had friends, Manslayer, just watchers, to make sure you did what they wanted. And now, when it is too late, you finally find out. I love it!"

Laughing wickedly, T'asha continued, "I guess that means I must also suppose that you are just as clueless to the fact that even the seers think that you are the returning king."

Daniel looked at T'asha in total disbelief and then looked at Eric, who was not denying any of it. His mind was spinning as he thought, *Eric is a seer? All this time he's been spying on me and only pretended to be a friend so he could be close?*

T'asha sneered at all three of them. "Look at him," she said, pointing at Daniel. "He is taken completely off guard by some trivial facts." Turning to glare at Kromsing, she continued, "And you and your pathetic order thought this bastard thief would one day rule the entire Westward? You are as blind and diluted, as the healers have always said you were!"

She slowly walked over to Alssa and pulled Alssa's knife out of it sheath. She then turned and stood in front of Eric. Reaching up with her right hand, she grabbed his hair on the back of his head and pulled it back. She then violently drove the tip of the knife blade into his left eye. As Eric screamed in pain from behind the gag, T'asha proclaimed, "You seers have always held the Three Sisters back from their rightful destiny, with your prophecies of a returning king, but no more."

Daniel lunged forward, struggling against the guards that held him, but they knocked him to the ground.

Alssa screamed out, "What are you doing?"

T'asha smiled and said, "Why sister, I am righting the wrongs that have been done to us by these men." Turning back to Eric, she grabbed his hair once again and jabbed the tip of the blade into his right eye, giving the blade a twist.

Eric passed out, with blood running down his face from both eye sockets. His body went limp in the guard's hands, and they let him fall to the floor.

T'asha nudged his head with her bare feet and spoke to the guards. "If or when he wakes up, let him crawl back to his little island, if he can find it. Let his kind know that their well-laid plans have failed completely."

Anger filled T'asha's eyes as she turned on Count Valkar. "I told you to leave the sword on the table. Why wasn't I obeyed?"

Valkar trembled just a bit as he said, "I thought…well, Your Majesty, I have seen this man fight with this weapon many times, and I felt it would be safer and easier for all of us if he wasn't able to get his hands on it."

T'asha scoffed, pointing at her captives. She said, "You are as big a fool as these three. Give him the sword."

Valkar was stunned and exclaimed, "What! Are you crazy? He would easily kill half of us before we could subdue him!"

T'asha spun around, swinging her left hand in a wide circle, Alssa's knife still firmly in her grasp. The tip sliced into Valkar's left cheek, causing blood to squirt all over the guard standing beside him. He dropped the sword on the floor and grabbed his face. As Valkar yelped, Daniel pulled free of those holding him and dived toward the sword. Deftly grabbing the pommel of his beloved weapon, he rolled through his dive and came to his feet in a fighting stance. All the guards started to rush him, but T'asha called them off. She reached out with her right hand and filled her fingers with Alssa's blond hair. Dragging Alssa to her knees, she placed Alssa's own knife against her throat.

Smiling wickedly at Daniel, she said, "Go ahead, kill as many as you like, but your sweet princess will bleed to death in front of you before you die."

Daniel had started to attack but froze in his tracks. He could see the silver blade open a little cut on Alssa's throat.

T'asha laughed again, looking down at her sister. She said, "You see, dear, he does really love you. How sweet, two star-crossed lovers who are too timid and shy to speak their true feelings for each other." T'asha raised her right foot and kicked Alssa in the middle of the back, knocking her face-first onto the floor. Looking at Daniel, she spit out, "You two disgust me!"

Daniel wasted no time but lunged at T'asha. The tip of his sword started to glow as it raced toward her heart. T'asha lifted her clenched right fist, with her palm facing Daniel. She then flicked her fingers open. Daniel flew straight back through the air, slamming against the wall, knocking the wind out of him and causing him to drop the sword. It clanged on the wooden floor. Daniel hung suspended two feet off the ground; he was unable to move.

Alssa pulled herself up onto her hands and knees, blood running from her nose. She looked at Eric, who appeared to be dead. The guards had all stepped back, their eyes filled with shock and fear. Alssa's mind raced. *What is happening here?*

T'asha spoke with evil humor, "You see, Count, there was never anything to fear from this bastard thief and his flaming sword."

On hands and knees, Alssa noticed that Daniel's sword had bounce toward her when he dropped it. Concentrating, she began to chant in a whisper.

T'asha slowly walked toward Daniel with her left hand extended. She was holding him off the ground without touching him. As she lowered her hand, he slid down the wall until his feet were only inches off the floor. She turned her head to look at Alssa and said, "It really is too bad that you and he didn't get a chance to express you true feelings for each other, heart to heart, before he lost his." With that, T'asha stabbed Alssa's knife into the center of Daniel's chest with all her strength. Daniel's back arched, he cried out with no sound, then went limp and fell front first to the floor.

T'asha turned to face her sister and mockingly said, "Well, pretty princess, what are you going to do now without all your big strong men to protect you?"

Alssa's eyes were filled with tears and her ears filled with her sister's taunts as she spoke the chant out loud. The blade burst into flames as she seized the handle. With all her strength, she pushed off the floor swinging the blade at T'asha's neck.

Slow to react because of the flaming blade T'asha was only able to lift her right hand and deflect it. So instead of cutting into her neck and slicing off her head, it cut off two of her fingers and the flat of the blade slapped against her face with an explosion of light. The force of the blast wave knocked everyone in the room down and rendered them unconscious.

CHAPTER 45

T'asha rose from the floor dazed and confused. She remembered the bright flash of light before she was knocked off her feet. She recalled her sister swinging the sword at her. She lifted her left hand up to her face. The sword had severed her two small fingers off clean, but the burning blade had cauterized the wound. Looking around she could see that all the rest of the people in the room were still unconscious.

Holding her left hand up in front of her face again to examine it more closely she caught a glimpse of herself in the wall mirror. A Shocked and horrified face stared back at her. The face of the woman in the mirror was split in half; the right side was smooth and beautiful with long red hair hanging down to below the shoulder. But the left side was a grotesque twisted mess. The hair was burned stubble short; the skin was charred, and the ear was missing. Her face looked as if it had melted, and she had a freshly cauterized scar on her neck. She grabbed her face and ran screaming from the room.

* * *

Alssa sat up, unsure of where she was. Her head pounded with the rhythm and intensity of a blacksmith's hammer. She could not open her eyes; everything was black. The joints in her hands and arms ached. She rubbed her hands up and down her arms to bring some comfort to her pain. Reaching up, she touched her face and realized her eyes were open. Panic struck her as she thought, *I am blind! Where am I? What happened to me?* She could not seem to force herself to remember.

Getting up on her hands and knees, she began to crawl forward hoping to find something to hold onto to lift herself up. She had only crawled a few feet when her hands bumped into something soft but firm. She began to grope around; it was clearly a body, but why was it here? What had happened? She could not remember. She had started feeling the body at the legs, so she worked her way up to the torso. Whoever it was, they were facedown. She rolled the body over, and her hands felt a warm sticky liquid.

Fear rose inside her as she thought, *Is this blood?* As her hands moved further up the body, she felt something hard sticking out of the chest. Her hands grasped it; she recognized what it was. It was the handle of a knife, her knife, and that is when the memories all came flooding back to her. The body and blood belonged to Daniel.

Holding Daniel's head, she shifted her body so she could hold it in her lap. Her mind raced as she began to recall all that had happened. The last thing she remembered was swinging the flaming sword at T'asha's neck. Then an explosion of light when the flat of the blade hit her sister's face. Working back from there, she remembered her sister stabbing Daniel in the heart and cutting out Eric's eyes. They were both dead. Her grief over their loss was overwhelming. The realization that this had all been a trap and they had walked into it totally unaware caused even more grief. This also meant that Captain Jovan and his men were riding into a trap.

Alssa began to sob. Not only had they not recovered the sword or captured T'asha, but everyone will be lost. All but her, and she was blind and a captive. Fear and desperation consumed her soul. She wept hard, uncontrollable tears, wishing for death.

She looked up and cried out to the God of her childhood, the one she and Cally had prayed to when they were in trouble, the one she had never believed in.

Now she called out to the light, "I pray that this day never have happened."

But she knew it had, and now all was lost. She cried out in anger, desperate for something, anything that might change what had befallen them.

She thought, *If only Cally were here, she had faith. She believed in things that could not be seen, things that could not happen. Cally always seemed to walk in this world and be in another at the same time.*

Alssa had never understood, thinking it was Cally's youthful playfulness. When Cally did not like what was happening, she would slip into another place and float through the events surrounding her. Alssa could never do that.

Alssa only believed in what was real. Things you could see and touch—they were real. *Well,* she thought, *what is real now, Daniel and Eric are dead, and I am alone. Trapped in this building with my traitorous sister. My sister, who had killed two men I had come to trust and one who I love.*

A wave of anguish overcame her, and she broke down again. She wept hard and long, covering Daniel's blood-soaked shirt with her tears.

After a time, her crying and grief turned back to anger. Looking up again at her nonexistent god, she said, "Why have you forsaken us? Why are you never here when I need you?"

She looked down at Daniel and then back up and cried, "This was him. This was the promised one. He is the one we had waited three hundred years for, and now he is dead, dead because of me. If he had let T'asha kill me, he could have gotten away. He could have killed her and taken his place on the throne. The Darkness would have been pushed back. But now, it will run rampant through the lands of the Westward. All is lost because of me."

Alssa sat, her head resting on Daniel's chest, her hair matted with his blood. Quietly she looked back up and shuddered, "Lord of light, you should have taken me and not him. He is the one who needs to live. God of light, restore his life and take mine in his place. I want to die in his place, give him back the spark of life."

Alssa cried out in desperation, believing if she could only exert the faith necessary, Daniel would live and she would die. She began to cry again, begging her God to exchange her life for his. She cried until she once again passed out.

After a long while, she opened her eyes, she was in the same room, she still could see nothing, but she could feel Daniel draped across her legs, and he was still dead. Nothing had changed.

It was more than she could take; overwhelmed, her heart began to burst in pain. She could feel the light of life inside of her rushing from her heart up through her throat. As the light exploded from her mouth, she could see its intensity. Her head pounded with a thousand stabbing pains. The tears began to flow one more time and right before she lost consciousness. She could see that her tears looked like liquid diamonds filled with the light of the brightest sun, and then she, too, was dead.

CHAPTER 46

Daniel, Alssa and Eric all awoke at the same time. They were back in Jovan's cave. Daniel was confused, His mind was fuzzy, but it did not hurt. His memories were jumbled; they did not make sense. He finally was able to hold on to the last solid thing he remembered. It was being stabbed in the chest by T'asha. He looked at Alssa who was staring at him with a look of disbelief and Eric, poor eric was sitting on a rock looking straight forward. His eye sockets were covered over with skin and showed no signs of scarring.

Daniel asked them both, "Do you know how we Got here?"

They both shook their heads no.

Jovan stepped out of the shadows and said, "Sergeant Black saw you go into the inn. Then much later saw T'asha run out through the same door you went in. She ran toward the small woods to the north of town. He decided to check up on you and when he found you, you were all lying unconscious in the second-floor meeting room. Nobody else was in the room with you. He loaded you all in a wagon and brought you back here."

Alssa asked Jovan, "What happened with your part of our plan?"

"Fortunately," Jovan answered, "before we could start our attack my last trooper who I had left in town in the beginning finally found us. He informed me that Sergeant Black had told him that T'asha had made arrangements with the Infantry colonel to set up a trap for us, as T'asha had guest our intentions."

"How can she be one step ahead of us all the time," Daniel asked to no one in particular?

Jovan said, "This is getting stranger and stranger. What happened in the inn?"

Alssa told what happened as best she could. When she was done, Jovan asked, "Wait a bit, let me get this straight. You're telling me that T'asha plunged a knife into Daniel's heart. You struck T'asha with the sword. You were knocked unconscious. When you woke up, T'asha was gone, Daniel was dead, and Eric, who is really a seer, had his eyes cut out. You then passed out again, and you woke up here."

Daniel spoke up. "She left out the part where she cried tears of light over my dead body, which pulled me back from death. Then she prayed to the light that I would not die but that life would be restored to my body. Which it was!"

Alssa turned her head slowly to give Daniel a startled look and said, "How can you know that? You were dead."

"I don't know how. I just watched you from above or at least I think I did. The memory is starting to fade. I was floating above you in a place that was filled with light. You were holding my head in your lap. I saw you collapse with your head on my chest as your tears flowed onto my body. There was a flash of light, and I felt like I was dragged through a wall of darkness, then I woke up in your arms."

Daniel smile at her in a way that he had never smiled at a woman before.

"What are you grinning at?" Alssa questioned.

Daniel responded sheepishly, "Nothing…well, you, you're amazing."

"Stop it! You are freaking me out. Why do you keep looking at me like that?" Alssa demanded.

Daniel smiled and said, "It is like I am seeing you for the first time, or at least in a way that I never saw you before. Something's changed about you. You're different." Daniel rubbed his chin, looked away from her, then looked back again. He walked around her, looking her up and down. Then he remarked, "Yes, something has changed. There is more of you, or more to you. Something has been added. It is like a shell broke open, and what was inside is now on the outside." Daniel stopped walking and stared at her.

"Stop that, you are acting really strange. I have not changed. If anyone has changed it is, you!" Alssa retorted as she started to walk away, but then she stopped and looked back and just stared.

After what seemed like forever to all of them, Jovan cleared his throat and said, "Um, if you two are done doing whatever it is you are doing, I still do not understand what happened. How can any of this be? You are talking about a miracle. How did this happen?"

Both Daniel and Alssa responded as one and said, "It happened because she/he is the fulfillment of the prophecy!"

Jovan and the rest of them were stunned.

Alssa reacted first and said, "You are the one who was dead and came back to life!"

"But only because of you," Daniel retorted. "You brought me back to life!"

"What did I do?" Alssa countered. "Hold you in my lap and cry like a baby? Some fulfilment!"

Daniel snorted and said, "I wasn't even able to stop T'asha from killing me. Not much of an all-powerful king."

Eric stood up from the stone he was sitting on, stared blankly in their direction, and spoke out, "Okay, you're both useless and the promised king. Now would you both please shut up. Can we focus on what our next move is going to be?"

Jovan kept looking back and forth between Daniel and Alssa, then said, "What's with all of you? I don't see how any of this matters. We failed to capture T'asha, and she has successfully allied herself with the local Pact of Brothers troops. We are completely surrounded, and to top it off, the wards on the Troll Hills have failed."

Alssa did a double take and said, "What! How would you know that the wards have failed?"

Jovan gave her a haggard look and replied, "You three have been unconscious for three days. During that time, T'asha's small army has been joined by thousands of Beasts."

Daniel ran his hand through his hair and asked, "Which Beasts?"

Jovan replied, "There are hadrac, Man-orcs and goblins. It Looks like the Pact of Brothers infantry regiment has decided to stay in L'ke L'fe, but she has her own troops. They have us trapped on top of this mountain and we are outnumbered by thousands. I do not see how we are going to get out of this one."

Alssa stepped away from Daniel with on last glance then addressed the group, she said, "Cally will be on her way back with our army. When she arrives, we will be easily able to deal with my traitorous sister and these dark creatures she has allied herself with.

Eric said, "We arranged to meet Cally at Simpkins Grotto not on top of this mountain. She would never know to look for us here."

Turning to look at Jovan, Eric asked, "If your messengers were able to get through to the Pact of Brothers, do you believe that your king will send troops to help?"

Jovan shuffled his feet and did not look up when he answered, "My messengers were not going to St. Michaels. They were going to H'la."

"That should still be sufficient. Are there not more Holy Land troops in H'la?" Alssa asked.

Jovan replied, "Remember, I sent for help before the incident at the inn. The person I sent my messenger too turned out to be the major who took part in the ambush with T'asha. The lieutenant colonel who is in command in H'la wants to see me hang. So I am not sure that help is coming from that direction."

Daniel was shocked and asked, "Why does the lieutenant colonel want to hang you?"

Jovan didn't look up as he replied, "He believes that I was derelict in my duties and disobedient to my orders, because I went after you and the sword instead of building up the defenses around H'la."

Daniel smirked and said, "So I am a thief, but you are a dishonored lancer waiting to be court marshaled?"

Jovan struggled with his answer, "You're half right. I am a dishonored Lancer, but it is quite clear now that you are no thief."

Daniel laughed and patted Jovan on the shoulder and said, "I wouldn't worry about it. Like you said we a probably not going to get off this mountain anyway."

Alssa repeated, "I think we should put a little more trust in Cally. She will figure out what is going on and find us."

Daniel interjected, "We cannot make a plan counting on outside help. We can only plan with what we have. Let us figure out how to get off this mountain and go to the grotto where we planned to meet Cally."

Jovan thought for some time and then said, "We can create a diversion. That would allow most of us to get away, and hopefully, those creating the diversion would also have a chance to escape in the confusion."

Daniel listened as the group past around many ideas. Back and forth they argued sometimes heatedly, sometimes to the point of absurdity. When everyone had exhausted all their ideas Daniel said, "It is true that we are surrounded and T'asha is seeking to destroy our little band, but her allies, such as they are, have only one thing on their minds, capturing and destroying the sword of light. I feel if we offer them the opportunity, they will not be able to restrain themselves. They will be drawn to the sword like a moth to a flame."

The entire group raised their voices as one. "We cannot take that kind of chance. Look what we risked getting it back when it was lost the last time."

All but Alssa who could see where Daniel was headed with his thoughts. She smiled knowingly at him.

Jovan, on the other hand, could only see the potential loss of the sword, so he said, "We would be crazy to expose the sword to those beasts. Imagine the devastation they could cause if they had control of it."

"Why do you think that?" Daniel asked. "I do not believe they have the ability to wield it. It would only be another sharp hunk of metal in their hands."

"How do you know that?" responded Jovan.

"I guess I don't know it for sure, but if evil could activate the sword, don't you think that T'asha would have used it?"

Jovan grunted, "I do not know the answer to that, but the risk of losing the sword and it being used by the Dark forces is too great. I am opposed to it."

Eric spoke up and said, "Whether evil can use the sword of power is not the real issue. The sword is a symbol of authority. It is a symbol of the great queen and the right to rule as her offspring. Without it, I do not believe we can unite the Westward nations against the coming darkness. I, too, am against it."

One by one each person expressed their concerns. Except Daniel and Alssa, who had said nothing, they all agreed; they could not take the risk of losing the sword.

Daniel was sure that this diversion was the only way out of the trap they were in, but he had another idea. Daniel smiled as he said, "So it is agreed, no sword. But how about this: Who do they all know carries the sword? Me! I will be the diversion. I will expose myself to the horde, they will assume I have the sword, and they will pursue me. Allowing all of you to escape. Being alone, I believe I will be able to elude capture and then join you at the rendezvous point."

When no objected to Daniel's suggestion, he was a little hurt; were they more worried about the sword than him?

Alssa smiled at Daniel and said, "It's an idea, or at least half an idea, but to truly make sure it works, I need to go with him. That way, even my sister will want to chase after us."

An outcry broke out among the others, "We cannot afford to lose you also."

Daniel choked out, "What!"

Eric consoled Daniel, "Relax, Daniel, both of you can now activate the sword. Alssa proved that at the inn. We need at least one of you to survive for the sword to retain its value."

"Thanks, Eric, that is real touching. I feel so needed," Daniel chided.

Alssa said, "Cally has the same blood flowing through her veins as me. Of the three of us, she is by far more righteous and is purer." Smiling at Daniel, she said, "No offense."

"None taken," he replied.

CHAPTER 47

After more arguing, it was finally agreed that both Alssa and Daniel would be the diversion using a normal sword coated with tar to make it burn with a flame. Everyone else would flee to Simpkins Grotto to meet Cally and the Three Sisters army.

After darkness fell, Alssa and Daniel slipped out of the camp with a pack full of provisions and two common swords. Working their way around to the other side of the mountain, they found a place on a protruding rock. The stone jutted out from the side of the mountain and made a flat ledge they could both fit on.

The ledge sat above the trees that filled the forest below them. At this elevation on the mountain, the trees were spread farther apart so they could easily see if anyone approached them from below. It also offered them a quick egress when it came time to escape.

They both sat down and began to wait. Their plan was to ambush a small patrol that would be probing for a way to assault the main camp. They were sure they would not have long to wait. They sat in the dark listening for the dark beasts, but only heard crickets.

Alssa quietly asked, "What was that all about back in the cave?"

"What are you talking about?" Daniel replied while keeping a watch over the forest below.

"Oh, come on, the looks, the stares, what was going on?" Alssa prodded.

"Nothing is going on, I just…" Daniel struggled with what to say: "I Just think things are different since the inn."

"Of course they are, it was horrible. We all almost died."

"One of us did!" Daniel exclaimed.

Alssa laughed. "Yeah, right." Then she continued, "When something like that happens, it's bound to affect us and change us."

Alssa reached out and gently touched him on the shoulder and said, "But it does seem that there is something else?"

Daniel thought, *'there is something else. I have never felt this way before, but I don't even know what it is. How can I possibly explain something I don't understand myself? I want to tell her that I see her differently, that I feel differently about her, but that is stupid she probably sees me as weak, after all she had to rescue me.'*

Alssa rubbed his shoulder and said, "It is okay, Daniel. Tell me what you feel, what you were trying to say back in the cave."

Daniel turned away to hide his face and replied, "I said it. With the light flowing through you and the ability to bring someone back from the dead. I believe you are the promised one. The one to save the Westward from the growing darkness."

Alssa let her hands drop into her lap. She then stood up and moved to the edge of the overlook as a tear escaped her eye and ran down her cheek. She wiped her face and turned quickly around, "I am just going to say it. I cannot hold it in any longer. Daniel I…"

Daniel held up his hand and said, "Shush."

Alssa slapped his hand down, "Don't shush me."

Daniel stood up and stepped to the edge of the rock holding up his hand again and said, "Quiet!"

Alssa started to protest, but then realized that Daniel was listening intently, then asked, "Do you hear something?"

Moving his head from side to side sniffing the air he said, "I smell something. It smells like hadrac pus."

"Curse the dark one," Alssa said as she started picking up their belongings, "I had hoped we would encounter orcs or goblins. Hadrac are relentless in their pursuit once they get your sent. They will be much harder to evade then the others would have been."

Daniel stepped back toward her and leaned in close and said, "We will need to kill them all but one before we reveal ourselves."

As they both watched together, they spied the ugly beasts moving between the trees. They were not being very stealthy, of course, hadrac never were. Being quiet or sneaky was not their style. Brute force was their go to.

Daniel Whispered. "I count five, how about you?"

"I Agree." Just like Daniel, Alssa had slipped in into her warrior mindset. "I will get their attention while you slip in behind them."

Daniel looked at her with admiration and thought, *'This is why I love her, she gets it. She understands the situation and plans accordingly.'*

Daniel pointed to a small clearing just a little way above their perch and said, "Try to get them to follow you up into that clearing."

Alssa said, "Okay," as she fumbled for something in her bedroll. Daniel's eyes were on the hadrac as she continued, "But you should use this."

Daniel turned back to her to see she was holding his sword, the sword of Light. As he took it from her, he said absently, "I love you."

Alssa jerked it back in surprise.

Daniel, seeing the look on her face realized what he had just said, stammered, "I mean, for sneaking the sword away from Eric."

Recovering her composure, Alssa handed the sword to Daniel and said, "I didn't sneak it, Eric gave it to me. He felt we had a better chance of surviving with the sword then without it." She than began to work her way toward the clearing'

Daniel watched her walk away and thought, *'That was dumb, why did I say that?'* He started moving noiselessly through the trees, but his thoughts kept returning to Alssa, *'Do I love her? I am not even sure I know what that means. Do I like her? for sure, she has become a friend. I have never had many female friends, actually, none. Truth be told I don't have many friends at all. Eric was possibly the closest, but I've known him for years and never knew he was a seer. How close of a friend can he be. The old man, Nathan, wasn't a friend, he was more like a father, what would I know what a father was like I never had one. I have spent my entire life moving around, working for rich people who were only interested in my ability to keep them alive. These last five years I have been running from bounty hunters. That tells it all right there, the one man I have the most in common with is Count Valkar and he has been trying to kill me.'*

With that revelation Daniel stopped in his tracks, which was a good thing. He was so absorbed in his thoughts he almost ran into the last hadrac in line.

Daniel could see that their leader was heading them away from the little clearing and more toward their rock out cropping. He was about to deviate from their plan when Alssa ran in front of the leader. With a loud guttural snort, the leader ran after her, the others quickly followed.

Daniel Chased after them in a trot. The beasts were making so much noise, grunting and snorting, they never heard him coming up behind them. It was a quick chase as Alssa stopped at the top of the clearing.

Nocking an Arrow in her bow she waited for the hadrac to stop to plan, but it was not happening. They just charged her instead, that was, until Daniel emerged from the bottom of the clearing and spoke the chant to ignite the sword. It burst into a bright flame the lite the entire clearing causing the hadrac to turn around. With that Alssa let her arrow fly, it struck the leader squarely between the shoulder blades. She quickly nocked another arrow and shot the second in line.

Daniel walked slowly toward the other three. They seemed mesmerized by the burning sword. Lifting it above his head, he thought he heard one of them say, "It's the Banisher," as they turned to run away. If their hope was to escape, they failed, because Alssa shot two more of them. The last one stopped, looking from Alssa to Daniel. He froze, like he did not know what to do.

Daniel started working his way up toward Alssa. Circling around the hadrac leaving him a way to escape. It did not work, the thing just stood there terrified. It could not take its eyes off the sword, eyes that Daniel could see were filled with terrifying fear and tears. *Tears, tears do hadrac cry?* What in the name of the light was going on? This was not in the plan. They wanted the beast to run away and tell the others where they were. But this guy was not moving. Alssa looked on with amazement. She could hear the hadrac muttering to himself, "Banisher, Banisher," over and over.

Looking at Daniel, she said, "What do we do?"

Daniel responded by extinguishing the sword and slapping the hadrac on the butt with the flat of the blade. The beast seemed to regain its limited senses. It snarled at them and then ran down the hill screeching.

Alssa walked over to Daniel and said, "That is the strangest thing I have ever seen. Did you hear the beast call it the Banisher?"

"I heard the beasts say it when we were in the Ebony forest, but I don't know what it means," Daniel replied. Then he asked, "Have you ever heard the term before?"

Alssa thought for a moment before she said, "No, I never have." Thinking some more, she continued, "Wait, I do remember the teachers referring to the great queen as the Banisher. I always thought it was in relationship to her having banished the dark lords to the Island of Exile."

Daniel spun the sword in his hand, turned it all around, then addressed it, "I have always called you the sword of light, but from this time forward, you will be known as the Banisher."

With a laugh, Alssa shrugged her shoulders and said, "Oh, give me a break!" Turning to walk up the hill, she admonished, "We had better get moving. They will be back, and with a lot more of them than five."

Daniel turned the sword over a couple mort times, smiled, and followed Alssa up the hill.

Chapter 48

Jovan called the other leaders together after his scouts reported that the enemy had moved off toward the other side of the mountain. Once they were all assembled, he said, "There are a couple of hours until dawn, and it appears Daniel and Alssa have attracted a lot of attention in a short time. We have a chance to get off this mountain and escape to Simpkins Grotto."

Gallant spoke up. "That's a long walk, Captain, and since the enemy ran off all our horses when they first arrived, we are going to have a hard time outrunning them. It is almost twenty miles to the grotto!"

Jovan nodded and responded, "I agree, so when we get off the mountain it will be best if we break up into small groups and go by different routes. We should only move at night and hide during the day. I think we should all be able to cover the distance in two or at the most three days and hopefully Cally and her army will be there when we arrive."

The group moved out of the cave. They had only walked for a short distance when they stumble upon a herd of sleeping orcs. Jovan had the group move around them quietly. He did not want to announce their movements to soon. T'asha was going to realize soon enough what was going on and they need as much of lead as they could get.

After walking for twenty more minutes, they reached the base of the mountain. One of his scouts informed him that there were corrals in front of them. The corrals were filled with horses, both theirs and those of T'asha's mounted troops. Jovan stopped the group and said, "This is too good of an opportunity to pass up. If we can obtain mounts and drive off the rest, we will have a great advantage in getting away safely."

Dividing his force into three groups, he gave orders, "Gallant, you will capture the horses. Sergeant Sharon, you will procure the tack. I will lead the last group to capture the camp and their commander."

Jovan entered the camp looking for the tent of the commander. They subdue the few women they encountered without having to kill any of them. He soon found the tent he was looking for. He was hoping if he were able to capture their leader, they would not have to draw undue attention while at the same time obtain some needed information. They surrounded the tent and confronted the orderly who was standing guard.

Jovan said, "If you do not resist, we will not kill you."

The orderly looked at him calmly and said, "Could you wait here a moment?" She then lifted the flap to the tent and announced, "They are here, Commander. Would you like me to show them in?"

"Yes, please do," came the reply.

The orderly motioned with her hand for Jovan to enter the tent and said to those with him, "The captain only, if the rest of you would please remain here?"

Jovan motioned for the rest of them to stay where they were and then entered the tent. Jovan took in the sparse furnishings of the tent. A Pact of Brothers commander's tent would have twice the room, a real bed, not a cot. There would be a writing desk, a large clothing chest along with other fineries like carpets on the floor.

He shifted his focus to the commander and stepped back in shock. The woman who sat waiting for him was fully dressed in her battle armor and with her sword laying on her camp table. And to his surprise, he also knew her; it was the officer he had helped when he first arrived in L'ke L'fe.

Jovan wondered if she remembered him. Not knowing, he said, "Hello, Commander! Who do I have the pleasure of addressing?"

Commander Westolve smiled at him and said, "Welcome, Captain Jovan. You know full well who I am. I have been expecting you."

Jovan's surprise showed when he said, "You remember me? I didn't think you would, you were not in good of shape the last time we met."

"You were kind to me that day. I have not found that to be the case with most Pact of Brothers officers," the commander replied.

Jovan frowned and nodded saying, "Most of our officers have little regard for you female soldiers in general, and a lot of animosity toward officers. That Animosity I do not share."

Commander Westolve smiled and asked, "And why is that Captain?"

Jovan replied quickly, "I have met your soldiers on patrols to Devil's Pass. I have heard the stories about your fighting skills and now I have spent time with your Princess Alssa, she is truly impressive."

Westolve twitched with the reference to Alssa being *her* princess but covered it up with the sign of blessing and then said, "Yes, she is, isn't she? Well, now that you are here, what shall we do?"

Jovan replied, "I am not sure what you mean, my people have captured all your troops. I think I will restrain all of you, and then me and my men will ride out of here on your horses."

At that moment Sergeant Sharon and Gallant barged into the tent and declared that they were the first one to accomplish their task. Jovan smiled.

Westolve said, "What enthusiastic Sergeants. Who do we have here?" Her eyes scanned Gallant. "Captain Jovan, who is this Hulking specimen of a trooper?" They then shifted to Sergeant Sharon, and she exclaimed, "Sergeant Sharon of the House J'ta Royal Guard, I am glad to see you are still alive."

Jovan began to speak when he was interrupted by Sergeant Sharon drawing her sword and pushing the tip against Commander Westolve's chest. The sergeant cursed out, "By the dark lords, you traitorous bitch, I should kill you now."

She said to Jovan, "This is the commander of the garrison at the Castle in the Gorge and T'asha's second-in-command. She plotted with T'asha to kill Alssa and Cally. She is a traitor and a murderer. It is because of her I lost my entire company to the goblins." Sharon began to cry, "All my friends, women who I have known and loved."

She put both hands on the handle of her sword and began to push. Tears flowed from her eyes, as her hands shook with rage and grief.

Jovan reached out with his right hand and set it on Sergeant Sharon's shoulder, and with his left, he pushed the blade of her sword down and said, "It is okay, she is not resisting. Justice will be served."

Falling to her knees, the sergeant began to cry uncontrollably. Jovan had Gallant take her outside as Commander Westolve commented, "Sergeant Sharon seems to be a bit unstable. Is this your influence? A Three Sisters trooper would normally have more self-control than this."

Gallant burst back into the tent and pointed his finger at the commander and said, "You will have nothing to say about Sergeant Sharon or my captain. You have aligned yourself with agents of evil and the dark lords." Gallant grabbed the commander around the throat and began to squeeze.

Jovan yelled at Gallant, "Restrain yourself! We have what we need. Go round up all the Three Sisters troopers and tie them up. Then get everyone mounted up so we can leave immediately."

As Gallant left, Commander Westolve looked at Jovan with a confident smile and said, "You Don't see it do you? You are so arrogant. Do you really think we were just sitting here, unaware of your plans? Queen T'asha knew that Alssa would try something like this, she and her entire Royal guard are waiting for you out on the plains. They mean to annihilate your whole force as you ride away from this mountain."

Jovan looked at her in disbelief. "You want me to believe that she left you and your troopers here to be captured? To be sacrificed so that she could catch us out in the open?"

"Again, you underestimate my Queen," Westolve said with a grimace. "She wanted us to be sacrificed, yes, but she has no intentions of us being captured. We were ordered to fight to the death to make it look more convincing."

"That's ridiculous. Why would she sacrifice her second-in-command for just a ruse?"

Westolve looked away and, in a whisper, said, "You don't know my queen, she can be severe. After your escape from the ambush at the inn, she has become even more ruthless. Besides, I have failed her many times, so she clearly has decided my services were no longer needed."

"Then I am even more confused, why have you not resisted us, and why are you telling me all of this?" Jovan asked.

"Because, though I love my Queen, and have little respect for the two usurpers, I will not be cast aside so easily. I am offering to lead you around the ambush to safety, after which, we will part ways."

Jovan rubbed his chin. The stubble that had been growing had turned into a beard in the last few weeks. He had really grown lax on his personal discipline since running from H'la. And he was tired, finding it hard to concentrate. This situation was not at all what he expected, and he was not sure what to do. So he called for Gallant and gave him an order. "Please go find the seer and bring him here." He then said to the commander, "We will let the seer determine if you are telling me the truth or not."

A few minutes later Eric followed Gallant into the tent and asked, "How can I help you, Captain?" But then stopped and sniffed the air. He stepped around the large sergeant and, with a big smile, said, "Commander Westolve, I am surprised to find you here, and even more surprised that the captain and his soldiers overcame you troopers so easily."

The commander was taken aback by the seer's familiarity and asked, "Do I know you?"

"Ah, yes, the mask." Reaching up, he lifted the cloth off his head that hid his now skin-covered eye sockets, "Does this help?"

Taking a step back, Commander Westolve sputtered, "You're the seer that T'asha…" Westolve shivered and choked out, "Whose eyes she cut out."

"That is true, but you still don't recognize me?" Eric smile was horrifying without eyes.

"No, should I?" The face before her stared at her and drove the realization of what T'asha had become, deeper into her soul. She still did not know who he was, but she said something that even she was surprised by, "I am sorry that this happened to you."

Now Eric was surprised and said, "The commander Westolve who I knew, was not capable of empathy, especially for a man."

Reaching out, he touched Jovan's arm and said, "Something strange is happening here."

Then to Commander Westolve, he said, "I spent six months in Castle in the Gorge with my men, up until you and your mistress started this mess, we are all in now."

Recognition came to Westolve's eyes, and she proclaimed, "You are Captain Kromsing, the leader of the mercenaries that Count Gravelet hired. Captain Jovan, this man is a mercenary, a sword for hire. He is no seer!"

Jovan replied, "You are mistaken. Both Daniel and Princesa Alssa say he is a seer. I have seen his handiwork. He clearly has the powers of a seer."

Westolve retorted, "If that is true, why did he spend a half of a year in Castle in the Gorge disguised as a mercenary?"

"It wasn't a disguise." Eric countered, "I have been a mercenary many a time, as well as an innkeeper, a tailor, a scribe and for a short time, a romancer of wealthy women. Not real proud of that one, but a man has got to do what a man has got to do."

"So it was you who helped that fat fool escape, where is he now?" Commander Westolve asked.

Eric replied, "I would have thought you would know better than me, He left our company to return to Jukeele with Cally a week ago."

Jovan interrupted, "This conversation will need to wait for another time." Looking at the seer, he asked, "Commander Westolve claims that T'asha has set a trap for us and is waiting for us out on the plains. The commander says she is willing to help us escape. Do you believe we can trust her?"

"Trust her, never!" Eric sniffed the air again and whispered to himself, "Darkness dispelled, light reveals, freedom comes from truth." Cocking his head to the side, he seemed to listen intently, then said, "The commander here, by nature, is all but incapable of lying. But her past loyalty to T'asha has never been in question."

Jovan sighed. "You're telling me that she will not lie, but that she will also not betray T'asha. Not much help Eric."

Eric replied, "I said her past loyalties, Not her present. I can tell you she isn't lying about the trap or her desire to get away from T'asha."

"Hey, I am standing right here guys. Why don't you ask me where my loyalties now lie?" Westolve asked.

Jovan smirked, "This is stupid. Okay, where do they lie, Commander?"

"I am not sure! Though I have little regard for Princess Alssa and Cally, Queen T'asha has become even more erratic and vindictive as of late. And she did leave me here to die. I believe my loyalties, for the time being, lie with me not getting dead."

Eric chuckled, "I told you she cannot lie."

Jovan said, "I am not sure that helps me very much in making my decision."

Eric countered, "What decision is to be made. We trust her lead us to safety or maybe into a trap. Or we ride off without her into a trap."

Looking at Commander Westolve, Jovan shook his head and said, "Okay, with the stipulation that your troopers go with us and they go bound to their horses and without their armor."

Westolve smile knowingly, "They will all go with us, I personally chose the ones who were to stay here with me, but they will not like having to travel without their armor."

CHAPTER 49

The trip off the mountain was uneventful, and Commander Westolve was true to her word. They saw no sign of T'asha or her troops. They made it to the grotto in a day. All the way there Jovan could not reconcile the thought that Lieutenant Colonel Barnes and the infantry Major had joined forces with T'asha. Did they not see that she was in league with the dark beasts? That fact alone should have been enough for them to realize that their original orders were out of date with the situation. Could they not see that they needed to let Brother Samuel know what was really happening in the Middle Kingdom?

These events convinced him that he was the only officer in the Pact of Brothers north of the Barrier Mountains that was still following the Holy Writ. Because of that he decided to put on his uniform regardless of what Lieutenant Colonel Barnes thought. When he informed his men, they all followed his example declaring that they would proudly fight the hordes of darkness as Holy Lancers.

Though Captain Jovan was not totally surprised with their decision, he was extremely pleased by it. He and his men had been together for almost a year and they all knew what evil was.

He was even more pleased and surprised that Commander Westolve and her troopers decided to stay with him. At first, they were going to go their own way. That was until they saw the devastation and carnage that T'asha and her allies had brought on all the people living in the area. There was not one farmhouse or outbuilding that had not been torn down and if the people had been there, they were killed.

Upon arriving at the rendezvous point Captain Jovan surveyed the Grotto; it was not what he expected. He thought it would be a big hole in the ground Where slabs of rock had been cut out to use for building. Instead, there were giant monolithic rock formations that had large pieces chiseled and cut away. He could still see large slabs of cut stone scattered all around. They had been discarded during the quarrying process. There was a lot of undergrowth and trees now filling the grotto. It was clear that it had been a long time since anyone had used the quarry.

Commander Westolve rode up to Captain Jovan and said, "I do not see anyone waiting for us. Did you not expect them to be here when we arrived?"

Jovan looked at her skeptically, "Yes, that was the plan."

"What do we do know?" asked the commander.

"We wait, Alssa and Daniel started out on foot, so I expected them to take longer than us. I have no Idea where Cally could be."

The commander looked away, biting her lower lip and said, "I would not but too much hope in Cally's returning."

"Why would you say that?" Captain Jovan asked.

Commander Westolve responded, "Queen T'asha has many different plans all working at the same time. I don't even know them all."

Both the commander and Captain Jovan dismounted. They handed the reins to waiting troopers then the commander continued, "One of the plans had to do with the queen mothers, another with the sitting women of the House of the People. As you have seen all of T'asha plans to this point have not been healthy for the people involved."

Jovan just looked at the commander in stunned disbelief. He did not know what to say or what question to ask so he turned and walked away.

* * *

Jovan had sat down on a large slab of stone to think. He was lost in thought as his mind swam with all the things that had gone wrong in the last two weeks and all the things that could still go wrong in the future. He lost track of time and must have dozed off. He was startled awake by a dream that they were under attack. Awake now, he knew he needed to do something, but he was not sure what it was. Then he thought about what Daniel had said in the cave, "We cannot make a plan counting on outside help. We can only plan with what we have."

Considering all that Commander Westolve had said, he thought, *If she is right, I better prepare a defense with what I do have.* He surveyed the Grotto and decided it was going to be an easy place to defend, but he also could see that it was not going to be an easy place to escape from if the time came that they needed to.

* * *

Daniel and Alssa came running into the camp just as Jovan finished figuring out a defense strategy. Both Daniel and Alssa were breathing hard and were drenched with sweat.

Upon seeing them, Captain Jovan ordered a man to fetch some water for them. As they approached, he said, "You made it. I am relieved that you are okay and even more relieved that you are here?"

Alssa took another deep breath and said, "We have been running with little rest the whole time. There is a band of about twenty goblins and man-orcs following us."

As Alssa took another deep breath, Daniel continued, "Captain, you need to send some archers to the south side of the quarry to meet them."

Captain Jovan called Sergeant Gallant over and gave orders. "Take five swordsmen and five bow women to the south side of the grotto and prepare for an attack."

Alssa looked at Jovan in surprise and said, "Ten! You need to send more than ten?"

"I agree but that is all we have," Jovan replied.

Now it was Daniel's turn to be surprised as he said, "All, what do you mean that is all. Isn't Cally here with the army?"

Jovan shook his head no and then said, "She has not arrived yet; we have had no word from her. But that is not our only problem, Follow me."

Jovan led the two of them to where commander Westolve and her forty troopers were being watched over. As Daniel and Alssa approached, Commander Westolve arose from the rock she was sitting on.

Alssa saw her first and demanded, "What is she doing here?"

Jovan held up his hand and said, "Before you say any more, you need to know that Commander Westolve helped us escape the trap set up by T'asha. Without her help I don't think any of us would be here at all."

Daniel thought to himself, *'This is Commander Westolve? Both Eric and Alssa had describe her to him, but she was nothing like the picture he had in his mind. She did not look the hard-as-iron officer they had described. He had imagined her older, not as attractive and smaller. The only thing that was like he pictured was her eyes. They were as hard and as piercing as they said.'*

Commander Westolve did a short bow as she came up to their group and then spoke. "Princess Alssa, I am Commander Westolve, Garrison Commander of the Castle in the Gorge."

"I know who you are. Why are you here, and not with my traitorous sister?" Alssa asked with disdain in her voice.

"I decided that serving her was not in the best interest of the Three Sisters realm, nor in that of my troops or myself," Westolve answered confidently.

"And what do you expect from me?" Alssa asked dismissively.

Westolve said nothing.

Alssa continued. "Do you expect me to receive you with open arms and act like nothing has happened! You have plotted with T'asha from the beginning to start this rebellion. Do you know how many of our women we lost at the lava fields to those hideous lizards? Everywhere we turned, your beasts have been there to thwart us. Too many of your sisters-in-arms have been killed because of you and your plans. And now I discover that you and T'asha have found a way to remove the wards that protected the Middle Kingdom. I should hang you here and now for what you have done."

Daniel could see that Alssa was working herself into a rage, which was not surprising having spent the last twenty-four hours running for their lives from those same horrible beasts, and now to confront one of the implementors of the planned coup. But he knew they did not have time for a confrontation right now.

He was about to say something when Captain Jovan interrupted, "Alssa, I have given the commander my parole if she agreed to come along with us peacefully, which she has, and if she helped us escape, which she did."

Alssa spun around to face Captain Jovan and screamed, "Your parole! Who are you to give this traitor your parole? What does your parole have to do with the Three Sisters? I will not be bound by an agreement that was set up by a Pact of Brothers officer who he himself has been labeled a traitor."

Daniel could hear the sound of battle as the bow-women engaged the beast at a distance. He stepped in between Captain Jovan and Alssa and said, "We will need to continue this argument later. Those troops that Jovan sent will not last long without help."

Westolve spoke up, "Give us our weapons we will fight."

Alssa snapped back, "Not a chance, you will stay right where you are."

Commander Westolve sat back down on her rock and motioned for her troopers to do the same. Captain Jovan instructed the four men watching them to continue to do so. But he shook his head and said under his breath, "This might be a mistake."

Daniel heard him and said quietly, "Be patient captain things may change quickly."

Both men ran to catch up with Alssa at the south end of the quarry. When they arrived, they found every trooper engaged in the fight. They drew their swords and entered the fray.

It was not long before Daniel realized that there were a lot more than the twenty beasts that had chased them. Fighting his way over to Alssa, he called out, "We are going to need help, there are too many of them, we need to get Westolves troopers armed and into the fight."

But as he said that the beast withdrew from the battle leaving the humans to recover lost ground. A quick count showed that they had only lost two men, both from Eric's mercenary company. That meant they were down to thirty-two not counting the one guarding Westolve and her women.

Daniel, Alssa, Eric, Captain Jovan, Sergeant Sharon, and Sergeant Gallant gathered to discuss what they were going to do.

Daniel spoke first, "I know we came her to meet Cally, but she is not here. So we will have to make do with what we have. The Grotto is an excellent place to defend. We can easily defeat a force three times our number, but they have more of their kind joining them all the time. If they had not quit the field when they did, they may have overrun us. Them leaving only means they are letting their numbers grow and then they will attack again. Any suggestion on what we should do?"

Alssa said, "We must put our trust in Cally. She will be here."

"Yes, but will it be in time. I agree with Daniel we will not survive another attack with our present forces," Captain Jovan said as he looked directly at Alssa. Then he continued, "I think we should arm Commander Westolve and her troopers."

"Absolutely not!" barked Alssa. "They cannot be trusted."

Captain Jovan pressed, "I think her helping the us to escape showed she no longer loyal to T'asha. We need her and her bowwomen if we hope to survive through this day."

Alssa stood shaking her head no and was about to start talking again when Eric interjected, "I must agree with the captain. Something has changed in Commander Westolve. She is no longer the same woman she was before she left the Castle in the Gorge."

"I will not listen to this." Alssa said firmly, "This woman is a traitor and cannot be trusted. This is ridiculous, I will not continue this discussion."

"Your Highness may I speak?" Sergeant Sharon asked.

"Of course, you can Sergeant, please try to speak some sense into these men," Alssa encouraged.

I know what Commander Westolve has done, and because of her, I have lost some good friends and many good troopers, but that cannot be held against her troopers. I have spent time talking to them on the ride here and they have just been following orders of their officers and Princess T'asha. The troopers who were stationed at castle in Gorge are some of the best in the Three Sisters army. Having forty of them helping us will even the odds. Plus, they all have the new Rodeneese Crossbow, which will make them even more effective in this situation. Sergeant Sharon continued to explain, "These new crossbows can fire a full quiver in about two minutes, their range is limited, but in this quarry it will not matter."

Alssa questioned the sergeant, "You think we can trust these women after all that has happened?"

"I don't know how much we can trust them, but I do know that they have spent their entire military career training and fighting these beasts, and they will fight this battle I am sure," the sergeant said confidently.

"Okay, we will rearm the troopers," Alssa conceded, "but I want Westolve in irons."

Sergeant Sharon looked to Captain Jovan for help, but he just shook his head. "Your Highness," Sergeant Sharon replied, "we do not have irons, and we have not restrained her up to this point and it has not been a problem."

"Do you not have any rope?" Alssa said with derision. "Why are you all fighting me on this? She is a traitor!"

Daniel stepped up and said, "Okay, we will leave Commander Westolve restrained, but the rest of her troopers will be rearmed. We can only spare one of the wounded men to watch her and we will give him instructions to let her loose if it looks like he will be over run. I will not leave anyone defenseless to face these beasts."

Alssa faced away from the group but did not leave the gathering. Daniel began to outline his thought on how they will run their defense of the Grotto. "We need to try to cause a shift in their attack to the east. So we will put the bulk of our forces on the west side of our present position. Hopefully, this will allow the beasts to flow to the east. That area of the grotto is more open, and it will allow our bowwomen greater range and more opportunities. The force in the west will push east and then flank them."

* * *

As the battle was joined it played out much like Daniel had hope it would. On the first day Daniel's Band was able to flank the beast army as they vainly tried to close in on the bowwomen. The slaughter was great. The beasts lost hundreds to the Bowwomen's bolts and Daniel's band only lost one swordsman. This carnage continued for three more days and hundreds more beast died to only four humans wounded.

On the fifth day as the human's strength began to tire, things grew worse and though the humans continued to slaughter beasts, ten troopers were killed and twenty-five were wounded. Daniel estimated that they were now fighting at twenty to one odds and that their ultimate defeat was not a matter of if, but of when. And when was tomorrow?

Daniel approached Jovan privately to discuss their situation. "We have put ourselves in quite a predicament."

Jovan sighed heavily. "You're right, and although this place is easy to defend there is no easy way out of here. In any direction we go we will be out in open plains. Now that they have us completely surrounded, we are without many choices."

Daniel nodded his head in agreement. "Since that is the case, then I suggest we set up our defenses in such a way that we kill as many of these foul beasts as possible before we die."

Eric had been sitting nearby listening to their conversation. So he joined in, "May I have a say into our final demise?" He chuckled, "I think I see a way out of this little mess we have created for ourselves."

Captain Jovan scoffed. "You see a way out! You see way out? This is not the time for your crazy sense of humor, Eric. We are not going to get out of this one, seer."

Daniel did a double take at Captain Jovan and asked, "What did you just say?"

"I said that we are not getting out of this trap. No matter what this crazy seer thinks," Jovan answered.

Turning to Eric, Daniel said, "So, crazy seer, do you really see away out?"

Eric rubbed his chin and smiled. "I do, we attack! Straight north out onto the plains. They will not expect it, and we will catch them by surprise."

Captain Jovan questioned, "And by doing this, you think we will be able to win or at least escape?"

Eric laughed. "No, we will probably all die, but it will be fun seeing their surprise as we do the unexpected."

Captain Jovan spit out, "You're nuts!"

Alssa asked, "Can a girl get in on this conversation?"

Captain Jovan told her what Eric wanted to do and said, "I think he has lost his mind along with his eyes."

Alssa said, "Cally is coming, I know it. Let's do it."

Daniel agreed, and Captain Jovan shrugged his shoulders and said, "It might be better than waiting here to die."

Daniel gathered all the leaders again and explained the plan. They all fully understood the situation and agreed they would rather die trying to win than resign themselves to death and defeat.

With the healthy swordsman leading the way and the bow-women forming a circle around the walking wounded, Alssa finally agreed to let Commander Westolve have a weapon to help defend the wounded. With everyone arranged, they struck heading straight north.

Their plan worked; they caught the beast totally by surprise, and their initial momentum carried them a few miles out of the quarry. But their own exhaustion and the overwhelming numbers of the enemy caused them to come to a stop on a small knoll overlooking the northern plains of the Middle Kingdom. They were surrounded on all four directions. To the west, the army of hadrac. To the south were the cliff orcs of the Deep River Ravine. The east were the vicious Man-orcs, and to the north lay the goblins and their direwolf pets. It was clear to all that they were going to die on this little hill.

Alssa and Daniel found themselves standing together during a small break in the fighting. Alssa commented, "My bowwomen are almost completely out of bolts with no chance to replenish their supply."

Daniel responded, "It looks like we're almost out of time, Princess."

Alssa gave a weak smile, paused for a moment, and said, "You know, standing here on this hill reminds me of the original Three Sisters on the Katan Hill waiting for the final attack of the Four Lords of Darkness."

"You told me about that when we first met. It's unfortunate we do not have three sides of this hill protected by a raging river. It would have been even better if we had started out with allot more soldiers too." Daniel looked off to the east with longing and then continued. "I want to tell you that I think you're really amazing. In fact, thee most amazing woman I have ever met." Looking back at her, he realized that she was not listening.

She was looking off to the north, and then she said, "They did not win because of those reasons. They overcame the dark lords with their faith. It was their faith in the light that allowed them to see beyond the impossible circumstances to find a way to victory. We must put our faith in the light, and we will find away, a path out of the darkness into the light." As she finished talking, she saw a change in Daniel's expression. His frown of dread had turned into a smile. She asked, "Do you feel it too, the faith welling up inside of you?"

Daniel pointed to the north and said, "I am not sure about the faith inside of me, but I am sure of that large dust cloud working its way south. It can only be one thing, fast-moving horses, lots of them."

Alssa could see it too. She blessed the light and yelled command to their remaining troops, "Make a square, archers and wounded in the middle! Hope is on the way."

* * *

It took only a matter of minutes to see the source of Alssa's hope. A thousand Three Sisters lancers crashed into the rear of the goblin horde. Another five hundred circled to the west and flanked the hadrac army sending them to flight. On the east another five hundred lancers overran the Man-orc position and drove them mercilessly south into the Deep River. The carnage was great and at the loss of only two hundred lancers. The army of darkness was sent fleeing, and the plains were filled with the bodies of thousands of the beasts.

Cally rode up to Alssa and Daniel, who were leaning on each other for support. As she dismounted, she removed her helmet and said, "I see the two of you cannot seem to stay out of trouble without me."

Alssa rushed over and put her arms around Cally and said, "Oh sister, I am glad to see you and you have arrived just in time."

Daniel wanted desperately to hug them both but refrained himself until the two sisters opened space and encouraged him to come join them. As they hugged him, Daniel thought, *I have never felt anything like this in my life. Is this what family feels like? This is nice.*

After pulling apart, Alssa gushed, "Cally, I finally understand what you have always said about faith. Somehow, I knew you would arrive and that we would be okay. Isn't that wonderful?"

"Yes, sister, it is," Cally replied as she burst into tears. "But I have terrible news."

Daniel was concerned and confused as he moved closer to Cally. Alssa reached out and placed her hands of her sister's shoulders and said, "What is it, Cally? What has happened?"

Cally cried for a couple of minutes then collected her wits and said, "While we were escaping from the goblins and fleeing through the Ebony forest, T'asha returned to Jukeele. She reported to them that we were dead and that she was the new queen. When our mothers resisted her, she had them executed for treason. Along with all our natural siblings. She then placed Megan on the throne as Stewart and gathered more troops and returned here to the Middle Kingdom with the excuse to of meeting the promised heir."

Daniel could not believe his ears, and Alssa had collapsed to the ground, as Cally continued, "That is why it has taken me so long to return. I had Megan arrested and thrown in prison. I then had to convince the Royal Court to allow me to take the army with me. I was only able to do that by promising to march south and apprehend T'asha. They had little hope that you would still be alive. But even in that they want me to send most of the troops back as there are rumors of a Ramaahian invasion."

Daniel knelt and took Alssa in his arms as she cried uncontrollably, and because he did not know what to say, he said nothing but thought to himself, *How can you go from the ecstasy of winning to losing what feels like almost everything so quickly?*

CHAPTER 50

After informing Cally of all that had happened while she was gone, the two princesses stood toe to toe arguing about which one of them should return to Jukeele with the bulk of the army and which one should stay and proceed to Queens Castle Home to greet the returning king.

Cally reiterated her main point, "You have always been the one destined to be the true leader of the Three Sisters, why are you fighting it now?"

Alssa reacted to Cally's last statement, "We have a triumvirate, with T'asha, you and me as the leaders. Why would you want that to change?"

Cally was indignant as she said, "Want it to change? What are you talking about? T'asha is trying to kill us both. She murdered are mothers. Everything has already changed. The triumvirate is gone. It was gone when Megan was not allowed to become queen. It was gone when T'asha murdered our families. The triumvirate is gone, and it isn't coming back. None of us have any children. If we die, there is no one to replace us. If you die out here, no one will be there to take the authority as queen. You must return to Jukeele with the army and establish your family as the rulers before even a greater disaster befalls us."

Alssa replied, "You are right, the time has come for change, and you are the one who can bring it about. You have always had the head for politics and the ability to get along with others. You are also much more intelligent than I am. I am only a warrior, not a stateswoman. The ladies in court will listen to you, and the people all love you."

"That is a lot of Ptroc dung, and you know it. You are the natural leader, and they will do as you say they all respect you."

"You mean fear me," Alssa stated.

Cally protested, "No, I don't. They don't fear you, they feared T'asha, but you they respect."

"And you they love," Alssa quickly answered.

Daniel had heard enough, "Okay, you two have established that everyone loves Cally, they all respect Alssa and T'asha is the bad seed. Can we get on with solving our real problems that we have right here, right now? We need to reach Queens Castle Home and let you guys prepare for the arrival of you long lost king. And when he shows up, will it not resolve all these problems, since he will be ruler of all the Westward?"

Alssa and Cally looked at each other and said at the same time, "You're the king, you big oaf! You just don't want to admit it."

Daniel's frustration overcame him, and he said, "Look you two, I am not a king. I have no idea who I am. I know that I am an orphan, passed around and abandoned by everyone I encounter. You have no idea what I have been through. You grew up in a palace with more parents they knew what to do with. I have never had a mother or a father. I am a nobody, so let it go. I am not your king."

Both ladies shrugged their shoulders and walked off. Daniel turned around and kicked the ground and thought, *That was totally unproductive and stupid. Why am I even involved in all of this? I should just get on a horse and ride out of here. This whole thing is really none of my affair. I am not responsible for any of these people nor any of this situation. They talk about evil and darkness like it is a new thing. The Eastward is an evil and dark place that is why I left. At least here evil is found in the form of dark beasts. In the Eastward all of those beasts look human.*

As Daniel struggled with the pain of his past, Eric and Captain Jovan approached him, and Jovan said, "Are you all right, Daniel? You look like the weight of the world is on your shoulders."

Daniel shook his head disgustedly and said, "It does feel like someone is trying to put the weight of the world on my shoulders, that is for sure."

Eric asked, "What does that mean?"

"Never mind," Daniel replied then continued, "It's nothing I can't handle, nothing new anyway. Except for maybe these crazy princess arguing with each other about which one should go back home, and which one should stay."

Jovan chuckled and said, "Maybe they are just watching out for each other. Siblings do that, you know."

Daniel snapped back, "No, I wouldn't know."

Before Jovan could respond to Daniel, Eric said strongly, "Neither one can go home. They both need to be here. They both must stay. I need to tell them." Looking at Daniel, he said, "You need to tell them they must both stay."

Daniel looked at Eric, held up both hands, and said, "Yeah, okay, calm down. We can tell them they both need to stay."

Eric seemed to relax and then kiddingly said to Daniel, "Maybe they were really fighting over which one gets to stay here with you?"

"That's crazy!" Daniel replied, and as he walked away, he said, "I am done with this conversation. We need to figure out how we are going to get from here to Queens Castle Home."

Eric punched Captain Jovan lightly in the shoulder and smiled as he said, "I don't even have eyes and I can see it, why is he so blind?"

Shaking his head, Captain Jovan replied, "I don't know, but I suppose he has his reasons. Let's go help him talk some sense into the princess and make a plan."

* * *

For some unspoken reason, Alssa and Cally quickly agreed that they would both stay, and they sent all but five hundred of the Lancers back to Jukeele. Then after spending a great deal of time discussing their options, they all agreed to take the mountain route through the Highguard Pass. It was an old road from Queens Castle Home through the towering mountains to the Rodeneese highlands.

At some point in the past, there was an earthquake that dropped a mountain on the road and made it impassable. The road was no longer traveled except for a few people from the northern plains who took a spur that joined the old road south of the earthquake sight.

Their trip was totally uneventful as they passed through the mountains. As Daniel looked around, there was almost no vegetation just mile after mile of rocks. At some point, Daniel started feeling like they were being watched. But no matter how hard he looked he saw no one, nothing but rocks.

They arrived at Queens Castle Home with five hundred lancers, two Hundred bowwomen, and the few men left from Eric's and Captain Jovan's companies. Fortunately, there was no sign of T'asha or her beast army.

Daniel approached Captain Jovan with a question, "With this lull in the fighting, do you think we could send another one of your troopers to the Pact of Brothers and see if they can send some help?"

"I was thinking the same thing. But I believe we need to do two things if we are to be successful," Captain Jovan replied. "First, we need to send Sergeant Gallant. He has a reputation of being a worthy man, and most of all, I trust him explicitly. He and I have been together for a few years."

"And second?" Daniel asked.

Jovan hesitated and then said, "We convince Alssa and Cally to write a letter to Brother Samuel requesting his assistance."

Daniel rubbed his chin and said, "That will be a hard sell. As far as I can tell, there is no great fondness between your two kingdoms. I am not sure the princesses will be willing. What makes you think Lord Samuel would want to help?"

"Greed! Simple as that. I believe Brother Samuel will see this as an opportunity. If he rescues the leaders of the Three Sisters, they will be beholding to him. That will make him feel like he has the right to annex the Middle Kingdom and all its potential riches."

"Sounds like a plan. You right the letter and round up Sergeant Gallant. I will talk to Alssa and Cally."

CHAPTER 51

When Daniel went into talk to Alssa and Cally, he was surprised to see they were with Eric and Commander Westolve. The discussion was quite intense, and he was not sure he should interrupt.

When Alssa saw him, she called him over and said, "We want your opinion on a matter."

He was sure he did not want to get involve considering how sharply they had been arguing and it was obvious to him that it must be over the commander, but he replied, "How can I help?"

Cally asked, "The seer has brought Commander Westolve here to petition for her release and to return her to service. What do you think?"

"What do I think? I think that it is none of my business. Commander Westolve is your officer and her actions effected you two, more than anyone else. I say you two decide."

Alssa showed a bit of frustration as she said, "We will decide! We do not want you to make a decision. We want you to look at the situation and give us your advice."

Daniel thought for a moment and was not going to say anything, but a niggling thought sat in the back of his mind, *Westolve will be needed in the coming battle, she is critical to its outcome.* Daniel shook his head and thought, *Now where did that come from?* Daniel turned to Eric and asked, "Why do you think she should be reinstated?"

Eric smiled at Daniel and replied, "I am the one who said that they should ask you, but I do feel like that it is important somehow."

Daniel looked for a long moment at Commander Westolve and then turned to the princess and said, "I agree with Eric. I believe it is critical that she be with you in the coming days. I don't know why; I just feel that it is."

"I agree with Daniel and Eric." Cally commented then said, "I know it is a big risk sister, but if both the seer and Daniel feel that we should take it then we must."

The look on Alssa face told everyone that she was not happy with the situation, but she said, "Okay, I will go along with the three of you." Turning to Commander Westolve, she warned, "I am not at all comfortable with this, Commander. I do not trust you and I will not forgive you for what you have done. But these three people, who I do trust, have petitioned for you and I will acquiesce to their counsel. But I warn you, if I see any wavering in loyalty of behavior, I will kill you myself. Do you understand me?"

Commander Westolve looked shaken and confused as she replied, "I do understand you, Your Majesty. I am both humbled and perplexed. I did not expect this opportunity, but I will not let you down."

After Alssa dismissed Eric and the commander, she asked Daniel, "What was it that you needed?"

"Captain Jovan is drafting a letter to send to Brother Samuel requesting assistance and Jovan felt it would be extremely hard for Samuel to turn down if yours and Cally's signature was on the request."

"I bet he would. Do you know what you are asking? He would hold this over us forever." Alssa replied.

Cally cautioned, "Sister, remember everything is changing we must change with it. Besides, if we don't get help, we may not live to have him be able to use it against us any way."

Alssa smiled in agreement with Cally and then turned to Daniel and said, "I think you should sign the letter too."

"Me! What for? It will mean nothing to him. He doesn't even know who I am?" Daniel replied incredulously.

"He will know soon enough and by that time what you say will mean a great deal to him," Cally interjected.

Daniel looked at the floor and shook his head and started to say, "You two can't let it go can you…"

But before he could finish, Captain Jovan came into the room with Sergeant Gallant and interrupted, "The sergeant is ready to go, and here is the letter. Are you ladies going to sign it?"

Alssa signed the letter and as she handed it to Cally, she commented, "I am having to do a great many things I am uncomfortable with lately and this is just another one of them."

Cally signed the letter and smiled as she handed it to Daniel. He took it reluctantly and was about to protest again, but then instead, He signed it with "THE MANSLAYER" and handed it back to Jovan who read it and laughed.

CHAPTER 52

It had been over eight days since Sergeant Gallant had left for the Pact of Brothers kingdom. Cally had been sending out patrols farther and farther from the castle each day looking for any sign of the enemy. Hope was starting to build that the brutal slaughter inflicted on the beast army during the Simpkins Grotto battle had dispersed them for good. No one really believed it, but they did hope.

On the afternoon of the eighth day Cally's scouts discovered the enemy assembling in an open plain about ten miles from the castle. The scouts reported that there was over a thousand orcs and hadrac gathered but no goblins. After a brief discussion it was decided to send out the Three Sisters' lancers to attack them and whittle down their numbers before there were too many to deal with. As the Lancers were forming up Daniel notice that Cally was mounting up to lead them.

Daniel called out, "Cally, what are you doing? You are not planning on going into battle with them, are you?"

Cally glared at him and continued to mount up.

Daniel hurried over to her and put his hand on her thigh and said, "You cannot put yourself in such danger. Your kingdom needs you. Your sister needs you!"

Everyone needs me! What about what I need? What about what you need?" Cally asked.

Daniel paused confused then said, "What I need? I don't know what you are talking about?"

Cally gave him an exasperated look and said, "No, I suppose you don't!" Then spinning her horse around, she said, "I seem to recall that it was I who led the attack that saved you and my sister at the Grotto. The odds were far greater then then now. Moreover, Three Sisters Royalty always lead from the front. We would never ask our soldiers to face anything that we ourselves would not be willing to face. Goodbye, Daniel. Help Alssa win this war." With that, she set off at a trot to lead her women into battle.

Daniel watched her ride away and thought, *That was a bit weird, is she thinking she will not come back? Does she not want to come back? I guess she did just lose her mother and her sister is trying to have everyone she cares about killed.* As Cally rode out of sight, Daniel whispered, "May the light go with you, Cally L'se."

Daniel found Alssa standing in the throne room that had not been used for three hundred years. When Alssa noticed him, she said, "Imagine, the great queen sat here and handed out justice and mercy for over one hundred years."

Daniel let out a whistle as he said, "That is a long time to live."

"She never died you know." Alssa boasted, "She just left, and no one ever saw her again."

Daniel nodded and said, "But she is certainly dead by now. She would be well over four hundred years old. That is not possible, is it?"

Alssa had a far-off look in her eyes as she said, "With man it is not possible, but when one dwells in the light...who knows?"

CHAPTER 53

As all the leaders gathered to discuss how they will defend against the coming horde, Daniel noticed that their hopes were higher than they had been in a long time.

His thoughts were confirmed when Sergeant Sharon, who had been promoted to Commander Sharon, said, "After Her Majesty, Cally L'se, disperses the rabble that has gathered on the Ten Mile plain. It will be the end of this war. We have easily killed five to seven thousand of these beasts. Their numbers have to be greatly reduced."

The Three Sisters Commander of the Brigade of Bowwomen, Halen J'te, agreed with the commander and add, "I think we probably only have the mopping up to do to clean these beasts out of the Westward,"

Commander Sharon cautiously expressed concern as she asked, "What about Princess T'asha, we do not know what became of her after the confrontation at the inn and our escape from the mountain cave?"

Eric Kromsing spoke up, "I, Like the rest of you, do not know what happened to T'asha. But I can see one of two possibilities. One, After the battle at Simpkins Grotto she has gone into hiding, or two, she has access to darkness that we are not aware of and at this moment she is amassing another enormous army to oppose us. I personally think it is the latter and that we are in for a long, difficult war."

Commander Halen complained, "So we are going to sit here in fear of what might be happening with no proof that it is. We should strike out and see what is out there."

Captain Jovan responded, "We do know what is out there. A thousand hadrac and orcs."

"Princess Cally and the lancers will deal with that rabble." Commander Halen proclaimed, "I say we from up our remaining troops and attack the Ebony forest and the Three Brides Valley and cleanse them of the rest of these vile creatures. Then we can all go home."

For a long time, the room grew quiet as each leader thought over their options. The silence was shattered as princess Cally and her officers pushed through the doors into the throne room. They were all covered in sweat and dirt looking like they had been riding hard.

Commander Sharon greeted them, "You are back quickly. It did not take you long to drive them away?"

Cally Slumped exhausted into a chair offered to her and said, "We did not drive any one away, we never even engaged with them."

"What!" exclaimed Commander Halen. "How can that be?"

"It be, because we were outnumbered by more than twenty to one," Cally said forlornly.

"What has happened?" Alssa asked patiently.

"We were all set up to attack and it clearly appeared that the beasts had no idea we were there. But before I gave the order, I felt compelled to send out scouts onto the ridge that paralleled our line of attack. It was only by the grace of the light that we averted disaster."

"What did your scouts fine?" Daniel asked.

The adjacent valley and hill filled with all manner of beast, some the scouts did not recognize, along with T'asha's traitorous army and Ramaahian infantry.

"Ramaahian infantry! That settles it!" Commander Halen exclaimed. "We must warn the court in Jukeele and inform the Pact of Brothers and call for their help before we are totally overcome."

Alssa motioned for everyone to calm down and said, "I agree with the commander on the first part, we must send a messenger back to Jukeele and to all the other nation. It is now clear that the

Darkness the prophecy spoke of is rising. We must also tell the Seers to check on the Isle of Exile and the four dark lords. But! On the second part I disagree, we will not be overcome."

Cally responded indignantly, "Do you propose that we flee and let T'asha, and her beast army overrun the Middle Kingdom?"

Alssa proclaimed, "Not in the least, sister, I propose we stay and fight and win!"

Captain Jovan called out, "We are outnumbered twenty to one, and you believe we can win?"

"That is correct, Captain. It is because I believe! I believe in all of you. I believe that we fight for what is right and true. And most of all, I have faith in the light. Faith that it will guide us to victory over darkness."

Now Daniel spoke up, "That is an inspiring speech, but just how do we obtain such a victory?"

"That I do not know, but I am confident that a way will be revealed," Alssa replied.

Commander Sharon asked, "And what are we supposed to do until the light reveals this miracle? Because that is what it will be if we win. It will have been a miracle?"

"You are right commander, it will be a miracle, but since you cannot not count on a miracle. We will make the best battle plan we can." Alssa replied and then continued, "In the beginning we will have our lancers meet them out as far away as possible, but only to harass them and slow them down. We try to inflict as may casualties as we can, but not at the cost of becoming engaged in a full battle. The lancers will then fall back to the defensive line we will set up on our side of the river at which point they will dismount and fight on foot."

Captain Jovan caught on to Alssa idea and added, "My men along with Eric's and a fourth of the bowwomen will dig traps and defensive trenches on the far side of the river. This will give the lancers cover fire as they retreat across the river. We will only engage with bows then we will also cross the river."

Eric spoke up I can help with some defensive deterrence's as well as a big surprise at the bridge.

Daniel could see the plan developing but could also see the futility in it and said, "Two things, first as good as this plan is it will hardly slow them down, and second, what will I be doing while all this is happening?"

Amazingly, Alssa and Cally answered together again, "Nothing, you will stay on this side of the river. You are the whole reason we are all here. You of all of us must survive so that you can take you place as the returning King."

Daniel looked at both in great frustration but did not say anything he just turned and walked out of the room.

CHAPTER 54

Daniel found himself standing on the bridge that spanned the Deep River thinking about their predicament and the princess's insistence that he was the foretold heir of M'tin. He was not sure how long he had stood there deep in thought when he felt a tug back into reality. He could see movement to the South. It was still some distance away, but he was sure he could see something coming down the road leading off the long slope that descended from the ridge. He quickly called for one of the guards to bring Alssa and Captain Jovan.

By the time Alssa and Captain Jovan arrived Daniel could see that it was a column of Horsemen and marching infantry.

Captain Jovan stepped up beside Daniel and said, "That the Fifth Lancers brigade and the Twenty-first Infantry regiment of the Pact of Brothers. It looks like they have seen some fighting. There will not be more than Five hundred men with them. I wonder why Brother Samuel sent so few troops?"

As the major leading the column of the Fifth Lancers Brigade crossed the bridge, he motioned for Sergeant Gallant to join him as he stopped next to Daniel's small group. Looking at Jovan, he said, "You must be the captain that Sergeant Gallant has told us about?"

Captain Jovan Saluted and said, "Yes, sir, and may I introduce you to Her Majesty, Alssa Martina Anna J'ta, Queen of the Three Sisters and this is my good friend Daniel Manslayer."

The major and Sergeant Gallant quickly dismounted and dropped to one knee in front of Alssa and said, "It is my honor to meet you Your Majesty. I am Major Ambrose of the Fifth Royal Lancers and I believe you already know Sergeant Gallant."

Alssa motion for him to rise and said, "Thank you, Major Ambrose, it is a pleasure to meet you, and yes, I am quite familiar with the good Sergeant. I am also pleased the Brother Samuel assented to sending you and your men."

The major glanced at Sergeant Gallant then back at Alssa and said, "I am sorry, but you are mistaken, Brother Samuel did not send me. Sergeant Gallant was unable to get into see the King nor any of his representatives. He then came to me. I guess, for two reasons, first, I am married to his sister and he thought he might have better luck getting to talk to me." The major turned and smiled at Sergeant Gallant. "The second, I was closer to you then any other unit as we were station in the Southern Barrier Mountains at St. Nicholas Pass."

Captain Jovan looked at the sergeant and said, "You were not able to talk to Brother Samuel or Colonel Campbell?"

Sergeant Gallant shook his head no and said, "They would not see me. I insisted to the point that the sergeant at Arms had me removed from the palace, with some difficulty I might add. That is when I thought of Joanas here." Sergeant Gallant pointed his thumb at the major and then saw a look of disapproval on his brother-in-law's face and said, "Sorry, Major, that is when I thought of Major Ambrose."

The major then added, "Although I have not been ordered here, I am theoretically responsible to secure everything north of St. Nicholas Pass. That normally means the northern foothills, but I have the personal discretion to extend my reach, So I have. I brought my company of lancers, two hundred strong, and A full regiment of infantry numbering five hundred."

"Well, we are grateful that you and your men are here. I only wish it could have been more," Alssa commented.

"You are welcome, Your Majesty," the major replied, "but according to the sergeant, you are only facing a few hundred hadrac and orc. My men are more than up for handling that. In fact, we did run into a couple of small bands of orc on the way here, but they gave us no trouble."

Daniel entered the conversation by saying, "That was the situation when the sergeant left. But now, we face twenty thousand of the beasts. There is also a mix of traitorous Three Sisters royal guard troops and a full regiment of Ramaahian infantry."

The shock on the major's face was complete as he said, "Ramaahian Infantry you say? Could you tell if they were Donnolian or Ramaahian? I have faced both on the eastern frontier and if their Donnolians they are hard to kill. They are brutes, big, strong and determined. Good fighters and very skilled." Addressing Captain Jovan, he asked, "What kind and how many troops do we have to stand against them?"

"Counting the ones, you brought, about fifteen hundred," Captain Jovan replied.

"Well, I hate to tell you this Captain, but that ain't enough. Not nearly enough." The major called a lieutenant over to him as he pulled the letter that Jovan had given Sergeant Gallant out of his satchel. He quickly added his name to the bottom of it and said, "Lieutenant, take a squad of lancers and this letter and ride as fast and as hard as you can to St. Michael's Keep. Do not go to the palace. Go to the Headquarters of the Fifth Lancers and give it to Colonel Glass. Nobody else, Just Colonel Glass, tell him our situation, he will know what to do."

As they all watched the lieutenant and four other lancers ride away, the major asked Captain Jovan again, "What kind of troops do we have?"

The captain told him and then explained their defensive plan modifying it to include the new arrivals. The major then observed, "That is a good plan, considering your limited resource and the terrain. We still do not stand a chance without reinforcements, but it is a good plan."

CHAPTER 55

After two Days of hard labor, made much quicker with the help of the new arrivals they had all the defensive fortifications dug. Many of the men, once they heard who they were fighting, commented that they were more than likely digging their own graves. Commander Sharon informed them that if they lose, graves will not be necessary as goblins will eat the dead.

On the morning of the third day, Scouts had notified everyone that the Beast army was on the move coming their way. Daniel was leaning against a tree looking across the river at the defensive works waiting for the battle to start.

He was talking out loud to himself, "I guess this will be as far east as I get. I sure wanted to see Giants Wall and the Western Highlands, but that probably isn't going to happen now."

He then heard a melodic rumble. It was like a song being made by stones, which made no sense to him, then another sound was laced into the melodic rumble, a sound he had heard before. Daniel looked around and whispered, "Oaklawn?"

The tree he was leaning on began to laugh, a laugh that brought tears of joy to Daniel's face as he said, "Oaklawn it is you! Isn't it?"

Then tree partially morphed into a Tree Troll as it said, "It is I Lightbearer, I and my friends have come to assist you in your battle with darkness."

Daniel looked out across the river, then realized that there were far more trees than had been there only a few days earlier, and he turned to Oaklawn and said, "How many of you have come?"

"As many as we could spare," Oaklawn replied, but then he gave out another one of his low laughs and said, "But it is not only us who has come. On your way to the castle of light, you woke up some of my cousins who also decided to join in the fun of squashing darkness. They watched you march through the mountains."

Oaklawn let out a long low howling sound like the wind blowing through a narrow canyon. Daniel again looked across the river expecting to see other trees responding, but instead a large rock partially morphed into a somewhat human from and Daniel could have sworn that a small pile of stone next to it lifted like a hand and wave at him.

Daniel shifted his gaze to the Tree Troll and asked, "Rock Trolls?"

"Yes, Lightbearer," Oaklawn responded, "the Creation of the light has come to battle the coming darkness." With that Oaklawn turned back into a tree.

Daniel almost ran back into the castle and up onto the ramparts where the rest of the leaders were gathered. As he approached, Cally asked him, "What has happened? You look excited for the first time in a long while."

"Where is Alssa? She needs to hear this." Daniel asked.

Cally replied, "She is reading some old book she found. Why?"

"We are going to win…" was all he got out before his voice was drowned out by the sound of Pact of Brother's trumpets announcing that the beast army had crossed the ridge and were coming down the slope toward the river.

They all watched as a seven hundred lancers made up of Three Sisters women and Pact of Brothers men attacked them from the flanks. The lancers made charge after charge into the horde of beasts. Each charge inflicting more and more casualties on the enemy before they had to withdraw from the field and retreated to the north side of the river.

Then it was the Bowwomen and Eric's mercenaries' turn. The women rained down flight after flight of Crossbow bolts down on the beasts. Again, inflicting heavy casualties on the enemy, but the onslaught was hardly slowed as those beasts coming from behind marched over the bodies of their fallen fellows.

As the bowwomen prepared to withdraw across the bridge the beast horde suddenly stopped as the unmistakable sound of trees groaning and boulders tumbling filled the river basin. The bowwomen froze in their tracks as both tree and stone turned into giant manlike beasts and marched out to meet the army of darkness. The bowwomen quickly stopped, turned and fire off their small reserve of arrows before they fled across the bridge. The giant trolls tossed hadrac, orc, and goblin into the air like twigs. The beast horde began to give way under the onslaught. The humans cheered as row after row of beasts fell like wheat before a reapers blade.

The Horde suddenly parted as giant grotesque ogres crossed the ridge and entered individual combat with the trolls. The beast army slowly started moving forward. Bypassing pockets of fighting trolls and ogres. As they moved into the area where the defensive battlements were built a new sound joined the grunts and howls of ogre and troll. The sound of thunder filled the air as huge pockets of dirt were thrown into the air filled with beast body parts. Explosion after explosion erupted on the far side of the river, and though the beast body count continued to rise, the horde kept coming. They moved all the way up to the edge of the river.

It was then that those on the ramparts saw the charging Ramaahian infantry coming at a run toward the bridge. Major Ambrose and Commander Halen had anticipated this, so they had held some bowwomen in reserve. Using the Rodones crossbows, they fired volley after volley into the on-rushing infantry. But these were not normal Ramaahian infantry; they were Donnolian heavy infantry, able to wear armor that was twice as thick as normal armor and though many of them fell to arrows not nearly enough.

It appeared that the bridge would be taken and if it were the battle was as good as over. Eric called out to Major Ambrose, "Move the troops away from the bridge."

The major called back, "We must defend it with the sword, or all will be lost."

Eric ordered, "Major, trust me we will not lose the bridge. Pull the troops back."

The major did as he was ordered, and as the last trooper moved away from the bridge, Eric lifted his arms in the air, waved his hands around, and said a silent prayer. And nothing happened.

Major Ambrose was beside himself he glared at Eric as the heavy infantry filled the bridge. Eric smiled at the major and snapped his fingers, and the bridge exploded into a million splinters killing all the troops on the bridge and many on the other side of the river. The smoke from the burning bridge and the dust and dirt blown into the air by the explosion hid the south side of the river from those in the and around the castle.

Everyone was congratulating Eric, including Commander Halen, "Seer Kromsing, I was unaware that the seer held such magic. I wish I would have been informed of its existence and that you planned on using it on the bridge."

Eric responded to the commander, "There was no magic. Seers are not magicians. We are diligent observers of everything around us. You are aware of the fire fountains that abound in the Wasteland? What happens there is what happened here, only on a smaller and controlled scale. No magic."

"Well, that stopped them," remarked Major Ambrose. "They will have to go all the way to the upper ford above L'ke L'fe. That will take them days."

As the smoke and dust settled on the south side of the river those on the north side had their hopes crushed. To their dismay they saw four tall, wheeled siege towers. Each tower had three levels and each level had twenty, Three Sisters bowwomen on them. Up until this point their enemy how not used missile weapons.

There were also ten giant wheeled machines that had turtle like tops. The machines held massive logs suspended under their roof like shells. The logs were sharpened to a point and were long enough to span the river. As the defenders looked on the giant turtles rolled forward, pushed by Man-orcs. They gained speed as they approached the river. The giant turtles crashed into the river and the Logs swung out from underneath. Seven out of the ten logs impaled themselves on the north side of the river making away for the beast to cross.

Major Ambrose sent twenty-man squads to each log to await the oncoming beast. Half of his men died before they could get to the logs. The siege tower archers picking them off one by one. The major sent squad after squad but T'asha's archers and the beast prevailed.

Alssa appeared on the parapet and commanded, "Major, withdraw your troops and have everyone return to the castle."

No one had noticed that she had not been with them. Daniel ran up to her and asked, "What are you doing? Where have you been?"

Alssa held up a book. Daniel read the title, "The Book of Light. You have been reading this whole time? Why?"

Alssa looked down to see if everyone was inside the castle and that the gate was locked. She then began to chant some words from the book, "Benevolent Light protect this place. Shield it in your blazing light."

As Daniel looked out over the wall is seemed to shimmer. The shimmer moved down the wall reaching the ground as the first beast arrived. The stood up their scaling ladders, and the first one began to climb, but then they started to shake and would fall off the ladder. This happened to all of them; some would try to find a handhold on the wall, but as soon as they touched it, they would fall off and shake for a moment on the ground. All who fell got back up but soon they all quit trying.

The people in the castle were amazed and could not understand what was happening but were also delighted that it was.

As they rejoiced, they heard a shrill cry from the other side of the river, "So, sister, you finally figured it out." It was T'asha; she stood sideways on the top tier of one of the siege towers. Her long red hair blowing in the wind, her alabaster skin shining through the smoke and dust. "I always told you that we were different, and that it would be us who would rule, not men."

Alssa challenged back, "T'asha why have you let the darkness take your soul? You know the great queen destined the Middle Kingdom and the Westward to be ruled by the heir of M'tin."

T'asha laughed and said, "You mean that worthless mercenary and his glowing sword. Clearly with what you have done to protect the castle you now know that the power is not in the sword but in the blood."

Alssa ignored her taunts and begged, "T'asha, please! Let this go. Turn away from the dark road and come back home to those who love you. It does not have to be this way."

The smile on T'asha's face became a wicked twisted grimace as she turned to face them head on. Alssa reacted in horror at the sight of her sister. The right side of T'asha's head was as beautiful as it had always been, but the left side was a twisted melted black mess, her hair was gone, her ear was melted onto her head and most of her cheek was missing so you could see her teeth.

"Look what your love has done to me. You struck out at me because I killed your lover. You and Cally have never loved me. You conspired against me all the time we were growing up, always off in your little huddle, laughing and giggling talking about me. Well, now you will find out what I was doing all the time that I spent alone." With that she raised her hands above her head and said words only spoken by the dark lords.

Dark clouds formed overhead, and lightening crashed down striking the turrets of the castle. Then the shimmering on the walls ceased and the beast began to climb the scaling ladders. As they reach the top, the soldiers would stab and knock them off. the beast began to pour across the log bridges again.

Alssa looked up into the sky and said, "The light cleanses the water and the water flows to the sea, the water cleanse the land, light come and cleanse the land,"

When she was done the river seem to rise and from into Multiple bodies that reached out and grabbed the log bridges and through them out into the plains. With giant hands of water, they swept the beast off the north side of the river.

Once again it looked like they were safe as Daniel remarked, "Water trolls!"

Alssa smiled at him and then called out to T'asha, "Please, sister, let's end this. The light can restore all things."

"I agree it is time to end this." She once again called out in the strange tongue and tornado funnels formed in the air and then became narrow spinning arrow-like shafts that flew down and struck the water trolls ripping them into tiny droplets that were carried off into all different directions. This was accompanied by a shrieking sound like water boiling in a kettle. Only a thousand times louder and far more forlorn.

A low rumbling and cracking sound emerged from the rock and tree trolls that were on the north side of the river. They threw themselves at T'asha and her tower to no avail as she called down Thunderclaps of sound that shattered the Rock trolls into tiny pebbles. This was followed by columns of fire that incinerated the tree trolls.

All who watched were mesmerized by the horror and frozen in fear. All but the beast army, it renewed its attack, crossing the river on the two log bridges that were left. They began to climb the scaling ladders.

Daniel ordered the remaining troops that were left into the inner keep. He had to drag Alssa as she was horrified by what here sister had done. Once they reached the keep, they ascended to the top to watch as the beast broke through the gate and over ran the outer castle area. T'asha called down storm clouds that darkened the sky and the rain poured down in torrents. T'asha had crossed the river and was standing on the parapet looking up at Alssa, Cally, Daniel, and Eric.

She was laughing maniacally as she said, "I see we are all together again, just like at the inn. Cally, my dear little sister, you missed the first time, but you will not be left out this time. And this time, dear sister, the outcome will be much different. T'asha again raised her hands and spoke. The tower began to shake and the air around the four of them crackled like fire and the tower walls were covered with climbing grunting orcs."

Eric said, "Alssa, it is time, she will not relent you must fight her."

Alssa turned to Daniel and said, "Draw your sword and raise it above your head." As he did, Alssa chanted, "By the Light all are set free, by the Light all can see. By the Light the darkness is dispelled, by the Light, the evil is repelled. The Light joins the spirit to soul, the light separates the soul from body. Strike now, oh Light, and separate the darkness from light."

Daniel had seen his sword change from glowing to a flame since he had arrived in the Lands of Chaos, but now it transformed again into a light brighter than the sun, pure energy, and then there was an explosion of light.

* * *

When they all awoke, they were laying on the top of the keep. Daniel stood up and looked around, there were no beasts. No orcs on the wall, no hadrac, no goblins, no ogres, only humans. The Ramaahian infantry as well as T'asha's troopers were wandering around as if they were lost. Alssa was standing next to T'asha, tears running down her face, neither one of them was moving. It was as if both of them were frozen in place. T'asha face of stuck in a disbelieving stare, and Alssa's eyes were open, but clearly, she was not there. Eric was standing beside Daniel, so he asked, "What happened, Eric?"

Eric surveyed the castle and the area around it with his nonexistent eyes and said, "The Banisher happened Daniel, the Banisher has returned, and now things will change."

CHAPTER 56

As they recovered from the battle, they discovered a great many things had changed. Alssa was in a coma sitting staring straight ahead with eyes open.

Colonel Campbell had arrived with the entire first lancer's division and the king's infantry corps over a ten thousand troops. He had also brought the news that Brother Samuel had dropped dead on the day of the Battle of Light, which is what everyone was calling it. The royal court of the Three Sisters had also sent an entire corps of Troops, but they too had arrived too late to help. With entire armies sitting outside of Queens Castle Home, tensions were high as they all waited for decisions to be made.

Daniel peered into Alssa's unflinching eyes. She was staring straight ahead, and he was sitting directly in front of her. Nevertheless, her stare went right through him as though she was looking somewhere else at a place no one else could see.

His heartbeat faster the normal, fear building inside of him. He was reluctant to speak what was in his heart even in this situation, but he was so desperate to have her back.

"Alssa, I don't know if you can hear me, but I need you back here with me, I have never known anyone like you. I do not know how I can continue without you. You were able to see me for who I really am. I love you Alssa, do you hear me? I love you."

Daniel heard the door behind him open. Looking out of the corner of his eye, Daniel could see the official green flowing cloak and yellow sash of the seers. Despite the cowl hiding his face, the halting stride of the wearer told Daniel that it was Eric Kromsing. The picture was a hard one for Daniel to accept; Eric just did not look right in the pious robes he wore.

Eric asked, "Has she moved or shown any sign of understanding what you are saying?"

Daniel's chest heaved. "No, not a twitch or a sound." Daniel hid his tearful face. "Do you believe she will?" he asked.

Eric replied, "I don't know, Daniel. She went along way into the light. I am not even sure she would want to come back if she could. Walking in the fullness of the light is an addictive thing to humans. Do you remember how you felt when you stepped into the light during your time in the crook? Where Alssa went to defeat, her sister was far deeper than that."

Daniel asked, "I don't understand, why would this happen? Why would the light hold onto her like this? Why will it not let her go?"

Eric turned away from Daniel and looked out the window and said, "Daniel, it isn't the light that is holding her. It is her who is holding onto the light. It is her choice. The fact that she hasn't gone completely is a sign that part of her wants to return."

Daniel stood up, walked over to the window, and stared into the darkness of the night. After a few moments, he spun around and said, "What can I do? What must I do to get her back?"

Eric put his hands together in front of his face and breathed a heavy sigh and replied, "I don't know. However, I do know this, the longer she is gone the less likely it will be that she will ever return."

Daniel walked back over to Alssa and looked deep into her eyes one more time. He could see no change, no acknowledgement that he was even there. A tear trickled down his cheek and into his beard.

Eric noticed and said, "Daniel, there might be—"

Daniel interrupted, "There might be what?"

Eric continued, "There are those among the seers who believe that the ancient wielders of the light still exist. In fact, they believe that the great queen was a light wielder, not just a Lightbearer."

Daniel asked, "What good is that to us now?"

"Well, they would be able to bring Alssa back," Eric stated.

"What? Where are they? How do I find them," Daniel begged?

Eric answered, "It is said they dwell in the east."

Daniel gave a great loud snort and said, "Eric, I have been in every country in the east. I grew up there. There are no light wielders living in the Twelve Kingdoms."

"I didn't say they were in the Twelve Kingdoms," Eric replied.

Daniel asked, "If not the Twelve Kingdoms, then where?"

Eric did not say anything; he just looked at Daniel.

Daniel continued, "That leaves only the Rafeal Waste. No one can travel even a few miles into that inferno before it kills them. I know, I have skirted the edges many times. It isn't possible, nothing lives in the Rafeal Waste."

Eric smiled and said, "What about in the center of the waste?"

The door opened, and two soldiers of the Three Sisters entered and quickly stepped to one side. They were followed by Cally, Captain Jovan, and Colonel Campbell.

Cally Looked at her sister with a mix of sympathy and pain. She drew herself up and composed her emotions. Turning to the men in the room, she said, "We need to talk. We must decide. We have won a great victory. I am afraid we will lose all we have gained if we do not act quickly."

Cally's eyes pleaded with Daniel as she continued. "I know you feel that Alssa is the Heir of M'tin, and thus, the rightful ruler of the Westward. But as all of us can see my sister is no longer capable of ruling. Kromsing and the seers have established your linage. You are a descendant of the great queen through M'tin. The sword obeys you and the people will follow you. You must accept your destiny."

Before Daniel could respond, Colonel Campbell spoke up, "Lightbearer, she is right, even the trolls call out for you to lead. You are the man who has been chosen by the light to lead us through the coming darkness."

Daniel dropped his chin and shook his head and said, "I cannot, I will not, I am not a king. There are other things I must do." He undid his shoulder harness and slid the sword and scabbard off his back and handed it to Cally and said, "You need to take your sister's place. The light is in you too!"

Cally's face went white, and she staggered back and said, "Me? No, no I am the last person who should take the throne."

Eric spoke softly as he said, "Cally, Daniel is right. You may not realize it, but you are now the sole ruler of the Three Sisters. Neither T'asha nor Alssa have heirs. The Family L'se is now the only ruling line left in your kingdom. The time of the triumvirate has come to an end. This new era has been brought into alignment by the light. You must not run from your destiny."

Cally spun around pointed at Daniel and yelled, "What about him? He is running away, fleeing from his destiny!"

Eric gave her a comforting smile and attempted to give her a hug, but she pulled away. Then he said, "Is he? Are you so sure of the will of the light that you know that? Search your heart, because you know deep down that the light has made a choice and you are it." Eric turned to face everyone else. "Cally is already the sole Queen of the Three Sisters domain, and as of today, the Seers have proclaimed her as the new monarch of the Middle Kingdom. All that is left, is for Brother Samuel's heir to make the decision to bring the Pact of Brothers in under her banner. Cally will then rule over all the great queen's realm."

Cally pulled the sword of light from its scabbard, lifted it above her head and began to chant. The blade burst into blinding light.

The men in the room bent down on one knee and said to together, "We pledge our hearts to our Queen. May the light illume her."

Cally lowered the blade and slammed it back into the scabbard. "Get off your knees and stop this nonsense." She handed the sword back to Daniel. Standing tall, she proclaimed, "I will accept this responsibility that is being forced upon me, but I will not do it as a Monarch. I will only act as a steward over the Middle Kingdom. And when this vagabond comes to his senses, he can be king." Cally continued, "My sister will recover so I will not abolish the triumvirate. I will maintain it until she returns." Cally turned and walked out of the room followed by her two guards. Colonel Campbell followed Cally out the door with a sly smile on his face.

Daniel sat back down on the stool that faced Alssa, who had not moved at all.

Eric lamented, almost to himself. "This is not good. This was unforeseen. Who would have thought that upon the return of the sword of light no one would sit on the thrown of power?" Turning to Daniel, he almost begged, "Why do you refuse to take this mantle upon yourself?"

Daniel took his time to answer and said, "Eric, you know I have felt compelled to go east through the highlands into the interior and now you have shown me why."

Jovan, who had sat silent until now, exclaimed, "You what? You're going to try to go beyond the giants-wall?"

"Not only the giants-wall, but beyond the Impenetrable Mountains if need be." He turned and looked at Alssa. "I must, for myself, and for her."

Jovan looked at him in stunned disbelief. "No one who has gone beyond the wall has ever lived to return. And there is no way through those mountains, that's why they are called impenetrable." Jovan turned to Kromsing, "Tell him Eric, tell him that this is crazy." Eric just shrugged his shoulders and looked at the floor. Jovan continued, "Daniel you can't do this. You will die if you try."

Daniel looked at Jovan and said softly, "That matters not, I must go."

* * *

The next morning Daniel, Jovan and Eric Kromsing went to meet with Cally, and Colonel Campbell in the throne room. Cally had ordered a common chair to be brought in and had it placed in front of the Dias that held the throne of power. She sat on the common chair with Colonel Campbell at her side. She studied the newcomers for a moment and settled her eyes on Daniel. "I have, with the advice of Colonel Campbell, made a decision concerning T'asha.

I am having her banished to the Island of Exile until the true ruler of the Middle Kingdom decides to return."

Jovan spoke up first with a loud cry. "No! She must die, she has communed with the dark lords and has joined with the orcs and hadrac. She unleashed the goblin horde on her own people she must suffer death for her crimes."

"That maybe so, but it will not be by my hand," Cally replied.

"And your plan is to send her to the Isle of Exile?" Kromsing questioned.

"Yes, that is what I said. I thought since she joined herself with the Lords of Darkness, she could spend her last days with them."

"This is not wise, my lady. We should speak to the seer's council before doing such a rash thing."

"You are free to talk to whomever you like, but I have made my decision. Colonel Campbell and the Pact of Brothers seers will transport T'asha to the Isle of Exile where she will be bound and tossed into the crater with her Lords. You are the ones who have made me steward, so that is my decision."

Colonel Campbell quickly interjected, "Captain Jovan will accompany me to the Isle where he will be a witness and then he will go on to St. Michaels Keep receiving the hero's welcome he deserves."

Jovan reluctantly replied, "Colonel Campbell, I must decline. I will be resigning my commission and I will be going with Daniel on his journey."

Cally appeared indifferent to his announcement, but Colonel Campbell exploded with rage. "By what authority do you think you can do this? You have a duty to your country, to your people. What about your loyalty to your King and to your family?"

Jovan smirked. "I have no family left. They have all been killed in service to their king. There is no longer a king in the Pact of Brothers, nor is there one here. So I resign by the only authority left, my own, and I will follow the only king I know, Daniel."

Daniel gave Jovan a sour look but addressed Cally, "What will you do with Alssa?"

Cally shifted nervously in her chair. "I am returning to Jukeele and Alssa will accompany me. I think it will be best if she is with her family."

Now Kromsing spoke up. "I agree with you, Your Majesty, being with her family will help, but I beg you don't take her from the boundaries of the castle. The thin thread of life she clings to is anchored here if you take her from it, she will surely die."

Cally sneered, "What do you suggest I do, seer?"

"You should move you're throne to Queens Castle Home. Set up your reign here and move your family to the Middle Kingdom. This is what destiny demands."

"Is it my destiny or the mechanizations' of the Seers?" Cally's face was hard. "I will not risk my sister's life; she will remain here with a permanent guard and caretakers. But I will not stay here. You will not force me into your plans."

Daniel was relieved and wanted to say something, but since he was leaving, he did not feel it was his place to comment into the situation; instead he announced, "I will be departing tomorrow."

Cally's countenance softened just a little as she asked, "Daniel, I still do not understand why you feel you must go away? We need you here. I need you here. Why do you resist what is clearly your destiny?"

"I must be faithful to my heart and the desires that have been placed there by the Light. I will not discuss it anymore, I must leave tomorrow, I am sorry for the grief it may cause."

Eric announced to the room, "I have bound myself to Daniel so I will also be going with the Lightbearer on his journey."

Daniel's heart soared when he heard Eric's decision. "I am honored by your choice, Eric Kromsing." Turning to Jovan, he continued, "And you, Jovan De Rean, I am humbled by your sacrifice. I wish I could guarantee our success, but I cannot, though I will assure you that I will honor your heart."

Under his breath, Colonel Campbell chuckled to himself as he turned and walked out of the room. "This looks like the start of a bad joke, a blind seer, a dishonored lancer, and a common thief go on an adventure."

EPILOGUE

When the morning sun rose over the mountain peaks, the army of the Three Sisters Marched out of Queens Castle Home with Cally in the lead.

Colonel Campbell, two seers and the division of Lancers guarded an Ox cart loaded with an iron cage. It held T'asha K'jo as she was being transported to the Isle of Exile.

Daniel, Jovan and Eric Kromsing watched them leave. After the columns wound out of sight Daniel walked back into Alssa's chambers. He sat in front of her and looked deep into her blue eyes for any sign of recognition. He found none. Slowly he bent over and kissed her softly on the cheek. Standing quickly, he turned and strode out the door. His abrupt exit prevented him from seeing the single tear the welled up and slowly ran down Alssa's left cheek.

* * *

Colonel Campbell watched from the guard tower on the edge of the volcano crater as two seers and T'asha were lowered down into the pit. The seers lifted her out of the basket and walked her to a cave opening. They removed the iron bars that blocked the opening and moved T'asha inside. T'asha had not said a word the entire trip from the Middle Kingdom. But as they shut the bars closed, she simply said, "Thank you." As they both stood and stared at her horribly disfigured face, a wicked smile crept across her lips. Fear started to fill their hearts as the two seers ran for the wicker basket.

Deep in the bowels of the mist-filled crater, the four Lords of darkness thought, *One step closer to freedom.*

About the Author

The author was born in Montana and grew up in a small farming town. He became a veracious reader in eighth grade when his English teacher convinced him and his friends to read Frank Hubert's *Dune* in a speed-and-comprehension challenge. He didn't win, but it changed his attitude about reading and learning for the rest of his life. Science fiction / fantasy captured his imagination, and he went on to read J. R. R. Tolkien's *The Hobbit* and the Lord of the Rings trilogy, along with all the Conan genre he could find. His discovery of Isaac Asimov's Foundation series sealed the deal. He has been collecting books all his life and has a physical library of over a thousand books and an untold number of digital downloads.

The author worked in the lumber and construction industry for many years until returning to school. He taught junior high and high school along with coaching football, wrestling, basketball, and volleyball. While teaching, he would make up stories to help his students understand the subjects at hand, and it was during this time that his students encouraged him to write his stories down.

The author loves to meet new people and listen to their unique stories about their personal adventures. Spending time with his children and grandchildren and raising fruit and nut trees. With the tremendous encouragement of his wife, he has built a tree house office / writing room to spend all his free time creating new worlds and introducing new and exciting characters into the world.

CPSIA information can be obtained
at www.ICGtesting.com
Printed in the USA
LVHW040426090222
710541LV00004B/33

9 781662 463709